MP   2006 Anaheim
WorldCon

D0952116

JOE HALDEMAN

A Separate War and Other Stories

ACE BOOKS, NEW YORK

THE BERKLEY PUBLISHING GROUP
Published by the Penguin Group
Penguin Group (USA) Inc.
375 Hudson Street, New York, New York 10014, USA
Penguin Group (Canada), 90 Eglinton Avenue East, Suite 700, Toronto, Ontario M4P 2Y3, Canada
(a division of Pearson Penguin Canada Inc.)
Penguin Books Ltd., 80 Strand, London WC2R 0RL, England
Penguin Group Ireland, 25 St. Stephen's Green, Dublin 2, Ireland
(a division of Penguin Books Ltd.)
Penguin Group (Australia), 250 Camberwell Road, Camberwell, Victoria 3124, Australia
(a division of Pearson Australia Group Pty. Ltd.)
Penguin Books India Pvt. Ltd., 11 Community Centre, Panchsheel Park, New Delhi—110 017, India
Penguin Group (NZ), Cnr. Airborne and Rosedale Roads, Albany, Auckland 1310, New Zealand
(a division of Pearson New Zealand Ltd.)
Penguin Books (South Africa) (Pty.) Ltd., 24 Sturdee Avenue, Rosebank, Johannesburg 2196,
South Africa

Penguin Books Ltd., Registered Offices: 80 Strand, London WC2R 0RL, England

This is a work of fiction. Names, characters, places, and incidents either are the product of the author's imagination or are used fictitiously, and any resemblance to actual persons, living or dead, business establishments, events, or locales is entirely coincidental. The publisher does not have any control over and does not assume any responsibility for author or third-party websites or their content.

First edition: August 2006

Library of Congress Cataloging-in-Publication Data

Haldeman, Joe W.
  A separate war and other stories / Joe Haldeman.—1st ed.
      p.   cm.
  ISBN 0-441-01407-0 (hardcover)
  1. Science fiction, American.   I. Title.

  PS3558.A353S47 2006
  813'.54—dc22

                                        2006006120

PRINTED IN THE UNITED STATES OF AMERICA

10   9   8   7   6   5   4   3   2   1

For my students, MIT and Clarion;
may their ideas be just crazy enough.

Contents

Meet Joe Haldeman

The first time I ever met Joe Haldeman . . .

That's how you're supposed to begin these things, isn't it? With an anecdote about how you first met? But, as is the case with many of my favorite authors, the first time I ever met Joe Haldeman was in the aisles of the public library, where I found his wonderful novel, *The Forever War.*

I read science fiction avidly all through my teenage years, beginning with Robert A. Heinlein, so I'd already read *Time for the Stars* and *Starship Troopers* and lots and lots of science fiction about faster-than-light travel and futuristic soldiers and intergalactic war.

But I had never read anything like this. *The Forever War* was a riveting adventure story about a threatening and exciting future, the very stuff of science fiction, but it was much more than that. It actually tried to deal with all the complexities, horrors, and paradoxes of war. (Some critics see the book as a rebuttal to *Starship Troopers,* and I definitely think it is, but that's only one aspect of the book.) It was filled with irony—because of the time jumps involved, a soldier could find himself obsolete during the course of a single war, or a single battle, and eternally separated from the things he was ostensibly fighting for—and compassion for the human condition without an ounce of sentimentality.

But it was still unmistakably a science-fiction novel, which used a standard SF device—the relativistic effects of faster-than-light space travel—as a metaphor for the displacement and alienation of soldiers returning to a society with which they can no longer connect. And it was an adult novel, in the best sense of the word, which didn't flinch at harsh realities or harsher conclusions about who and what we are as a species and what sort of universe it is we inhabit.

In short, it was an amazing book, and an unforgettable one. In the years since I first read it, I've thought of it often, most recently when I read about the lack of armor for the soldiers in Iraq. (In *The Forever War*, the "collapsar" time jumps the soldiers make can render their weapons and armor fatally outdated.) More than anything else I've ever read or seen, it gave me insight into the Vietnam War and the experience of the soldiers who were there (Joe was wounded in the war, where he served as a combat engineer). And all wars before and since.

The war novel it most reminded (and reminds) me of is Erich Maria Remarque's *All Quiet on the Western Front*, and that's the highest compliment I can pay it. I fell completely in love with it, immediately read all the Joe Haldeman I could find, and hoped someday I'd be lucky enough to meet him in person.

A few years later I did, and fell in love all over again. This is not always the case. Meeting authors you admire is often disillusioning and sometimes disastrous. But Joe Haldeman was everything his stories had led me to believe he would be—intelligent, thoughtful, charming, and funny.

And gracious. He's nice to everyone, fans and students (he teaches writing at MIT) and fellow writers alike, and there's not an ounce of nasty competitiveness in him. He was wonderful to me the first time I met him (I was awestruck and awkward and, as I recall, gushed something eloquent like, "Oh, gosh, Mr. Haldeman, I love your books!"), and every time since, and I consider myself lucky to be a friend of his. And extraordinarily lucky to have been allowed to present him a richly deserved Nebula Award.

Before I went to Spain the first time, he sent me a list of helpful travel tips, one of which kept me from ordering raw meat (Joe: "*Carpaccio* means uncooked"), getting lost ("Always carry a card with the hotel's name and address on it so you can show it to the taxi driver if all else fails"), and generally making an idiot of myself in a foreign country. And everyone who knows him has stories just like that, of considerate things Joe has done.

He's also modest, even though he's one of the most respected and admired writers I know. He has won any number of awards, including the Nebula Award (given by the Science Fiction Writers of America) and the Hugo Award (voted on by the membership of the World Science Fiction Convention), has been president of SFWA, and is one of science fiction's most famous writers. But you'd never know it if you met him.

Joe never touts his own accomplishments, never boasts, never talks about his advances or his sales or his awards. Or his books. Besides *The Forever War*, he's the author of *Mindbridge*, *Tool of the Trade*, *Buying Time*, *All My Sins Remembered*, and the acclaimed *Worlds* series. He's just as famous for his short stories, including "Out of Phase," the Hugo-winning "Tricentennial," and the stories in this volume. He's also edited several anthologies, among them, *Cosmic Laughter* and *Study War No more*, and has had a long and distinguished career.

Which is much harder to do than he makes it look. Writing careers tend to be nasty, brutish, and short, and Joe had the additional problem of sudden fame. When *The Forever War* was published, it was instantly recognized as a science-fiction classic. It won the Nebula Award, the Hugo Award, and the Australian Ditmar Award, and ever since has been regarded (and rightly so) as one of the most important and groundbreaking books of the field.

Which it is. If I were asked to rank it, I would put it on a *very* short list of novels along with Frank Herbert's *Dune,* Walter M. Miller, Jr.'s *A Canticle for Leibowitz*, and Philip K. Dick's *Do Androids Dream of Electric Sheep?*, all of which deal with serious and timeless societal and philosophical issues and which transcend the conventions of the genre at the same time they employ them.

It also catapulted Joe to stardom, with all its attendant difficulties. Writing a classic, especially early in your career, is not necessarily a blessing—look at J. D. Salinger and Truman Capote. Writers who've risen to sudden prominence frequently fret about "topping" their previous work so much that they work themselves into terminal writer's block. Or turn into pretentious, preening jerks. Or settle into a deadly routine of repeating themselves or writing endless sequels to please readers who want more of the same.

Joe Haldeman hasn't fallen into any of those traps, or, to my knowledge, even given them any thought: He simply writes what he's interested in and passionate about, from Hemingway to poetry to the human condition, and that intensity has resulted in novels and short stories all very different from each other, except in quality. He writes about traditionally science-fictional subjects—from telepathy to orbiting space colonies to black holes to immortality—but he employs them in uniquely nontraditional ways to explore what it means to be human in a variety of identity-splintering environments.

My personal favorite is *The Hemingway Hoax*, an eloquent novel about the torments and inescapabilities of the writing life and of life in general. It's beautifully researched and even more beautifully written. It uses a traditional science-fiction trope, the alternate history, which imagines the very different world that would result from a single different action at some point in the past. Alternate history has a long and noble history, beginning with Ward Moore's *Bring the Jubilee*, but it's often used to play shallow historical chess games or advance pet political agendas. But Joe Haldeman uses it to explore all the choices and chances of our lives, and the near impossibility of keeping our footing when the ground continually shifts beneath us.

This attempt to keep one's footing, to find meaning in the world even if it is a world without meaning, and the beyond-difficult task of defining morality in such a world, are what Joe Haldeman's work is all about. His intense belief in that search for meaning permeates everything he writes.

He cares deeply, passionately about his writing, and at the same time is a total professional. He's dedicated to the art and craft of writing. He writes every day, working meticulously to get each sentence absolutely perfect before he goes on to the next. And that devotion to craft, to detail, is what makes his work so good.

All of his work is painstakingly researched, but it's never nitpicking or pedantic. I talked before about *The Hemingway Hoax*. Reading the story, it's obvious Joe knows every single detail there is to know about Hemingway, but it doesn't stop there. He has also made a real effort to understand the man *and* the writer.

Every single work of his reflects that same dedication to detail. One of my favorite stories about Joe is the one Sheila Williams, the editor of *Asimov's Science Fiction Magazine*, tells about dealing with Joe and a first-time-out author on the same day. She left phone messages one after the other for both, asking them to check on possible errors in both their stories. The first-time author called back to complain about the arrogance of an editor daring to touch his deathless prose and to whine, "I don't see what difference it makes. The readers will never notice." (Not true, his mistake was both major and inexcusable.) Multi–award winner Joe Haldeman, on the other hand, whose error really was minor, complained not at all. Instead, he called back in the late afternoon with his changes and to say he was sorry he'd taken so long to get back to Sheila, but the necessary book had been checked out of his local library, so he'd ridden his bike fifteen miles into the city to the main library to find it. "That's why he's Joe Haldeman," Sheila says admiringly.

It is. He's a complete professional, from the seemingly minor details of a story to its larger emotional truths, from teaching to signing books for fans (some of whom interrupt him in the middle of dinner), from his stories to his friendships. He'll expend any amount of effort to get it right.

Which is why I still find opening a Joe Haldeman book (like this new collection of short stories) just as exciting as finding *The Forever War* in the library and meeting Joe Haldeman for the first time. I know you will, too. It's a gem. Just like Joe Haldeman.

—Connie Willis

Introduction: The Secret of Writing

When I was too young to check books out of the adult section of the local library, I spent a lot of weekend time sitting there and reading the forbidden texts. There was one officious librarian who would always shoo me back to the children's section (and try to make me read something besides that science fiction trash), but most of them tolerated my intrusion.

My favorite adult book was a fat red tome called *Henley's Twentieth Century Book of Formulas, Processes, and Trade Secrets*. "Secrets" is the dramatic and operative word there. How to make your own root beer or nitroglycerin. Cure asthma or constipation in canaries. I would bicycle away from the library aglow with secret wisdom. Things I knew my parents didn't know.

Any letter of the alphabet would yield marvels: Bear fat, bookbinder's varnish, bust reducer, British champagne, broken bones (a test for), blasting powder, Bowl of Fire trick. "Burning Brimstone" is not a trick you'll find in contemporary manuals of magic: "Wrap cotton around two small pieces of brimstone and wet it with gasoline; take between the fingers, squeezing the surplus liquid out, light it with a candle, throw back the head well, and put it on the tongue blazing. Blow fire from mouth, and observe that a freshly blown-out candle may be lighted from the flame."

The book was full of advice that might or might not help one survive into adulthood: "The warning as to the danger of experimenting with the manufacture of ordinary gunpowder applies with renewed force when nitro-glycerine is the subject of the experiment."

It was old then, more than fifty years ago, and that was a large part of its charm. Even as a boy, I could appreciate the innocence and earnestness of that bygone day, when there was a secret formula for everything.

But did it have a secret formula for writing? You bet it did: Make a solution of alum in strong vinegar and, using a fine-tipped brush, write a message on an egg. When the vinegar dries, the message will disappear. But hard-boil the egg and break it open—and there it is again, inside!

Which brings us around to the point of this little essay.

When I put together my first collection of short stories—*Infinite Dreams*, back in 1978, I introduced each story with a paragraph or two about where I thought it had come from—admitting that I knew that some people didn't care for that kind of blather, but we put it in a different typeface, easy to skip.

In the next collection (*Dealing in Futures*, 1985), I refined the idea by dividing the introduction into one piece before the story, carefully not giving anything away, and then a "coda" piece after the story, which assumed the reader had read it, and would segue into the intro to the next story.

That was a little too complicated. In the third one (*None So Blind*, 1996), I wrote plain afterwords, commenting on the extent to which each story had been affected by actual events.

Ten years later, I wonder whether I've told anybody anything as useful as how to hide a message in an egg.

Anybody who's interested knows that there's no "secret formula" to writing fiction, at least fiction that aspires to accomplishing anything beyond filling time for the reader. Of course some forms of fiction are more or less formulaic, like sin-and-suffer confessions and pornography. When I was in graduate school in computer science, a friend and I put together a string-manipulation program that churned out WWI Flying Ace Stories, and, for the genre, I don't think they were half-bad. But most of us would rather read and write fiction that requires something more subtle than a random number generator to decide what happens next.

It occurs to me, assembling this fourth collection, that the typographical tradition of restricting story introduction and afterwords to a hundred or so words, and separating them by the stories themselves, limits what the author can say about each story, as well as how the stories might be related. So this time I'm assembling all of that stuff, I mean wit and wisdom, into one section in the back of the book, "Notes on the Stories." If nothing else, it will make it convenient for people who, like me, flip through and read all the introductions first, as well as for those who want to ignore everything but the stories.

All of these stories are collected here for the first time, but (for reasons explained in "Notes on the Stories") they cover a thirty-six-year span of writing, from my very first published story to one that I wrote while putting this book together. For perspective, I've added the year of writing to the end of each story.

Finally, the long average of nine years between story collections, from a person who writes for a living, ought to be addressed. Why don't you write more than two stories per year? It's not just that they pay less, per word or per hour of writing, than novels—in fact, they can sometimes pay more, if they're sold to a top market and often reprinted. But they represent an interruption, a distraction.

E. L. Doctorow caught the pace of a novelist's life with a driving metaphor: "Writing a novel is like driving at night. You can only see as far as your headlights will let you, but you can make the whole trip that way." Writing a short story, then, is like taking the car out for an afternoon spin, to visit an interesting place or person.

But the two don't mix well. Most writers can't just take time off from a novel, knock off a short story, and then come back and pick up the novel where they left it. The time and concentration that go into the story make you lose momentum on the novel. Run out of gas, there in the night.

So most of the stories here were written in between novels or in periods when I've suspended work on a novel in order to teach (which I do every fall semester). I admire people who can write novels and teach at the same time, but for me it's like holding down two jobs, both of which seem to draw on the same source of energy, and I only do it when forced to by deadlines. While I'm teaching I usually write only poetry, articles, and short stories, which don't require the level of engagement that a novel imposes.

Most of the stories here were written to order in one sense or another—challenges or requests from friends and editors. "I'm putting together an anthology of stories about the future of fruitcakes, and naturally I thought of *you* first." That's a lot different from my first two collections, which are mostly made up of stories that just happened. (The third one was about half and half, sui generis versus on-request.)

I remember those days with a certain wistfulness. I'd have several projects going at once, and when I got up in the morning, while fixing coffee, would decide which was most appealing, and then have at it.

It's been some years since I've had that freedom, which I've traded, conventionally, for security: like most of the people I know who write fiction for a living, I sign novel contracts with deadlines and write books more or less on schedule. If I get an idea for a short story while I'm working on a novel, I put it in a "Crazy Ideas" file, actually an old cigar box, which I sort through every now and then. I'm often startled to find that I've used one of those ideas in a novel—I'd forgotten jotting it down, but remembered at the deep level where stories must ultimately come from.

I suppose that's why it doesn't bother me that most of the short stories I write now are done on request. The answer to the question "Where do your crazy ideas some from?"—which really is the sought-after Secret of Writing—is not the editors who want a story about A.D. 3001 or terraforming or Future Washington or fruitcakes. I think if you're a storyteller, you have a myriad of more or less unformed stories simmering away, waiting for a reason to be told. The request frees the story to tell—perhaps to find out—what it's about.

—Joe Haldeman

A Separate War

1

Our wounds were horrible, but the army made us well and gave us Heaven, temporarily.

The most expensive and hard-to-replace component of a fighting suit is the soldier inside of it, so if she or he is crippled badly enough to be taken out of the fight, the suit tries to save what's left. In William's case, it automatically cut off his mangled leg and sealed the stump. In my case it was the right arm, just above the elbow.

That was the Tet-2 campaign, which was a disaster, and William and I lay around doped to the gills with happyjuice while the others died their way through the disaster of Aleph-7. The score after the two battles was fifty-four dead, thirty-seven of us crips, two head cases, and only twelve more or less working soldiers, who were of course bristling with enthusiasm. Twelve is not enough to fight a battle with, unfortunately, so the *Sangre y Victoria* was rerouted to the hospital planet Heaven.

We took a long time, three collapsar jumps, getting to Heaven. The Taurans can chase you through one jump, if they're at the right place and the right time. But two would be almost impossible, and three just couldn't happen.

(But "couldn't happen" is probably a bad-luck charm. Because of the relativistic distortions associated with travel through collapsar jumps, you never know, when you greet the enemy, whether it comes from your own time, or centuries in your past or future. Maybe in a millennium or two, they'll be able to follow you through three collapsar jumps like following footprints. One of the first things they'd do is vaporize Heaven. Then Earth.)

Heaven is like an Earth untouched by human industry and avarice, pristine forests and fields and mountains—but it's also a monument to human industry, and avarice, too.

When you recover—and there's no "if"; you wouldn't be there if they didn't know they could fix you—you're still in the army, but you're also immensely wealthy. Even a private's pay rolls up a fortune, automatically invested during the centuries that creak by between battles. One of the functions of Heaven is to put all those millions back into the economy. So there's no end of things to do, all of them expensive.

When William and I recovered, we were given six months of "rest and recreation" on Heaven. I actually got out two days before him, but waited around, reading. They did still have books, for soldiers so old-fashioned they didn't want to plug themselves into adventures or ecstasies for thousands of dollars a minute. I did have $529,755,012 sitting around, so I could have dipped into tripping. But I'd heard I would have plenty of it, retraining before our next assignment. The ALSC, "accelerated life situation computer," which taught you things by making you do them in virtual reality. Over and over, until you got them right.

William had half again as much money as I did, since he had outranked me for centuries, but I didn't wait around just to get my hands on his fortune. I probably would have wanted his company even if I didn't love him. We were the only two people here born in the twentieth century, and there were only a handful from the twenty-first. Very few of them, off duty, spoke a language I understood, though all soldiers were taught "premodern" English as a sort of temporal *lingua franca*. Some of them claimed their native language was English, but it was extremely fast and seemed to have lost some vowels along the way. Four centuries. Would I have sounded as strange to a Pilgrim? I don't think so.

(It would be interesting to take one of those Pilgrim Fathers and show him what had evolved from a life of grim piety and industriousness. Religion on Earth is a curiosity, almost as rare as heterosex. Heaven has no

God, either, and men and women in love or in sex with people not of their own gender are committing an anachronistic perversion.)

I'd already arranged for a sumptuous "honeymoon" suite on Skye, an airborne resort, before William got out, and we did spend five days there, amusing each other anachronistically. Then we rented a flyer and set out to see the world.

William humored my desire to explore the physical, wild, aspects of the world first. We camped in desert, jungle, arctic waste, mountaintops, deserted islands. We had pressor fields that kept away dangerous animals, allowing us a good close look at them while they tried to figure out what was keeping them from lunch, and they were impressive—evolution here had not favored mammal over reptile, and both families had developed large swift predators in a variety of beautiful and ugly designs.

Then we toured the cities, in their finite variety. Some, like the sylvan Threshold, where we'd grown and trained our new limbs, blended in with their natural surroundings. This was a twenty-second-century esthetic, too bland and obvious for modern tastes. The newer cities, like Skye, flaunted their artificiality.

We were both nervous in Atlantis, under a crushing kilometer of water, with huge, glowing beasts bumping against the pressors, dark day and dark night. Perhaps it was too exact a metaphor for our lives in the army, the thin skins of cruiser or fighting suit holding the dark nothingness of space at bay while monsters tried to destroy you.

Many of the cities had no function other than separating soldiers from their money, so in spite of their variety there was a sameness to them. Eat, drink, drug, trip, have or watch sex.

I found the sex shows more interesting than William did, but he was repelled by the men together. It didn't seem to me that what they did was all that different from what we did—and not nearly as alien as tripping for sex, plugging into a machine that delivered to you the image of an ideal mate and cleaned up afterwards.

He did go to a lesbian show with me, and made love with unusual energy that night. I thought there was something there besides titillation; that he was trying to prove something. We kidded each other about it— "Me Tarzan, you Jane," "Me Tarzan, you Heathcliff." Who on this world would know what we were laughing about?

Prostitution had a new wrinkle, with empathy drugs that joined the servicer and customer in a deep emotional bond that was real while it lasted, I suppose to keep in competition with the electronic fantasy. We told each other we weren't inclined to try it, though I was curious, and probably would have done it if I'd been alone. I don't think William would have, since the drugs don't work between men and women, or so one of them told us, giggling with wide-eyed embarrassment. The very idea.

We had six months of quiet communion and wild, desperate fun, and still had plenty of money left when it suddenly ended. We were having lunch in an elegant restaurant in Skye, watching the sun sparkle on the calm ocean a klick below, when a nervous private came up, saluted, and gave us our sealed orders.

They were for different places. William was going to Sade-138, a collapsar out in the Greater Magellanic Cloud. I was going to Aleph-10, in the Orion group.

He was a major, the Yod-4 Strike Force commander, and I was a captain, the executive officer for Aleph-10.

It was ridiculous. We'd been together since Basic—five years or half a millennium—and neither of us was leadership material. The army had abundant evidence of that. Yet he was leaving in a week, for Stargate. My Strike Force was mustering here, in orbit around Heaven, in two days.

We flew back to Threshold, half the world away, and got there just as the administrative offices were opening. William fought and bought his way to the top, trying at the very least to have me reassigned as his XO. What difference could it make? Most of the people he'd muster with at Stargate hadn't even been born yet.

Of course it was not a matter of logic; it was a matter of protocol. And no army in history had ever been so locked in the ice of protocol. The person who *signed* those orders for the yet unborn was probably dead by now.

We had a day and a night together, sad and desperate. At the end, when I had to go into isolation three hours before launch, we were almost deferential with one another, perhaps the way you act in the presence of beloved dead. No poet who ever equated parting with death had ever had a door slam shut like that. Even if we had both been headed for Earth, a few days apart, the time-space geometry of the collapsar jump would guarantee that we arrived decades or even centuries from one another.

And this wasn't Earth. There were 150,000 light-years between Sade-138 and Aleph-10. Absolute distance means nothing in collapsar geometry, they say. But if William were to die in a nova bomb attack, the tiny spark of his passing would take fifteen hundred centuries to crawl to Orion, or Earth. Time and distance beyond imagination.

The spaceport was on the equator, of course, on an island they called Pærw'l; Farewell. There was a high cliff, actually a flattened-off pinnacle, overlooking the bay to the east, where William and I had spent silent days fasting and meditating. He said he was going there to watch the launch. I hoped to get a window so that I could see the island, and I did push my way to one when we filed into the shuttle. But I couldn't see the pinnacle from sea level, and when the engines screamed and the invisible force pushed me back into the cushions, I looked but was blinded by tears, and couldn't raise a hand to wipe them away.

2

Fortunately, I had six hours' slack time after we docked at the space station Athene, before I had to report for ALSC training. Time to pull myself together. I went to my small quarters and unpacked and lay on the bunk for a while. Then I found my way to the lounge and watched the planet spin below, green and white and blue. There were eleven ships in orbit a few klicks away, one a large cruiser, presumably the *Bolivar*, which was going to take us to Aleph-10.

The lounge was huge and almost empty. Two other women in unfamiliar beige uniforms, I supposed Athene staff. They were talking in the strange fast Angel language.

While I was getting coffee, a man walked in wearing tan-and-green camouflage fatigues like mine. We weren't actually camouflaged as well as the ones in beige, in this room of comforting wood and earth tones.

He came over and got a cup. "You're Captain Potter, Marygay Potter."

"That's right," I said. "You're in Beta?"

"No, I'm stationed here, but I'm army." He offered his hand. "Michael Dobei, Mike. Colonel. I'm your Temporal Orientation Officer."

We carried our coffee to a table. "You're supposed to catch me up on this future, this present?"

He nodded. "Prepare you for dealing with the men and women under you. And the other officers."

"What I'm trying to deal with is this 'under you' part. I'm no soldier, Colonel."

"Mike. You're actually a better soldier than you know. I've seen your profile. You've been through a lot of combat, and it hasn't broken you. Not even the terrible experience on Earth."

William and I had been staying on my parents' farm when we were attacked by a band of looters; Mother and Dad were killed. "That's in my profile? I wasn't a soldier then. We'd quit."

"There's a lot of stuff in there." He raised his coffee and looked at me over the rim of the cup. "Want to know what your high-school advisor thought of you?"

"You're a shrink."

"That used to be the word. Now we're 'skinks.'"

I laughed. "That used to be a lizard."

"Still is." He pulled a reader out of his pocket. "You were last on Earth in 2007. You liked it so little that you reenlisted."

"Has it gotten better?"

"Better, then worse, then better. As ever. When I left, in 2318, things were at least peaceful."

"Drafted?"

"Not in the sense you were. I knew from age ten what I was going to be; everybody does."

"What? You knew you were going to be a Temporal Adjustment Officer?"

"Uh-huh." He smiled. "I didn't know quite what that meant, but I sure as hell resented it. I had to go to a special school, to learn this language—SoldierSpeak—but I had to take four years of it, instead of the two that most soldiers do.

"I suppose we're more regimented on Earth now; crèche to grave control, but also security. The crime and anarchy that characterized your Earth are ancient history. Most people live happy, fulfilling lives."

"Homosexual. No families."

"Oh, we have families, parents, but not random ones. To keep the population stable, one person is quickened whenever one dies. The new one goes to a couple that has grown up together in the knowledge that they have a talent for parenting; they'll be given, at most, four children to raise."

"'Quickened'—test-tube babies?"

"Incubators. No birth trauma. No real uncertainty about the future. You'll find your troops a pretty sane bunch of people."

"And what will they find *me*? They won't resent taking orders from a heterosexual throwback? A dinosaur?"

"They know history; they won't blame you for being what you are. If you tried to initiate sex with one of the men, there might be trouble."

I shook my head. "That won't happen. The only man I love is gone, forever."

He looked down at the floor and cleared his throat. Can you embarrass a professional skink? "William Mandella. I wish they hadn't done that. It seems . . . unnecessarily cruel."

"We tried to get me reassigned as his XO."

"That wouldn't have worked. That's the paradox." He moved the cup in circles on the table, watching the reflections dance. "You both have so much time in rank, objective and subjective, that they had to give you commissions. But they couldn't put you under William. The heterosex issue aside, he would be more concerned about your safety than about the mission. The troops would see that, and resent it."

"What, it never happens in your brave new world? You never have a commander falling in love with someone in his or her command?"

"Of course it happens; het or home, love happens. But they're separated and sometimes punished, or at least reprimanded." He waved that away. "In theory. If it's not blatant, who cares? But with you and William, it would be a constant irritant to the people underneath you."

"Most of them have never seen heterosexuals, I suppose."

"None of them. It's detected early and easy to cure."

"Wonderful. Maybe they can cure me."

"No. I'm afraid it has to be done before puberty." He laughed. "Sorry. You were kidding me."

"You don't think my being het is going to hurt my ability to command?"

"No, like I say, they know how people used to be—besides, privates aren't supposed to *empathize* with their officers; they're supposed to follow their orders. And they know about ALSC training; they'll know how well prepared you are."

"I'll be out of the chain of command, anyhow, as executive officer."

"Unless everybody over you dies. It's happened."

"Then the army will find out what a mistake it made. A little too late."

"You might surprise yourself, after the ALSC training." He checked his watch. "Which is coming up in a couple of hours."

"Would you like to get together for lunch before that?"

"Um, no. I don't think you want to eat. They sort of clean you out beforehand. From both ends."

"Sounds . . . dramatic."

"Oh, it is, all of it. Some people enjoy it."

"You don't think I will."

He paused. "Let's talk about it afterwards."

3

The purging wasn't bad, since by that time I was limp and goofy with drugs. They shaved me clean as a baby, even my arms and cheeks, and were in the process of covering me with feedback sensors when I dozed off.

I woke up naked and running. A bunch of other naked people were running after me and my friends, throwing rocks at us. A heavy rock stung me under the shoulder blade, knocking my breath away and making me stumble. A chunky Neanderthal tackled me and whacked me on the head twice with something.

I knew this was a simulation, a dream, and here I was passing out in a dream. When I woke up a moment later, he had forced my legs apart and was about to rape me. I clawed at his eyes and rolled away. He came after me, intention still apparent, and my hand fell on his club. I swung it with both hands and cracked his head, spraying blood and brains. He ejaculated in shuddering spurts as he died, feet drumming the ground. God, it was supposed to be realistic, but couldn't they spare me a few details?

Then I was standing in a phalanx with a shield and a long spear. There were men in front of our line, crouching, with shorter spears. All of the weapons were braced at the same angle, presenting a wall of points to the horses that were charging toward us. This is not the hard part. You just stand firm, and live or not. I studied the light armor of the Persian enemy as they approached. There were three who might be in my area if we unhorsed them, or if their horses stopped.

The horse on my left crashed through. The one on the right reared up and tried to turn. The one charging straight at us took both spears in the breast, breaking the shaft of mine as it skidded, sprawling, spraying blood and screaming with an unearthly high whine, pinning the man in front of me. The unhorsed Persian crashed into my shield and knocked me down as I was drawing my short sword; the hilt of it dug in under my ribs and I almost slashed myself getting it free of the scabbard while I scrambled back to my feet.

The horseman had lost his little round shield, but his sword was coming around in a flat arc. I just caught it on the edge of my shield and *as I had been taught* chopped down toward his unprotected forearm and wrist—he twisted away, but I nicked him under the elbow, lucky shot that hit a tendon or something. He dropped his sword and as he reached for it with his other hand, I slashed at his face and opened a terrible wound across eye, cheek, and mouth. As he screamed a flap of skin fell away, exposing bloody bone and teeth, and I shifted my weight for a backhand, aiming for the unprotected throat, and then something slammed into my back and the bloody point of a spear broke the skin above my right nipple; I fell to my knees dying and realized I didn't have breasts; I was a man, a young boy.

It was dark and cold and the trench smelled of shit and rotting flesh. "Two minutes, boys," a sergeant said in a stage whisper. I heard a canteen gurgle twice and took it when it was passed to me, warm gin. I managed not to cough and passed it on down. I checked in the darkness and still didn't have breasts and touched between my legs and that was strange. I started to shake and heard the man next to me peeing, and I suddenly had to go, too. I fumbled with the buttons left-handed, holding on to my rifle, and barely managed to get the thing out in time, peeing hotly onto my hand. "Fix bayonets," the sergeant whispered while I was still going *and instinct took over* and I felt the locking port under the muzzle of my Enfield and held it with my left hand while my right went back and slid the bayonet from its sheath and clicked it into place.

"I shall see you in Hell, Sergeant Simmons," the man next to me said conversationally.

"Soon enough, Rez. Thirty seconds." There was a German machine-gun position about eighty yards ahead and to the right. They also had at least one very good sniper and, presumably, an artillery observer. We were hoping for some artillery support at 1:17, which would signal the beginning of our charge. If the artillery didn't come, which was likely, we were to charge anyhow, riflemen in two short squads in front of grenadiers. A suicide mission, perhaps, but certain death if your courage flags.

I wiped my hand on the greasy, filthy fatigues and thumbed the safety off the rifle. There was already a round chambered. I put my left foot on the improvised step and got a handhold with my left. My knees were water, and my anus didn't want to stay closed. I felt tears, and my throat went dry and metallic. *This is not real.* "Now," the sergeant said quietly, and I heaved myself up over the lip of the trench and fired one-handed in the general direction of the enemy, and started to run toward them, working the bolt, vaguely proud of not soiling myself. I flopped on the ground and took an aimed shot at the noise of the machine gun, no muzzle flash, and then held fire while squad two rushed by us. A grenadier skidded next to me, and said, "Go!" It became "Oh!" when a bullet smacked into him, but I was up and running, another round chambered, four left. A bullet shattered my foot, and I took one painful step and fell.

I pulled myself forward, trying to keep the muzzle out of the mud, and rolled into a shallow crater half-filled with water and parts of a swollen decaying body. I could hear another machine gun starting, but I couldn't breathe. I pushed up with both arms to gasp some air above the crater's miasma, and a bullet crashed into my teeth.

It wasn't chronological. I went from there to the mist of Breed's Hill, on the British side of what the Americans would call the Battle of Bunker Hill. The deck of a ship, warding off pirates while sails burned; then another ship, deafened by cannon fire while I tried to keep a cool lead on the kamikaze Zero soaring into us.

I flew cloth-winged biplanes and supersonic fighters, used lasers and a bow and arrow and leveled a city with the push of a button. I killed with bullets and bolos and binary-coded decimals. Every second, I was aware that it was a training exercise; I felt terror and sorrow and pain, but only for minutes or hours. And I slept at least as many hours as I was awake, but there was no rest—somehow while sleeping, my brain was filled with procedures, history, regulations.

When they unplugged me after three weeks I was literally catatonic. That was normal, though, and they had drugs that pulled you back into the world. They worked for more than 90 percent of the new officers. The others were allowed to drift away.

4

We had two weeks of rest and rehabilitation—in orbit, unfortunately, not on Heaven—after the ALSC experience. While we were sweating it out in the officers' gym, I met the other line officers, who were as shaken and weak as I was, after three weeks' immersion in oxygenated fluorocarbon, mayhem, and book learning.

We were also one mass of wrinkles from head to toe, the first day, when our exercises consisted of raising our arms above our heads and trying to stand up and sit down without help. The wrinkles started to fade in the sauna, as we conversed in tired monosyllables. We looked like big muscular pink babies; they must have shaved or depilated us during the three weeks.

Three of us were male, which was interesting. I've seen lots of naked men, but never a hairless one. I guess we all looked kind of exposed and diagrammatic. Okayawa had an erection, and Morales kidded him about it, but to my relief it didn't go any further than that. It was a socially difficult situation anyhow.

The commander, Angela Garcia, was physically about ten years older than me, though of course by the calendar she was centuries younger. She was gruff and seemed to be holding a lot in. I knew her slightly, at least by sight; she'd been a platoon leader, not mine, in the Tet-2 disaster. Both her legs had the new-equipment look that my arm did. We'd come to Heaven together, but since her regrowth took three times as long as mine, we hadn't met there. William and I were gone before she was able to come into the common ward.

William had been in many of my ALSC dreams, a shadowy figure in some of the crowds. My father sometimes, too.

I liked Sharn Taylor, the medical officer, right off. She had a cheerful fatalism about the whole thing, and had lived life to the hilt while on Heaven, hiring a succession of beautiful women to help her spend her fortune. She'd run out of money a week early, and had to come back to Threshold and live on army rations and the low-power trips you could get for free. She herself was not beautiful; a terrible wound had ripped off her left arm and breast and the left side of her face. It had all been put back, but the new parts didn't match the old parts too well.

She had a doctor's objectivity about it, though, and professional admiration for the miracles they could accomplish—by the current calendar, she was more than 150 years out of medical school.

Her ALSC session had been totally different from ours, of course; an update of healing skills rather than killing ones. "Most of it is getting along with machines, though, rather than treating people," she told me while we nibbled at the foodlike substance that was supposed to help us recover. "I can treat wounds in the field, basically to keep someone alive until we can get to a machine. But most modern weapons don't leave enough to salvage." She had a silly smile.

"We don't know how modern the enemy is going to be," I said. "Though I guess they don't have to be all *that* modern to vaporize us." We both giggled, and then stopped simultaneously.

"I wonder what they've got us on," she said. "It's not happyjuice; I can feel my fingertips and have all my peripheral vision."

"Temporary mood elevator?"

"I hope it's temporary. I'll talk to someone."

Sharn found out that it was just a euphoriant in the food; without it, ALSC withdrawal could bring on deep depression. I'd almost rather be depressed, I thought. We *were*, after all, facing almost certain doom. All but one of us had survived at least one battle in a war where the average survival rate was only 34 percent per battle. If you believed in luck, you might believe we'd used all of ours up.

We had the satellite to ourselves for eight days—ten officers waited on by a staff of thirty support personnel—while we got our strength back. Of course friendships formed. It was pretty obvious that it went beyond friendship with Chance Nguyen and Aurelio Morales; they stuck like glue from the first day.

Risa Danyi and Sharn and I made up a logical trio, the three officers out of the chain of command. Risa was the tech officer, a bit older than Sharn and me, with a Ph.D. in systems engineering. She seemed younger, though, born and raised on Heaven. Not actually born, I reminded myself. And never traumatized by combat.

Risa's ALSC had been the same as mine, but she had found it more fascinating than terrifying. She was apologetic about that. She had grown up tripping, and was accustomed to the immediacy and drama of it—and she didn't have any real-life experiences to relate to the dream combat.

Both Risa and Sharn were bawdy by nature and curious about my heterosex, and while we were silly with the euphoriants I didn't hold back anything. When I was first in the army, we'd had to obey a rotating "sleeping roster," so I slept with every male private in the company more than once, and although sleeping together didn't mean you had to have sex, it was considered unsporting to refuse. And of course men are men; most of them would have to go through the motions, literally, even if they didn't feel like it.

Even on board ship, when they got rid of the sleeping roster, there was still a lot of switching around. I was mainly with William, but neither of us was exclusive (which would have been considered odd, in our generation). Nobody was fertile, so there was no chance of accidental pregnancy.

That notion really threw Sharn and Risa. Pregnancy is something that happens to animals. Sharn had seen pictures of the process, medical history, and described it to us in horrifying detail. I had to remind them that I was born that way—I did *that* to my mother, and she somehow forgave me.

Risa primly pointed out that it was actually my father who did it to my mother, which for some reason we all thought was hilarious.

One morning when we were alone together, just looking down at the planet in the lounge, she brought up the obvious.

"You haven't said anything about it, so I guess you've never loved a woman." She cleared her throat, nervous. "I mean had sex. I know you loved your mother."

"No." I didn't know whether to elaborate. "It wasn't that common; I mean I *knew* girls and women who were together. That way."

"Well." She patted my elbow. "You know."

"Uh, yes. I mean yes, I understand. Thanks, but I . . ."

"I just meant, you know, we're the same rank. It's even legal." She laughed nervously; if all the regulations were broken that enthusiastically, we'd be an unruly mob, not an army.

I wasn't quite sure what to say. Until she actually asked, I hadn't thought about the possibility except as an abstraction. "I'm still grieving for William." She nodded and gave me another pat and left quietly.

But of course that wasn't all of it. I could visualize her and Sharn, for instance, having sex; I'd seen it on stage and cube often enough. But I couldn't put myself in their place. Not the way I could visualize myself being with one of the men, especially Sid, Isidro Zhulpa. He was quiet, introspective, darkly beautiful. But too well balanced to contemplate a sexual perversion involving me.

I was still jangled about fantasy, imagination; real and artificial memories. I knew for certain that I had never killed anyone with a club or a knife, but my body seemed to have a memory of it, more real than the mental picture. I could still feel the ghost of a penis and balls, and breastlessness, since all of the ALSC combat templates were male. Surely that was more alien than lying down with another woman. When I was waiting for William to get out of his final range-and-motion stage, reading for two days, I'd had an impulse to try tripping, plugging into a lesbian sex simulation, the only kind that was available for women.

For a couple of reasons, I didn't do it. Now that it's too late—the only trips on Athene are ALSC ones—I wish I had. Because it's not as simple as "I accept this because it's the way they were brought up," with the implied condescension that my pedestal of normality entitles me.

Normality. I'm going to be locked up in a can with 130 other people for whom my most personal, private life is something as exotic as cannibalism. So rare they don't even have an epithet for it. I was sure they'd come up with one.

TABLE OF ORGANIZATION
Strike Force Beta
Aleph-10 Campaign

1ECHN	MAJ Garcia		COMM Sidorenko
2ECHN	1LT Nguyen		
3ECHN	1LT Zhulpa		
4ECHN	CPT Potter	XO	
	2LT Darnyi	TO	
	2LT Taylor, MD	MO	

	1	2	3	4
5ECHN	2LT Sadovyi	2LT Okayawa	2LT Mathes	2LT Morales
6ECHN	SSgt Baron	SSgt Troy	SSgt Tsuruta	SSgt Hencken
7ECHN	Sgt Naber	Sgt Kitamura	Sgt Yorzyk	Sgt Verdeur
8ECHN	Cpl Roth	Cpl Gross	Cpl Bruner	Cpl Graef
	Cpl Sieben	Cpl Simeony	Cpl Ritter	Cpl Henkel
	Cpl Korir	Cpl Sadovyi	Cpl Loader	Cpl Catherwood
	Cpl Montgomery	Cpl Popov	Cpl Hajos	Cpl Hamay
	Cpl Daniels	Cpl Kahanamoku	Cpl Miyzaki	Cpl Csik
	Cpl Son	Cpl Daniels	Cpl Taylor	Cpl Hopkins
	Cpl Devitt	Cpl Schollander	Cpl Winden	Cpl Spitz
	Cpl Gammoudi	Cpl Akii-Bua	Cpl Beiwat	Cpl Keino
	Cpl Armstrong	Cpl Kariuki	Cpl Brir	Cpl Keter
	Cpl Kostadinova	Cpl Ajunwa	Cpl Roba	Cpl Keimo
	Cpl McDonald	Cpl Balas	Cpl Reskova	Cpl Mayfair
	Cpl Zubero	Cpl Furniss	Cpl Kopilakov	Cpl Gross
	Cpl Myazaki	Cpl Roth	Cpl Pakratov	Cpl Lopez
	Cpl Ris	Cpl Scholes	Cpl Ris	Cpl Henricks
	Cpl Russell	Cpl Rozsa	Cpl Moorhouse	Cpl Lundquist
	Cpl Shiley	Cpl Csak	Cpl Coachman	Cpl Brand
	Cpl Ackerman	Cpl Pankritov	Cpl Nesty	Cpl O'Brien
	Pvt Darryl	Pvt Gyenji	Pvt Crapp	Pvt Hong
	Pvt Biondi	Pvt Stewart, M.	Pvt Baumann	Pvt Stewart, J.
		Pvt Engel-Kramer	Pvt Min	Pvt Mingxia

Supporting: 1LT Otto (NAV), 2LTs Wennyl and Van Dykken (MED), Durack (PSY), Bleibkey (MAINT), Lackey (ORD), Obspowich (COMM), Madison (COMP); 1Sgts Mastenbroek (MED), Anderson (MED), Szoki (MED), Fraser (MED), Henne (PSY), Neelson (MAINT), Ender (ORD); SSgts Krause (MED), Steinseller (MED), Hogshead (MED), Otto (MED), Yong (MAINT), Jingyi (CK), Meyer (COMP); Sgts Gould (MED), Bonder (MAINT), Kraus (ORD), Waite (REC); Cpls Friedrich (MED), Haislett (MED), Poll (SEX), Norelius (SEX), Gyenge (ORD); Pvts Curtiss (MAINT), Senff (CK), Harup (ORD).

APPROVED STFCOM STARGATE 12 Mar 2458   FOR THE COMMANDER:
                                                       Olga Torischeva BGEN STFCOM

The lounge was a so-called plastic room; it could re-form itself into various modes, according to function. One of the Athene staff had handed over the control box to me—my first executive function as executive officer.

When the troop carriers lined up outside for docking, I pushed the button marked "auditorium," and the comfortable wood grain faded to a neutral ivory color as the furniture sank into the floor, and then rose up again, extruding three rows of seats on ascending tiers. The control box asked me how many seats to put on the stage in front. I said six and then corrected myself, to seven. The Commodore would be here, for ceremony's sake.

As I watched the Strike Force file into the auditorium, I tried to separate the combat veterans from the Angels. There weren't too many of the latter; only fourteen out of the 130 were born on Heaven. For a good and unsettling reason.

Major Garcia waited until all the seats were filled, and then she waited a couple of minutes longer, studying the faces, maybe doing the same kind of sorting. Then she stood up and introduced the Commodore and the other officers, down to my echelon, and got down to business.

"I'm certain that you have heard rumors. One of them is true." She took a single note card from her tunic pocket and set it on the lectern. "One hundred sixteen of us have been in combat before. All wounded and brought here to Heaven. For repairs and then rest.

"You may know that this concentration of veterans is unusual. The army values experience, and spreads it around. A group this size would normally have about twenty combat veterans. Of course this implies that we face a difficult assignment.

"We are attacking the oldest known enemy base." She paused. "The Taurans established a presence on the portal planet of the collapsar Aleph-10 more than two hundred years ago. We've attacked them twice, to no effect."

She didn't say how many survivors there had been from those two attacks. I knew there had been none.

"If, as we hope, the Taurans have been out of contact with their home planet for the past two centuries, we have a huge technological advantage. The details of this advantage will not be discussed until we are under weigh." An absurd but standard security procedure. A spying Tauran could no more disguise itself and come aboard than a moose could. No one here could be in the pay of the Taurans. The two species had never exchanged anything but projectiles.

"We are three collapsar jumps away from Aleph-10, so we will have eleven months to train with the new weapon systems . . . with which we will defeat them." She allowed herself a bleak smile. "By the time we reach them, we may be coming from four hundred years in their future. That's the length of time that elapsed between the defeat of the Spanish Armada and the first nuclear war."

Of course relativity does not favor one species over the other. The Taurans on Aleph-10 might have had visitors from their own future, bearing gifts.

The troops were quiet and respectful, absorbing the fraction of information that Major Garcia portioned out. I supposed most of them knew that things were not so rosy, even the inexperienced Angels. She gave them a few more encouraging generalities and dismissed them to their temporary billets. We officers were to meet with her in two hours, for lunch.

I spent the intervening time visiting the platoon billets, talking with the sergeants who would actually be running the show, day by day. I'd seen their records but hadn't met any of them except Cat Verdeur, who had been in physical therapy with me. We both had right-arm replacements, and as part of our routine we were required to arm wrestle every day, apologetic about the pain we were causing each other. She was glad to see me, and said she would have let me win occasionally if she'd known I was going to outrank her.

The officers' lounge was also a plastic room, which I hadn't known. It had been a utilitarian meeting place before, with machines that dispensed simple food and drink. Now it was dark wood and intricate tile; linen napkins and crystal. Of course the wood felt like plastic and the linen, like paper, but you couldn't have everything.

Nine of us showed up on the hour, and the major came in two minutes later. She greeted everyone and pushed a button, and the cooks Jengyi and Senff appeared with real food and two carafes of wine. Aromatic stir-fried vegetables and zoni, which resembled large shrimp.

"Let's enjoy this while we can," she said. "We'll be back on recycled Class A's soon enough." Athene had room enough for the luxury of hydroponics and, apparently, fish tanks.

She asked us to introduce ourselves, going around the table's circle. I knew a little bit about everyone, since my XO file had basic information on the whole Strike Force, and extensive dossiers of the officers and noncoms. But there were surprises. I knew that the major had survived five battles, but didn't know she'd been to Heaven four times, which was a record. I knew her second-in-command, Chance Nguyen, came from Mars, but didn't know he was from the first generation born there, and was the first person drafted from his planet—there had been a huge argument over it, with separatists saying the Forever War was Earth's war. But at that time, Earth could still threaten to pull the plug on Mars. The red planet was self-sufficient now, Chance said, but he'd been away for a century, and didn't know what the situation was.

Lillian Mathes just came from Earth, with less than twenty years' collapsar lag, and she said they weren't drafting from Mars at that time; it was all tied up in court. So Chance might be the only Martian officer in service.

He had a strange way of carrying himself and moving, wary and careful, swimming through this unnaturally high gravity. He told me he'd trained for a Martian year, wearing heavier and heavier weights, before going to Stargate and his first assignment.

All of them were scholarly and athletic, but only Sid, Isidro Zhulpa, had actually been both a scholar and an athlete. He'd played professional baseball for a season, but quit to pursue his doctorate in sociology. He'd gotten his appointment as a junior professor the day before his draft notice. His skin was so black as to be almost blue; with his chiseled features and huge muscularity, he looked like some harsh African god. But he was quiet and modest, my favorite.

I mainly talked with him and Sharn through the meal, chatting about everything but our immediate future. When everything was done, the cooks came in with two carts and cleared the table, leaving tea and coffee. Garcia waited until all of us had been served and the privates were gone.

"Of course we don't have the faintest idea of what's waiting for us at Aleph-10," the major said. "One thing we have been able to find out, which I don't think any of you have been told, is that we know how the second Strike Force bought it."

That was something new. "It was like a minefield. A matrix of nova bombs in a belt around the portal planet's equator. We're assuming it's still there."

"They couldn't detect it and avoid it?" Risa asked.

"It was an active system. The bombs actually chased them down. They detonated four, coming closer and closer, until the fifth got them. The drone that was recording the action barely got away; one of the bombs managed to chase it through the first collapsar jump.

"We can counter the system. We're being preceded by an intelligent drone squad that should be able to detonate all of the ring of nova bombs simultaneously. It should make things pretty warm on the ground, as well as protecting our approach."

"We don't know what got the first Strike Force?" Sid asked.

Garcia shook her head. "The drone didn't return. All we can say for sure is that it wasn't the same thing."

"How so?" I asked.

"Aleph-10's easily visible from Earth; it's about eighty light-years away. They would have detected a nova bomb 120 years ago, if there'd been one. The assumption has to be that they attacked in a conventional way, as ordered, and were destroyed. Or had some accident on the way."

Of course they hadn't beamed any communication back to Earth or Stargate. We still didn't. The war was being fought on portal planets, near collapsars, which were usually desolate, disposable rocks. It would only take one nova bomb to vaporize the Stargate station; perhaps three to wipe out life on Earth.

So we didn't want to give them a road map back.

6

A lot of the training over the next eleven months had to do with primitive weapons, which explained why so much of my ALSC time had been spent practicing with bows and arrows, spears, knives, and so forth. We had a new thing called a "stasis field," which made a bubble inside which you *had* to use simple tools: no energy weapons worked.

In fact, physics itself didn't work too well inside a stasis field; chemistry, not at all. Nothing could move faster than 16.3 meters per second inside—including elementary particles and light. (You could see inside, but it wasn't light; it was some tachyon thing.) If you were exposed to the field unprotected, you'd die instantly of brain death—no electricity—and anyhow freeze solid in a few seconds. So we had suits made of stuff like tough crinkly aluminum foil, full of uncomfortable plumbing and gadgets so that everything recycled. You could live inside the stasis field, inside the suit, indefinitely. Until you went mad.

But one rip, even a pinprick, in the fabric of the suit, and you were instantly dead.

For that reason, we didn't practice with the primitive weapons inside the field. And if you had a training accident that caused the smallest scratch, on yourself or anyone else, you got to meditate on it for a day in solitary confinement. Even officers; my carelessness with arrow points cost me a long anxious day in darkness.

Only one platoon could fit in the gym at a time, so at first I trained with whoever was using it when I got a few hours off from my other duties. After a while I arranged my schedule so that it was always the fourth platoon. I liked both Aurelio Morales, the squad leader, and his staff sergeant, Karl Hencken. But mainly I liked Cat Verdeur.

I don't remember a particular time when the chumminess suddenly turned into sex; there was nothing like a proposition and a mad fling. We were physically close from the beginning, because of our shared experience at Threshold. Then we were natural partners for hand-to-hand combat practice, being about the same physical age and condition. That was a rough kind of intimacy, and the fact that officers and noncoms had a shower separate from the other men and women gave us another kind.

Aurelio and Karl took one side, and Cat and I took the other. We sort of soaped each other's backs, and eventually fronts.

Being a sergeant, Cat didn't have her own billet; she slept in a wing with the other women in her platoon. But one night she showed up at my door on the verge of tears, with a mysterious problem we'd both been dealing with: sometimes the new arm just doesn't feel like it belongs. It obeys your commands, but it's like a separate creature, grafted on, and the feeling of its separateness can take over everything. I let her cry on my shoulder, the good one, and then we shared my narrow bed for the night. We didn't do anything that we hadn't done many times in the shower, but it wasn't playful. I lay awake thinking, long after she fell asleep with her cheek on my breast.

I still loved William, but barring a miracle I would never see him again. What I felt for Cat was more than just friendship, and by her standards and everyone else's there was nothing odd about it. And there was no way I could have had a future with Sid or any of the other men.

When I was young there'd been a sarcastic song that went "If I can't be with the one I love, I'll love the one I'm with." I guess that sort of sums it up.

I went to Elise Durack, the Strike Force psychologist, and she helped me through some twists and turns. Then Cat and I went together to Octavia Poll, the female sex counselor, which wound up being a strange and funny four-way consultation with Dante Norelius, the male counselor. That resulted in a mechanical contrivance that we giggled about but occasionally used, which made it more like sex with a man. Cat sympathized with my need to hold on to my past, and said she didn't mind that I was remembering William when I was with her. She thought it was romantic, if perverse.

I started to bring the subject up with the major, and she brushed it off with a laugh. Everyone who cared aboard ship knew about it, and it was a good thing; it made me seem less strange to them. If I had been in Cat's platoon, above her in the direct chain of command, she would be routinely assigned to another platoon, which had been done several times.

(The logic of that is clear, but it made me wonder about Garcia herself. If she became in love with another woman, there wouldn't be any way to put that woman someplace outside of her command. But as far as I knew, she didn't have anybody.)

Cat more or less moved in with me. If some people in her platoon resented it, more were just as glad not to have their sergeant watching over them every hour of the day. She usually stayed with them until first lights-out, and then walked down the corridor to my billet—often passing other people on similar missions. Hard to keep secrets of that sort in a spaceship, and not many tried.

There was an element of desperation in our relationship, doomed souls sharing a last few months, but that was true of everybody's love unless they were absolutely myopic one-day-at-a-timers. If the numbers held, only 34 percent of us had any future beyond Elephant, which is what everybody called Aleph-10 by the time we angled in for our second collapsar jump.

William had tried in a resigned way to explain the physics of it all, the first time we did a jump, but math had defeated me in college long before calculus kicked me permanently into majoring in English. It has to do with acceleration. If you just fell toward a collapsar, the way normal matter does, you would be doomed. For some reason you and the people around you would seem to be falling forever, but to the outside world, you would be snuffed out instantly.

Well, sure. Obviously nobody ever did the experiment.

Anyhow, you accelerate toward the collapsar's "event horizon," which is what it has instead of a surface, at a precalculated speed and angle, and you pop out of another collapsar umpty light-years away—maybe five, maybe five million. You better get the angle right, because you can't always just reverse things and come back.

(Which we hoped was all that happened to the first Elephant Strike Force. They might be on the other side of the galaxy, colonizing some nice quiet world. Every cruiser did carry a set of wombs and a crèche, against that possibility, though the major rolled her eyes when she described it. Purely a morale device, she said; they probably didn't work. I wondered whether, in that case, people might be able to grit their teeth and try to make babies the old-fashioned way.)

Since we were leaving from Heaven, we were required to make at least two collapsar jumps before "acquiring" Elephant. That soaked up two centuries of objective time, if such a thing exists. To us it was eleven fairly stressful months. Besides the training with the old-fashioned weapons, the troops had to drill with their fighting suits and whatever specialized weapon system they were assigned to, in case the stasis field didn't work or had been rendered useless by some enemy development.

Meanwhile, I did my executive officer work. It was partly bookkeeping, which is almost trivial aboard ship, since nothing comes in and nothing goes out. The larger part was a vague standing assignment to keep up the troops' morale.

I was not well qualified for that; perhaps less qualified than anybody else aboard. Their music didn't sound like music to me. Their games seemed pointless, even after they'd been relentlessly explained. The movies were interesting, at least as anthropology, and the pleasures of food and drink hadn't changed much, but their sex lives were still pretty mysterious to me, in spite of my affection for Cat and the orgasms we exchanged. If a man and a woman walked by, I was still more interested in the man. So I did love a woman, but as an actual lesbian I was not a great success.

Sometimes that gave me comfort, a connection to William and my past. More often it made me feel estranged, helpless.

I did have eight part-time volunteers, and one full-time subordinate, Sergeant Cody Waite. He was not an asset. I think the draft laws on Earth, the Elite Conscription Act, were ignored on Heaven. In fact, I would go even further (to make a reference that nobody on the ship would understand) and claim that there was a Miltonian aspect to his arrival. He had been expelled from Heaven, for overweening pride. But he had nothing to be proud of, except his face and muscles. He had the intelligence of a hamster. He did look like a Greek god, but for me what that meant was that every time I needed him to do something, he was down in the gym working out on the machines. Or off getting his rectum reamed by some adoring guy who didn't have to talk with him. He could read and write, though, so eventually I found I could keep him out of the way by having him elaborate on my weekly reports. He could take "This week was the same as last week," and turn it into an epic of relentless tedium.

I was glad to be out of the chain of command. You train people intensively for combat and then put them into a box for eleven months of what? More training for combat. Nobody's happy and some people snap.

The men are usually worse than the women—or, at least, when the women lose control it tends to be a shouting match rather than fists and feet. Cat had a pair who were an exception, though, and it escalated to attempted murder in the mess hall.

This was ten days before the last collapsar jump—everybody on the ragged edge—between Lain Mayfair and "Tiny" Keimo, who was big enough to take on most of the men. Lain tried to cut her throat, from behind, and Tiny broke her arm at the elbow while everybody else was diving for cover, and was seriously strangling her—trying to kill her before she herself bled to death—when the cook, J. J., ran over and brained the big woman with a frying pan.

While they were still in the infirmary there was a summary court-martial. With the consistent testimony of forty witnesses, Major Garcia didn't have any choice: she sentenced Lain Mayfair to death for attempted murder. She administered the lethal injection herself.

I was required to be a witness, and more, and it was not the high point of my day. Mayfair was bedridden and, I think, slightly sedated. Garcia explained the reason for the verdict and asked Mayfair whether she would prefer the dignity of taking the poison herself. She didn't say anything, just cried and shook her head. Two privates held her down by the shoulders while Garcia took her arm and administered the popper. Mayfair turned pale and her eyes rolled up. She shook convulsively for a few seconds and was dead.

Garcia didn't show any emotion during the ordeal. She whispered to me that she would be in her quarters if anybody really needed her, and left quickly.

I had to supervise the disposal of the body. I had two medics wrap her tightly in a sheet and put her on a gurney. We had to roll it down the main corridor, everybody watching. I helped the two of them carry her into the airlock. She was starting to stiffen, but her body wasn't even cold.

I had a friend read a prayer in Mayfair's language, and asked the engineer for maximum pressure in the airlock, and then popped it. Her body spun out into its lonely, infinite grave.

I went back to the infirmary and found Tiny inconsolable. She and Mayfair had been lovers back on Stargate. Everything had gone wrong, nothing made sense, why why why why? My answer was to have Sharn give her a tranquilizer. I took one myself.

7

We came tearing out of the Elephant's collapsar about one minute after the defense phalanx, the ten high-speed intelligent drones that had multiple warheads, programmed to take out the portal planet's nova-bomb minefield.

The first surprise was that the minefield wasn't there. The second surprise was that the Taurans weren't, either. Their base seemed intact but long deserted, cold.

We would destroy it with a nova bomb, but first send a platoon down to investigate it. Garcia asked that I go along with them. It was Cat's platoon. It would be an interesting experience to share, so long as a booby trap didn't blow us off the planet. The deserted base could be bait.

We would have a nova bomb with us. Either Morales or I could detonate it if we got into a situation that looked hopeless. Or Garcia could do it from orbit. I was sure Garcia could do it. Not so sure about me or Aurelio.

But while we were down in the prep bay getting into our fighting suits, there came the third surprise, the big one. I later saw the recording. The main cube in the control room lit up with a two-dimensional picture of a young man in an ancient uniform. He popped in and out of three dimensions while he spoke: "Hello, Earth ship. Do you still use this frequency? Do you still use this language?"

He smiled placidly. "Of course you won't respond at first; neither would I. This could be a trap. Feel free to investigate at long range. I am calling from a different portal planet. I'm currently 12.23 million kilometers from you, on the plane of the ecliptic, on an angle of 0.54 radians with respect to the collapsar. As you probably know by now.

"I am a descendant of the first Strike Force, nearly half a millennium ago. I await your questions." He sat back in his chair, in a featureless room. He crossed his legs and picked up a notebook and began flipping through it.

We immediately got a high-resolution image of the portal planet. It was small, as they usually are; cold and airless except for the base. It was actually more like a town than a base, and it was as obvious as a beacon. It wasn't enclosed; air was evidently held in by some sort of force field. It was lit up by an artificial sun that floated a few kilometers above the surface.

There was an ancient cruiser in orbit, its dramatic, sweeping streamlined grace putting our functional clunkiness to shame. There were also two Tauran vessels. None of them was obviously damaged.

All of us 5-and-above officers were on the bridge when we contacted the planet. Commodore Sidorenko sat up front with Garcia; he technically outranked her in this room, but it was her show, since the actual business was planetside.

I felt a little self-conscious, having come straight from the prep bay. Everyone else was in uniform; I was just wearing the contact net for the fighting suit. Like a layer of silver paint.

Garcia addressed the man in the chair. "Do you have a name and a rank?"

It took about forty seconds for the message to get to him, and another forty for his response: "My name is Eagle. We don't have ranks; I'm here because I can speak Old Standard. English."

You could play a slow chess game during this conversation, and not miss anything. "But your ancestors defeated the Taurans, somehow."

"No. The Taurans took them prisoner and set them up here. Then there was another battle, generations ago. We never heard from them again."

"But we lost that battle. Our cruiser was destroyed with all hands aboard."

"I don't know anything about that. Their planet was on the other side of the collapsar when the battle happened. The people here saw a lot of light, distorted by gravitational lensing. We always assumed it was some robotic assault, since we didn't hear anything from either side, afterwards. I'm sorry so many people died."

"What about the Taurans who were with you? Are there Taurans there now?"

"No; there weren't any then, and there aren't any now. Before the battle they showed up now and then."

"But there are—" she began.

"Oh, you mean the Tauran ships in orbit. They've been there for hundreds of years. So has our cruiser. We have no way to get to them. This place is self-sufficient, but a prison."

"I'll contact you again after I've spoken to my officers." The cube went dark.

Garcia swiveled around, and so did Sidorenko, who spoke for the first time: "I don't like it. He could be a simulation."

Garcia nodded. "That assumes a lot, though. And it would mean they know a hell of a lot more about us than we do about them."

"That's demonstrable. Four hundred years ago, they were supposedly able to build a place for the captives to stay. I don't believe we would have any trouble simulating a Tauran, given a couple of hundred captives and that much time for research."

"I suppose. Potter," she said to me, "go down and tell the fourth platoon there's a slight change of plans, but we're still going in ready for anything. I think the best thing we can do is get over there and make physical contact as soon as possible."

"Right," Siderenko said. "We don't have the element of surprise anymore, but there's no percentage in sitting here and feeding them data, giving them time to revise their strategy. If there *are* Taurans there."

"Have your people prepped for five gees," Garcia said to me. "Get you there in a few hours."

"Eight," Siderenko said. "We'll be about ten hours behind you."

"Wait in orbit?" I said, knowing the answer.

"You wish. Let's go down to the bay."

We had a holo of the base projected down there and worked out a simple strategy. Twenty-two of us in fighting suits, armed to the teeth, carrying a nova bomb and a stasis field, surround the place and politely knock on the door. Depending on the response, we either walk in for tea or level the place.

Getting there would not be so bad. Nobody could endure four hours of five-gee acceleration, then flip for four hours of deceleration, unprotected. So we'd be clamshelled in the fighting suits, knocked out and superhydrated. Eight hours of deep sleep and then maybe an hour to shake it off and go be a soldier. Or a guest for tea.

Cat and I made the rounds in the cramped fighter, seeing that everybody was in place, suit fittings and readouts in order. Then we shared a minute of private embrace and took our own places.

I jacked the fluid exchange into my hip fitting and all of the fear went away. My body sagged with sweet lassitude, and I let the soft nozzle clasp my face. I was still aware enough to know that it was sucking all of the air out of my lungs and then blowing in a dense replacement fluid, but all I felt was a long low-key orgasm. I knew that this was the last thing a lot of people felt, the fighter blown to bits moments or hours later. But the war offered us many worse ways to die. I was sound asleep before the acceleration blasted us into space. Dreaming of being a fish in a warm and heavy sea.

8

The chemicals won't let you remember coming out of it, which is probably good. My diaphragm and esophagus were sore and tired from getting
rid of all the fluid. Cat looked like hell and I stayed away from mirrors,
while we toweled off and put on the contact nets and got back into the
fighting suits for the landing.

Our strategy, such as it was, seemed even less appealing, this close to
the portal planet. The two Tauran cruisers were old models, but they
were a hundred times the size of our fighter, and since they were in syn-
chronous orbit over the base, there was no way to avoid coming into
range. But they did let us slide under them without blowing us out of the
sky, which made Eagle's story more believable.

It was pretty obvious, though, that our primary job was to be a target, for those ships and the base. If we were annihilated, the *Bolivar*
would modify its strategy.

When Morales said we were going to just go straight in and land on
the strip beside the base, I muttered, "Might as well be hung for a sheep
as a goat," and Cat, who was on my line, asked why anyone would hang
a sheep. I told her it was hard to explain. In fact, it was just something my
father used to say, and if he'd ever explained it, I'd forgotten.

The landing was loud but featherlight. We unclamped our fighting
suits from their transport positions and practiced walking in the one-
third gee of the small planet. "They should've sent Goy," Cat said, which
is what we called Chance Nguyen, the Martian. "He'd be right at home."

We moved out fast, people sprinting to their attack positions. Cat
went off to the other side of the base. I was going with Morales, to knock
on the door. Rank and its privileges. The first to die, or be offered tea.

The buildings on the base looked like they'd been designed by a careful child. Windowless blocks laid out on a grid. All but one were sand-
colored. We walked to the silver cube of headquarters. At least it had
"HQ" in big letters over the airlock.

The shiny front door snicked up like a guillotine in reverse. We went
through with dignified haste, and it slammed back down. The blade, or
door, was pretty massive, for us to "hear" it in a vacuum; vibration
through our boots.

Air hissed in—that we *did* hear—and after a minute a door swung open. We had to sidle through it sideways, because of the size of our fighting suits. I suppose we could have just walked straight through, enlarging it in the process, and in fact I considered that as I sidled. It would prevent them from using the airlock until they could fix it.

Then another door, a metal blast door half a meter thick, slid open. Seated at a plain round table were Eagle and a woman who looked like his twin sister. They wore identical sky-blue tunics.

"Welcome to Alcatraz," Eagle said. "The name is an old joke." He gestured at the four empty chairs. "Why not get out of your suits and relax?"

"That would be unwise," Morales said.

"You have us surrounded, outside. Even if I were inclined to do you harm, I wouldn't be that foolish."

"It's for your own protection," I extemporized. "Viruses can mutate a lot in four hundred years. You don't want us sharing your air."

"That's not a problem," the woman said. "Believe me. My bodies are very much more efficient than yours."

"'My bodies'?" I said.

"Oh, well." She made a gesture that was meaningless to me, and two side doors opened. From her side a line of women walked in, all exact copies of her. From his side, copies of him.

There were about twenty of each. They stared at us with identical bland expressions, and then said in unison, "I have been waiting for you."

"As have I." A pair of naked Taurans stepped into the room.

Both our laserfingers came up at once. Nothing happened.

"I'm sorry I had to lie to you," one of the women said.

I braced myself to die. I hadn't seen a live Tauran since the Yod-4 campaign, but I'd fought hundreds of them in the ALSC. They didn't care whether they lived or died, so long as they died killing a human.

"There is much to be explained," the Tauran said in a thin, wavering voice, its mouth-hole flexing and contracting. Its body was covered with a loose tunic like the humans', hiding most of the wrinkled orange hide and strange limbs, and the pinched antlike thorax.

The two of them blinked slowly in unison, in what might have been a social or emotional gesture, a translucent membrane sliding wetly down over the compound eyes. The tassels of soft flesh where their noses should have been stopped quivering while they blinked. "The war is over. In most places."

The man spoke. "Human and Tauran share Stargate now. There is Tauran on Earth and human on its home planet, J'sardlkuh."

"Humans like you?" Morales said. "Stamped out of a machine?"

"I come from a kind of machine, but it is living, a womb. Until I was truly *one*, there could be no peace. When there were billions of us, all different, we couldn't understand peace."

"Everyone on Earth is the same?" I said. "There's only one kind of human?"

"There are still survivors of the Forever War, like yourselves," the female said. "Otherwise, there is only one human. As there is only one Tauran. I was patterned after an individual named Khan. I call myself Man."

There were sounds to my left and right, like distant thunder. Nothing in my communicator.

"Your people are attacking," the male said, "even though I have told them it is useless."

"Let me talk to them!" Morales said.

"You can't," the female said. "They all assembled under the stasis field, when they saw the Taurans through your eyes. Now their programmed weapons attack. When those weapons fail, they will try to walk in with the stasis field."

"This has happened before?" I said.

"Not here, but other places. The outcome varies."

"Your stasis field," a Tauran said, "has been old to us for more than a century. We used a refined version of it to keep you from shooting us a minute ago."

"You say the outcome varies," Morales said to the female, "so sometimes we win?"

"Even if you killed me, you wouldn't 'win'; there's nothing to win anymore. But no, the only thing that varies is how many of you survive."

"Your cruiser *Bolivar* may have to be destroyed," a Tauran said. "I assume they are monitoring this conversation. Of course they are still several light-minutes away. But if they do not respond in a spirit of cooperation, we will have no choice."

Garcia did respond in less than a minute, her image materializing behind the Taurans. "Why don't we invite *you* to act in a spirit of cooperation," she said. "If none of our people are hurt, none of yours will be."

"That's beyond my control," the male said. "Your programmed weapons are attacking; mine are defending. I think that neither is programmed for mercy."

The female continued. "That they still survive is evidence of our good intentions. We could deactivate their stasis field from outside." There was a huge *thump* and Man's table jumped up an inch. "Most of them would be destroyed in seconds if we did that."

Garcia paused. "Then explain why you haven't."

"One of my directives," the male said, "is to minimize casualties among you. There is a genetic diversity program, which will be explained to you at Stargate."

"All right," Garcia said. "Since I can't communicate with them otherwise, I'll let you deactivate the stasis field—but at the same time, of course, you have to turn off your automatic defenses. Otherwise they'd be slaughtered."

"So you invite us to be slaughtered instead," he said. "Me and your two representatives here."

"I'll tell them to cease fire immediately."

All this conversation was going on with a twenty-second time lag. So "immediately" would be a while in coming.

Without comment, the two Taurans disappeared, and the forty duplicate humans filed back through the dome.

"All right," Eagle said, "perhaps there is a way around this time lag. Which of you is the ranking officer here?"

"I am," I said.

"Most of my individuals have returned to an underground shelter. I will turn off your stasis field and our defenses simultaneously.

"Tell them they must stop firing immediately. If we die, our defenses resume, and they won't have the protection of the stasis field."

I chinned the command frequency, which would put me in contact with Cat and Sergeant Hencken as soon as the field disappeared.

"I don't like this," Morales said. "You can turn your weapons on and off with a thought?"

"That's correct."

"We can't. When Captain Potter gives them the order, they have to understand and react."

"But it's just turning off a switch, is it not?" There was another huge bang, and a web of cracks appeared in the wall to my left. Man looked at it without emotion.

"First a half dozen people have to understand the order and decide to obey it!"

The male and female smiled and nodded in unison. "Now."

Thumbnail pictures of Karl and Cat appeared next to Morales. "Cat! Karl! Have the weapons units cease fire immediately!"

"What's going on?" Karl said. "Where's the stasis field?"

"They turned it off. Battle's over."

"That's right," Morales said. "Cease fire."

Cat started talking to the squads. Karl stared for a second and started to do the same.

Not fast enough. The left wall exploded in a hurricane of masonry and chunks of metal. The two Men were suddenly bloody rags of shredded flesh. Morales and I were knocked over by the storm of rubble. My armor was breached in one place; there was a ten-second beep while it repaired itself.

Then vacuum silence. The one light on the opposite wall dimmed and went out. Through the hole our cannon had made, the size of a large window, the starlit wasteland strobed in silent battle.

The three thumbnails were gone. I chinned down again for command freek. "Cat? Morales? Karl?"

Then I turned on a headlight and saw that Morales was dead, his suit peeled open at the chest, lungs and heart in tatters under ribs black with dried blood.

I chinned sideways for the general freek and heard a dozen voices shouting and screaming in confusion.

So Cat was probably dead, and Karl, too. Or maybe their communications had been knocked out.

I thought about that possibility for a few moments, hoping and rejecting hope, listening to the babble. Then I realized that if I could hear all those privates, corporals, they could hear me.

"This is Potter," I said. "*Captain* Potter," I yelled.

I stayed on the general freek and tried to explain the strange situation. Five did opt to stay outside. The others met me under the yellow light, which framed the top of a square black blast door that rose out of the ground at a forty-five-degree angle, like our tornado shelter at home, thousands of years ago, hundreds of light-years away. It slid open, and we went in, carrying four fighting suits whose occupants weren't responding but weren't obviously dead.

One of those was Cat, I saw as we came into the light when the air-lock door closed. The back of the helmet had a blast burn, but I could make out VERDEUR.

She looked bad. A leg and an arm were missing at shoulder and thigh. But they had been snipped off by the suit itself, the way my arm had been at Tet-2.

There was no way to tell whether she was alive, since the telltale on the back of the helmet was destroyed. The suit had a biometric readout, but only a medic could access it directly, and the medic and his suit had been vaporized.

Man led us into a large room with a row of bunks and a row of chairs. There were three other Men there, but no Taurans, which was probably wise.

I popped out of my suit and didn't die, so the others did the same, one by one. The amputees we left sealed in their suits, and Man agreed that it was probably best. They were either dead or safely unconscious: if the former, they'd been dead for too long to bring back; if the latter, it would be better to wake them up in the *Bolivar*'s surgery. The ship was only two hours away, but it was a long two hours for me.

As it turned out, she lived, but I lost her anyhow, to relativity. She and the other amputees were loaded, still asleep, onto the extra cruiser, and sent straight to Heaven.

They did it in one jump, no need for secrecy anymore, and we went to Stargate in one jump aboard *Bolivar*.

When I'd last been to Stargate it had been a huge space station; now it was easily a hundred times as large, a man-made planetoid. Tauran-made, and Man-made.

We learned to say it differently: *Man*, not man.

Inside, Stargate was a city that dwarfed any city on the Earth I remembered—though they said now there were cities on Earth with a billion Men, humans, and Taurans.

We spent weeks considering and deciding on which of many options we could choose to set the course of the rest of our lives. The first thing I did was check on William, and no miracle had happened; his Strike Force had not returned from Sade-138. But neither had the Tauran force sent to annihilate them.

I didn't have the option of hanging around Stargate, waiting for him to show up; the shortest scenario had his outfit arriving in over three hundred years. I couldn't really wait for Cat, either; at best she would get to Stargate in thirty-five years. Still young, and me in my sixties. If, in fact, she chose to come to Stargate; she would have the option of staying on Heaven.

I could chase her to Heaven, but then *she* would be thirty-five years older than me. If we didn't pass one another in transit.

But I did have one chance. One way to outwit relativity.

Among the options available to veterans was Middle Finger, a planet circling Mizar. It was a nominally heterosexual planet—het or home was now completely a matter of choice; Man could switch you one way or the other in an hour.

I toyed with the idea of "going home," becoming lesbian by inclination as well as definition. But men still appealed to me—men not Man—and Middle Finger offered me an outside chance at the one man I still truly loved.

Five veterans had just bought an old cruiser and were using it as a time machine—a "time shuttle," they called it, zipping back and forth between Mizar and Alcor at relativistic speed, more than two objective years passing every week. I could buy my way onto it by using my back pay to purchase antimatter fuel. I could get there in one collapsar jump, having left word for William, and if he lived, could rejoin him in a matter of months or years.

The decision was so easy it was not a decision; it was as automatic as being born. I left him a note:

11 Oct 2878

William—
All this is in your personnel file. But knowing you, you might just chuck it. So I made sure you'd get this note.
    Obviously, I lived. Maybe you will, too. Join me.
    I know from the records that you're out at Sade-138 and won't be back for a couple of centuries. No problem.
    I'm going to a planet they call Middle Finger, the fifth planet out

*from Mizar. It's two collapsar jumps, ten months subjective. Middle
Finger is a kind of Coventry for heterosexuals. They call it a "eugenic
control baseline."*

*No matter. It took all of my money, and all the money of five other
old-timers, but we bought a cruiser from UNEF. And we're using it as
a time machine.*

*So I'm on a relativistic shuttle, waiting for you. All it does is go
out five light-years and come back to Middle Finger, very fast. Every
ten years I age about a month. So if you're on schedule and still alive,
I'll only be twenty-eight when you get here. Hurry!*

*I never found anybody else, and I don't want anybody else. I don't
care whether you're ninety years old or thirty. If I can't be your lover,
I'll be your nurse.*

—Marygay

9

From *The New Voice*, Paxton, Middle Finger 24–6
14/2/3143
OLD-TIMER HAS FIRST BOY

Marygay Potter-Mandella (24 Post Road, Paxton) gave birth Friday last to a fine
baby boy, 3.1 kilos.

Marygay lays claim to being the second-"oldest" resident of Middle Finger,
having been born in 1977. She fought through most of the Forever War and then
waited for her mate on the time shuttle, 261 years.

The baby, not yet named, was delivered at home with the help of a friend of the
family, Dr. Diana Alsever-Moore.

(1998)

Diminished Chord

When I was married I played in a pretty good band and made pretty good money, but when the marriage went south so did I. Wound up being a sideman in a college town in Florida. Jazz and swing and rock, whatever—need a banjo, I can frail along; pluck a mandolin.

Or a lute. How I got the lute, and the lute got me, is a story.

A sideman's a musical hired gun, and a chameleon. You learn to pick up the lead's style really fast and get under it. You make them happy and you get more work; word gets around.

I was a noodler as a kid, with a no-name classical guitar my father left sitting around. Always had a good ear. When a song came up on the radio I'd pick up that soft-string and just start playing along somewhere in the middle of the fingerboard. I learned how to read music with piano lessons, but the main thing was always ear to fingers without too much brain in between. That turned out to serve me well.

I also did a little teaching at a local music store, classical on Wednesdays and rock on Thursdays. That eked out my sideman income, which was irregular all the time and shrank to almost nothing in the summer—bands that book college towns when the students are away don't make enough money to hire someone like me. (Someone who's the best damned guitar player in town, and modest besides.)

The teaching gig is how I met Laura, got the lute, fell in love, and turned my life into something mad and magical. And I do mean madness and magic, not metaphor.

I later found out that Laura had seen me perform at a gig that turned out to be a kind of one-man-band freak show. It was a pretty good folk-rock quintet that changed its name about once a week. When I worked for them they were Jerry & the Winos, though if you've ever heard of them it was probably as Baked Alaska, with their hit single and album "Straighten Up and Die Right." Cheerful bunch.

Anyhow, one of Jerry's winos was poleaxed with something like Montezuma's Revenge—they'd just come from New Mexico and figured the spices might have gotten him, not to mention the thirty-two-hour drive. So they hired me to pick up for the guy, who doubled on twelve-string and electric bass, no problem.

(I have an apartment so full of musical instruments that you have to move one to sit down. That's relevant.)

It turned out that it wasn't the food, though, but a bug, and the quintet that had become a quartet wound up being just Jerry and me, with the rest of his band in the hospital. Jerry may have beaten the the thing because he was such a total drug addict that he couldn't tell the difference between being sick and being well. Or maybe the heroin killed off all those microorganisims before it finally killed Jerry, six or seven years later.

But that was one hell of a gig. He had the lungs and the energy of his namesake Garcia, and a kind of stoned concentration that was a marvel to watch. The afternoon three of his guys took a fast cab to join their buddy in the GI ward, Jerry and his sound man laid out all their arrangements on the floor of the stage and we walked down the line, the two of them basically arguing about what instrument I was going to play when. Jerry knew I could play anything from a Roland to a rattle, and he decided to make a virtue out of a necessity—not to mention saving a few hundred bucks by not hiring another sideman or three.

I was in seventh heaven. I also got a lot of ego gratification and local publicity out of it, because Jerry was generous in explaining what had happened and how I'd saved his sorry butt. So I just danced from keyboard to fingerboard; frets to fretless—if there'd been a saxophone onstage I would've tried to learn it. We had it set up so Jerry went between electric and acoustic while I went from one music stand to the next, reading like a son of a bitch on five instruments. Jerry vetoed the sound man when he wanted to use the Roland's computer-generated percussion, which was good. Jerry did rhythm while I did lead, and vice versa. By the end of the second night we were playing like we'd been together forever, and Jerry said if the other guys weren't pals, he'd leave 'em in the hospital and we could hit the road together.

But he and the Winos moved on, and I went back to doing what I did, with one huge difference: Laura had been there both nights. Friday with a date, and then Saturday alone.

I hadn't seen her—with the lights you don't see a lot past the stage—and if I had, I probably wouldn't have taken special notice. She was one of those women who could be beautiful when she wanted to be, but preferred the anonymity of being plain. A kind of protective coloration: whatever she was, it wasn't ordinary.

She showed up the next Wednesday at the store and asked about classical lessons. No, she didn't have a guitar, which was good; my secondary function at the place, maybe my primary one, was to sell guitars to my defenseless students.

I'm a reasonable guy and usually start them out with something good but not too expensive. An expert can get a pretty good sound out of anything, but a beginner can't; on the other hand, you don't want to talk somebody into a thousand-dollar guitar that she'll be stuck with if she quits in a month.

Nobody'd ever done what she did. She asked me what my favorite chord was—an open A major seventh in the fourth position—and listened to me play it on every classical guitar in the store. She didn't buy the most expensive one, but she was close, a custom-made three-quarter-size that a luthier up in Yellow Springs had made for a guy who died before it could be delivered.

I said it had a haunting tone. She said maybe that was because it was haunted.

She was clumsy the first day, but after that she learned faster than anyone I've ever taught. Once a week wasn't enough; she wanted lessons on the weekends, too. Sometimes at the store on Saturday; sometimes elsewhere on Sunday, when the store was closed. We practiced down at the lake on campus when the weather was fine; otherwise her place.

Her apartment was as plain and neat as mine was cluttered and, well, not neat. Mine looked like a bachelor had lived there alone for five years. Hers looked like no one lived there at all. It had the understated rightness of a Japanese Sumi-e painting—a few pieces of furniture, a few pieces of art, all in harmony. I wondered what was hidden behind the closed bedroom door. Maybe I hoped the room was heaped high with junk.

When I did see it, I found it was as simple as the rest of the place. A low bed, a table and chair, and a place to hang our clothes.

She was no groupie. I'd had plenty of experience with them, both before and (unfortunately) during my marriage. Sidemen don't get groupies, though, and groupies don't approach you with quiet seriousness and explain that it was time to move your relationship to a higher spiritual plane.

I hesitated because of age—I'd just turned forty and she seemed half that—and I did respect her and not want to hurt her. She smiled and said that if I didn't hurt her, she would try to return the favor.

Later I would remember "try to." She must have known.

Our first night was more than a night, in both time and consequence. She revealed her actual beauty for the first time, and gave me more physical pleasure than any woman ever had, and took the same in return. I didn't question where she could have learned all that she knew. Sometime around noon, she left me exhausted in her bed, and it was getting dark again when she gently shook me awake. She said she had a present for me.

There were two candles on her table, with wine and cheese, bread and fruit. She lit a few other candles around the room while I opened the bottle, and then brought over her gift, a large angular thing in a cotton sack. When I took it from her, it knocked against the table with a soft discordant jangle.

It was a big ornate lute-like thing, which she called a chitarrone. At least that's what the antique dealer had called it when she bought it at the big flea market in Waldo.

It didn't sound very musical, missing some strings and not in tune with the rusty ones it did have, but even in its beat-up state it was an impressive piece of work, a cross between a lute and a kind of string bass.

The wood was inlaid in a neat pattern, and there were three ornately carved sound holes. It came with a diagram showing how the strings should be tuned, drawn with brown ink on paper that felt like soft animal skin, a kind of hokey attempt at antiquity, I thought. The notes were square, but the staffs were recognizable. I knew I could string it with modern mandolin, guitar, and cello strings.

It couldn't possibly be as old as it looked, and not be in a museum, and she said no, the dealer only claimed it was a twentieth-century copy. It hadn't cost enough to be that old. I looked forward to trying it out; I could get strings at the store the next day and tune it up between students—maybe I'd have it sounding like something when she came in for her four o'clock lesson.

She said she'd look forward to it, and we got to work on the wine and food. We talked of this and that, and then I played her some old ballads on her small guitar. The food of love, the poet said, and we moved back into her rumpled bed.

I woke to the smell of coffee, but she was already gone; a note by the pot said she had an eight o'clock class. I made a breakfast of leftover cheese and bread and cleaned up a bit, feeling unnaturally domestic. Went back to my place sort of drifting in a state of *I-don't-deserve-this-but-who-does?* Shaved and showered and found a clean shirt, and got to the store an hour and a half before my first pupil.

The chitarrone looked authentically old in the cold fluorescent light of the store's workroom. I cleaned it carefully with some Gibson guitar spray, but resisted waxing it. That would make it prettier, but would have a muting effect on the sound, and I was intensely curious about that.

Over the course of the day, during two dead hours and my lunch break, I replaced the strings one at a time and kept tuning them up as they relaxed. I tuned the thing two whole tones low, since it obviously hadn't been played in some time, and I didn't want to stress it.

It had a good sound, though, tuning: plangent, archaic. It was a real time trip. They don't make them like that anymore—or they do, but not for working musicians like yours truly. A twenty-one–string nightmare, I don't think so.

The other guys at the store were fascinated by it, though, and so were two of my students. But not the one I wanted to see and hear it. She didn't make her four o'clock.

I called and her phone had been disconnected. After work, I rushed over and found her apartment door open, the living room and bedroom bare. The super, miffed because I'd interrupted her dinner preparations, said the place had been empty since June, two months. When I tried to explain, she looked wary and then scared, and eased the door shut with two loud clicks.

The chitarrone, lying diagonally across the car's backseat, was solid and eerily real. As I drove home it played itself at every bump in the road, a D diminished, slightly out of tune.

Amazon.com didn't have *The Chitarrone for Idiots*, or for madmen, but there were plenty of lute books with medieval and Renaissance music, and it was easy to incorporate the instrument's bass drone strings into the melodies. There wasn't much call for it in jazz and rock gigs, but I brought it along when folk groups were amenable. I'd worked out some slightly anachronistic pieces like "Scarborough Fair" and "Greensleeves" that were easy to play along with, and singable, and they led to the unlikely gig that demonstrated the thing's true power.

I got a call from a music professor who asked whether I really had a chitarrone, and he got all excited when I demonstrated it over the phone. Could I clear up two weekends in February and play with his consort at the upcoming Medieval Faire?

In fact I was free those weekends. We set up a couple of practice dates, and he faxed me some sheets. They were lute and therobo parts, and it was easy to cobble them together into something that used the instrument's resonant bass strings.

We met at the professor's crumbling-but-genteel Victorian mansion. He'd gathered eleven students who played an assortment of modern replicas of period string, wind, and percussion instruments, and they were all enthralled by my medieval Rube Goldberg machine. The professor, Harold Innes, was especially impressed, not only at the workmanship but the careful aging of the instrument—could it possibly be a "misplaced" museum piece? I told him it came from the Waldo flea market, and God knows where it might originally have been stolen from.

Innes's wife Gladys was a piece of work, setting out tea and cookies with a kind of smoldering resentment. If she had ever been charmed by her husband's fascination with old music (and perhaps with young students), it had not withstood the test of time. Maybe it was the unfortunate choice of a husband whose last name made a jingling rhyme with her first—thirty or forty years of being "Gladys Innes" might push you toward being "Gladys Anything Else."

Halfway though the rehearsal, they had a quiet but intense argument in the kitchen. One of the students wondered aloud where they would rehearse if Gladys got the house, and the others just nodded sourly.

Gladys did know music, though. She asked me intelligent questions about various tunings and techniques for playing the thing, and when Harold asked me to do a couple of solo numbers, she came out and listened with rapt attention.

I got the job, and looked forward to it even though the six days would pay less than a normal weekend, and I would have to rent and wear a ridiculous houppelande thing, tied around the waist with a rope, that made me look and feel like Falstaff.

A curious thing happened at the second rehearsal, which was a dress rehearsal. Gladys was all smiles and flirting, with me and the students, but especially with Harold. He himself wore a kind of stunned honeymooner look. Their marriage was obviously off the rocks, and the consort responded to that with more than relief; their playing was superbly controlled and had a new emotional depth.

There was another emotional aspect. After the tea break, I played a couple of pieces, a solo of "Twa Corbies" and a duet of "Lord Randal" with a young man who harmonized with a doom-laden tenor recorder. Neither is exactly romantic, plucking eyes and poisoning your lover with eel-broth, but the students paired up while they listened, mostly boy-girl but also a pair of men who leaned together, touching each other shoulder to knee, and two women who held hands and whispered quietly.

It wasn't my singing, which a critic once neatly pinned as "accurate," but some quality of the chitarrone's sound. The damned thing was aphrodisiac, at least in that setting, the old musty Victorian parlor with everyone dressed up for a passion play. The passion was so thick you could bottle it and sell it online.

The Medieval Faire was the killer, though. I was prepared to endure it—thee-ing and thou-ing everyone, wearing a quarter inch of beard and the woolen houppelande, not exactly made for Florida spring—but I did wind up enjoying the phony ambience, not just because the concert tent was next to the mead tent. I've never played to a more appreciative audience.

The pattern of the gig settled down to this: we would rotate among three sets of period music, during which I would play lute parts with my regular classical guitar. That would be about forty minutes' worth. Then I would pick up the chitarrone, holding it like a mandolin on steroids, and play a couple of tunes with light accompaniment.

Crowds would form in those last ten minutes, crowds that filled the tent and spilled out into the muddy mess outside. The crowd was composed completely of pairs, doing body language as if it were an Olympic sport.

Two successful CDs later, I shouldn't complain, but I will. Laura left me with a magical gift, and a hole in my heart that grows deeper every time I use it. Not just because I miss her, though I miss her like a wounded soldier must miss his lost limb.

I watch people while I play; I watch them go all soft and fall in love. But never with the player. Never with me.

(2004)

Giza

I hope you already know all this. I hope it's nothing but a redundant, overly dramatic gesture. But in case there's nothing left tomorrow, in case the ones in orbit don't survive, there will at least be this record, buried beneath the rubble, sending out radio beeps for about a million years, until the power source decays away.

This is how it came about.

When we bred the first ghosts—giza, as they came to call themselves—there was a predictable outcry from conservative folk all over the world. Playing God, making monsters, yammer yammer. They do seem to have turned into monsters, after all, of a certain kind. Though they started out fairly human.

Nobody could argue with the practical aspect then, almost eighty years ago. If we were going to proceed with space industrialization, we needed people in space—lots of people, even though the physical work was done by machines.

Back then, you didn't normally keep people in orbit for more than eighteen months at a time. Even with mandatory exercise and diet supplements, most started to weaken and waste away before a year had gone by. But when we started mining the earthgrazing asteroids, the most accessible source of metals for space manufacturing, a merely yearlong tour was out of the question. The rocks do come close to the Earth's orbit, by definition, but they spend most of their orbits far away, and distance means time, and money.

We needed people who could live in space permanently. So we made some.

Biological engineering was perfectly legal and routine by 2050. Almost nobody in the most prosperous half of the world was born without some degree of intervention. Who would take a chance on having children mentally or physically crippled from birth? There were limits, in most of the world—you couldn't have a child born with four arms, in hopes of selling him to the circus, any more than you could today.

Unless you lived in Spain. Their starting-from-scratch revolution in 2042 left a huge loophole in local laws controlling how profoundly parents could manipulate the genetic makeup of their potential children. The Basques, forever proud of their difference from the rest of the world, took advantage of the law with a vengeance, first with children capable of superhuman athletic prowess, and then stranger talents. By the time the loophole was forced shut in 2063, there were Basques with wings and gills and tentacles, who could breed true if they could find mates. Most of them did.

Though banned from professional sports, there were other niches where the engineered Basques had no competition. Barrel-chested giants with uncanny balance carried girders in high steel. Thousands of arrain, the fat, gilled ones, took over sectors of marine engineering and the fishing industries. And of course the ghosts took over space.

A normal human of average size needs eighteen hundred kilocalories of energy every day just to lie in bed. That's about a loaf of bread. If you're up and working all day, you need twice as much. Working in null gee, inside an asteroid, doesn't take as much energy as working on Earth, but you can't get around that 1800-k-calorie minimum. Unless you're very small.

The giza were not just bred small; they were bred weak. Spindly muscle and porous bone, so they needed only meager amounts of protein and calcium and phosphorous. They look like translucent skinny six-year-olds with adult faces on adult-sized heads, but ten of them use the same mass of food and water and air as one of you.

The first ghosts had mothers born on Earth, of course, but the first generation was born in low-Earth orbit, in a small hospital-and-nursery satellite run by Hispania Interspacial. For consenting to such extreme genetic engineering, the families were paid one hundred thousand eurams per child, half in cash and half in a trust fund in the child's name.

It was not a lot of money at the time, in prosperous Spain—a down payment on a decent city flat—but the Basques didn't do it for the money, and they didn't want the city. They did want space, to conquer space, and they almost succeeded.

H.I. guaranteed each child a technical education, at their orbital university, if they qualified. If they didn't, or flunked out, there was room in orbit for people to do other kinds of work. The only thing they couldn't do was go back to Earth, against whose gravity they could hardly breathe, let alone walk. Even lunar gravity would be dangerous to their flimsy bones.

They lived fairly well, though, in the hive they carved inside the ferrous asteroid Quetzalcoatl. A small city was in place when the first ones arrived, and it expanded naturally, as the mining machines ground their automatic way through the iron and nickel.

It was spartan in many ways, but the Earth sent much of their required carbon, hydrogen, and oxygen in the form of food. They ate well. When it costs a thousand eurams to send a kilo of food, it might as well be caviar as beans. They had closed-cycle agriculture, too, so those kilos of caviar and pâté and artichoke hearts became soil for less exotic fare.

The ghosts were able to bear children at the age of ten, and large families were rewarded, since H.I. needed workers, and it was expensive to orbit pregnant women from Earth. Their population doubled and redoubled. They doubled and quadrupled the number of machines, though, and honeycombed the asteroid, making interior real estate as well as profit for H.I.

Giza culture diverged from Earth's, most strikingly in religion: their terrestrial parents had mostly been agnostic or Nuevo Catolico, but the giza regressed to (or rediscovered) the Neolithic Basque worship of the Goddess, Mari, who, like them, lived in caves.

The discovery of warm fusion revolutionized ghost society; cheap spaceflight brought tourism into their otherwise closed economy. Earthling tourists brought money, of course, but they were also required to bring food, water, and air enough to support them during their stay—which resources of course remained within the asteroid's recirculating biome.

The stranger the ghosts appeared, the more interesting they were to tourists, and what started as a more or less cynical exploitation of this became a jarringly swift transformation of their culture into a kind of juvenile primitivism. A female could have six or seven children before she was eighteen, and many did. So you had children being led and taught by children, more or less supervised by a small core of technologically elite, who prospered from the display of the children's charming and strange naïveté, set against their high-tech environment.

And then it stopped. The ninth generation was sterile. Every single one of them.

To the giza, it was obvious that the whole thing had been set up from the time the first one of them had been delivered custom-made into space. They bred true down to the very last manufactured gene, and that last gene was a time bomb that doomed them as a species.

They had been invented, they said, to spend a century setting up a comfortable civilization in space. And then die off and get out of your way. You have always hated the Basques, anyway.

Ridiculous, the Spanish authorities said. Nobody could be so malicious and heartless. It had been an extreme experiment in an inexact science, and a mistake was made.

The ghosts didn't answer. The only communication Earth got from them was a continuous loop of a long prayer to Mari in an obscure Basque dialect. None of the tourists there got through to Earth, either, and none returned. We've just learned, in a final message, that they were all told to leave at once, and crowded into airlocks. When the warning bell rang and the airlocks opened, there was nothing on the other side but vacuum. They may have gotten off easy.

For months, we heard nothing from Quetzalcoatl but recorded prayer. Then we saw that it was being moved, the giza using warm-fusion steering rockets to bend its orbit. When it became obvious that it was aiming toward Earth collision, we started to take measures.

Ghost psychology was not necessarily the same as human psychology, but the planners had known enough about human nature to allow for extremes. H.I. had a huge bomb capable of diverting the asteroid, in case a maniac got ahold of it and decided humans should go the way of the dinosaurs. The diversion would destroy the asteroid and all its inhabitants, of course; still, the decision to launch was no decision.

But the giza either knew about the defense or had deduced it. When the bomb-carrying missile was halfway there, they sent a vicious farewell message and committed suicide, blowing themselves up.

It was a careful, calculated act. They had prepared the asteroid with their burrows so that rather than blowing apart into random fragments, it cracked into twenty-one pieces, any one of them large enough to doom life on Earth, all continuing along roughly the same path. Our bomb pulverized one piece.

The fragment blew up at nighttime here, and it was quite a sight, as bright as the full moon for some seconds. We can't see its dark companions yet. I suppose the first and last thing people will see of them will be the bright flash of impact.

I'm going down into the basement of this building, turn on the beacon, and lock this record in its safe. Then I'll come back up and wait for the light.

(2001)

Foreclosure

When you're in real estate you have to be a people person. Often that means nodding and smiling through people's delusions, waiting to talk them back down into something they can actually afford.

But financial delusions are one thing, and actual nutcases are something else. That's what I thought I was in for the day Baldy walked into my life.

I'd only been an actual broker for a couple of months, though I'd been in real estate for many years part-time, and more than two years full-time, since my husband passed away. So I would have told you by then that nothing could surprise me.

I could usually tell if customers were serious before they even opened their mouths, as soon as they walked through the door. Single males were usually not. So when a balding, portly middle-aged man walked in one hot August day, sweating profusely and fanning himself with a newspaper, I just put on my neutral smile and decided to let him enjoy the air-conditioning for a while.

He didn't respond to my greeting, but just plopped down in the chair in front of me and stared, brow furrowed. He didn't blink, and he seemed not to have any eyebrows.

When he spoke, his lips barely moved. "You deal in the transfer of land."

"Well, sure. We help landowners—"

"Owners." He shook his head stiffly. "No one owns anything. You sit on our land and spoil it."

I looked at him closely. "Are you a Native American?"

He leaned forward, peering. I thought about the pepper spray in my bag in the bottom drawer.

"One of you? No. I just look this way. Just for now."

"I'm afraid I don't follow."

He nodded again. "You will follow." He reached inside his sweat-stained seersucker suit and my hand dropped—casually, I hoped—toward the bottom drawer.

He brought out a cylinder that was actually three rolled-up photographs. When he unrolled them, they somehow snapped as flat and stiff as plastic place mats.

He dealt them out in front of me like three large playing cards. I took one look and my heart actually stopped for a couple of beats.

They were three-dimensional and moving. Not like 3-D movies or comics or any such foolery. Each picture was like a window.

He tapped on the first one, hard. "This is what was here when we first . . . arranged for the land." It was a volcanic wasteland, like I saw on a National Geographic special on Hawaii. "When it was first ceded." Ceded or seeded?

He thumped the second one, which was an edenic forest. "This is here now, a few hundred, maybe one hundred times ago. Just yesterday."

He pushed the third one toward me.

"This is what you have done." It was downtown, a couple of blocks from my office, the lunchtime traffic jam. I could almost smell the exhaust.

I picked up the picture and brought it closer to my face. I *could* smell the exhaust! There was a muted sound of traffic. The other two had faint aromas, too, arboreal humus and sharp brimstone.

"Impressive." I stacked them together and put them in the middle of the table. I didn't know what else to say.

"You are an accident. This is not your fault. But this place was clean and perfect, the way we made it. Hundreds of millions of times ago, years ago, when we seeded. It grew green and did oxygen, as we planned. We didn't plan you, though, and you're undoing it."

"Wait." This was something out of my husband's pulp magazines. "You mean the whole planet?"

He nodded. "The place, the planet." He closed his eyes. You could hear the wheels turning in his head. His eyes snapped open again. He still hadn't blinked. "We bought it. We fixed it up. Long before I was born. Now we're ready to move in. But we find *you* here."

"So you're from another planet."

He tilted his head. "Another place. Another time and place. Now *you* have to go to another place."

"I don't get it." Though I was getting it, and not liking it. "Who are you, anyhow?"

"I am like you; I facilitate the transfer of property."

"A *real estate* agent?"

"Yes. Perhaps more like a lawyer." He closed his eyes again, thinking, or maybe translating. "You are undesirable parasites, but you are also sentient creatures. This makes my function more difficult.

"If you were not sentient, we could simply be rid of you. Like you do with bugs. But there are protocols. Laws we have to obey."

"Wait. You could just . . . get rid of us, like bugs?"

"Easier, really. Bugs are tough. But, as I say, protocols. We have to allow you to leave. To establish yourselves someplace that is not . . . here and now. Especially here."

"Wait. Move to another planet?"

"Sure. You haven't done that?"

I shook my head. "Well, *no*." This was 1967, the year before the first moon landing.

"I do it all the time. Nothing to it." He took another cylinder out of his pocket and snapped it flat. "This is the agreement."

I stared at it. "What is this, Chinese?"

He nodded. "There are 763 million Chinese on your planet. More than any other people. So that is the language of default. Touch the agreement."

I did, and it suddenly turned to English. "How'd you do that?"

"I don't know." He stood up. "It's not my concern anymore." Without even saying good-bye, he started for the door.

I looked at the document. My name was on the bottom line. It gave us fifty years: on August 14, 2017, all humans remaining on Earth would be exterminated.

"Wait!" I said. "Who am I supposed to give this to?"

"I don't care. I just had to give it to you."

"I want to talk to your boss." I tried to keep the panic out of my voice. "Your supervisor."

"I don't have a boss."

I picked up the document. *"Someone gave this to you!"*

"Oh. The Council." He clapped twice.

Two old women and an old man appeared, seven feet tall, skinny, dressed in black robes. Their eyes went up and down instead of sideways. "What is it this time?" one of the women said.

"She doubts the authority of the foreclosure."

She looked at me very severely. "It is similar to your own laws about land. They were given permission to change its ecology; to develop it. Once developed, they may take possession."

"What about *us*?"

"Sad. Accidents are often sad."

"We don't have any rights?"

She looked at the other two, and then back at me. "Why would you have rights? To put it in your terms, you didn't buy the land. You didn't develop it. You have to move off." The three of them disappeared.

I looked at Baldy. "That's *it*?"

"Simple enough." He opened the door.

"But I'm just a *real estate* agent!"

"So am I." He stepped out into the brightness and faded away like vapor. There was nothing but the hot smell of the street.

It might have been a minute later before I looked down at the document again. It was cool to the touch, and not hard or slick like plastic. My name and address were at the bottom, below two other things that might have been signatures, followed by something like Morse code, dots and dashes. The dashes changed in length, though, when I moved my head.

I thought about calling a lawyer. But the language was clear enough, way more clear than a real estate contract. On August 14, 2017, any humans remaining on Earth would be exterminated. That was the word they used, too; no euphemisms. I would probably be around, at seventy-eight; my family was long-lived on both sides.

Call the police? They'd lock me up.

I opened the filing cabinet and took out my husband's old address book. I took it back to my desk, hands shaking, and finally found the number I wanted, under the letter "J"—Jeremiah. Jeremiah Phipps, the science-fiction writer. I'd never actually met him, but he and my husband used to play pool together.

It was almost noon, but the phone obviously woke him up. I don't suppose writers keep bankers' hours, or real estate agents'.

I told him I needed advice about a mysterious object and asked whether I might meet him for lunch and get his opinion. My treat, I said, at Leonardo's, a pretty good Italian restaurant. That got his interest; he agreed to meet me there at one.

I called another agent to come cover for me, and when she showed up at quarter to one, I took the three photographs and contract in a large envelope and went down to Leonardo's. I'd normally walk the seven blocks, but it was a hundred degrees out. I turned the car's air conditioner on high and went back to the office for a few minutes. I guess I was helping to ruin the fellow's atmosphere, but it was evidently too late to worry about that.

I was inside Leonardo's cool, enjoying a Coke in a booth that looked out on the parking lot, when I saw the apparition that was Jeremiah Phipps. He had a shaggy grey beard and a mane of grey hair tied back in a ponytail, riding a rusty old bike, wearing cutoff jeans and a Florida Gators T-shirt. On his way in, he asked the waitress for two Buds.

"Very weird." I didn't show him the pictures and contract right off, but first told him how the man had walked in and started talking cryptic nonsense. The two mugs of beer came, and I paused while he drained one of them. I ordered a large deluxe pizza, figuring he could take the leftovers home.

"I was getting scared," I said. "I thought his manner was threatening. But I guess it was just a language thing."

"He some kind of foreigner?"

"Some kind." I took out the three pictures and laid them down. "How about *that*?"

He picked up one of them, looked at it closely, held it up to the light, looked at the other side. "Hmm."

"Ever seen anything like that?"

He looked at the other two and raked his fingers through his beard. "I don't get it. Three sheets of plastic?"

"What? No, look—this is a prehistoric scene, and this is the traffic at Sixth and University, and this . . ."

He was looking at me in a funny way. "You see that stuff on them?"

"*In* them! They're three-dimensional, moving. You can even *smell* them!" I picked up the prehistoric one and sniffed deeply, and thrust it at him. "Fire and brimstone!"

He sniffed it gingerly and put it down. "Yeah, um, look . . . I don't want to pry, but is this maybe an acid flashback? I know how—"

"I've never taken drugs in my life!" The nerve.

He held up a placating hand. "Just tryin' to be scientific here." He handed them back. "Study 'em. They're still the same?"

"Except this one." I turned it over. "You had it upside down." I took the contract out of the envelope. It hadn't changed. "How about this?"

He stared at it, both sides, then sighted down it as if looking for dust on the surface. "Another picture?"

"No. This is a contract. It gives the human race fifty years to get off the Earth."

"Not gonna happen." He squinted at it and then rubbed his beard, calculating. "Three and a half billon people, that's about two hundred thousand a day, call it eight thousand per hour. You couldn't move 'em across town in a bus in that time. Let alone to Mars or wherever." He shook his head and sort of laughed through his nose. "Ain't gonna happen."

"You think I'm crazy."

He riveted me with his eyes, coal black and bloodshot. "I don't say that about people. We all got different ways with reality."

The pizza came. I ordered two more beers and grabbed one as soon as they came.

He was a pizza-consuming machine, six slices to my two. He couldn't have weighed a hundred-twenty. Maybe he only ate when somebody else was paying.

"What you want to do," he said, lingering over the last piece, "is get some scientists interested in this plastic. There can't be any plastic on Earth that does what you say."

"You believe me."

"Provisionally, yeah. Why would you lie to me? I don't have any money or prestige. Not gonna get any in this life."

He touched the middle one, leaving a little smear of grease. "This is Sixth and University."

"That's right." I dabbed away the fingerprint.

"What you're seeing is the traffic going by there now?"

"Yes. Or I think so. It could be anytime recent, this time of day."

He got up. "Order me another beer. I'm gonna bicycle down there and hold up a certain number of fingers. Then I come back and you tell me how many."

I watched him pedal laboriously away, and ordered another beer and a cannoli. Maybe I could finish it before he got back, using the beer as a distraction.

A few minutes later, he showed up at the intersection. He held up three fingers. He turned around, and behind his back, two fingers in a V.

I'd finished most of the cannoli by the time he returned. "You want the rest of that?"

I pushed it toward him. "You held up three fingers and had two behind your back."

He nodded slowly and nibbled at the pastry. "Suppose you don't tell people about the intergalactic real estate man. Suppose you just say 'I'm psychic. You go do anything at the corner of Sixth and University, and I'll look at this piece of plastic and tell you what it is.'"

"They'd say I had a hidden camera."

He sipped his beer. "Wouldn't do you any good if you were sitting in a newspaper office. A television station."

"A laboratory," I said. "I want scientists to pay attention."

"Uh-huh. First you got to *get* their attention." He drank half the beer and set it down hard. "What time you get off work?"

"Five."

"Got a card? A business card?" I fished through my purse and gave him one. "I know some people," he said. "I'll call you."

He showed up right at five in a car driven by a younger man. It was a dusty old black Chevrolet with a magnetic sign on the door advertising a local television station. A black car in Florida? Cheap, I presumed.

The boy had a big smile, and I couldn't blame him for that. Looking forward to some fun. He said they had a thing, a "spot," scheduled for right after the six-thirty commercial. I said that was fine and reached in to shake his hand. That's when I saw the second young man in the back with a bulky camera.

"Randall Armitage," the driver said to me. "Have you ever met me before?"

"No," I said apologetically. "I don't watch much television. What is this?"

"He's taking a movie of you, uncut from now until the demonstration. Is that all right? John Buford Marshall."

I shrugged. He didn't have air-conditioning, but it wasn't that far to the station. I got in and sneezed from the dust. "Let's go," I said. "Don't spare the horses."

We parked near the entrance to the TV station and the driver helped the cameraman, carrying a heavy battery for him. They both walked backwards, taking a picture of me crunching down the gravel walk. "This is not going to be very exciting," I said. "Walking."

"It's not part of the show," Jeremiah Phipps said. "It's for the scientists afterwards." Randall gave an unambiguous smirk. That firmed my resolve. I wanted to see the look on their faces later.

We sat down in a studio that was shabby everywhere the camera couldn't see. The announcer's desk itself was clean and smelled of lemon furniture polish. "Can I get you a coffee?" Randall asked, and I nodded, laying out the three pictures. A woman with a clipboard sat down behind us all without introducing herself.

The coffee smelled great, but as I raised it to my lips I asked, "Will I be able to go to the bathroom?"

" 'Fraid not," the cameraman said. "Not until after the thing."

I set it down. "I'll explain about the three pictures," I said.

"Just the one, please," John Buford said. "The one we can verify."

"Okay." I peered into it. "It's rush hour, of course. Tourists crawl up Sixth Avenue and find they can't turn left on University. Horns honking, as if *that* ever did any good." I looked up. "Of course anybody could tell you that.

"There's a short man wearing a straw boater walking a huge dog across the street. It's a Great Dane."

"You should send someone out with a walkie-talkie," Jeremiah said.

Randall nodded but said no. "This is a television thing. Not a radio thing."

"We can do it later," the cameraman said neutrally. "Can you explain how this happened?"

"Sure." I wondered which one of them was in charge. I talked to the camera. "About eleven-thirty today, a strange-looking man walked into my real estate office. I'm a realtor for Star Realty on Thirteenth Street." A plug wouldn't hurt.

So I just plunged into the story and told it as accurately as I could remember. I held the sheet up to the camera and described what I could see and smell and hear. Randall looked at me sort of like he was studying a bug. Marshall looked more charitable. The silent woman with the clipboard left.

"We're going to do a simple test first," he said. "I'm going to stand at the intersection and write something on this big sheet of paper." A poster board, actually. "Nobody knows what I'm going to write—*I* don't even know, yet. You tell us what you see. Then our other portable camera, like this one, will show it."

"Okay. Just point the paper north on Sixth. Or turn it around a couple of times."

He left with a teenage boy. "Kind of stupid," I said. "He could have left a note behind. He could have told me hours ago what he was going to write."

The cameraman smiled. "You don't know television, ma'am. People trust the camera."

"They do," Jeremiah said. "Not like they read books anymore." I could hear a woman reading the news to the camera in the next room.

After a few minutes, John Buford Marshall smoothed his tie and another man came in to operate the camera. Bright lights snapped on. "Ma'am?" I went up to join him, and a woman powdered us both. While she was doing it, he said, "Let me have an oblique two-shot here with space in the lower corner for Randall's insert."

"You got it, boss." Maybe he was the boss. After a minute, the man in the shadows said, "In five." Three green lights, an orange and then a red.

"Thank you, Thelma," he said, and conspicuously looked at his watch, in spite of the fact that there were clocks everywhere. "Thank you for the explanation of this ordinary woman's extraordinary talent. Do you see our reporter, Mrs. Hockfield?"

"Oh, yes. He's standing on the sidewalk outside the music store on University. He's talking to the cameraman." I held the plastic close. "Can't quite hear. Still a lot of traffic."

"He should start writing . . . now." He did, a moment later, and then turned the board around. "It doesn't make any sense."

"Just tell us what you think it says."

"No 'think' about it. It says SHE IS A THETAN."

Jeremiah Phipps said a word I don't think they allow on television.

"Ten seconds now, and the external camera." I was watching his face instead of the monitor. His eyes bugged out in a most gratifying way. "How . . . how did you . . . what's a Thetan?"

"I'm sure I don't know. I'm certainly *not* one! I'm a member of the Daughters of the American Revolution."

"Here come the phones," Jeremiah Phipps said. One in the main office rang stridently. Two in the studio blinked angry red lights. "I think you're going to find out more than you ever wanted to know about Thetans."

———

It was kind of a joke. It turned out that Jeremiah Phipps knew Randall through science fiction—he was a "fan," not a writer, and Randall decided to play a little science-fictional joke on Phipps.

Over the next few days I heard a lot about Thetans and L. Ron Hubbard, another science-fiction writer who discovered this religion, or made it up, Dianetics or Scientology. After news of the message "SHE IS A THETAN" got around—especially after the networks picked it up—I had twenty or thirty Scientologists a day come by the office.

As I say, you have to be a people person in this business, and part of that is to live and let live when it comes to religion. In my heart of hearts I don't suppose I really *believe* any of it, not even the Episcopalianism I grew up with—that dried up when my husband died young—but anything that gets you through the day is all right by me. These Scientologists had some pretty strange things to say, and I don't pretend I could follow it all, but they seemed moral and good-hearted.

And they believed me. I couldn't get any scientists past the Thetan thing, but that was all right. The Scientologists believed me. And they bought houses. Boy, did they buy houses. I got gold pins for most property sold every year from 1967 until I retired in 1981. Houses weren't that easy to sell in Gainesville then, in the middle of the state, equally far from the ocean and the Gulf.

After I retired, the Scientologists would still come by. They'd look at the pictures, which I had hanging on the wall, and some of them would claim to see things. Maybe, I don't know.

The picture that was the near past started to change as workers appeared and put a railroad through. That would be back in the 1850s, right in the same place, what would become Sixth and University. If I lived to be into my nineties, I'd see the Civil War come in. They had a battle there.

That wouldn't show up, though, until after August 14, 2017. When we'd all be exterminated, if old Baldy was to be believed. I hadn't been able to get anybody but Jeremiah Phipps interested in that, and he passed long ago.

But before he died, he gave me an idea. It might work.

————

I turned seventy-eight in 2017, some the worse for wear but no complaints. On August 14 I put on my best Sunday dress and sat in the living room with a pitcher of iced tea.

Just before noon, Baldy knocked on the door and then walked through it, like mist. He hadn't changed.

"Do not get up. I can see it is not easy."

"Thank you." He mopped at his face with a big handkerchief and looked around my rather crowded house. Never could get rid of stuff.

"So what's it going to be?" I said. "Big explosion? Poison gas?"

"What would you prefer?"

"Ice, I suppose, like the poet said. It's been so damned hot."

"I could ask for ice." He sat down on the couch. "May I?"

"Help yourself." He poured a glass of iced tea and drank most of it.

He patted his lips with the handkerchief. "We might as well begin the . . ."

"Wait. I want to talk to the Council again."

"To what end? You will just bother them."

"You brought them before. This is much more serious."

"Oh, not really. Not to me." He looked annoyed, but he clapped his hands twice. The Council appeared, two seated next to him and a third, perhaps the one I spoke to half a century before, standing in front of the coffee table.

"What is it *this* time?" she said with asperity.

"When last we talked," I said carefully, "you said that your property laws were similar to ours."

"In some ways, yes."

"We have a thing called 'adverse possession.' Squatter's rights."

"I know of this," she said.

"You live on a piece of property for a length of time, continuously, without permission of the owner. 'Open and notorious.' Is that us?"

"That could be argued, of a species that accidentally evolved on a planet owned by someone else. But the agreement with *his* species"—she nodded at Baldy—"is the primary one, and was only contingent on their profoundly changing the environment. The ecology."

"That's what he said." I got to my feet, joints popping, and crossed over to the window. I threw the curtains open with a dramatic swoosh.

The sea glittered on the horizon.

"This was a hundred miles inland fifty years ago. Now it's an island. In fifty years, we've changed the Earth's ecology more than his people did in fifty thousand. Five hundred thousand."

She looked out over the sea and nodded.

"But we *planned* it," Baldy said.

"So did we," I said. "Everybody knew it was going to happen." Perhaps not so soon, I didn't say.

She looked at me, and her brow furrowed. "She's telling the truth." To Baldy: "Her case is stronger than yours." The three of them disappeared.

Baldy sat in silence for a moment. He finished his tea and stood up. He went to the window, and nodded.

"Clever. But we do have time on our side. We will return after you are extinct." He stepped to the door. "You will have your ice by then, I think."

He disappeared in a wisp.

I guess we can handle the ice when it happens.

It's a funny thing. When you live on the beach you hardly ever go swimming. I thought this afternoon I might.

(2004)

Four Short Novels

REMEMBRANCE OF THINGS PAST

Eventually it came to pass that no one ever had to die, unless they ran out of money. When you started to feel the little aches and twinges that meant your body was running down, you just got in line at Immortality, Incorporated, and handed them your credit card. As long as you had at least a million bucks—and eventually everybody did—they would reset you to whatever age you liked.

One way people made money was by swapping knowledge around. Skills could be transferred with a technology spun off from the immortality process. You could spend a few decades becoming a great concert pianist, and then put your ability up for sale. There was no shortage of people with two million dollars who would trade one million to be their village's Van Cliburn. In the sale of your ability, you would lose it, but you could buy it back a few decades or centuries later.

For many people this became the game of life—becoming temporarily a genius, selling your genius for youth, and then clawing your way up in some other field, to buy back the passion that had rescued you first from the grave. Enjoy it a few years, sell it again, and so on ad infinitum. Or *finitum*, if you just once made a wrong career move, and wound up old and poor and bereft of skill. That happened less and less often, of course, Darwinism inverted: the un-survival of the least fit.

It wasn't just a matter of swapping around your piano-playing and brain surgery, of course. People with the existential wherewithal to enjoy century after century of life tended to grow and improve with age. A person could look like a barely pubescent teenybopper, and yet be able to out-Socrates Socrates in the wisdom department. People were getting used to seeing acne and *gravitas* on the same face.

Enter Jutel Dicuth, the paragon of his age, a raging polymath. He could paint and sculpt and play six instruments. He could write formal poetry with his left hand while solving differential equations with his right. He could write formal poetry *about* differential equations! He was an Olympic-class gymnast and also held the world record for the javelin throw. He had earned doctorates in anthropology, art history, slipstream physics, and fly-tying.

He sold it all.

Immensely wealthy but bereft of any useful ability, Jutel Dicuth set up a trust fund for himself that would produce a million dollars every year. It also provided a generous salary for an attendant. He had Immortality, Incorporated, set him back to the apparent age of one year, and keep resetting him once a year.

In a world where there were no children—where would you put them?—he was the only infant. He was the only person with no useful skills and, eventually, the only one alive who did not have nearly a thousand years of memory.

In a world that had outgrown the old religions—why would you need them?—he became like unto a god. People came from everywhere to listen to his random babbling and try to find a conduit to the state of blissful innocence buried under the weight of their wisdom.

It was inevitable that someone would see a profit in this. A consortium with a name we would translate as Blank Slate offered to "dicuth" anyone who had a certain large sum of what passed for money, and maintain them for as long as they wanted. At first people were slightly outraged, because it was a kind of sacrilege, or were slightly amused, because it was such a transparent scheme to gather what passed for wealth.

Sooner or later, though, everyone tried it. Most who tried it for one year went back for ten or a hundred, or, eventually, forever. After some centuries, permanent dicuths began to outnumber humans—though those humans were not anything you would recognize as people, crushed as they were by nearly a thousand years of wisdom and experience. And jealous of those who had given up.

On 31 December, A.D. 3000, the last "normal" person surrendered his loneliness for dicuth bliss. The world was populated completely by total innocents, tended by patient machines.

It lasted a long time. Then one by one, the machines broke down.

CRIME AND PUNISHMENT

Eventually it came to pass that no one ever had to die, unless they were so horrible that society had to dispose of them. Other than the occasional horrible person, the world was in an idyllic state, everyone living as long as they wanted to, doing what they wanted to do.

This is how things got back to normal.

People gained immortality by making copies of themselves, farlies, which were kept in safe places and updated periodically. So if you got run over by a truck or hit by a meteorite, your farlie would sense this and automatically pop out and take over, after prudently making a farlie of itself. Upon that temporary death, you would lose only the weeks or months that had gone by since your last update.

That made it difficult to deal with criminals. If someone was so horrible that society had to hang or shoot or electrocute or inject him to death, his farlie would crop up somewhere, still bad to the bone, make a farlie of itself, and go off on another rampage. If you put him in jail for the rest of his life, he would eventually die, but then his evil farlie would leap out, full of youthful vigor and nasty intent.

Ultimately, if society felt you were too horrible to live, it would take preemptive action: check out your farlie and destroy it first. If it could be found. Really bad people became adept at hiding their farlies. Inevitably, people who were really good at being really bad became master criminals. It was that, or die forever. There were only a few dozen of them, but they moved through the world like neutrinos: effortless, unstoppable, invisible.

One of them was a man named Bad Billy Beerbreath. He started the ultimate crime wave.

There were Farlie Centers where you would go to update your farlie—one hundred of them, all over the world—and that's where almost everybody kept their farlies stored. But you could actually put a farlie anywhere, if you got together enough liquid nitrogen and terabytes of storage and kept them in a cool dry place out of direct sunlight.

Most people didn't know this; in fact, it was forbidden knowledge. Nobody knew how to make Farlie Centers anymore, either. They were all built during the lifetime of Joan Farlie, who had wandered off with the blueprints after deciding not to make a copy of himself, himself.

Bad Billy Beerbreath decided to make it his business to trash Farlie Centers. In its way, this was worse than murder, because if a client died before he or she found out about it, and hadn't been able to make a new farlie (which took weeks)—he or she would die for real, kaput, out of the picture. It was a crime beyond crime. Just thinking about this gave Bad Billy an acute pleasure akin to a hundred orgasms.

Because there were a hundred Bad Billy Beerbreaths.

In preparation for his crime wave, Bad Billy had spent years making a hundred farlies of himself, and he stored them in cool dry places out of direct sunlight, all around the world. On 13 May 2999, all but one of those farlies jump-started itself and went out to destroy the nearest Farlie Center.

By noon, GMT, police and militia all over the world had captured or killed or subdued every copy (but one) of Bad Billy, but by noon every single Farlie Center in the world had been leveled, save the one in Akron, Ohio.

The only people left who had farlies were people who had a reason to keep them in a secret place. Master criminals like Billy. Pals of Billy. They all were waiting at Akron, and held off the authorities for months, by making farlie after farlie of themselves, like broomsticks in a Disney cartoon, sending most of them out to die, or "die," defending the place, until there were so many of them the walls were bulging. Then they sent out word that they wanted to negotiate, and during the lull that promise produced, they fled en masse, destroying the last Farlie Center behind them.

They were a powerful force, a hundred thousand hardened criminals united in their contempt for people like you and me, and in their loyalty to Bad Billy Beerbreath. Somewhat giddy, not to say insane, in their triumph after having destroyed every Farlie Center, they went on to destroy every jail and prison and courthouse. That did cut their numbers down considerably, since most of them only had ten or twenty farlies tucked away, but it also reduced drastically the number of police, not to mention the number of people willing to take up policing as a profession, since once somebody killed you twice, you had to stay dead.

By New Year's Eve, A.D. 3000, the criminals were in charge of the whole world.

Again.

WAR AND PEACE

Eventually it came to pass that no one ever had to die, unless they wanted to, or could be talked into it. That made it very hard to fight wars, and a larger and larger part of every nation's military budget was given over to psychological operations directed toward their own people: *dulce et decorum est* just wasn't convincing enough anymore.

There were two elements to this sales job. One was to romanticize the image of the soldier as heroic defender of the blah blah blah. That was not too hard; they'd been doing that since Homer. The other was more subtle: convince people that every individual life was essentially worthless—your own and also the lives of the people you would eventually be killing.

That was a hard job, but the science of advertising, more than a millennium after Madison Avenue, was equal to it, through the person of a genius named Manny O'Malley. The pitch was subtle, and hard for a person to understand who hasn't lived for centuries, but shorn of Manny's incomprehensible humor and appeal to subtle pleasures that had no name until the thirtieth century, it boiled down to this:

A thousand years ago, they seduced people into soldiering with the slogan, "Be all that you can be." But you have *been* all you can be. The only thing left worth being is *not* being.

Everybody else is in the same boat, O'Malley convinced them. In the process of giving yourself the precious gift of nonexistence, share it with many others.

It's hard for us to understand. But then we would be hard for them to understand, with all this remorseless getting and spending laying waste our years.

Wars were all fought in Death Valley, with primitive hand weapons, and the United States grew wealthy renting the place out, until it inevitably found itself fighting a series of wars *for* Death Valley, during one of which O'Malley himself finally died, charging a phalanx of no-longer-immortal pikemen on his robotic horse, waving a broken sword. His final words were, famously, "Oh, shit."

Death Valley eventually wound up in the hands of the Bertelsmann Corporation, which ultimately ruled the world. But by that time, Manny's advertising had been so effective that no one cared. Everybody was in uniform, lining up to do their bit for Bertelsmann.

Even the advertising scientists. Even the high management of Bertelsmann.

There was a worldwide referendum, utilizing something indistinguishable from telepathy, where everybody agreed to change the name of the planet to Death Valley, and on the eve of the new century, A.D. 3000, have at each other.

Thus O'Malley's ultimate ad campaign achieved the ultimate victory: a world that consumed itself.

THE WAY OF ALL FLESH

Eventually it came to pass that no one ever had to die, so long as just one person loved them. The process that provided immortality was fueled that way.

Almost everybody can find someone to love him or her, at least for a little while, and if and when that someone says good-bye, most people can clean up their act enough to find yet another.

But every now and then you find a specimen who is so unlovable that he can't even get a hungry dog to take a biscuit from his hand. Babies take one look at him and get the colic. Women cross their legs as he passes by. Ardent homosexuals drop their collective gaze. Old people desperate for company feign sleep.

The most extreme such specimen was Custer Tralia. Custer came out of the womb with teeth, and bit the doctor. In grade school he broke up the love-training sessions with highly toxic farts. He celebrated puberty by not washing for a year. All through middle school and high school, he made loving couples into enemies by spreading clever vicious lies. He formed a Masturbation Club and didn't allow anybody else to join. In his graduation yearbook, he was unanimously voted "The One Least Likely to Survive, If We Have Anything to Do with It."

In college, he became truly reckless. When everybody else was feeling the first whiff of mortality and frantically seducing in self-defense, Custer declared that he hated women almost as much as he hated men, and he reveled in his freedom from love, his superior detachment from the cloying crowd. Death was nothing compared to the hell of dependency. When, at the beginning of his junior year, he had to declare what his profession was going to be, he wrote down "hermit" for first, second, and third choices.

The world was getting pretty damned crowded, though, since a lot of people loved each other so much they turned out copy after copy of themselves. The only place Custer could go and be truly alone was the Australian outback. He had a helicopter drop him there with a big water tank and crates of food. They said they'd check back in a year, and Custer said don't bother. If you've decided not to live forever, a few years or decades one way or the other doesn't make much difference.

He found peace among the wallabies and dingoes. A kangaroo began to follow him around, and he accepted it as a pet, sharing his rehydrated KFC and fish and chips with it.

Life was a pleasantly sterile and objectless quest. Custer and his kangaroo quartered the outback, turning over rocks just to bother the things underneath. The kangaroo was loyal, which was a liability; but at least it couldn't talk, and its attachment to Custer was transparently selfish, so they got along. He taught it how to beg, and, by not rewarding it, taught it how to whimper.

One day, like Robinson Crusoe, he found footprints. Unlike Robinson Crusoe, he hastened in the opposite direction.

But the footprinter had been watching him for some time, and outsmarted him. Knowing he would be gone all day, she had started miles away, walking backwards by his camp, and knew that his instinct for hermitage would lead him directly, perversely, back into her cave.

Parky Gumma had decided to become a hermit, too, after she read about Custer's audacious gesture. But after about a year she wanted a bath, and someone to love her so she wouldn't die, in that order. So under the wheeling Milky Way, on the eve of the thirty-first century, she stalked backwards to her cave and squandered a month's worth of water sluicing her body, which was unremarkable except for the fact that it was clean and the only female one in two hundred thousand square miles.

Parky left herself unclothed and squeaky clean, carefully perched on a camp stool, waiting for Custer's curiosity and misanthropy to lead him back to her keep. He crept in a couple of hours after sunrise.

She stood up and spread her arms, and his pet kangaroo boinged away in terror. Custer himself was paralyzed by a mixture of conflicting impulses. He had seen pictures of naked women, but never one actually in the flesh, and honestly didn't know what to do.

Parky showed him.

The rest is the unmaking of history. That Parky had admired him and followed him into the desert was even more endearing than the slip and slide that she demonstrated for him after she washed him up. But that was revolutionary, too. Custer had to admit that a year or a century or a millennium of that would be better than keeling over and having dingos tear up your corpse and spread your bones over the uncaring sands.

So this is Custer's story, and ours. He never did get around to liking baths, so you couldn't say that love conquers all. But it could still conquer death.

(1998)

For White Hill

———

•

———

I am writing this memoir in the language of England, an ancient land of Earth, whose tales and songs White Hill valued. She was fascinated by human culture in the days before machines—not just thinking machines, but working ones; when things got done by the straining muscles of humans and animals.

Neither of us was born on Earth. Not many people were, in those days. It was a desert planet then, ravaged in the twelfth year of what they would call the Last War. When we met, that war had been going for over four hundred years, and had moved out of Sol Space altogether, or so we thought.

Some cultures had other names for the conflict. My parent, who fought the century before I did, always called it the Extermination, and their name for the enemy was "roach," or at least that's as close as English allows. We called the enemy an approximation of their own word for themselves, Fwndyri, which was uglier to us. I still have no love for them, but have no reason to make the effort. It would be easier to love a roach. At least we have a common ancestor. And we accompanied one another into space.

One mixed blessing we got from the war was a loose form of interstellar government, the Council of Worlds. There had been individual treaties before, but an overall organization had always seemed unlikely, since no two inhabited systems are less than three light-years apart, and several of them are over fifty. You can't defeat Einstein; that makes more than a century between "How are you?" and "Fine."

The Council of Worlds was headquartered on Earth, an unlikely and unlovely place, if centrally located. There were fewer than ten thousand people living on the blighted planet then, an odd mix of politicians, religious extremists, and academics, mostly. Almost all of them under glass. Tourists flowed through the domed-over ruins, but not many stayed long. The planet was still very dangerous over all of its unprotected surface, since the Fwndyri had thoroughly seeded it with nanophages. Those were submicroscopic constructs that sought out concentrations of human DNA. Once under the skin, they would reproduce at a geometric rate, deconstructing the body, cell by cell, building new nanophages. A person might complain of a headache and lie down, and a few hours later there would be nothing but a dry skeleton, lying in dust. When the humans were all dead, they mutated and went after DNA in general, and sterilized the world.

White Hill and I were "bred" for immunity to the nanophages. Our DNA winds backwards, as was the case with many people born or created after that stage of the war. So we could actually go through the elaborate airlocks and step out onto the blasted surface unprotected.

I didn't like her at first. We were competitors, and aliens to one another.

When I worked through the final airlock cycle, for my first moment on the actual surface of Earth, she was waiting outside, sitting in meditation on a large flat rock that shimmered in the heat. One had to admit she was beautiful in a startling way, clad only in a glistening pattern of blue and green body paint. Everything else around was grey and black, including the hardpacked talcum that had once been a mighty jungle, Brazil. The dome behind me was a mirror of grey and black and cobalt sky.

"Welcome home," she said. "You're Water Man."

She inflected it properly, which surprised me. "You're from Petros?"

"Of course not." She spread her arms and looked down at her body. Our women always cover at least one of their breasts, let alone their genitals. "Galan, an island on Seldene. I've studied your cultures, a little language."

"You don't dress like that on Seldene, either." Not anywhere I'd been on the planet.

"Only at the beach. It's so warm here." I had to agree. Before I came out, they'd told me it was the hottest autumn on record. I took off my robe and folded it and left it by the door, with the sealed food box they had given me. I joined her on the rock, which was tilted away from the sun and reasonably cool.

She had a slight fragrance of lavender, perhaps from the body paint. We touched hands. "My name is White Hill. Zephyr-meadow-torrent."

"Where are the others?" I asked. Twenty-nine artists had been invited; one from each inhabited world. The people who had met me inside said I was the nineteenth to show up.

"Most of them traveling. Going from dome to dome for inspiration."

"You've already been around?"

"No." She reached down with her toe and scraped a curved line on the hard-baked ground. "All the story's here, anywhere. It isn't really about history or culture."

Her open posture would have been shockingly sexual at home, but this was not home. "Did you visit my world when you were studying it?"

"No, no money, at the time. I did get there a few years ago." She smiled at me. "It was almost as beautiful as I'd imagined it." She said three words in Petrosian. You couldn't say it precisely in English, which doesn't have a palindromic mood: *Dreams feed art and art feeds dreams.*

"When you came to Seldene I was young, too young to study with you. I've learned a lot from your sculpture, though."

"How young can you be?" To earn this honor, I did not say.

"In Earth years, about seventy awake. More than one-forty-five in time-squeeze."

I struggled with the arithmetic. Petros and Seldene were 22 light-years apart; that's about 45 years' squeeze. Earth is, what, a little less than 40 light-years from her planet. That leaves enough gone time for someplace about 25 light-years from Petros, and back.

She tapped me on the knee, and I flinched. "Don't overheat your brain. I made a triangle; went to ThetaKent after your world."

"Really? When I was there?"

"No, I missed you by less than a year. I was disappointed. You were why

I went." She made a palindrome in my language: *Predator becomes prey becomes predator?* "So here we are. Perhaps I can still learn from you."

I didn't much care for her tone of voice, but I said the obvious: "I'm more likely to learn from you."

"Oh, I don't think so." She smiled in a measured way. "You don't have much to learn."

Or much I could, or would, learn. "Have you been down to the water?"

"Once." She slid off the rock and dusted herself, spanking. "It's interesting. Doesn't look real." I picked up the food box and followed her down a sort of path that led us into low ruins. She drank some of my water, apologetic; hers was hot enough to brew tea.

"First body?" I asked.

"I'm not tired of it yet." She gave me a sideways look, amused. "You must be on your fourth or fifth."

"I go through a dozen a year." She laughed. "Actually, it's still my second. I hung on to the first too long."

"I read about that, the accident. That must have been horrible."

"Comes with the medium. I should take up the flute." I had been making a "controlled" fracture in a large boulder and set off the charges prematurely, by dropping the detonator. Part of the huge rock rolled over onto me, crushing my body from the hips down. It was a remote area, and by the time help arrived I had been dead for several minutes, from pain as much as anything else. "It affected all of my work, of course. I can't even look at some of the things I did the first few years I had this body."

"They are hard to look at," she said. "Not to say they aren't well-done, and beautiful, in their way."

"As what is not? In its way." We came to the first building ruins and stopped. "Not all of this is weathering. Even in four hundred years." If you studied the rubble, you could reconstruct part of the design. Primitive but sturdy, concrete reinforced with composite rods. "Somebody came in here with heavy equipment or explosives. They never actually fought on Earth, I thought."

"They say not." She picked up an irregular brick with a rod through it. "Rage, I suppose. Once people knew that no one was going to live."

"It's hard to imagine." The records are chaotic. Evidently the first people died two or three days after the nanophages were introduced, and no one on Earth was alive a week later. "Not hard to understand, though. The need to break something." I remembered the inchoate anger I felt as I squirmed there helpless, dying from *sculpture*, of all things. Anger at the rock, the fates. Not at my own inattention and clumsiness.

"They had a poem about that," she said. "'Rage, rage against the dying of the light.'"

"Somebody actually wrote something during the nanoplague?"

"Oh, no. A thousand years before. Twelve hundred." She squatted suddenly and brushed at a fragment that had two letters on it. "I wonder if this was some sort of official building. Or a shrine or church." She pointed along the curved row of shattered bricks that spilled into the street. "That looks like it was some kind of decoration, a gable over the entrance." She tiptoed through the rubble toward the far end of the arc, studying what was written on the faceup pieces. The posture, standing on the balls of her feet, made her slim body even more attractive, as she must have known. My own body began to respond in a way inappropriate for a man more than three times her age. Foolish, even though that particular part is not so old. I willed it down before she could see.

"It's a language I don't know," she said. "Not Portuguese; looks like Latin. A Christian church, probably, Catholic."

"They used water in their religion," I remembered. "Is that why it's close to the sea?"

"They were everywhere: sea, mountains, orbit. They got to Petros?"

"We still have some. I've never met one, but they have a church in New Haven."

"As who doesn't?" She pointed up a road. "Come on. The beach is just over the rise here."

I could smell it before I saw it. It wasn't an ocean smell; it was dry, slightly choking.

We turned a corner and I stood staring. "It's a deep blue farther out," she said, "and so clear you can see hundreds of metras down." Here the water was thick and brown, the surf foaming heavily like a giant's chocolate drink, mud piled in baked windrows along the beach. "This used to be soil?"

She nodded. "There's a huge river that cuts this continent in half, the Amazon. When the plants died, there was nothing to hold the soil in place." She tugged me forward. "Do you swim? Come on."

"Swim in *that*? It's filthy."

"No, it's perfectly sterile. Besides, I have to pee." Well, I couldn't argue with that. I left the box on a high fragment of fallen wall and followed her. When we got to the beach, she broke into a run. I walked slowly and watched her gracile body, instead, and waded into the slippery heavy surf. When it was deep enough to swim, I plowed my way out to where she was bobbing. The water was too hot to be pleasant, and breathing was somewhat difficult. Carbon dioxide, I supposed, with a tang of halogen.

We floated together for a while, comparing this soup to bodies of water on our planets and ThetaKent. It was tiring, more from the water's heat and bad air than exertion, so we swam back in.

• •

We dried in the blistering sun for a few minutes and then took the food box and moved to the shade of a beachside ruin. Two walls had fallen in together, to make a sort of concrete tent.

We could have been a couple of precivilization aboriginals, painted with dirt, our hair baked into stringy mats. She looked odd but still had a kind of formal beauty, the dusty mud residue turning her into a primitive sculpture, impossibly accurate and mobile. Dark rivulets of sweat drew painterly accent lines along her face and body. If only she were a model, rather than an artist. Hold that pose while I go back for my brushes.

We shared the small bottles of cold wine and water and ate bread and cheese and fruit. I put a piece on the ground for the nanophages. We watched it in silence for some minutes, while nothing happened. "It probably takes hours or days," she finally said.

"I suppose we should hope so," I said. "Let us digest the food before the creatures get to it."

"Oh, that's not a problem. They just attack the bonds between amino acids that make up proteins. For you and me, they're nothing more than an aid to digestion."

How reassuring. "But a source of some discomfort when we go back in, I was told."

She grimaced. "The purging. I did it once, and decided my next outing would be a long one. The treatment's the same for a day or a year."

"So how long has it been this time?"

"Just a day and a half. I came out to be your welcoming committee."

"I'm flattered."

She laughed. "It was their idea, actually. They wanted someone out here to 'temper' the experience for you. They weren't sure how well traveled you were, how easily affected by . . . strangeness." She shrugged. "Earthlings. I told them I knew of four planets you'd been to."

"They weren't impressed?"

"They said well, you know, he's famous and wealthy. His experiences on these planets might have been very comfortable." We could both laugh at that. "I told them how comfortable ThetaKent is."

"Well, it doesn't have nanophages."

"Or anything else. That was a long year for me. You didn't even stay a year."

"No. I suppose we would have met, if I had."

"Your agent said you were going to be there two years."

I poured us both some wine. "She should have told me you were coming. Maybe I could have endured it until the next ship out."

"How gallant." She looked into the wine without drinking. "You famous and wealthy people don't have to endure ThetaKent. I had to agree to one year's indentureship to help pay for my triangle ticket."

"You were an actual slave?"

"More like a wife, actually. The head of a township, a widower, financed me in exchange for giving his children some culture. Language, art, music. Every now and then he asked me to his chambers. For his own kind of culture."

"My word. You had to . . . *lie* with him? That was in the contract?"

"Oh, I didn't have to, but it kept him friendly." She held up a thumb and forefinger. "It was hardly noticeable."

I covered my smile with a hand, and probably blushed under the mud.

"I'm not embarrassing you?" she said. "From your work, I'd think that was impossible."

I had to laugh. "That work is in reaction to my culture's values. I can't take a pill and stop being a Petrosian."

White Hill smiled, tolerantly. "A Petrosian woman wouldn't put up with an arrangement like that?"

"Our women are still women. Some actually would like it, secretly. Most would claim they'd rather die, or kill the man."

"But they wouldn't actually *do* it. Trade their body for a ticket?" She sat down in a single smooth dancer's motion, her legs open, facing me. The clay between her legs parted, sudden pink.

"I wouldn't put it so bluntly." I swallowed, watching her watching me. "But no, they wouldn't. Not if they were planning to return."

"Of course no one from a civilized planet would want to stay on ThetaKent. Shocking place."

I had to move the conversation onto safer grounds. "Your arms don't spend all day shoving big rocks around. What do you normally work in?"

"Various mediums." She switched to my language. "Sometimes I shove little rocks around." That was a pun for testicles. "I like painting, but my reputation is mainly from light and sound sculpture. I wanted to do something with the water here, internal illumination of the surf, but they say that's not possible. They can't isolate part of the ocean. I can have a pool, but no waves, no tides."

"Understandable." Earth's scientists had found a way to rid the surface of the nanoplague. Before they reterraformed the Earth, though, they wanted to isolate an area, a "park of memory," as a reminder of the Sterilization and these centuries of waste, and brought artists from every world to interpret, inside the park, what they had seen here.

Every world except Earth. Art on Earth had been about little else for a long time.

Setting up the contest had taken decades. A contest representative went to each of the settled worlds, according to a strict timetable. Announcement of the competition was delayed on the nearer worlds so that each artist would arrive on Earth at approximately the same time.

The Earth representatives chose which artists would be asked, and no one refused. Even the ones who didn't win the contest were guaranteed an honorarium equal to twice what they would have earned during that time at home, in their best year of record.

The value of the prize itself was so large as to be meaningless to a normal person. I'm a wealthy man on a planet where wealth is not rare, and just the interest that the prize would earn would support me and a half dozen more. If someone from ThetaKent or Laxor won the prize, they would probably have more real usable wealth than their governments. If they were smart, they wouldn't return home.

The artists had to agree on an area for the park, which was limited to a hundred square kaymetras. If they couldn't agree, which seemed almost inevitable to me, the contest committee would listen to arguments and rule.

Most of the chosen artists were people like me, accustomed to working on a monumental scale. The one from Laxor was a composer, though, and there were two conventional muralists, paint and mosaic. White Hill's work was by its nature evanescent. She could always set something up that would be repeated, like a fountain cycle. She might have more imagination than that, though.

"Maybe it's just as well we didn't meet in a master-student relationship," I said. "I don't know the first thing about the techniques of your medium."

"It's not technique." She looked thoughtful, remembering. "That's not why I wanted to study with you, back then. I was willing to push rocks around, or anything, if it could give me an avenue, an insight into how you did what you did." She folded her arms over her chest, and dust fell. "Ever since my parents took me to see Gaudí Mountain, when I was ten."

That was an early work, but I was still satisfied with it. The city council of Tresling, a prosperous coastal city, hired me to "do something with" an unusable steep island that stuck up in the middle of their harbor. I melted it judiciously, in homage to an Earthling artist.

"Now, though, if you'd forgive me . . . well, I find it hard to look at. It's alien, obtrusive."

"You don't have to apologize for having an opinion." Of course it looked alien; it was meant to evoke *Spain*! "What would you do with it?"

She stood up and walked to where a window used to be, and leaned on the stone sill, looking at the ruins that hid the sea. "I don't know. I'm even less familiar with your tools." She scraped at the edge of the sill with a piece of rubble. "It's funny: earth, air, fire, and water. You're earth and fire, and I'm the other two."

I have used water, of course. The Gaudí is framed by water. But it was an interesting observation. "What do you do, I mean for a living? Is it related to your water and air?"

"No. Except insofar as everything is related." There are no artists on

Seldene, in the sense of doing it for a living. Everybody indulges in some sort of art or music, as part of "wholeness," but a person who only did art would be considered a parasite. I was not comfortable there.

She faced me, leaning. "I work at the Northport Mental Health Center. Cognitive science, a combination of research and . . . is there a word here? *Jaturnary*. 'Empathetic therapy,' I guess."

I nodded. "We say *jådr-ny*. You plug yourself into mental patients?"

"I share their emotional states. Sometimes I do some good, talking to them afterwards. Not often."

"It's not done on Petrosia," I said, unnecessarily.

"Not legally, you mean."

I nodded. "If it worked, people say, it might be legal."

"'People say.' What do you say?" I started to make a noncommittal gesture. "Tell me the truth?"

"All I know is what I learned in school. It was tried but failed spectacularly. It hurt both the therapists and the patients."

"That was more than a century ago. The science is much more highly developed now."

I decided not to push her on it. The fact is that drug therapy is spectacularly successful, and it *is* a science, unlike *jådr-ny*. Seldene is backward in some surprising ways.

I joined her at the window. "Have you looked around for a site yet?"

She shrugged. "I think my presentation will work anywhere. At least that's guided my thinking. I'll have water, air, and light, wherever the other artists and the committee decide to put us." She scraped at the ground with a toenail. "And this stuff. They call it 'loss.' What's left of what was living."

"I suppose it's not everywhere, though. They might put us in a place that used to be a desert."

"They might. But there will be water and air; they were willing to guarantee that."

"I don't suppose they have to guarantee rock," I said.

"I don't know. What would you do if they did put us in a desert, nothing but sand?"

"Bring little rocks." I used my own language; the pun also meant courage.

She started to say something, but we were suddenly in deeper shadow. We both stepped through the tumbled wall, out into the open. A black line of cloud had moved up rapidly from inland.

She shook her head. "Let's get to the shelter. Better hurry."

We trotted back along the path toward the Amazonia dome city. There was a low concrete structure behind the rock where I first met her. The warm breeze became a howling gale of sour steam before we got there, driving bullets of hot rain. A metal door opened automatically on our approach and slid shut behind us. "I got caught in one yesterday," she said, panting. "It's no fun, even under cover. Stinks."

We were in an unadorned anteroom that had protective clothing on wall pegs. I followed her into a large room furnished with simple chairs and tables, and up a winding stair to an observation bubble.

"Wish we could see the ocean from here," she said. It was dramatic enough. Wavering sheets of water marched across the blasted landscape, strobed every few seconds by lightning flashes. The tunic I'd left outside swooped in flapping circles off to the sea.

It was gone in a couple of seconds. "You don't get another one, you know. You'll have to meet everyone naked as a baby."

"A dirty one at that. How undignified."

"Come on." She caught my wrist and tugged. "Water is my specialty, after all."

· · ·

The large hot bath was doubly comfortable for having a view of the tempest outside. I'm not at ease with communal bathing—I was married for fifty years and never bathed with my wife—but it seemed natural enough after wandering around together naked on an alien planet, swimming in its mud-puddle sea. I hoped I could trust her not to urinate in the tub. (If I mentioned it, she would probably turn scientific and tell me that a healthy person's urine is sterile. I know that. But there is a time and a receptacle for everything.)

On Seldene, I knew, an unattached man and woman in this situation would probably have had sex even if they were only casual acquaintances, let alone fellow artists. She was considerate enough not to make any overtures, or perhaps (I thought at the time) not greatly stimulated by

the sight of muscular men. In the shower before bathing, she offered to
scrub my back, but left it at that. I helped her strip off the body paint
from her back. It was a nice back to study, pronounced lumbar dimples,
small waist. Under more restrained circumstances, it might have been *I*
who made an overture. But one does not ask a woman when refusal
would be awkward.

Talking while we bathed, I learned that some of her people, when
they become wealthy enough to retire, choose to work on their art full-
time, but they're considered eccentric, even outcasts, egotists. White Hill
expected one of them to be chosen for the contest, and wasn't even going
to apply. But the Earthling judge saw one of her installations and tracked
her down.

She also talked about her practical work in dealing with personality
disorders and cognitive defects. There was some distress in her voice
when she described that to me. Plugging into hurt minds, sharing their
pain or blankness for hours. I didn't feel I knew her well enough to bring
up the aspect that most interested me, a kind of ontological prurience:
what is it like to actually *be* another person; how much of her, or him, do
you take away? If you do it often enough, how can you know which parts
of you are the original you?

And she would be plugged in to more than one person at once, at
times, the theory being that people with similar disorders could help each
other, swarming around in the therapy room of her brain. She would fade
into the background, more or less unable to interfere, and later analyze
how they had interacted.

She had had one particularly unsettling experience, where through a
planetwide network, she had interconnected more than a hundred con-
genitally retarded people. She said it was like a painless death. By the time
half of them had plugged in, she had felt herself fade and wink out. Then
she was reborn with the suddenness of a slap. She had been dead for
about ten hours.

But only connected for seven. It had taken technicians three hours to
pry her out of a persistent catatonia. With more people, or a longer period, she might have been lost forever. There was no lasting harm, but the
experiment was never repeated.

It was worth it, she said, for the patients' inchoate happiness afterwards. It was like a regular person being given supernatural powers for

half a day—powers so far beyond human experience that there was no way to talk about them, but the memory of it was worth the frustration.

After we got out of the tub, she showed me to our wardrobe room: hundreds of white robes, identical except for size. We dressed and made tea and sat upstairs, watching the storm rage. It hardly looked like an inhabitable planet outside. The lightning had intensified so that it crackled incessantly, a jagged insane dance in every direction. The rain had frozen to white gravel somehow. I asked the building, and it said that the stuff was called *granizo* or, in English, hail. For a while it fell too fast to melt, accumulating in white piles that turned translucent.

Staring at the desolation, White Hill said something that I thought was uncharacteristically modest. "This is too big and terrible a thing. I feel like an interloper. They've lived through centuries of this, and now they want *us* to explain it to them?"

I didn't have to remind her of what the contest committee had said, that their own arts had become stylized, stunned into a grieving conformity. "Maybe not to *explain*—maybe they're assuming we'll fail, but hope to find a new direction from our failures. That's what that oldest woman, Norita, implied."

White Hill shook her head. "Wasn't she a ray of sunshine? I think they dragged her out of the grave as a way of keeping us all outside the dome."

"Well, she was quite effective on me. I could have spent a few days investigating Amazonia, but not with her as a native guide." Norita was about as close as anyone could get to being an actual native. She was the last survivor of the Five Families, the couple of dozen Earthlings who, among those who were offworld at the time of the nanoplague, were willing to come back after robots constructed the isolation domes.

In terms of social hierarchy, she was the most powerful person on Earth, at least on the actual planet. The class system was complex and nearly opaque to outsiders, but being a descendant of the Five Families was a prerequisite for the highest class. Money or political power would not get you in, although most of the other social classes seemed associated with wealth or the lack of it. Not that there were any actual poor people on Earth; the basic birth dole was equivalent to an upper-middle-class income on Petros.

The nearly instantaneous destruction of ten billion people did not destroy their fortunes. Most of the Earth's significant wealth had been offplanet, anyhow, at the time of the Sterilization. Suddenly it was concentrated into the hands of fewer than two thousand people.

Actually, I couldn't understand why anyone would have come back. You'd have to be pretty sentimental about your roots to be willing to spend the rest of your life cooped up under a dome, surrounded by instant death. The salaries and amenities offered were substantial, with bonuses for earthborn workers, but it still doesn't sound like much of a bargain. The ships that brought the Five Families and the other original workers to Earth left loaded down with sterilized artifacts, not to return for exactly one hundred years.

Norita seemed like a familiar type to me, since I come from a culture also rigidly bound by class. "Old money, but not much of it" sums up the situation. She wanted to be admired for the accident of her birth and the dubious blessing of a torpid longevity, rather than any actual accomplishment. I didn't have to travel 33 light-years to enjoy that kind of company.

"Did she keep you away from everybody?" White Hill said.

"Interposed herself. No one could act naturally when she was around, and the old dragon was never *not* around. You'd think a person her age would need a little sleep."

"'She lives on the blood of infants,' we say."

There was a phone chime, and White Hill said *"Bono"* as I said *"Chä."* Long habits. Then we said Earth's *"Hola"* simultaneously.

The old dragon herself appeared. "I'm glad you found shelter." Had she been eavesdropping? No way to tell from her tone or posture. "An administrator has asked permission to visit with you."

What if we said no? White Hill nodded, which means yes on Earth. "Granted," I said.

"Very well. He will be there shortly." She disappeared. I suppose the oldest person on a planet can justify not saying hello or good-bye. Only so much time left, after all.

"A physical visit?" I said to White Hill. "Through this weather?"

She shrugged. "Earthlings."

After a minute there was a "ding" sound in the anteroom, and we walked down to see an unexpected door open. What I'd thought was a hall closet was an airlock. He'd evidently come underground.

Young and nervous and moving awkwardly in plastic. He shook our hands in an odd way. Of course we were swimming in deadly poison. "My name is Warm Dawn. Zephyr-boulder-brook."

"Are we cousins through Zephyr?" White Hill asked.

He nodded quickly. "An honor, my lady. Both of my parents are Seldenian, my gene-mother from your Galan."

A look passed over her that was pure disbelieving chauvinism: *Why would anybody leave Seldene's forests, farms, and meadows for this sterile death trap?* Of course she knew the answer. The major import and export, the only crop, on Earth, was money.

"I wanted to help both of you with your planning. Are you going to travel at all, before you start?"

White Hill made a noncommittal gesture. "There are some places for me to see," I said. "The Pyramids, Chicago, Rome. Maybe a dozen places, twice that many days." I looked at her. "Would you care to join me?"

She looked straight at me, wheels turning. "It sounds interesting."

The man took us to a viewscreen in the great room and we spent an hour or so going over routes and making reservations. Travel was normally by underground vehicle, from dome to dome, and if we ventured outside unprotected, we would of course have to go through the purging before we were allowed to continue. Some people need a day or more to recover from that, so we should put that into the schedule, if we didn't want to be hobbled, like him, with plastic.

Most of the places I wanted to see were safely under glass, even some of the Pyramids, which surprised me. Some, like Ankgor Wat, were not only unprotected but difficult of access. I had to arrange for a flyer to cover the thousand kaymetras, and schedule a purge. White Hill said she would wander through Hanoi, instead.

I didn't sleep well that night, waking often from fantastic dreams, the nanobeasts grown large and aggressive. White Hill was in some of the dreams, posturing sexually.

By the next morning the storm had gone away, so we crossed over to Amazonia, and I learned firsthand why one might rather sit in a hotel room with a nice book than go to Ankgor Wat, or anywhere that required a purge. The external part of the purging was unpleasant enough, even with pain medication, all the epidermis stripped and regrown. The inside part was beyond description, as the nanophages could be hiding out anywhere. Every opening into the body had to be vacuumed out, including the sense organs. I was not awake for that part, where the robots most gently clean out your eye sockets, but my eyes hurt and my ears rang for days. They warned me to sit down the first time I urinated, which was good advice, since I nearly passed out from the burning pain.

White Hill and I had a quiet supper of restorative gruel together, and then crept off to sleep for half a day. She was full of pep the next morning, and I pretended to be at least sentient, as we wandered through the city making preparations for the trip.

After a couple of hours I protested that she was obviously trying to do in one of her competitors; stop and let an old man sit down for a minute.

We found a bar that specialized in stimulants. She had tea and I had bhan, a murky warm drink served in a large nut shell, coconut. It tasted woody and bitter, but was restorative.

"It's not age," she said. "The purging seems a lot easier the second time you do it. I could hardly move, all the next day, the first time."

Interesting that she didn't mention that earlier. "Did they tell you it would get easier?"

She nodded, then caught herself and wagged her chin horizontally, Earth-style. "Not a word. I think they enjoy our discomfort."

"Or like to keep us off guard. Keeps them in control." She made the little kissing sound that's Lortian for agreement and reached for a lemon wedge to squeeze into her tea. The world seemed to slow slightly, I guess from whatever was in the bhan, and I found myself cataloging her body microscopically. A crescent of white scar tissue on the back of a knuckle, fine hair on her forearm, almost white, her shoulders and breasts moving in counterpoised pairs, silk rustling, as she reached forward and back and squeezed the lemon, sharp citrus smell and the tip of her tongue between her thin lips, mouth slightly large. Chameleon hazel eyes, dark green now because of the decorative ivy wall behind her.

"What are you staring at?"

"Sorry, just thinking."

"Thinking." She stared at me in return, measuring. "Your people are good at that."

After we'd bought the travel necessities we had the packages sent to our quarters and wandered aimlessly. The city was comfortable, but had little of interest in terms of architecture or history, oddly dull for a planet's administrative center. There was an obvious social purpose for its blandness—by statute, nobody was *from* Amazonia; nobody could be born there or claim citizenship. Most of the planet's wealth and power came there to work, electronically if not physically, but it went home to some other place.

A certain amount of that wealth was from interstellar commerce, but it was nothing like the old days, before the war. Earth had been a hub, a central authority that could demand its tithe or more from any transaction between planets. In the period between the Sterilization and Earth's token rehabitation, the other planets made their own arrangements with one another, in pairs and groups. But most of the fortunes that had been born on Earth returned here.

So Amazonia was bland as cheap bread, but there was more wealth under its dome than on any two other planets combined. Big money seeks out the company of its own, for purposes of reproduction.

· ▲

Two other artists had come in, from Auer and Shwa, and once they were ready, we set out to explore the world by subway. The first stop that was interesting was the Grand Canyon, a natural wonder whose desolate beauty was unaffected by the Sterilization.

We were amused by the guide there, a curious little woman who rattled on about the Great Rift Valley on Mars, a nearby planet where she was born. White Hill had a lightbox, and while the Martian lady droned on we sketched the fantastic colors, necessarily loose and abstract because our fingers were clumsy in clinging plastic.

We toured Chicago, like the Grand Canyon, wrapped in plastic. It was a large city that had been leveled in a local war. It lay in ruins for many years, and then, famously, was rebuilt as a single huge structure from those ruins. There's a childish or drunken ad hoc quality to it, a scarcity of right angles, a crazy-quilt mixture of materials. Areas of stunning imaginative brilliance next to juryrigged junk. And everywhere bones, the skeletons of ten million people, lying where they fell. I asked what had happened to the bones in the old city outside of Amazonia. The guide said he'd never been there, but he supposed that the sight of them upset the politicians, so they had them cleaned up. "Can you imagine this place without the bones?" he asked. It would be nice if I could.

The other remnants of cities in that country were less interesting, if no less depressing. We flew over the east coast, which was essentially one continuous metropolis for thousands of kaymetras, like our coast from New Haven to Stargate, rendered in sterile ruins.

The first place I visited unprotected was Giza, the Great Pyramids. White Hill decided to come with me, though she had to be wrapped up in a shapeless cloth robe, her face veiled, because of local religious law. It seemed to me ridiculous, a transparent tourism ploy. How many believers in that old religion could have been offplanet when the Earth died? But every female was obliged at the tube exit to go into a big hall and be fitted with a *chador* robe and veil before a man could be allowed to look at her.

(We wondered whether the purging would be done completely by women. The technicians would certainly see a lot of her uncovered during that excruciation.)

They warned us it was unseasonably hot outside. Almost too hot to breathe, actually, during the day. We accomplished most of our sightseeing around dusk or dawn, spending most of the day in air-conditioned shelters.

Because of our special status, White Hill and I were allowed to visit the Pyramids alone, in the dark of the morning. We climbed up the largest one and watched the sun mount over desert haze. It was a singular time for both of us, edifying but something more.

Coming back down, we were treated to a sandstorm, *khamsin*, which actually might have done the first stage of purging if we had been allowed to take off our clothes. It explained why all the bones lying around looked so much older than the ones in Chicago; they normally had ten or twelve of these sandblasting storms every year. Lately, with the heat wave, the *khamsin* came weekly or even more often.

Raised more than five thousand years ago, the Pyramids were the oldest monumental structures on the planet. They actually held as much fascination for White Hill as for me. Thousands of men moved millions of huge blocks of stone, with nothing but muscle and ingenuity. Some of the stones were mined a thousand kaymetras away, and floated up the river on barges.

I could build a similar structure, even larger, for my contest entry, by giving machines the right instructions. It would be a complicated business, but easily done within the two-year deadline. Of course there would be no point to it. That some anonymous engineer had done the same thing within the lifetime of a king, without recourse to machines—I agreed with White Hill: that was an actual marvel.

We spent a couple of days outside, traveling by surface hoppers from monument to monument, but none was as impressive. I suppose I should have realized that and saved Giza for last.

We met another of the artists at the Sphinx, Lo Tan-Six, from Pao. I had seen his work on both Pao and ThetaKent, and admitted there was something to be admired there. He worked in stone, too, but was more interested in pure geometric forms than I was. I think stone fights form, or imposes its own tensions on the artist's wishes.

I liked him well enough, though, in spite of this and other differences, and we traveled together for a while. He suggested we not go through the purging here, but have our things sent on to Rome, because we'd want to be outside there, too. There was a daily hop from Alexandria to Rome, an airship that had a section reserved for those of us who could eat and breathe nanophages.

As soon as she was inside the coolness of the ship, White Hill shed the *chador* and veil and stuffed them under the seat. "Breathe," she said, stretching. Her white bodysuit was a little less revealing than paint.

Her directness and undisguised sexuality made me catch my breath. The tiny crease of punctuation that her vulva made in the bodysuit would have her jailed on some parts of my planet, not to mention the part of this one we'd just left. The costume was innocent and natural and, I think, completely calculated.

Pao studied her with an interested detachment. He was neuter, an option that was available on Petros, too, but one I've never really understood. He claimed that sex took too much time and energy from his art. I think his lack of gender took something else away from it.

We flew about an hour over the impossibly blue sea. There were a few sterile islands, but otherwise it was as plain as spilled ink. We descended over the ashes of Italy and landed on a pad on one of the hills overlooking the ancient city. The ship mated to an airlock so the normal-DNA people could go down to a tube that would whisk them into Rome. We could call for transportation or walk, and opted for the exercise. It was baking hot here, too, but not as bad as Egypt.

White Hill was polite with Lo, but obviously wished he'd disappear. He and I chattered a little too much about rocks and cements, explosives and lasers. And his asexuality diminished her interest in him—as, perhaps, my polite detachment increased her interest in me. The muralist from Shwa, to complete the spectrum, was after her like a puppy in its first heat, which I think amused her for two days. They'd had a private conversation in Chicago, and he'd kept his distance since, but still admired her from afar. As we walked down toward the Roman gates, he kept a careful twenty paces behind, trying to contemplate things besides White Hill's walk.

Inside the gate we stopped short, stunned in spite of knowing what to expect. It had a formal name, but everybody just called it Òssi, the Bones. An order of Catholic clergy had spent more than two centuries building, by hand, a wall of bones completely around the city. It was twice the height of a man, varnished dark amber. There were repetitive patterns of femurs and rib cages and stacks of curving spines, and at eye level, a row of skulls, uninterrupted, kaymetra after kaymetra.

This was where we parted. Lo was determined to walk completely around the circle of death, and the other two went with him. White Hill and I could do it in our imaginations. I still creaked from climbing the pyramid.

Prior to the ascent of Christianity here, they had huge spectacles, displays of martial skill where many of the participants were killed, for punishment of wrongdoing or just to entertain the masses. The two large amphitheaters where these displays went on were inside the Bones but not under the dome, so we walked around them. The Circus Maximus had a terrible dignity to it, little more than a long depression in the ground with a few eroded monuments left standing. The size and age of it were enough; your mind's eye supplied the rest. The smaller one, the Colosseum, was overdone, with robots in period costumes and ferocious mechanical animals re-creating the old scenes, lots of too-bright blood spurting. Stones and bones would do.

I'd thought about spending another day outside, but the shelter's air-conditioning had failed, and it was literally uninhabitable. So I braced myself and headed for the torture chamber. But as White Hill had said, the purging was more bearable the second time. You know that it's going to end.

Rome inside was interesting, many ages of archeology and history stacked around in no particular order. I enjoyed wandering from place to place with her, building a kind of organization out of the chaos. We were both more interested in inspiration than education, though, so I doubt that the three days we spent there left us with anything like a coherent picture of that tenacious empire and the millennia that followed it.

A long time later she would surprise me by reciting the names of the Roman emperors in order. She'd always had a trick memory, a talent for retaining trivia, ever since she was old enough to read. Growing up different that way must have been a factor in swaying her toward cognitive science.

We saw some ancient cinema and then returned to our quarters to pack for continuing on to Greece, which I was anticipating with pleasure. But it didn't happen. We had a message waiting: ALL MUST RETURN IM-MEDIATELY TO AMAZONIA. CONTEST PROFOUNDLY CHANGED.

Lives, it turned out, profoundly changed. The war was back.

▲

We met in a majestic amphitheater, the twenty-nine artists dwarfed by the size of it, huddled front row center. A few Amazonian officials sat behind a table on the stage, silent. They all looked detached, or stunned, brooding.

We hadn't been told anything except that is was a matter of "dire and immediate importance." We assumed it had to do with the contest, natu-rally, and were prepared for the worst: it had been called off; we had to go home.

The old crone Norita appeared, "We must confess to carelessness," she said. "The unseasonable warmth in both hemispheres, it isn't some-thing that has happened, ever since the Sterilization. We looked for at-mospheric causes here, and found something that seemed to explain it. But we didn't make the connection with what was happening in the other half of the world.

"It's not the atmosphere. It's the Sun. Somehow the Fwndyri have found a way to make its luminosity increase. It's been going on for half a year. If it continues, and we find no way to reverse it, the surface of the planet will be uninhabitable in a few years.

"I'm afraid that most of you are going to be stranded on Earth, at least for the time being. The Council of Worlds has exercised its emergency powers and commandeered every vessel capable of interstellar transport. Those who have sufficient power or the proper connections will be able to escape. The rest will have to stay with us and face . . . whatever our fate is going to be."

I saw no reason not to be blunt. "Can money do it? How much would a ticket out cost?"

That would have been a gaffe on my planet, but Norita didn't blink. "I know for certain that two hundred million marks is not enough. I also know that some people have bought 'tickets,' as you say, but I don't know how much they paid, or to whom."

If I liquidated everything I owned, I might be able to come up with three hundred million, but I hadn't brought that kind of liquidity with me; just a box of rare jewelry, worth perhaps forty million. Most of my wealth was thirty-three years away, from the point of view of an earthbound investor. I could sign that over to someone, but by the time they got to Petra, the government or my family might have seized it, and they would have nothing save the prospect of a legal battle in a foreign culture.

Norita introduced Skylha Sygoda, an astrophysicist. He was pale and sweating. "We have analyzed the solar spectrum over the past six months. If I hadn't known that each spectrum was from the same star, I would have said it was a systematic and subtle demonstration of the micro-stages of stellar evolution in the late main sequence."

"Could you express that in some human language?" someone said.

Sygoda spread his hands. "They've found a way to age the Sun. In the normal course of things, we would expect the Sun to brighten about six percent each billion years. At the current rate, it's more like one percent per year."

"So in a hundred years," White Hill said, "it will be twice as bright?"

"If it continues at this rate. We don't know."

A stocky woman I recognized as !Oona Something, from Jua-nguvi, wrestled with the language: "To how long, then? Before this Earth is uninhabitable?"

"Well, in point of fact, it's uninhabitable now, except for people like you. We could survive inside these domes for a long time, if it were just a matter of the outside getting hotter and hotter. For those of you able to withstand the nanophages, it will probably be too hot within a decade, here; longer near the poles. But the weather is likely to become very violent, too.

"And it may not be a matter of a simple increase in heat. In the case of normal evolution, the Sun would eventually expand, becoming a red giant. It would take many billions of years, but the Earth would not survive. The surface of the Sun would actually extend out to touch us.

"If the Fwndyri were speeding up time somehow, locally, and the Sun were actually *evolving* at this incredible rate, we would suffer that fate in about thirty years. But it would be impossible. They would have to have a way to magically extract the hydrogen from the Sun's core."

"Wait," I said. "You don't know what they're doing now, to make it brighten. I wouldn't say anything's impossible."

"Water Man," Norita said, "if that happens, we shall simply die, all of us, at once. There is no need to plan for it. We do need to plan for less extreme exigencies." There was an uncomfortable silence.

"What can we do?" White Hill said. "We artists?"

"There's no reason not to continue with the project, though I think you may wish to do it inside. There's no shortage of space. Are any of you trained in astrophysics, or anything having to do with stellar evolution and the like?" No one was. "You may still have some ideas that will be useful to the specialists. We will keep you informed."

Most of the artists stayed in Amazonia, for the amenities if not to avoid purging, but four of us went back to the outside habitat. Denli om Cord, the composer from Luxor, joined Lo and White Hill and me. We could have used the tunnel airlock, to avoid the midday heat, but Denli hadn't seen the beach, and I suppose we all had an impulse to see the Sun with our new knowledge. In this new light, as they say.

White Hill and Denli went swimming while Lo and I poked around the ruins. We had since learned that the destruction here had been methodical, a grim resolve to leave the enemy nothing of value. Both of us were scouting for raw material, of course. After a short while we sat in the hot shade, wishing we had brought water.

We talked about that and about art. Not about the Sun dying, or us dying, in a few decades. The women's laughter drifted to us over the rush of the muddy surf. There was a sad hysteria to it.

"Have you had sex with her?" he asked conversationally.

"What a question. No."

He tugged on his lip, staring out over the water. "I try to keep these things straight. It seems to me that you desire her, from the way you look at her, and she seems cordial to you, and is after all from Seldene. My interest is academic, of course."

"You've never done sex? I mean before."

"Of course, as a child." The implication of that was obvious.

"It becomes more complicated with practice."

"I suppose it could. Although Seldenians seem to treat it as casually as . . . conversation." He used the Seldenian word, which is the same as for intercourse.

"White Hill is reasonably sophisticated," I said. "She isn't bound by her culture's freedoms." The two women ran out of the water, arms around each other's waists, laughing. It was an interesting contrast; Denli was almost as large as me, and about as feminine. They saw us and waved toward the path back through the ruins.

We got up to follow them. "I suppose I don't understand your restraint," Lo said. "Is it your own culture? Your age?"

"Not age. Perhaps my culture encourages self-control."

He laughed. "That's an understatement."

"Not that I'm a slave to Petrosian propriety. My work is outlawed in several states, at home."

"You're proud of that."

I shrugged. "It reflects on them, not me." We followed the women down the path, an interesting study in contrasts, one pair nimble and naked except for a film of drying mud, the other pacing evenly in monkish robes. They were already showering when Lo and I entered the cool shelter, momentarily blinded by shade.

We made cool drinks and, after a quick shower, joined them in the communal bath. Lo was not anatomically different from a sexual male, which I found obscurely disturbing. Wouldn't it bother you to be constantly reminded of what you had lost? Renounced, I suppose Lo would say, and accuse me of being parochial about plumbing.

I had made the drinks with guava juice and ron, neither of which we have on Petrosia. A little too sweet, but pleasant. The alcohol loosened tongues.

Denli regarded me with deep black eyes. "You're rich, Water Man. Are you rich enough to escape?"

"No. If I had brought all my money with me, perhaps."

"Some do," White Hill said. "I did."

"I would too," Lo said, "coming from Seldene. No offense intended."

"Wheels turn," she admitted. "Five or six new governments before I get back. *Would* have gotten back."

We were all silent for a long moment. "It's not real yet," White Hill said, her voice flat. "We're going to die here?"

"We were going to die somewhere," Denli said. "Maybe not so soon."

"And not on Earth," Lo said. "It's like a long preview of Hell." Denli looked at him quizzically. "That's where Christians go when they die. If they were bad."

"They send their bodies to Earth?" We managed not to smile. Actually, most of my people knew as little as hers, about Earth. Seldene and Luxor, though relatively poor, had centuries' more history than Petros, and kept closer ties to the central planet. The Home Planet, they would say. Homey as a blast furnace.

By tacit consensus, we didn't dwell on death anymore that day. When artists get together they tend to wax enthusiastic about materials and tools, the mechanical lore of their trades. We talked about the ways we worked at home, the things we were able to bring with us, the improvisations we could effect with Earthling materials. (Critics talk about art, we say; artists talk about brushes.) Three other artists joined us, two sculptors and a weathershaper, and we all wound up in the large sunny studio drawing and painting. White Hill and I found sticks of charcoal and did studies of each other drawing each other.

While we were comparing them, she quietly asked "Do you sleep lightly?"

"I can. What did you have in mind?"

"Oh, looking at the ruins by starlight. The moon goes down about three. I thought we might watch it set together." Her expression was so open as to be enigmatic.

Two more artists had joined us by dinnertime, which proceeded with a kind of forced jollity. A lot of ron was consumed. White Hill cautioned me against overindulgence. They had the same liquor, called "rum," on

Seldene, and it had a reputation for going down easily but causing storms. There was no legal distilled liquor on my planet.

I had two drinks of it, and retired when people started singing in various languages. I did sleep lightly, though, and was almost awake when White Hill tapped. I could hear two or three people still up, murmuring in the bath. We slipped out quietly.

It was almost cool. The quarter-phase moon was near the horizon, a dim orange, but it gave us enough light to pick our way down the path. It was warmer in the ruins, the tumbled stone still radiating the day's heat. We walked through to the beach, where it was cooler again. White Hill spread the blanket she had brought, and we stretched out and looked up at the stars.

As is always true with a new world, most of the constellations were familiar, with a few bright stars added or subtracted. Neither of our home stars was significant, as dim here as Earth's Sol is from home. She identified the brightest star overhead as AlphaKent; there was a brighter one on the horizon, but neither of us knew what it was.

We compared names of the constellations we recognized. Some of hers were the same as Earth's names, like Scorpio, which we call the Insect. It was about halfway up the sky, prominent, imbedded in the galaxy's glow. We both call the brightest star there Antares. The Executioner, which had set perhaps an hour earlier, they call Orion. We had the same meaningless names for its brightest stars, Betelgeuse and Rigel.

"For a sculptor, you know a lot about astronomy," she said. "When I visited your city, there was too much light to see stars at night."

"You can see a few from my place. I'm out at Lake Påchlå, about a hundred kaymetras inland."

"I know. I called you."

"I wasn't home?"

"No; you were supposedly on ThetaKent."

"That's right, you told me. Our paths crossed in space. And you became that burgher's slave wife." I put my hand on her arm. "Sorry I forgot. A lot has gone on. Was he awful?"

She laughed into the darkness. "He offered me a lot to stay."

"I can imagine."

She half turned, one breast soft against my arm, and ran a finger up my leg. "Why tax your imagination?"

I wasn't expecially in the mood, but my body was. The robes rustled off easily, their only virtue.

The moon was down now, and I could see only a dim outline of her in the starlight. It was strange to make love deprived of that sense. You would think the absence of it would amplify the others, but I can't say that it did, except that her heartbeat seemed very strong on the heel of my hand. Her breath was sweet with mint, and the smell and taste of her body were agreeable; in fact, there was nothing about her body that I would have cared to change, inside or out, but nevertheless, our progress became difficult after a couple of minutes, and by mute agreement we slowed and stopped. We lay joined together for some time before she spoke.

"The timing is all wrong. I'm sorry." She drew her face across my arm, and I felt tears. "I was just trying not to think about things."

"It's all right. The sand doesn't help, either." We had gotten a little bit inside, rubbing.

We talked for a while and then drowsed together. When the sky began to lighten, a hot wind from below the horizon woke us up. We went back to the shelter.

Everyone was asleep. We went to shower off the sand, and she was amused to see my interest in her quicken. "Let's take that downstairs," she whispered, and I followed her down to her room.

The memory of the earlier incapability was there, but it was not greatly inhibiting. Being able to see her made the act more familiar, and besides, she was very pleasant to see, from whatever angle. I was able to withhold myself only once, and so the interlude was shorter than either of us would have desired.

We slept together on her narrow bed. Or she slept, rather, while I watched the bar of sunlight grow on the opposite wall and thought about how everything had changed.

They couldn't really say we had thirty years to live, since they had no idea what the enemy was doing. It might be three hundred; it might be less than one—but even with bodyswitch that was always true, as it was in the old days: sooner or later something would go wrong and you would die. That I might die at the same instant as ten thousand other people and a planet full of history—that was interesting. But as the room filled with light, and I studied her quiet repose, I found her more interesting than that.

I was old enough to be immune to infatuation. Something deep had been growing since Egypt, maybe before. On top of the pyramid, the rising Sun dim in the mist, we had sat with our shoulders touching, watching the ancient forms appear below, and I felt a surge of numinism mixed oddly with content. She looked at me—I could only see her eyes—and we didn't have to say anything about the moment.

And now this. I was sure, without words, that she would share this, too. Whatever "this" was. England's versatile language, like mine and hers, is strangely hobbled by having the one word, love, stand for such a multiplicity of feelings.

Perhaps that lack reveals a truth, that no one love is like any other. There are other truths that you might forget, or ignore, distracted by the growth of love. In Petrosian there is a saying in the palindromic mood that always carries a sardonic, or at least ironic, inflection: "Happiness presages disaster presages happiness." So if you die happy, it means you were happy when you died. Good timing or bad?

▲ •

!Oona M'vua had a room next to White Hill, and she was glad to switch with me, an operation that took about three minutes but was good for a much longer period of talk among the other artists. Lo was smugly amused, which in my temporary generosity of spirit I forgave.

Once we were adjacent, we found the button that made the wall slide away and pushed the two beds together under her window. I'm afraid we were antisocial for a couple of days. It had been some time since either of us had had a lover. And I had never had one like her, literally, out of the dozens. She said that was because I had never been involved with a Seldenian, and I tactfully agreed, banishing five perfectly good memories to amnesia.

It's true that Seldenian women, and men as well, are better schooled than those of us from normal planets, in the techniques and subtleties of sexual expression. Part of "wholeness," which I suppose is a weak pun in English. It kept Lo, and not only him, from taking White Hill seriously as an artist: the fact that a Seldenian, to be "whole," must necessarily treat art as an everyday activity, usually subordinate to affairs of the heart, of the body. Or at least on the same level, which is the point.

The reality is that it *is* all one to them. What makes Seldenians so alien is that their need for balance in life dissolves hierarchy: this piece of art is valuable, and so is this orgasm, and so is this crumb of bread. The bread crumb connects to the artwork through the artist's metabolism, which connects to orgasm. Then through a fluid and automatic mixture of logic, metaphor, and rhetoric, the bread crumb links to soil, sunlight, nuclear fusion, the beginning and end of the universe. Any intelligent person can map out chains like that, but to White Hill it was automatic, drilled into her with her first nouns and verbs: *Everything is important. Nothing matters.* Change the world but stay relaxed.

I could never come around to her way of thinking. But then I was married for fifty Petrosian years to a woman who had stranger beliefs. (The marriage as a social contract actually lasted fifty-seven years; at the half-century mark we took a vacation from each other, and I never saw her again.) White Hill's worldview gave her an equanimity I had to envy. But my art needed unbalance and tension the way hers needed harmony and resolution.

By the fourth day most of the artists had joined us in the shelter. Maybe they grew tired of wandering through the bureaucracy. More likely, they were anxious about their competitors' progress.

White Hill was drawing designs on large sheets of buff paper and taping them up on our walls. She worked on her feet, bare feet, pacing from diagram to diagram, changing and rearranging. I worked directly inside a shaping box, an invention White Hill had heard of but had never seen. It's a cube of light a little less than a metra wide. Inside is an image of a sculpture—or a rock or a lump of clay—that you can feel as well as see. You can mold it with your hands or work with finer instruments for cutting, scraping, chipping. It records your progress constantly, so it's easy to take chances; you can always run it back to an earlier stage.

I spent a few hours every other day cruising in a flyer with Lo and a couple of other sculptors, looking for native materials. We were severely constrained by the decision to put the Memory Park inside, since everything we used had to be small enough to fit through the airlock and purging rooms. You could work with large pieces, but you would have to slice them up and reassemble them, the individual chunks no bigger than two-by-two-by-three metras.

We tried to stay congenial and fair during these expeditions. Ideally, you would spot a piece, and we would land by it or hover over it long enough to tag it with your ID; in a day or two the robots would deliver it to your "holding area" outside the shelter. If more than one person wanted the piece, which happened as often as not, a decision had to be made before it was tagged. There was a lot of arguing and trading and Solomon-style splitting, which usually satisfied the requirements of something other than art.

The quality of light was changing for the worse. Earthling planetary engineers were spewing bright dust into the upper atmosphere, to reflect back solar heat. (They modified the nanophage-eating machinery for the purpose. That was also designed to fill the atmosphere full of dust, but at a lower level—and each grain of *that* dust had a tiny chemical brain.) It made the night sky progressively less interesting. I was glad White Hill had chosen to initiate our connection under the stars. It would be some time before we saw them again, if ever.

And it looked like "daylight" was going to be a uniform overcast for the duration of the contest. Without the dynamic of moving sunlight to continually change the appearance of my piece, I had to discard a whole family of first approaches to its design. I was starting to think along the lines of something irrational-looking; something the brain would reject as impossible. The way we mentally veer away from unthinkable things like the Sterilization, and our proximate future.

We had divided into two groups, and jokingly but seriously referred to one another as "originalists" and "realists." We originalists were continuing our projects on the basis of the charter's rules: a memorial to the tragedy and its aftermath, a stark sterile reminder in the midst of life. The realists took into account new developments, including the fact that there would probably never be any "midst of life" and, possibly, no audience, after thirty years.

I thought that was excessive. There was plenty of pathos in the original assignment. Adding another, impasto, layer of pathos along with irony and the artist's fear of personal death . . . well, we were doing art, not literature. I sincerely hoped their pieces would be fatally muddled by complexity.

If you asked White Hill which group she belonged to, she would of course say, "Both." I had no idea what form her project was going to take; we had agreed early on to surprise one another, and not impede each other with suggestions. I couldn't decipher even one-tenth of her diagrams. I speak Seldenian pretty well, but have never mastered the pictographs beyond the usual travelers' vocabulary. And much of what she was scribbling on the buff sheets of paper was in no language I recognized, an arcane technical symbology.

We talked about other things. Even about the future, as lovers will. Our most probable future was simultaneous death by fire, but it was calming and harmless to make "what if?" plans, in case our hosts somehow were able to find a way around that fate. We did have a choice of many possible futures, if we indeed had more than one. White Hill had never had access to wealth before. She didn't want to live lavishly, but the idea of being able to explore all the planets excited her.

Of course she had never tried living lavishly. I hoped one day to study her reaction to it, which would be strange. Out of the box of valuables I'd brought along, I gave her a necklace, a traditional beginning-love gift on Petros. It was a network of perfect emeralds and rubies laced in gold.

She examined it closely. "How much is this worth?"

"A million marks, more or less." She started to hand it back. "Please keep it. Money has no value here, no meaning."

She was at a loss for words, which was rare enough. "I understand the gesture. But you can't expect me to value this the way you do."

"I wouldn't expect that."

"Suppose I lose it? I might just set it down somewhere."

"I know. I'll still have given it to you."

She nodded and laughed. "All right. You people are strange." She slipped the necklace on, still latched, wiggling it over her ears. The colors glowed warm and cold against her olive skin.

She kissed me, a feather, and rushed out of our room wordlessly. She passed right by a mirror without looking at it.

After a couple of hours I went to find her. Lo said he'd seen her go out the door with a lot of water. At the beach I found her footprints marching straight west to the horizon.

She was gone for two days. I was working outside when she came back, wearing nothing but the necklace. There was another necklace in her hand: she had cut off her right braid and interwoven a complex pattern of gold and silver wire into a closed loop. She slipped it over my head and pecked me on the lips and headed for the shelter. When I started to follow she stopped me with a tired gesture. "Let me sleep, eat, wash." Her voice was a hoarse whisper. "Come to me after dark."

I sat down, leaning back against a good rock, and thought about very little, touching her braid and smelling it. When it was too dark to see my feet, I went in, and she was waiting.

▲ • •

I spent a lot of time outside, at least in the early morning and late afternoon, studying my accumulation of rocks and ruins. I had images of every piece in my shaping box's memory, but it was easier to visualize some aspects of the project if I could walk around the elements and touch them.

Inspiration is where you find it. We'd played with an orrery in the museum in Rome, a miniature solar system that had been built of clockwork centuries before the Information Age. There was a wistful, humorous, kind of comfort in its jerky regularity.

My mental processes always turn things inside out. Find the terror and hopelessness in that comfort. I had in mind a massive but delicately balanced assemblage that would be viewed by small groups; their presence would cause it to teeter and turn ponderously. It would seem both fragile and huge (though of course the fragility would be an illusion), like the ecosystem that the Fwndyri so abruptly destroyed.

The assemblage would be mounted in such a way that it would seem always in danger of toppling off its base, but hidden weights would make that impossible. The sound of the rolling weights ought to produce a nice anxiety. Whenever a part tapped the floor, the tap would be amplified into a hollow boom.

If the viewers stood absolutely still, it would swing to a halt. As they left, they would disturb it again. I hoped it would disturb them as well.

The large technical problem was measuring the distribution of mass in each of my motley pieces. That would have been easy at home; I could rent a magnetic resonance densitometer to map their insides. There was no such thing on this planet (so rich in things I had no use for!), so I had to make do with a pair of robots and a knife-edge. And then start hollowing the pieces out asymmetrically, so that once set in motion, the assemblage would tend to rotate.

I had a large number of rocks and artifacts to choose from, and was tempted to use no unifying principle at all, other than the unstable balance of the thing. Boulders and pieces of old statues and fossil machinery. The models I made of such a random collection were ambiguous, though. It was hard to tell whether they would look ominous or ludicrous, built to scale. A symbol of helplessness before an implacable enemy? Or a lurching, crashing junkpile. I decided to take a reasonably conservative approach, dignity rather than daring. After all, the audience would be Earthlings and, if the planet survived, tourists with more money than sophistication. Not my usual jury.

I was able to scavenge twenty long bars of shiny black monofiber, which would be the spokes of my irregular wheel. That would give it some unity of composition: make a cross with four similar chunks of granite at the ordinal points, and a larger chunk at the center. Then build up a web inside, monofiber lines linking bits of this and that.

Some of the people were moving their materials inside Amazonia, to work in the area marked off for the park. White Hill and I decided to stay outside. She said her project was portable, at this stage, and mine would be easy to disassemble and move.

After a couple of weeks, only fifteen artists remained with the project, inside Amazonia or out in the shelter. The others had either quit, surrendering to the passive depression that seemed to be Earth's new norm, or, in one case, committed suicide. The two from Wolf and Mijhøven opted for coldsleep, which might be deferred suicide. About one person in three slept through it; one in three came out with some kind of treatable mental disorder. The others went mad and died soon after reawakening, unable or unwilling to live.

Coldsleep wasn't done on Petrosia, although some Petrosians went to other worlds to indulge in it as a risky kind of time travel. Sleep until whatever's wrong with the world has changed. Some people even did it for financial speculation: buy up objects of art or antiques, and sleep for a century or more while their value increases. Of course their value might not increase significantly, or they might be stolen or co-opted by family or government.

But if you can make enough money to buy a ticket to another planet, why not hold off until you had enough to go to a really *distant* one? Let time dilation compress the years. I could make a triangle from Petrosia to Skaal to Mijhøven and back, and more than 120 years would pass, while I lived through only three, with no danger to my mind. And I could take my objects of art along with me.

White Hill had worked with coldsleep veterans, or victims. None of them had been motivated by profit, given her planet's institutionalized anti-materialism, so most of them had been suffering from some psychological ill before they slept. It was rare for them to come out of the "treatment" improved, but they did come into a world where people like White Hill could at least attend them in their madness, perhaps guide them out.

I'd been to three times as many worlds as she. But she had been to stranger places.

▲ • • •

The terraformers did their job too well. The days grew cooler and cooler, and some nights snow fell. The snow on the ground persisted into mornings for a while, and then through noon, and finally it began to pile up. Those of us who wanted to work outside had to improvise cold-weather clothing.

I liked working in the cold, although all I did was direct robots. I grew up in a small town south of New Haven, where winter was long and intense. At some level I associated snow and ice with the exciting pleasures that waited for us after school. I was to have my fill of it, though.

It was obvious I had to work fast, faster than I'd originally planned, because of the increasing cold. I wanted to have everything put together and working before I disassembled it and pushed it through the airlock. The robots weren't made for cold weather, unfortunately. They had bad traction on the ice, and sometimes their joints would seize up. One of them complained constantly, but of course it was the best worker, too, so I couldn't just turn it off and let it disappear under the drifts, an idea that tempted me.

White Hill often came out for a few minutes to stand and watch me and the robots struggle with the icy heavy boulders, machinery, and statuary. We took walks along the seashore that became shorter as the weather worsened. The last walk was a disaster.

We had just gotten to the beach when a sudden storm came up with a sandblast wind so violent that it blew us off our feet. We crawled back to the partial protection of the ruins and huddled together, the wind screaming so loudly that we had to shout to hear each other. The storm continued to mount and, in our terror, we decided to run for the shelter. White Hill slipped on some ice and suffered a horrible injury, a jagged piece of metal slashing her face diagonally from forehead to chin, blinding her left eye and tearing off part of her nose. Pearly bone showed through, cracked, at eyebrow, cheek, and chin. She rose up to one elbow and fell slack.

I carried her the rest of the way, immensely glad for the physical strength that made it possible. By the time we got inside she was unconscious and my white coat was a scarlet flag of blood.

A plastic-clad doctor came through immediately and did what she could to get White Hill out of immediate danger. But there was a problem with more sophisticated treatment. They couldn't bring the equipment out to our shelter, and White Hill wouldn't survive the stress of purging unless she had had a chance to heal for a while. Besides the facial wound, she had a broken elbow and collarbone and two cracked ribs.

For a week or so she was always in pain or numb. I sat with her, numb myself, her face a terrible puffed caricature of its former beauty, the wound glued up with plaskin the color of putty. Split skin of her eyelid slack over the empty socket.

The mirror wasn't visible from her bed, and she didn't ask for one, but whenever I looked away from her, her working hand came up to touch and catalogue the damage. We both knew how fortunate she was to be alive at all, and especially in an era and situation where the damage could all be repaired, given time and a little luck. But it was still a terrible thing to live with, an awful memory to keep reliving.

When she was more herself, able to talk through her ripped and pasted mouth, it was difficult for me to keep my composure. She had considerable philosophical, I suppose you could say spiritual, resources, but she was so profoundly stunned that she couldn't follow a line of reasoning very far, and usually wound up sobbing in frustration.

Sometimes I cried with her, although Petrosian men don't cry except in response to music. I had been a soldier once and had seen my ration of injury and death, and I always felt the experience had hardened me, to my detriment. But my friends who had been wounded or killed were just friends, and all of us lived then with the certainty that every day could be anybody's last one. To have the woman you love senselessly mutilated by an accident of weather was emotionally more arduous than losing a dozen companions to the steady erosion of war, a different kind of weather.

I asked her whether she wanted to forget our earlier agreement and talk about our projects. She said no; she was still working on hers, in a way, and she still wanted it to be a surprise. I did manage to distract her, playing with the shaping box. We made cartoonish representations of Lo and old Norita, and combined them in impossible sexual geometries. We shared a limited kind of sex ourselves, finally.

The doctor pronounced her well enough to be taken apart, and both of us were scourged and reappeared on the other side. White Hill was already in surgery when I woke up; there had been no reason to revive her before beginning the restorative processes.

I spent two days wandering through the blandness of Amazonia, jungle laced through concrete, quartering the huge place on foot. Most areas seemed catatonic. A few were boisterous with end-of-the-world hysteria. I checked on her progress so often that they eventually assigned a robot to call me up every hour, whether or not there was any change.

On the third day I was allowed to see her, in her sleep. She was pale but seemed completely restored. I watched her for an hour, perhaps more, when her eyes suddenly opened. The new one was blue, not green, for some reason. She didn't focus on me.

"Dreams feed art," she whispered in Petrosian; "and art feeds dreams." She closed her eyes and slept again.

▲ ■

She didn't want to go back out. She had lived all her life in the tropics, even the year she spent in bondage, and the idea of returning to the ice that had slashed her was more than repugnant. Inside Amazonia it was always summer, now, the authorities trying to keep everyone happy with heat and light and jungle flowers.

I went back out to gather her things. Ten large sheets of buff paper I unstuck from our walls and stacked and rolled. The necklace, and the satchel of rare coins she had brought from Seldene, all her worldly wealth.

I considered wrapping up my own project, giving the robots instructions for its dismantling and transport, so that I could just go back inside with her and stay. But that would be chancy. I wanted to see the thing work once before I took it apart.

So I went through the purging again, although it wasn't strictly necessary; I could have sent her things through without hand-carrying them. But I wanted to make sure she was on her feet before I left her for several weeks.

She was not on her feet, but she was dancing. When I recovered from the purging, which now took only half a day, I went to her hospital room, and they referred me to our new quarters, a three-room dwelling in a place called Plaza de Artistes. There were two beds in the bedroom, one a fancy medical one, but that was worlds better than trying to find privacy in a hospital.

There was a note floating in the air over the bed saying she had gone to a party in the common room. I found her in a gossamer wheelchair, teaching a hand dance to Denli om Cord, while a harpist and flautist from two different worlds tried to settle on a mutual key.

She was in good spirits. Denli remembered an engagement, and I wheeled White Hill out onto a balcony that overlooked a lake full of sleeping birds, some perhaps real.

It was hot outside, always hot. There was a mist of perspiration on her face, partly from the light exercise of the dance, I supposed. In the light from below, the mist gave her face a sculpted appearance, unsparing sharpness, and there was no sign left of the surgery.

"I'll be out of the chair tomorrow," she said, "at least ten minutes at a time." She laughed, "*Stop* that!"

"Stop what?"

"Looking at me like that."

I was still staring at her face. "It's just . . . I suppose it's such a relief."

"I know." She rubbed my hand. "They showed me pictures, of before. You looked at that for so many days?"

"I saw you."

She pressed my hand to her face. The new skin was taut but soft, like a baby's. "Take me downstairs?"

▲ ▲

It's hard to describe, especially in light of later developments, disintegrations, but that night of fragile lovemaking marked a permanent change in the way we linked, or at least the way I was linked to her: I've been married twice, long and short, and have been in some kind of love a hundred times. But no woman has ever owned me before.

This is something we do to ourselves. I've had enough women who *tried* to possess me, but always was able to back or circle away, in literal preservation of self. I always felt that life was too long for one woman.

Certainly part of it is that life is not so long anymore. A larger part of it was the run through the screaming storm, her life streaming out of her, and my stewardship, or at least companionship, afterwards, during her slow transformation back into health and physical beauty. The core of her had never changed, though, the stubborn serenity that I came to realize, that warm night, had finally infected me as well.

The bed was a firm narrow slab, cooler than the dark air heavy with the scent of Earth flowers. I helped her onto the bed (which instantly conformed to her) but from then on it was she who cared for me, saying that was all she wanted, all she really had strength for. When I tried to reverse that, she reminded me of a holiday palindrome that has sexual overtones in both our languages: Giving is taking is giving.

▲ ▲ ●

We spent a couple of weeks as close as two people can be. I was her lover and also her nurse, as she slowly strengthened. When she was able to spend most of her day in normal pursuits, free of the wheelchair or "intelligent" bed (with which we had made a threesome, at times uneasy), she urged me to go back outside and finish up. She was ready to concentrate on her own project, too. Impatient to do art again, a good sign.

I would not have left so soon if I had known what her project involved. But that might not have changed anything.

As soon as I stepped outside, I knew it was going to take longer than planned. I had known from the inside monitors how cold it was going to be, and how many ceemetras of ice had accumulated, but I didn't really *know* how bad it was until I was standing there, looking at my piles of materials locked in opaque glaze. A good thing I'd left the robots inside the shelter, and a good thing I had left a few hand tools outside. The door was buried under two metras of snow and ice. I sculpted myself a passageway, an application of artistic skills I'd never foreseen.

I debated calling White Hill and telling her that I would be longer than expected. We had agreed not to interrupt each other, though, and it was likely she'd started working as soon as I left.

The robots were like a bad comedy team, but I could only be amused by them for an hour or so at a time. It was so cold that the water vapor from my breath froze into an icy sheath on my beard and moustache. Breathing was painful; deep breathing probably dangerous.

So most of the time, I monitored them from inside the shelter. I had the place to myself; everyone else long since gone into the dome. When I wasn't working I drank too much, something I had not done regularly in centuries.

It was obvious that I wasn't going to make a working model. Delicate balance was impossible in the shifting gale. But the robots and I had our hands full, and other grasping appendages engaged, just dismantling the various pieces and moving them through the lock. It was unexciting but painstaking work. We did all the laser cuts inside the shelter, allowing the rock to come up to room temperature so it didn't spall or shatter. The air-conditioning wasn't quite equal to the challenge, and neither were the cleaning robots, so after a while it was like living in a foundry: everywhere a kind of greasy slickness of rock dust, the air dry and metallic.

So it was with no regret that I followed the last slice into the airlock myself, even looking forward to the scourging if White Hill was on the other side.

She wasn't. A number of other people were missing, too. She left this note behind:

I knew from the day we were called back here what my new piece would have to be, and I knew I had to keep it from you, to spare you sadness. And to save you the frustration of trying to talk me out of it.

As you may know by now, scientists have determined that the Fwndyri indeed have sped up the Sun's evolution somehow. It will continue to warm, until in thirty or forty years there will be an explosion called the "helium flash." The Sun will become a red giant, and the Earth will be incinerated.

There are no starships left, but there is one avenue of escape. A kind of escape.

Parked in high orbit there is a huge interplanetary transport that was used in the terraforming of Mars. It's a couple of centuries older than you, but like yourself it has been excellently preserved. We are going to ride it out to a distance sufficient to survive the Sun's catastrophe, and there remain until the situation improves, or does not.

This is where I enter the picture. For our survival to be meaningful in this thousand-year war, we have to resort to coldsleep. And for a large number of people to survive centuries of coldsleep, they need my jaturnary skills. Alone, in the ice, they would go slowly mad. Connected through the matrix of my mind, they will have a sense of community, and may come out of it intact.

I will be gone, of course. I will be by the time you read this. Not dead, but immersed in service. I could not be revived if this were only a hundred people for a hundred days. This will be a thousand, perhaps for a thousand years.

No one else on Earth can do jaturnary, and there is neither time nor equipment for me to transfer my ability to anyone. Even if there were, I'm not sure I would trust anyone else's skill. So I am gone.

My only loss is losing you. Do I have to elaborate on that?

You can come if you want. In order to use the transport, I had to agree that the survivors be chosen in accordance with the Earth's strict class system—starting with dear Norita, and from that pinnacle, on down—but they were willing to make exceptions for all of the visiting artists. You have until mid-Deciembre to decide; the ship leaves Januar first.

If I know you at all, I know you would rather stay behind and die. Perhaps the prospect of living "in" me could move you past your fear of coldsleep; your aversion to jaturnary. If not, not.

I love you more than life. But this is more than that. Are we what we are?

W. H.

The last sentence is a palindrome in her language, not mine, that I believe has some significance beyond the obvious.

● ● ■

I did think about it for some time. Weighing a quick death, or even a slow one, against spending centuries locked frozen in a tiny room with Norita and her ilk. Chattering on at the speed of synapse, and me unable to not listen.

I have always valued quiet, and the eternity of it that I face is no more dreadful than the eternity of quiet that preceded my birth.

If White Hill were to be at the other end of those centuries of torture, I know I could tolerate the excruciation. But she was dead now, at least in the sense that I would never see her again.

Another woman might have tried to give me a false hope, the possibility that in some remote future the process of *jaturnary* would be advanced to the point where her personality could be recovered. But she knew how unlikely that would be even if teams of scientists could be found to work on it, and years could be found for them to work in. It would be like unscrambling an egg.

Maybe I would even do it, though, if there were just some chance that, when I was released from that din of garrulous bondage, there would be something like a real world, a world where I could function as an artist. But I don't think there will even be a world where I can function as a man.

There probably won't be any humanity at all, soon enough. What they did to the Sun they could do to all of our stars, one assumes. They win the war, the Extermination, as my parent called it. Wrong side exterminated.

Of course the Fwndyri might not find White Hill and her charges. Even if they do find them, they might leave them preserved as an object of study.

The prospect of living on eternally under those circumstances, even if there were some growth to compensate for the immobility and the company, holds no appeal.

—
• ■
—

What I did in the time remaining before mid-Deciembre was write this account. Then I had it translated by a xenolinguist into a form that she said could be decoded by any creature sufficiently similar to humanity to make any sense of the story. Even the Fwndyri, perhaps. They're human enough to want to wipe out a competing species.

I'm looking at the preliminary sheets now, English down the left side and a jumble of dots, squares, and triangles down the right. Both sides would have looked equally strange to me a few years ago.

White Hill's story will be conjoined to a standard book that starts out with basic mathematical principles, in dots and squares and triangles, and moves from that into physics, chemistry, biology. Can you go from biology to the human heart? I have to hope so. If this is read by alien eyes, long after the last human breath is stilled, I hope it's not utter gibberish.

—
■
—

So I will take this final sheet down to the translator and then deliver the whole thing to the woman who is going to transfer it to permanent sheets of platinum, which will be put in a prominent place aboard the transport. They could last a million years, or ten million, or more. After the Sun is a cinder, and the ship is a frozen block enclosing a thousand bits of frozen flesh, she will live on in this small way.

So now my work is done. I'm going outside, to the quiet.

(1995)

Finding My Shadow

I used to love this part of the city. Jain and I had looked at a loft looking over the park toward Charles Street and the river, dreaming of escaping Roxbury. Not much here now.

My partner, Mark, pointed to the left. "Movement." I jammed the joystick left and up, and the tracks clattered over the curb into dirt, the dry baked ruin that used to be Boston Common.

It was a boy, trying to hide behind the base of a fallen equestrian statue.

I touched my throat mike. "Halt! Put your hands over your head." He took off like a squirrel, and I gunned it forward. There was no way he could outrun us.

"Taze or tangle?" Mason said.

"Taze." When we got within range, he scoped the kid and fired. A wire darted out, and the jolt knocked him flat. I braked with both feet, and we lurched forward into our harnesses.

We both stayed inside, looking around. "This stinks," he said, and I nodded. How did the boy get here without being seen, in the glare of the nightlights? Had to be a rabbit-hole nearby.

We waited a couple of minutes, watching. Jain and I used to walk through the Common when it was an island of calm in the middle of the Boston din. Flowers everywhere in the spring and summer, leaves in the fall. But I'd liked the winters best, at least when it snowed. The flakes sifting down in the dark, in the muffled quiet.

Never dark now, but always quiet. With occasional gunfire and explosions.

"The shock might have killed him," I said, "if he's in bad enough shape."

"Skin looks like—" Mason started, when there was a "thud" sound, and we were suddenly enveloped in flame. "Fire at will," I said, unnecessarily. Mason had the gatling on top screaming as it rotated, traversing blindly. It would probably get the kid.

My rear monitor was clear, so I jammed it into full reverse with the left track locked. We spun around twice in two seconds, harness jamming my cheek. No sign of whoever bombed us.

"Swan Pond?" Mason said.

"That's probably what they want us to do. Not that much fire; I can blow it out." Steering with the monitor, I stomped it in reverse. Braked once as we bumped off the curb, and then backed uphill at howling redline. The windshield cleared except for a smear of soot, and I stopped at the top of the hill, by the ruins of the Capitol.

A female voice from the radio: "Unit Seven, what was that all about? Did you engage the enemy?"

"After a fashion, Lillian," I said. "We were down in the Common, near the parking lot entrance. Kid came up, a decoy, and we tazed him."

"What, a child?" They were rare; the survivors were all sterile.

"Yeah, a boy about ten or twelve. While we were waiting for him to wake up, they popped us with a Molotov."

"I'd say flamer," Mason said. He was scanning the area down there with binoculars.

"Maybe a flamer. Couldn't see forward, so we laid down some covering fire and backed out. Wasn't enough to hurt the track; we're okay now."

"Kid's not there," Mason said. "Somebody retrieved him."

"Got a fire team zeroed on the coordinates where you started backing up," the radio said. "What do you want?"

I want to go home, I thought. "Sure he's gone?" I whispered to Mason.

He handed me the binoculars. "See for yourself." No kid, no blood trail.

"No one there now, at least on the surface," I said to Lillian. "Drill round, H.E., maybe."

"Roger." I could hear her keyboard. A few seconds later, the round came in with a sound like cloth tearing. It made a puff of dust where we'd been standing, and then a grey cloud of high-explosive smoke billowed out of the entrance to the underground lot, a couple of hundred yards away, the same time we heard the muffled explosion.

"On target," I said. Of course they'd be idiots to stick around right under where they'd hit us. That parking lot had tunnels going everywhere.

"Need more?" she asked.

"No, negative."

"Hold on." She paused. "Command wants you to go take a look. Down below, in the lot."

"Why don't *they* come and take a look?" That was really asking for it. They could pop us from any direction and scuttle back down their tunnels.

"So do you want more arty?"

"Yeah, affirmative. Two drill rounds with gas."

Wipers squeaked, cleaning the soot off the front as we rolled slowly down the hill. "What flavor? We got CS, VA, fog, big H and little H."

I looked at Mason. "Little H?"

He nodded. "Fog, too." I relayed that to Lillian. Little H was happy gas; it induced euphoria and listlessness. Fog was a persistent but breathable particulate suspension. Not that we'd be breathing it, with little H in the air.

(Big H was horror gas. It brought on such profound depression that the enemy usually suicided. But sometimes they wanted to take you with them.)

The two rounds thumped in while we were fitting the gas masks on. Track's airtight and self-contained, but you never know.

I tuned to infrared, and the ruins around us became even greyer. Spun to the left, and then left again, into the lot's down ramp. "Hold on." I gunned it forward and turned on glare lights all around.

"Jesus!" Mason flinched.

"Go IR," I said. To him it must have looked like I was speeding straight into an opaque wall. I slowed a little as we slid inside, sideways.

If you were looking in visible light, you wouldn't see anything *but* light, from our glare, in the swirling fog. In IR, it was just a thin mist.

A few derelict cars amid debris. The crater from her first round was still smoking. There were dozens of holes punched through the ceiling from previous drill rounds. I switched off the IR for a moment and saw nothing but blinding white. Clicked it back on and looked for movement.

"What do you see, Seven?"

"What am I looking for?" I said. "No obvious bodies where your H.E. came in. Nobody walking around in hysterics. No flamers."

"Power down, turn off your lights, and listen." I did. Turned up the ears and heard nothing but creaks and pops from our engine, cooling.

In infrared there was enough light to see in, just barely. Faint beams shone down through the arty holes, from the nightlights suspended over the city.

Someone laughed.

"We might have one," I whispered. Little H disperses fast, and it can penetrate deep into a tunnel if the air's moving in that direction.

The laugh continued, not crazy, just like responding to a joke. Except that it went on and on. A husky female voice, echoing.

It sounded like Jain's laugh.

"Sounds like she's in a tunnel," Mark said. "Over there." He pointed ahead and to the right.

"Yeah, good, a tunnel." This was probably the actual trap they'd used the boy as bait for.

Or maybe that *is* Jain, and she's bait. For me. I shook the notion off. How could they know I was in this track?

"Seven, you have backup coming in. Hold your position."

Hold our position against what, a laugh? "Keep an eye out, Mark. I'm gonna armor up." One of us was going to leave the track, for sure.

"Guess we both better." The armor was restricting and hot, but with it you could survive a flaming or a point-blank hit from a .65 machine gun. That would break a bone or two and knock you down, but you'd live.

Not much room in the track; no room for modesty. I had to stay half in the seat while I stripped down. Mark was watching my reflection. I didn't say anything. If I liked men, he'd be near the top of the list. Enjoy the flash.

The bottom half of the armor wasn't bad, heavy plastic mail, but the top was a bitch for women, if they had any breasts at all. Clamshell snaps along the right rib cage. I grunted at the last one.

"Hurts," Mark said.

"Join the army and have a walking mammogram. Go ahead." He stripped down quickly. I glanced, and was obscurely disappointed that he didn't have an erection. What am I, a toad? No, his partner and immediate superior.

While Mark was armoring up, our reinforcements came down the ramp, subtle as a rolling garbage can. An APC, armored personnel carrier. Here this soon, it must have been the one stationed up by the T entrance at Park.

"That you, Petroski?" I said on the combat scramble freek.

"No, it's Snow White and her fuckin' dwarfs," he said. "Mental dwarfs. They said you got movement down here?"

"Just someone laughing after the arty came in." I turned on the green spotting laser and cranked it around to where we'd heard the voice. It looked like an open freight-elevator door.

I told him about the boy and the flamer; he'd seen the smoke. "You see the green pointer? The elevator there?" It wasn't bright in IR.

"Yeah, but hang for a second. Got some boys and girls still fuckin' with their breathers."

"What?" APCs are open. "You got guys breathin' this stuff? Didn't they tell you—"

"Yeah, Little H. They've got 'em on, just checking the buddy valves. Command said get right down here, no time for the regular drill."

"Hope it's not that serious," I said. "So far we have the Disappearing Boy and the Laughing Woman. Don't think we have to call in the nukes yet."

The laugh again, and a chill down my spine. I clicked away from the scramble freek. "Mark, I could swear I know that voice."

"Anyone I know?"

"No, from before. Here in Boston."

"That's real likely." Only a fraction of one percent had survived the fever bomb. They were all carriers.

This time the laugh ended in something like a sob. "We lived together more than two years, inseparable. People called her my shadow. She was black."

"Lovers."

"Yeah, don't be shocked." Mark was straight as a ruler, but I thought he knew I wasn't, and didn't seem to care.

"Probably just wishful thinking," he said. "Projecting."

"I don't know. You learn someone's—"

"Ready to ride," Petroski said. "This is a kill, right?"

"No," I said hastily. "Play it by ear. We might want a capture."

"What the fuck for?" The quarantine camp in Newton was full to overflowing. And overflow was obviously what it mustn't do.

"Let's just triangulate on the sound. You go over left about a hundred yards and turn off your engine."

"I've gotta get authorization, not to kill."

"No, you don't," I said, improvising. "I'll go in with the nonlethals. You just back me up with a regular squad."

"In the dark with nonlethals?" Mark said. "You *are* fuckin' nuts."

"I'm not asking you to come along. Hand me that tangler." It was the size of a pistol but, instead of bullets, it fired a tightly wound ball of sticky monofilament that blossomed out to become a net. I started to take the Glock 11-mm. out of its holster.

"Christ, don't leave your *gun* behind!"

"I've got a squad backing me up."

"So they can kill whoever gets you, afterwards," he said roughly. "I don't want to break in a new partner. Take the fuckin' gun."

Well, that was touching. I left the pistol in place and tucked the tangler inside my web belt. "Satisfied?"

"Yeah, but you're still nuts. Those sickos just as soon kill you as look at you."

"Yeah, and we'd *rather* kill them than look at them." I opened the door and swung out into the fog.

The fever virus bomb had sprayed Boston Christmas morning. I was visiting my folks in Washington, or I would have joined the million who were dead before New Year's, bulldozed into mass graves. Or become one of the few who survived to be sickos, carriers.

I'd talked to Jain on Christmas and the next day. She'd gotten the cough a few hours after the bomb, and by the next day her lungs were so full she could hardly talk other than to say good-bye. On the third day, all the phones in Boston were dead.

I couldn't have gone to her. Every American city had been locked down Christmas Eve, when they learned what the bomb was, but not where. "A big city in the East." Soldiers and police running everywhere, in Washington. Our family had piled in a car and tried to get out, but every exit was blocked and guarded. Seemed like typical government nonsense at the time. But they must have known how infectious it was, and how fast it would spread.

Boston was dead by dawn of the third day. Of course when I "joined" the military, I was sent here. Supposedly I knew the city, but without the T, the subway, I was lost. And everything underground belonged to the sickos now.

One-half of one percent of a million people meant five thousand carriers—survivors, they called themselves—living off the ruins of the city.

I didn't think Jain could have survived, she'd been so near death when we last talked. Then I found out they all had to go through that stage, and I had some hope that she'd lived. Then I saw what happened to the survivors, and I more than half hoped she hadn't.

Her name hadn't been on the casualty list, but about a third of the bodies hadn't been identified. She always was walking out without her purse.

Petroski came up with a short squad of riflemen, all armored like me. Only one, a sniper, actually had a rifle. The three others had Remington shoot-'em-ups, fully automatic shotguns. And I would be between them and their target, a comforting thought.

"What's the call, Lieutenant?"

I thought about the geometry of it. "Put the sniper and one other under that truck there." I pointed. "The other two on the wall, maybe twenty yards left and right of the elevator. Hold fire until I give the order."

"Or you get creamed. You trust that armor?"

"So nuke 'em if I get creamed."

"If it's a flamer, Lieutenant," the sniper said, "get down fast. I'll be shooting straight in. Your armor wouldn't do squat against this." He patted his rifle with affection. It was a 60-mm. recoilless.

"Thanks. Try to aim a little high till I can get out of the way." I nodded at their sergeant and he said "Go."

They scurried off, darting from cover to cover as if it were a training exercise. They'd be safer tiptoeing. If the enemy had IR they would have fired at us already. They could hear them moving, though, and might fire at the sound.

Nothing happened. I started walking straight toward the elevator. I had an IR flashlight; transferred it to my left hand and drew the tangler.

By the time I was twenty feet away I could see that what sounded like a "tunnel" was a freight elevator with both front and rear doors open. Corridor beyond.

I chinned the command freek. "Lillian, get me a floor plan of this parking lot, and whatever's north on the same level. Am I walking into another big lot?"

She must have had it up already; it flashed onto my data side almost instantly, my own position a blue circle. "It's a service corridor," she said. "Keep walking straight and you'll wind up in the Big Dig. About a thousand places to hide along the way."

"They're not gonna have much fog in there. You want another round to the north? We can probably get the corridor."

"Not yet. Let me see what's what."

"Okay. Your funeral." Actually, there was a note of relief in her voice. She could shell an old target like the underground lot until Judgement Day, but every time they put a round in a new place, they had to follow up with an assessment team and file a damage report. This was still Boston that they were blowing up, and someday we'd have it back. What was left of it.

Moving as quietly as possible, I inched over to one side of the door and flashed the IR around it. Chinned the scramble freek: "It's an open elevator shaft, like eight feet to the door on the other side. No way I'm gonna try to jump it."

"Want a couple grenades?" the sergeant said.

"Not yet. I—" There was a loud crash, and I flattened myself against the wall.

"What the fuck's goin' on?" the sergeant said. "We're gonna lay down some—" There was a loud *crack* and a 60-mm. round screamed down the corridor.

"No! Wait for my command!"

Then a scraping sound. Someone had dropped a metal plate across the shaft, and was pushing it.

The voice that had laughed whispered, "That you, Ardis?"

She knew my name and there was no mistaking the Jamaican lilt. "Jain! Get away from the door!"

"I am. I'm on the floor over on the side. You comin' over?"

"Yeah. Of course." On the freek: "Everybody *hold fire* until I say otherwise!"

"Or if we lose your carrier wave," the sergeant said.

I popped once for affirmative and stepped toward the metal plate. Then I stopped. "How did you know it was me?"

She laughed, from the little H, then forced herself to stop. "We . . . we're not dumb cavemen, Ardis. Someone monitoring the military web recognized your name and told me. I found out you were in charge of Track Seven and what your duty schedule was. It was pretty easy to set up this meeting."

"Easy! What about the kid?"

"He volunteered. We were afraid you might kill an adult. Your partner, Mark, might. He has twenty-three kills, none of them children."

"How did you know it wouldn't be Mark coming after you here?"

"I know you, Ardis. You wouldn't send him. Come across."

The plate was about a foot wide. I had to look at it to place my feet, and tried not to think about how far down the shaft went. She took my hand for the last couple of steps.

"You be lookin' like Papa Legba," she said. The armor was shiny black and formidable.

The fog was thin in the corridor; I could see her well. She was wearing a shabby jumpsuit that covered most of her body. Her face had some of the hard striations that were the aftermath of the disease, but to me they were like a contour map of her familiar beauty.

I stepped toward her, stepping into a dream; gathered her into my hard breast. Everything blurred. "Alive," I said. "Jain."

"God, my darling," she sobbed and laughed. Then she held me at arm's length and stared into my faceplate. "Look, can anybody else hear what I'm saying?"

"Not unless I click them in."

"Fast, then." She took a deep breath. "Look, I'm not infectious. Nobody is."

"What? What about Newton?"

"Just a prison." She stifled a laugh. "Silly damned stuff. Look, we've had normal people live with us, they don't get no plague."

"Then why not just show them?"

"Once when we tried, they just took everyone to Newton. Second time, they killed everyone. Not sure why; what's goin' on.

"We need you; we need someone in the power loop. Come live with us—come live with me!—for a few months, and then get back in touch with your people."

I had a hundred questions. Then I got one myself: "Lieutenant! What the hell's goin' on in there?"

Without answering, I toed the steel plate and pushed it into the elevator shaft.

"Let's go," Jain said.

"Just a second." I took off the helmet, popped the cuirass, and stepped out of the armor. "They can home in on the armor." I kicked off the boots and piled it all up in the corner. "Get out of here fast," I whispered.

We slipped along the wall about fifty yards, and Jain lifted a piece of plasterboard that hid a hole big enough to wiggle through. "You first." I crawled into a dark room full of boxes, feeling a little merry and playful from the whiff of little H. She followed me and as she pulled the cover back, I heard a gas grenade rattling down the corridor; heard it pop and hiss. "This way." She took my hand.

We went through a silent door into another corridor, dark except for a cluster of three dim flashlights.

"Mission accomplished," Jain said quietly. "Anybody have something for her to wear?"

"Jacket," someone said, and handed it over, rustling. It was damp and smelled of rancid sweat, but at least it was warm. Sized for a large man, it came down to about six inches above my knees. It would look very fetching, if we ever got to somewhere with light.

We moved swiftly through the dark, too swiftly for barefoot me, afraid of tripping or stepping on something. But it gave me some time to think.

Jain wouldn't lie to me about this, but that doesn't mean that what she told me was true. She might unknowingly be passing on a lie, or she might know the truth and be in denial of it. In which case I was already walking dead.

I put that possibility out of my mind, not because it was unlikely but because there was nothing I could do about it. And I'd rather be uncertain and with Jain than safe in my track.

We stopped at a tall metal door. While everybody else played their lights on the bottom right corner of it, a big bare-chested man—my benefactor?—took a long crowbar to it. After several minutes of grunting and prising, the door popped open.

"This is a good defense," Jain said. "It opens and closes easily from the other side, but nobody's going to just walk through it from here. This'll be a long ladder." I followed the others to step backwards onto a metal ladder in the darkness.

It wasn't totally dark, though, looking down. There was a square, the floor, slightly less inky. I had an irrational twinge of modesty, my bare butt right above the stranger below me.

"Almost there," Jain said from over her shoulder above me. "Headquarters."

My foot hit carpeted concrete and I waited for Jain while the others went ahead. "So what's at headquarters?"

"Mostly supplies. Some low-tech communications gear. Everything's nine-volt solar power."

It was a large warehouse room with dim lights here and there. Crates of food and water. A child's crib was a grab bag of miscellaneous cans and boxes; Jain rummaged through it and got a Snickers bar. "Hungry?"

"No, more like naked. You got clothes down here?" She walked me down a few yards, and there were clothes of all kinds roughly folded and sorted by size. I stepped into some black pants and found a black jersey, a fit combination for my new job as revolutionary turncoat, except for the Bergdorf labels. A fancy outfit to be buried in.

A tall skinny man walked up and offered his hand. "You're Lieutenant Drexel?"

"I don't think I'm Lieutenant anyone anymore. Ardis." He was hard to look at. Besides the skin striations from the virus, a face wound had torn a hole in his cheek, exposing his back teeth.

He nodded. "I'm Wally, more or less in charge of this area. Has Jain filled you in?"

"Not much. You aren't actually carriers?"

"No. We may have been, right after we recovered. People who came in to help us died. We think it was leftover virus from the attack. But what we think doesn't make any difference.

"It left us weak. Old people who survived the attack all died in the first year; now people in their fifties and sixties are going the same way. Infections, pneumonia, bronchitis."

"Our immune systems are shot," Jain said. "If we don't get medical help, we'll all be dead in a few years."

"We don't really understand what's going on," Wally said. "They've got hundreds of us out at the Newton Center; we've seen them. You'd think by now they'd know that none of us are carrying the disease."

"Maybe they wouldn't know, if they're really strict about quarantine," I said.

"Not all of them are," Jain said. "The guards wear surgical masks, but we've seen some take them off to smoke, even when there were 'carriers' around."

"Could just be carelessness," Wally said. "We're trying to avoid a conspiracy mind-set here."

I nodded. "Hard to see how it's to anybody's advantage to maintain the status quo. All of Boston shut down needlessly? Who profits?"

"Who set off the bomb?" Jain asked.

"Well, we assume—"

"But we don't *know*, right? Has anybody claimed responsibility?"

"No. Presumably they don't want to be nuked to glowing rubble."

"What if it wasn't 'them'? What if it was us?"

"Jain," Wally said.

"Well, the bomb didn't go off in the business district or Back Bay. It went off in Roxbury, and if it hadn't been for the wind reversing, you wouldn't have had one percent white casualties. You don't like what that implies, Wally, and neither do I, but a fact is a fact."

"I didn't know that," I said.

"Well, they did find what might have been the bomb casing," Wally said, "in the back of a blown-up truck down in Roxbury. Texas license plates. But there was a lot of that kind of damage in the riots, before everybody was too weak to riot."

"I can take you down to see it. Pretty safe. Army doesn't do much down there."

"Nightlights?"

"Go during the day. We only go out at night to attract attention."

———

We did go out to see it the next day, and I could have made a case for or against Jain's suspicions. The Texas truck did have a tank in the back that had exploded, but the part that remained attached was identified as LP gas, which it seemed to have been using for fuel. Of course that might have been camouflage for a tank full of the mystery virus; the engine was set up to switch between LP and gasoline.

The driver had died in the explosion. Jain's theory for that wasn't simple suicide, but rather that he had driven around the black neighborhoods for hours, maybe a whole day, releasing the stuff slowly, making sure it would get to its target. He himself would have been one of the first infected. He survived through the initial symptoms, and when he was sure it was working, destroyed the evidence, killing himself.

You would think a nutcase like that would want people to know who had done it, get his name in the history books, but they don't always. The Oklahoma City bombing when I was a kid, and the St. Louis Arch.

Anyhow, my job wasn't to explain anything, but just to demonstrate. For that, I only had to stay alive.

After the first symptomless day, I was pretty sure. They wanted me to stay with them for a couple of weeks, to prove their point beyond a shadow of a doubt, which was no problem. I moved in with Jain, and we sort of picked up where we'd left off. She looked a little different, but it wasn't her looks that had attracted me to her.

And instead of the walk-up in Roxbury, we were living in a three-million-dollar suite overlooking the Charles. We could even have taken the twelfth-floor penthouse, but under the circumstances that wouldn't be practical. Without elevators, it was *still* a walk-up, and we had to carry all our water up from the river.

It was not a typical lovers' reunion. So much of the catching up was about the horrors she had survived and my own less dramatic horror of watching martial law and paranoaic isolationism erode the American way of life.

Or maybe this nightmare was the real America, stripped of cosmetic civilization. What my mother had called the Reaganbush jungle, the moneyed few in control, protecting their fortunes at any social cost. That was Jain's party line, too.

But the people who owned this huge suite would probably like to have it back. The Brahmins who owned Boston would definitely like it back.

And every day I remained uninfected made the situation more mysterious. Who was profiting from this big lie?

We would find out. In a way.

The mechanics of the exposé had to be a little roundabout. We couldn't just go on television and do a tell-all show. There were plenty of stations in Boston, but nobody knew the equipment well enough to juryrig it to work with our low-voltage sun power, or even knew whether it was possible.

It was easy enough to make a disk, though, a home video of uninfected me surrounded by survivors, telling my story and theirs. Then we made about a hundred copies of the disk and had them tossed over the fence all around the border of the infected area. Even if no civilians found them, guards would, and it would be easy for them to verify from military records that I was who I said I was.

Four people died in the process of trying to distribute the disks. Well, they were weapons of a sort. Against the status quo.

A couple of days after that, Jain and I were sitting at home reading, when I heard the whining sound of a track decelerating outside. I looked through the dirty window and it was Track Number Seven, my old one.

"Let's get out of here," Jain said. There was an escape route through a duct in the basement.

"You go," I said. "I think they want to talk."

"Yeah, they wanna talk." She grabbed my arm. "*Go!*"

I shook her off. "They know I'm here. If they wanted to hurt me they could have dropped one artillery round in our lap."

"You trust them?"

"They're just people, Jain." The doors of the track opened and three armored soldiers came out.

"People, shit." I heard her bare feet slapping down the stairs and fought the urge to follow her.

The three came up the outdoor steps, and I opened the door for them. They filed inside without a word.

One had captain's bars. When they were all in the living room he said, "This is her?"

"Yeah. That's her."

"Mark," I said. He turned around and left.

The captain grabbed one arm and then the other, and pinioned me. "Let's do it."

The other had red crosses on each shoulder. He or she pulled a syringe out of a web-belt pocket.

There was a huge explosion, and the medic went down, hard. The captain let go of me and spun around. Jain was standing at the top of the basement steps with an 11-mm. Glock. She and the captain fired at the same time. He hit her in the center of the chest. Her blood spattered the wall behind her and she was dead before she started to fall.

Her bullet staggered him, but the armor worked, and he recovered before I had time to do more than scream. He punched me in the side of the head and I collapsed.

He hauled me roughly to my feet. "Medic. Get the fuck up."

He moaned. "Jesus, man." He got up on one elbow. "Think she broke my sternum."

"I'll break more'n that. Do your job."

He got up slowly, painfully. Found the syringe on the floor.

"What's that?" Though I knew. He gave me an injection in the shoulder and threw the needle away.

The captain shoved me toward the door. "Let's go make another video."

———

I was in the Newton cell for about eight hours when I started to cough. By then I'd written most of this. Though I don't suppose anyone will ever see it. It will be burned with my clothes, with my body.

I'll never know whether Jain was completely right. She had at least part of the story.

My face is stiffening. The ridges don't show in the cell's dirty metal mirror, but I can feel them under the skin.

It's hard to make my jaw work to close my mouth. Before long it will stay a little bit open, then more, until it's wide as it can go. I know that from the pictures of the corpses. I wonder whether you die before the jaw breaks.

I'm isolated from everybody, but from the small window of my cell I can see the exercise yard, and I can see that Wally was right. There aren't any old people left among the survivors. Nobody over their midforties. Next year it might be midthirties. In a few years, Newton, like Boston, will be empty.

They can have their city back. Turn off the nightlights, repair the artillery damage. Scrub the dried blood off the walls, pick up the bones and throw them away.

Whenever I move, I can hear the little motors of the camera as it tracks me from the darkness of the corridor. Sometimes I see a glint of light from its lens.

I don't think there was any conspiracy. Just a status quo that perpetuated itself. Us versus them in a waiting game. With insignificant me poised for a few days in the middle: an us who was a them; a them who was an us.

Who lost and found and lost her shadow.

(2003)

Civil Disobedience

I'm old enough to remember when the Beltway was a highway, not a dike. Even then, there were miles that had to be elevated over low places that periodically flooded.

We lived in suburban Maryland when I was a child. I remember seeing on television the pictures of downtown Washington after Hurricane Hilda, with the Washington Monument and the Capitol and the Lincoln Memorial all isolated islands. My brother and I helped our parents stack sandbags around our Bethesda house, but the water rose over them. Good thing the house had two stories.

That was when they built the George W. Bush Dam to regulate the flow of the Potomac, after Hilda. (My grandfather kept mumbling "Bush Dam . . . Damn Bush.) That really was the beginning of the end for the UniParty, a symbol for all that went wrong afterwards.

The politicos claimed they didn't cause the water to rise—it was supposed to be a slow process, hundreds or even thousands of years before a greenhouse crisis. I guess they built the dam just in case they were wrong.

Then there were three hurricanes in four weeks, and they all made it this far north, so the dam closed up tight—and people in flooded Maryland and Virginia could look over the Beltway dike and see low-and-dry

Washington, and sort of resent what their tax dollars had bought. Maybe what happened was inevitable.

Over the next decade, the dikes also went up around New York, Boston, Philadelphia, and Miami. The Hamptons, Cape Cod. Temporary at first, but soon enough, as the water rose, bricked into permanence. While suburbs and less wealthy coastal towns from Maine to Florida simply drowned.

By the time the water got to rooftop level, of course all those towns were deserted, their inhabitants relocated inland, into Rehab camps if they couldn't afford anything else. We spent a couple of years in the Rockville one, until Dad had saved enough to get into an apartment in Frederick. It was about as big as a matchbox, but by then we two boys had gone off to college and trade school.

I was an autodidact without too much respect for authority, so I said the hell with college and became a SCUBA instructor, a job with a future. That was after I'd been in the Navy for one year, and the Navy brig for one week. Long enough in the service to learn some underwater demolition, and that's on my website, which brought me to the attention of Homeland Security, about a day and a half after the Bush Dam blew.

Actually, I'm surprised it took them that long. Most of my income for several years had been from Soggy Suburbs, diving tours of the drowned suburbs of Washington. People mostly come back to see what's become of the family manse, now that fish have moved in, and it does not generate goodwill toward the government. They've tried to shut me down a couple of times, but I have lawyers from both the ACLU and the Better Business Bureau on my side.

I returned to my dock with a boatload of tourists—only four, in the bitter January cold—and found a couple of suits and a couple of cops waiting, along with a Homeland Security helicopter. They had a federal warrant to bring me in for questioning.

It was an interesting ride. I'm used to seeing the 'burbs underwater, of course, but it was strange to fly over what had become an inland sea, inside the Beltway dike. The dam demolition had been a pretty thorough job, and in less than a day, it became as deep inside the Beltway as outside. They can fill up the collapsed part and pump the water out, but it will take a long time.

(The guy who did it called it "civil disobedience" rather than terrorism, which I thought was a stretch. But he did time the charges so that the flooding was gradual, and no one drowned.)

Since I was a suspected terrorist, I lost the protection of the courts, not to mention the ACLU and the Better Business Bureau. They didn't haul out the cattle prods, but they did lock me in a small room for twenty-four hours, saying, "We'll get to you."

It could have been worse. It was a hotel room, not a jail, but there was nothing to read or eat, no TV or phone. They took my shoulder bag with the book I was reading and my computer and cell.

I guess they thought that would scare me. It just made me angry, and then resigned. I hadn't really done anything, but since when did that matter, with the UniParty. And not doing anything was not the same as not knowing anything.

The smell of mildew was pervasive, and the carpet was squishy. When we landed on the roof, it looked like about four stories were above the waterline. I couldn't see anything from the room; the window was painted over with white paint from the outside.

Exactly twenty-four hours after they had brought me in, one of the suits entered through the hotel-room door, leaving a guard outside.

"What do you need a cop for?"

He gave me a look. "Full employment." He sat down on the couch. "First of all, where were you—"

"I get food, you get answers."

"You have that backward." He looked at the back of his hand. "Answers, then food. Can you prove where you were when the dam was sabotaged?"

"No, and neither can you."

"What do you mean by that?"

"Food."

Yet another look. He stood up without a word and knocked twice on the door. The guard opened it, and he left.

A few minutes later I tried knocking, myself. No result. But the man did come back eventually, bearing a ham sandwich on a Best Western plate.

I peeled back the white bread and looked at it. "What if I don't eat ham?"

"You left a package of sliced ham in your refrigerator on K Street.

You ordered a ham sandwich at Denny's for lunch on the twenty-eighth of November. I checked while they were making the sandwich."

Now *that* was scary, considering where my refrigerator was now. I tore into the sandwich even though it was probably full of truth serum. "If you know so much about me," I said between bites, "then you must know where I was at any given time."

"You said that neither you nor I could say where we were when the dam blew."

"No . . . you asked where I was when it was *sabotaged*. That could have been a week or a year before the actual explosions. The saboteurs were probably back in Albania or Alabama or wherever by then."

"So where were you when it blew?"

"At my girlfriend's place. It rattled the dishes and a picture fell off the wall."

"That's the tree house she's squatting in, out in Wheaton?"

"Home sweet home, yeah. Her original apartment is kind of damp. She paid a premium for ground floor. Wrong side of the Beltway."

"So we only have her word for where you were."

"And mine, yes. What, you don't have surveillance cameras out in Treetown yet?"

"None that show her place."

I guess it was my turn to respond, or react. I finished the sandwich instead, slowly, while he watched. He took the plate, I suppose so I couldn't Frisbee it at his head, take his keys and gun, subdue the guard, steal the helicopter, and go blow up the New York dike. Instead I posited: "If the saboteurs could have been anyplace in the world when it blew, what difference does it make where I was?"

"You weren't in town. It looks like you knew something was going to happen."

"Really."

"Yes, *really*. We got a warrant, and a Navy SEAL forensic team searched your apartment."

"Are my goldfish all right? Water's kind of cold."

"It's interesting what's missing. Not just toiletries and clothes, but boxes of books and pictures from the walls. Your computer system, not portable. All the paper having to do with your business. Your pistol and its registration. You moved them with four cab rides between your apartment and the Sligo dock, all two days before the Flood."

"So I moved in with my girlfriend. It happens."

"Not so conveniently."

I tried to look confused. "That's why you're on my case. I'm one of the dozens, hundreds, of people who moved out of D.C. that day or the next?"

"You're the only one with underwater demolition training. On that alone, we could haul you down to Cuba and throw away the key."

"Come on—"

"And you were already on a watch list for your attitude. The things you've said to customers."

"The apartment was too expensive, so I got back my deposit and moved out. My girlfriend—"

"A week before the first of the month."

"Sure. It was—"

"In a blizzard."

"Yeah, it was snowing. No problem. Or the cabbie's problem, not mine. We wanted to have Christmas together."

"For Christmas, you just sort of boated through twelve miles of blizzard. By compass, for the fun of it."

"Oh, bullshit. I just kept the Beltway to my left for ten-some miles and turned right at the half-submerged Chevron sign. Then about a hundred yards to a flagpole, bear left, and so forth. I've done it a hundred times. You try it with a compass. I want to watch."

He nodded without changing expression. "One of the things we lost when the dam blew was a really delicate sniffing machine. It can tell whether you've been anywhere near high explosives recently. The closest one's in our New York office."

"Let's go. I haven't touched anything like that since the Navy. Four or five years ago." I'd been in the same house with some, but I hadn't touched it.

He stood up very smoothly, one flex, not touching the arm of the couch. I wouldn't want to get into anything physical with him. "Get your coat."

I got it from the musty closet and shook it out, shedding molecules of mold and plastic explosive. How sensitive was that machine, really?

He knocked twice, and the cop took us to an open elevator. The buttons under 4 were covered with duct tape. The cop used a cylindrical fire department key to start it. "Roof?"

"Right."

"Where's my stuff?" I said. "I don't want to leave it here."

"We're not going anywhere." He buttoned up his coat and I zipped mine up. We got out of the elevator into a glassed-in waiting area and went out onto the roof. There was no helicopter on the pad. Not too cold, high twenties with no wind, and the air smelled really good, almost like the ocean.

I followed him over to the edge. There was water all the way to where the horizon was lost in bright afternoon haze, the tops of a few buildings rising like artificial islands in a science-fiction world. Behind us, the Beltway, with almost no traffic.

"It's quiet," I said. Faint rustle of ice slurry below us. I peered over the rusty guardrail and saw it rolling along the building wall.

"They said 'Power to the People.' This isn't power to anybody. It's like the country's been beheaded."

I didn't say that if you're ugly enough, extreme cosmetic surgery could help. I might be in enough trouble already.

"Whoever did this didn't think it through. It's not just the government, the bureaucracy. It's the country's history. Our connection to the past; our identity as America."

That was something Hugh was always on about. The way they wrap themselves in the flag and pretend to be the inheritors of a grand democratic tradition. While they're really alchemists, turning the public trust into gold.

"Hugh Oliver," he said, startling me.

"What about Hugh?"

"He disappeared the same time you did."

"What, like I disappeared? I left a forwarding address."

"Your parents' address."

"They knew where I was."

"So did we. But we've lost Mr. Oliver. Perhaps you know where to find him?"

"Huh-uh. We're not that close."

"Funny." He took a pair of small binoculars out of his coat pocket and switched them on. The stabilizers hummed as he scanned along the horizon. Still looking at nothing, he said, "A surveillance camera saw you go into a coffeehouse in Georgetown with him last Wednesday. The Lean Bean."

Oh shit. "Yeah, I remember that. So?"

"The camera didn't show either of you coming out. You're not still there, so you must have left through the service entrance."

"He was parked in the alley out back."

"Not in his own car. It had a tracer."

"So I'm not my brother's car's keeper. It must have been somebody else's. What did he—"

"Or a rental?"

That much, I could give up. "Not a rental. It was clapped-out and full of junk."

"You didn't recognize it?"

I shook my head. Actually, I'd assumed it was Hugh's. "Why did you have a tracer on his car?"

"What did you talk about?"

"Business. How bad it is." Hugh's a diver; not much winter work. Idle hands do the devil's work, I guess. "We just had a cup of coffee, and he drove me home."

"And what did you do when you got home?"

"What? I don't know. Made dinner."

He put the binoculars down on the railing and pulled out a little sound recorder. "This is what you did."

It was a recording of me phoning my landlord, saying I'd found a cheaper place and would be moving out before Christmas.

"That was at six twenty-five," he said. "When you got home from the coffeehouse, you must have gone straight to the phone."

I had, of course. "No. But I guess it was the same day. That Wednesday."

He picked up the binoculars again and scanned the middle distance. "It's okay, Johnson."

The big man slammed me against the guardrail, hard, then tipped me over and grabbed my ankles. I was gasping, coughing, trying not to vomit, dangling fifty feet over the icy water.

"Johnson is strong, but he can't hold on to you forever. I think it's time for you to talk."

"You can't . . . you can't do this!"

"I guess you have about a minute," he said, looking at his watch. "Can you hold on a minute?" I could see Johnson nod, his upside-down smile.

"Let me put it to you this way. If you can tell us where Hugh Oliver went, you live. If you can't, you have this little accident. It doesn't matter whether it's because you don't know, or because you refuse to tell. You'll just fall."

My throat had snapped shut, paralyzed. "I—"

"You'll either drown or freeze. Neither one is particularly painful. That bothers me a little. But I can't tell you how little guilt I will feel."

Not the truth! "Mexico. Drove to Mexico."

"No, we have cameras at every crossing, with face recognition."

"He knew that!"

"Can you let go of one ankle?" He nodded and did, and I dropped a sickening foot. "Mexico returns terrorists to us. He must have known that, too."

"He was going to Europe from there. Speaks French." *Quebec.*

He shrugged and made a motion with his head. The big man grabbed the other ankle and hauled me back. My chin snapped against the railing, and my shoulder and forehead hit hard on the gravel.

"Yeah, Europe. You're lying, but I think you do know where he is. I can send you to a place where they get answers." He rubbed his hands together and blew on them. "Maybe I'll go along with you. It's warm down there."

Cuba. Point of no return.

My stomach fell. Even if I knew nothing about Hugh, I knew too much about them.

They couldn't let me live now. They'll pull out their answers and bury me in Guantanamo.

Johnson picked me up roughly. I kicked him in the shin, tore loose, ran three steps, and tried to vault over the edge. My hurt shoulder collapsed, and I cartwheeled clumsily into space.

Civil disobedience. What would the water feel like?

Scalding. Then nothing.

(2005)

Memento Mori

She sat on the examination table, trying to hold the open back of the hospital robe closed. Everything was cold chrome and eggshell white and smelled of air-conditioning and rubbing alcohol. And of her, slightly.

The man stepped in and quietly closed the door behind him. He had a stethoscope and a name tag but was wearing all black.

He spoke her name and took her cold hand. His hand was warm and dry.

He listened for a heart and then for breathing. He put the stethoscope away in a drawer and left it open.

"You have to trust me completely," he said.

"Will it hurt?"

"Not really," he said. He wasn't actually lying. The pain would not belong to her.

"But people have died from it."

"People have died during it. Not many," he said. "What would death be to you?"

"I don't know. John Donne said something about it."

" 'Death, thou shalt die.' " He almost smiled. "Take off the robe."

She took it off and tried to fold it, then just dropped it.

He didn't react to her strange nakedness. "Lie down here." She did. "Hold still."

With his finger he traced a line from her navel to her breastbone. Her skin was gray and tight, room temperature and parchment smooth. He kept his finger pressed there, marking a place midway between her small breasts.

He painted something cold there.

"You will just barely feel this," he said. She looked away. He pressed a round fitting firmly into the bone, with a small snap.

He blotted for blood. There wasn't any. "That wasn't bad," he said. "Was it?"

She nodded, eyes tightly closed.

"How did you die?" he asked.

"I don't really know. I woke up like this."

He tapped the fitting a few times and wiggled it. "This must be your first time," he said.

"Yes; I'm only 110."

He bound her wrists and ankles to the table with metal clamps.

"Is that really necessary? I'm weak as a kitten."

"You never know," he said. "Sometimes there's a violent reaction, hysterical strength."

He put on a chain necklace with a heavy silver cross, with rubies at the stigmata points. She heard the metallic rattle and opened her eyes. "I'm not a Christian. Will it work?"

"You don't have to be a believer," he said. "And this is not an exorcism, except in some metaphorical way. Metaphorical, not metaphysical."

"Okay."

"Close your eyes again," he said. He reached into the open drawer and withdrew a black metal rod that tapered to a point. He gently inserted the point of the long black tool into the fitting in her chest. Then he moistened his fingertips with his tongue and touched her ears and then her eyes, whispering in Latin, "*Exorcizo te, omnis spiritus immunde, in nomine Dei . . .*"

"So why the Latin? If it's not an exorcism."

"It's a message to both our bodies," he said. "An incantation that initializes us as patient and healer."

"That sounds as bad as exorcism."

"It's science," he said. "The nanozooans that keep you immortal have gone into an emergency mode. Some imbalance has to be addressed. They can stay alive themselves, in aggregate, but they can't keep you alive, beyond oxygenating your brain.

"Together, they have the intelligence of a small child. But it's not easy to get them to do anything out of their routine. Like organic cells, most of them have a single function in terms of keeping your body going. But instead of dying when things go wrong, they go into shutdown mode and await instruction.

"We chose the old Latin rite as an instruction code because no one will run into it accidentally. If it were some common phrase, you might overhear it accidentally, and your body would start deconstructing itself. That would be frightening."

"I don't think I understand. I'm not a technical person. What is that black thing?"

"It's like medicine in the old days," he said. "Helping your body help itself. Try to let the Latin put you to sleep."

"Okay." She closed her eyes again.

"*. . . in nomine Domini nostri Jesu Christi eradicare, et effugare ab hoc plasmate Dei. Ipse tibi imperat, qui te de supernis caelorum in inferiora terrae demergi praecepit. Ipse tibi imperat, qui mari, ventis, et tempestatibus imperavit . . .*"

Her eyes snapped open, bright red, and she bucked against the restraints, howling. Lunging, she was almost able to bite him, with teeth suddenly long and sharp as fangs. He leaned into the short sword and pushed her back to the table. The door behind him banged open, and two big attendants in green started in and hesitated.

"It's okay," he said. "Get the cleaning 'bot."

Her mouth overflowed with black foam, and she shook her head violently, spraying the room. Yellow and gray worms came crawling out of her mouth and nose. Noxious gases rose out of her body and billowed into orange flame. Something like electricity crackled along her arms. Finally, she fell limp.

He had studied her carefully through the whole seizure. Now he rotated the black tool patiently between his palms, like a man trying to start a fire, but more slowly. Green vapors rose out of her chest for a minute, and then stopped, and there was a little bright blood there. He put down the tool and found a cap in the open drawer, and closed off the fitting with it.

He undid the restraints. "Okay, guys," he said. "She's ready for cleanup." The two big men came in and carried her away, while the cleaning robot scuttled around after wriggling worms and various excreta.

She came slowly back to consciousness seated in a lukewarm shower. There was a kindly looking matron in a candy-stripe uniform watching her. "Are you coming around?"

"Yes. Yes, I am." The dead gray skin sloughed off, and the skin underneath glowed bright healthy pink. "That didn't hurt at all."

The man in black appeared in the door. "Good thing. There'd be hell to pay."

(2004)

Faces

I think the universe would have been a much finer place if space travel had stayed expensive. Then it would never have involved me. So now I get to spend two years of my life doing "social observation" on a planet where, stepping out without a space suit, you wouldn't live long enough to take a second breath.

Social observation by a draftee with a gun. You couldn't call it war, since these woogies were still killing each other with sticks when we arrived—and besides, nobody really wants to hurt them. We just want to find out whether they have anything worth taking.

I do the reals and read books about the old days, my great-grandparents' time, when they spent more to put two men on the Moon than we spend to keep ten battalions on ten worlds. I try to feel what they felt, but I can't get there. It's not very glorious: step into the machine, step out on a woogie planet, try not to get into too much trouble, come back one month a year to spend your pay.

We call this one La-la Land, or just Lalande, because its star's real name was Lalande followed by some number. A sun with another sun pretty far away. Not much night, or none at all, for about half the year, which bothers some people. I grew up in Alaska, sun all night in the summer, and also lived there while getting my highly useful degree in art history. For some reason that seems to have qualified me to become a heavy equipment operator. With a gun, one must add, and a big gun, on the heavy equipment, which I would call a tank if I didn't know it was a GPV(E), General Purpose Vehicle (Exploration). Which spends half its time in the motor pool with mysterious ailments.

My partner in this dubious enterprise is Whoopie Marchand, whose name may affect her demeanor, with another appropriate degree: library science. We both wish the other was a mechanic. Whoopie comes from Jamaica, and likes to keep the machine about ten degrees hotter than I would choose, and in our tiny space cooks food so spicy it makes my eyes water. So except for the fact that I prefer the company of men and can hardly understand a word she says, we were just made for one another.

The Lalandians are a little more like humans, or at least other Earth creatures, than most woogies. (I have an older cousin who served on Outback, where the natives are like big spiders with metal shells.) They have the right number of eyes and ears and nostrils and a tiny mouth-thing, but six arm/legs. Their body chemistry is so different from ours that they breathe chlorine along with their oxygen. The water that comes out of their wells would kill you in a second.

Their heads are long and squashed-looking, with batwing ears and chins like axe blades. Bright red slanted eyes with nictitating membranes, set in deep sockets. Not easy to love.

They look sort of like nightmare centaurs, but their front, with the chest and "arms" and head, isn't always pointed forward. When they want to, those arms become the hind legs, and their butts rise up into the air, and they can use their former hind legs as arms. It's a defense thing, since from a distance the butt looks like the head, with dark spots for eyes and ears and mouth, but it's just a fat-and-water storage organ. If something bites it off, they can regenerate it.

It's an evolutionary anachronism now; their ancestors killed off all the large predators when they became tool-users. The old guys were pretty fierce, too, evidently. Sabretooth centaurs with big claws. They're more or less settled down now, though.

Whoopie and I are part of X Group, engineers, and normally stay in the compound that overlooks the town Nula. It's the biggest town on the continent, with maybe ten thousand natives. Hard to get a count, though; they're nomadic, and most of them are just in town temporarily, buying and selling and anxious to get back on the road. They ride six-legged things that aren't mammals but look like big soft camels, going from one oasis to another on this dry dustball of a world.

They couldn't send me someplace where the natives had art, like Kelsey or Pakkra; that would be too sensible. They probably send mechanics there. The Lalandians seem kind of plain and pragmatic; they have crafts like weaving and pottery, but everything's utilitarian. There are subtle and beautiful color variations in some of their fired pots, but they seem to be incidental, perhaps accidental. They're close to color-blind anyhow, with those huge red eyes.

So I was surprised and pleased to get what looked like an art assignment; the coordinator said an orbital survey showed what looked like statuary in the Badlands north of here, and Whoopie and I were to go out and take its measure. They didn't choose Whoopie on the off chance that there might be a library out there; it's just that we had trained together on the GPV in South Dakota and Antarctica. And we did get along all right except for gender, culture, language, diet, and all. Did I mention that she smokes? I don't. For the past month or so, she and I had been out for a couple of hours a day, gathering geological specimens to send back to Earth. This was going to be a really long one, so I made sure she had lots of weeds and chili powder.

We went into town first, to take on water, which is always a bit of a driving challenge, since the Lalandians are fascinated by the GPV, which bears a superficial resemblance to their camel things, since it's bulbous and has six wheels. Their culture lacks the concept of being squashed like a bug, though, lacking heavy machinery, and it takes a delicate touch on the joystick to keep from running over the juvenile natives.

I'm glad to let Whoopie drive in town, since she's better at it and enjoys it. I sort of enjoy riding along hanging on to the side. The kids wave like human kids would. I'd throw them candy except carbohydrates would kill them.

When we left the city limits, defined by a huge dirt wall, I swung inside through the double door, took off the breather helmet, and seatbelted myself into the command seat. "Hey, mon," Whoopie said.

"It's John," I said, not for the first time.

"Hey, John. You smell like the chlorine dust."

"Go ahead." She lit up a clove-smelling weed. The airco cranked max on her side and sucked up most of it.

"You don' want one."

"Thanks, no." I thought about my own opie but couldn't slap that until I was off duty. She could smoke the clove thing because regulations lag behind reality.

The inside of the GPV was bigger than a civilian van, but full enough of stuff that it felt crowded. Two bunks and a galley in front of us, and a little head with a privacy curtain that only pulled halfway. Weapons station at the very rear. Chatterguns and a big pulse cannon in case you were bothered by something far enough away to use it. We'd trained on both back earthside, but nobody had ever fired a shot on Lala. Probably a good thing. The chatterguns were almost as hard on the user as on the target, and the cannon could blow the front off the tank if you depressed it too far.

Whoopie put the thing on dumb auto, and we studied the chart on the screen. There weren't any roads headed for the artifact.

"How the hell they build this thing?" Whoopie said. "Gotta be twice the size of Mount Rushmore. They had roads and like explosives and jackhammers for Rushmore."

I didn't know what Mount Rushmore was, but then I was never actually an American, not since Alaska seceded when I was six. Neither was Whoopie, of course, but Jamaica was an American protectorate and just a hop away. She went there all the time.

She saw my expression and explained. "Mount Rushmore's in one of those states like Idaho? The big square ones, I always get mixed up. They got four and a half presidents' heads carved in the side of a mountain." She closed her eyes, trying to remember. "Washington, Jefferson, Lincoln. One of the Roosevelts. Then they try to add someone from the twenty-first, Reagan or Bush, and it collapses. Just a triangle of hair and part of one eye left. It looks kinda like a cunt."

I traced a possible route with my finger. "Maybe we should stay on this mesa? Just follow along the curve of the canyon lip."

She nodded. "Twice as long, but God knows what we get in the valley." Probably rubble, like leftover president chins. "You want to set it up, drive for a while?"

"Yeah, take a break." The weed usually made her sleepy. She went forward and scrunched into the sack.

I might have joined her if I was that way. She's kind of pretty. And we do like each other more than we let on.

I took the stylus and drew us a route that stayed along a level path, according to the elevation lines, an arc that went west and then north. That would be the default, in case I smoked a joint and fell asleep myself. But dumb auto won't go over five or six kays per hour. We'd run out of curry before we got there.

I shifted over and belted in and gave the dashboard a thumbprint and eyescan. Cranked it up to about fifty, sixty kays, bumpety bump.

"Don't you go too fast, mon," Whoopie mumbled.

"Sleep, my darling. I made Expert on this thing."

"Yah, that's what I mean. Be expert." I actually got ranked Expert on vehicles and weapons I'd never seen, let alone driven or shot. If you're not Expert all-around, they can't send you off planet. So there you go.

The trough we were in was kind of like a broad dry creek bed, pebbles and rocks. Sometimes boulders you had to maneuver around. At that speed it didn't even take half a brain.

I used the other half to paint mental pictures. I'm not a bad artist—just not an especially good one—and the paintings I do in my head work out better than the ones on paper or canvas. I did Whoopie's face, half in darkness, mysterious. The African goddess of Annoying Normal People.

The main sun set after about an hour and a half, but there was enough light from the little one, I didn't have to pop an eyepill. They always make me sweat, go figure. After about three hours, though, the light was getting green and weak. Whoopie got up and suggested we take it easy for a while, let the little bastard rise up out of the mists near the horizon.

It was good to stop. The shock absorbers on the tank were marvels of engineering, I'm sure, but I still felt like a pair of dice finally come to rest.

She'd soaked some dehydrated goat for a curry. Why did we take goat to the stars? It would never have occurred to me to eat one in the first place. She'd eat worms if they had curry and hot sauce on them, though in fact goat was big comfort food for her.

I did my usual escape, putting on a real and delaying my own dinner so I wouldn't have to share the smell of hers. I'd been on this one before, soaring like a condor over the Norwegian fjords in total winter, really like a bird, finding the weak thermals on the sun side and sliding along them, thinking of nothing but flight. Enjoying the deadly cold. At least there was plenty of oxygen and no exotic spices.

When I came out of it the air was cold and curry-free. "I turned up the airco," Whoopie said. "Where'd you go?"

I told her. "I could try that."

"Thought you didn't like cold." I handed her the headset.

She nodded. "Like the birds, though." She settled into the pilot seat and turned it on.

I zapped some chicken stew and read while she soared. A survey of Spanish architecture, post-Gaudi. I had a monograph linked to it, distilled from my Ph.D. thesis, and there were two latent hits I'd have to check when I went back earthside. Maybe a job offer, dream on.

It used to be that when you were drafted, the goddamned Confederación would make them keep your job for when you got back. That ended the year before I was offered the opportunity of service. I'll spend next month earthside trying to line something up, but there seem to be about five art historians for every nonteaching job. I'll wind up in some cow college trying to keep a roomful of Eskimos and myself awake while I drone on about Doric and Corinthian columns.

The phone chimed and I thumbed it. The lovely face of our immediate superior, Yobie Mercer. I sort of hated his tattoos, which looked amateur and self-inflicted. "Coordinator. What can I do for you?"

"You could start by telling me why your vehicle's not moving."

"It's dark. We took a break for chow and to wait for Junior to come up out of the mist."

"You have lights."

"With all respect, sir, the terrain is pretty uneven."

"It's not that bad. How far are you?"

I looked at the chart and measured out about two inches. "It looks like about seventy klicks, sir. Three hours in the dark."

"Well, do it. I want you there by main dawn."

"Yes, sir." If they're in such a goddamned hurry, why don't they fly someone out? "We'll certainly try."

"You'll more than try, Denham. You'll be there. We have civilian press coming at 0800."

"Press, sir? From Earth?"

"Just do it." He clicked off.

"What was that all about?" Whoopie had the helmet off.

"Fearless Leader wants us there at dawn, big dawn. Something about press."

"Press this." She grabbed her crotch. "You wanta drive?"

"I'd as soon you did. If you're rested enough."

"Sure, no prob." We shifted around and belted in. She dimmed the inside lights and snapped on the outside floods. The vague landscape jumped into sharp relief, mostly jumbled grey rocks. The bright light brought out subtle shadings, ochre and gamboge and rust.

She opened the med kit and looked at the eyepills, but put them back. I wouldn't want them either, with the high contrast. She shook out a stimmy and put it under her lower lip. "Hang on, mon." She edged the joystick forward.

She was pretty good, keeping it around a hundred, slithering on the turns occasionally, but she really was better at it than I was. It wasn't her fault that the machine crapped out on us.

There was a sudden really ominous sound, like metal grinding while an electric arc sputtered, and the GPV(E) stopped E-ing with a vengeance. It juddered to a stop, I think with all the tracks and wheels locked. The dim interior lights and the external floodlight went dark. Junior was high enough that we could see a little, though.

"Shit!" Whoopie rattled the joystick around and stomped on pedals, to no effect, and then sat and listened. The machine creaked and popped. Smell of hot metal and ozone.

"Mercer's going to love this," I said.

She tapped on the screen. Nothing. "If and when he finds out about it. We're in real trouble, mon. John."

"Try the suit radios?"

She nodded. "Better get into the suits, anyhow. I think we've got a leak." There might have been a little chlorine, masked by the ozone.

We stripped and helped each other into the suits, nice butt, and tried the airlock. We had to use the manual emergency levers, and the outside door stuck in the open position.

My heads-up said I had three and a half hours of air, normal activity. "Did you top off the spares?"

"Huh-uh." I hadn't either. They had maybe an hour each, if nobody'd been at them.

I followed her around the tank to the other side. She opened the three access panels to the engine, transmission, and fuel cells. "There you go."

The fuel cell terminals were fused, still hot and smoking. "What could do that?" I said. "Something short them out?"

"I can't imagine what. Maybe something inside? Do you know how fuel cells work?"

"You're the big driver."

"What the fuck is that supposed to mean?"

"Calm down, calm down. It's just that you know more about cars and things."

"Ya, ya. You want to call Fearless Leader?"

"Not especially." But I tapped out the home-base sequence on my wrist plate. "Shit."

"Nothing?"

"Not even static. Something's really wrong."

She tried hers and it didn't work, either. She looked north and raised a hand as if to scratch her nose. It clanked against the helmet. "Damn. It's only a few kilometers more. We could walk to it."

"Leave the tank? Our food and water—"

"Which don't do any good, you can't take off the helmet. This press thing is going to be there at eight o'clock. There will be a chopper."

"It might just be a remote camera."

"Even so."

I sank back onto the tank's fender. "This can't all be happening at once."

"Ya, well, when was the last time you check the suit radios? Topped off the reserve oxygen?" She shook her head, though I could only see the gesture because I was looking directly into her helmet. "Or me. The motor pool don't check, they don't get a written order."

"Look, Mercer knew when we stopped last night. He'll know we've stopped now, and call. When he doesn't get an answer, won't he send a chopper out?"

"I don' think so. What's gonna send the signal we stopped, we ain't got power?" She looked at her watch. "Unless he bothers to call before Press Time, it'll be two hours before he knows somethin's wrong. Then how long before they start lookin'?"

Knowing Mercer, he might go off to breakfast with the reporter, especially if she was female. Then chat her up while we learn to breathe chlorine. "Okay. Let's carry the spare oxygen."

I started to get up and instead fell to the ground. We said "Shit!" in unison; the tank was starting to move on without us. Whoopie ran around to the airlock side, and I followed as soon as I could get to my feet.

She was inside, both doors open. I swung up and staggered in, too.

"Damn! Nothing!" She was working the joystick with both hands. The tank continued to crawl along at a fast walk.

She leaned forward and looked at the dash. "I don' know what the hell. Where's it gettin' power?"

"Maybe it's some fail-safe thing," I said. "A backup power supply. Is it following the default path?"

"I don't think so—Jesus! It's headed for the edge!" I popped open the cabinet next to the airlock and unshipped the two reserve oxygen tanks. Whoopie grabbed one and we both half jumped, half fell out of the door. We sat and watched the machine crawl toward its doom.

But at the edge, it slowly spun left and continued on its way. We got to our feet and followed it.

"It's not headed back," Whoopie observed. "So it's not some kind of homing program."

"And it's not following the default I traced. But it is headed roughly in the right direction."

"That's where it's goin'." She checked her wrist compass and almost tripped over a rock. "Might even be a more direct route." It certainly wasn't afraid of skirting the edge of the canyon, something I'd avoided, mapping with the stylus. Maybe it did have a kind of homing "instinct," but toward its destination rather than back to the motor pool.

Keeping up with it was exhausting. The suits aren't uncomfortable in the short term, but they reminded me of when your mother overdressed you for playing in the snow: you walk kind of like a zombie in a movie. Very comical.

After stomping along for about an hour and a half, we topped a rise and could see the artifacts, which were impressive. Three identical Lalandian heads, maybe a hundred meters high. In another fifteen minutes, the GPV rolled as close to the artifacts as it could get, on the edge of a sheer cliff, and stopped.

It took us a while to get our breath, and it was about time to stop breathing so hard. My heads-up said thirty-eight minutes left.

"Whatta you make of it?"

"Been here a while. If they were on Earth, I'd say they were thousands of years old. This atmosphere's more corrosive, though. Um . . ."

We had stared at them for several minutes, in silence, before either of us realized it was odd.

"John," she said, still staring.

"Yeah," I said. "This is crazy."

"Let's both look away now. On the count of three."

"Hell with counting. Just look away."

It was like not looking at a beautiful painting, combined with not looking at a horrible accident. I looked at my feet, and every muscle in my neck was trying to make me raise my head.

"This is max bad," she said, and I could tell from her voice that her teeth were clenched.

Some kilometers away, I could hear the throb of a helicopter. With some effort I was able to look in its direction. It was the big cargo one, good. It would have at least six oxygen tanks.

Then it stopped. It was going thump-thump-thump and then nothing. I saw it autorotate about halfway to the ground, and then it stabilized and continued toward our position.

But the engine wasn't going; the blades weren't turning. It was evidently magicked the way our tank had been.

Whoopie and I lost interest in the chopper and stared back at the statues. They were a little more fascinating than anything I'd ever seen. When the helicopter landed next to us, we glanced at it, and then returned our attention to the three heads, ugly and compelling.

Mercer got out of the helicopter, followed by two Lalandians and another human, the newsie. Through her faceplate I could see she was beautiful. I looked back at the statues. I could hear Mercer breathing hard through the suit's external speakers.

"What is . . ." Mercer began. "What, um." He was staring at them, too.

One Lalandian was our translator, Moe. "I see it works on you, too," it said, lisping the esses and making a strange click-sound for the tees.

"What works?" the newsie mumbled.

"I told the Mercer. The three spirits."

"You said 'compelling.'" Mercer tried to look at the creature, but turned his attention back to the three.

"Are they not?" Mercer didn't answer.

I tried to concentrate. "How old are they?"

"Who knows? Old."

The newsie cleared her throat. "Do you know, build, what? Wait." You could hear her take a deep breath. "Do-you-know-who-built-them?"

Moe said something in his own language, and the other answered with a syllable. "They've always been. They're not like a building."

I tried to close my eyes but couldn't. It seemed to be getting worse. "Long? How long?"

"I'm sorry?" it said.

"How . . . long-does-it-last?" Whoopie said.

"It has lasted, how you calculate, thousands of thousands of days."

Both of the Lalandians flipped, their tail ends in the air. They stared at each other almost nose to nose. "Many died here, starve and thirst, before we learned the way."

"Die here," Mercer said. "People stand here till they die?"

"Not people; not humans. You are the first to be here."

"You didn't tell me!"

"No. If I had told you, you would not have brought us out here. These two, John and Whoopie, would have died if they didn't know the way. We like them."

"The way?" I said. "That's what you're doing now?"

"Yes," Moe said, and the two of them started moving away, stepping in unison.

"Wait!" Whoopie said. "We can't . . . we can't walk with our butts in the air!"

"I think it's not the way you do it," Moe said. "It's who you are with. This is my mate," and he said her name, which sounded like a digestive emanation.

"None of us have mates," Whoopie said. "Not here."

"It only has to be someone you are . . . attracted to? You concentrate on him. If he is also attracted to you, you can both walk away."

"Oh my God," Whoopie said, and half turned toward me. "You don't like women."

"I'm here," Mercer said, tattoos and jowls and all. Her complexion turned a little grey, and she shook her head slowly.

"Whoopie," I said softly. "Look at me." With a huge effort I stepped around, facing away from the statues. She took two steps toward me.

I stared into her blue eyes, so striking against her dark skin. Soft skin that I had to admit I'd wanted to touch. Her mouth opened slightly in an expression of surprise. "There's one woman I do like."

"You have a funny way of expressing it." Our faceplates clicked together, and she giggled and tried to put her arms around me. It was an awkward gesture in the clumsy suits, but unambiguous. The compulsion was suddenly gone, replaced by a more pleasant feeling. I returned her embrace, and we began to shuffle away.

"How far do we have to go?" I called to the Lalandians.

"Out of sight," Moe said.

"Wait!" the newsie shouted. "What the hell are we going to do?"

Good point. If I were in her position, I'd be doomed. "How much air do you have?" They each had four hours.

"We can't carry them," Whoopie said. "Maybe her, but not him."

"They might fight it, too." We whispered out a plan, trying to ignore Mercer's pleading with the woman, which would have been funny if it weren't a life-and-death situation.

We wound up waltzing back to the GPV, where we clumsily kicked open the front storage locker. There was a cable attached to a winch there. We managed to detach it and make a loop.

It served as a kind of lasso. We tried it on the woman first, looping it under her arms. She couldn't cooperate, but she didn't resist until we actually began to pull. She dug in and tried to stay, but after a couple of tugs she fell down. We dragged her as fast as we could, back down the rise that led to the ledge. After a couple of hundred meters, we reached the two Lalandians, and she said she was okay. Whoopie and I were free to look at something besides each other.

"You're a funny guy," she mumbled, looking at her feet.

"Just versatile," I said, though it was not something I'd known about myself. I felt intensely confused, but not unhappy.

"So now you go back and get Mr. Popularity?" the newsie said.

We looked at each other and laughed. "Don't even think it," Whoopie said.

He was a little more trouble, heavy and ornery. Once he was safe, we still had to go back and collect four air tanks.

Of course we still weren't completely out of trouble. The Lalandians said they thought our radios would work when we were sufficiently far away, but then they didn't really know anything about radios; they were no more or less magical than the statues.

We followed our GPV's tracks back to where we'd lost control of it, and a little way beyond, all of our radios started chattering. They had observed some of what was happening from orbit, and the commander of the Marine detachment was about to send an assault team after us, assuming the helicopter had been hijacked, though by whom and for what reason was not clear.

Whoopie and I were glad to leave the service the next year, resisting a fairly sizable reenlistment bonus in exchange for a degree of sanity. Ten years later, we're still together, with a normal kid and fairly normal jobs. As far as we know, the Lalande Effect is still a mystery.

In a universe full of mysteries, some of them wonderful.

(2004)

Heartwired

Margaret Stevenson walked up the two flights and came to a plain wooden door with the nameplate RELATIONSHIPS, LTD. She hesitated, then knocked. Someone buzzed her in.

She didn't know what to expect, but the simplicity surprised her: no receptionist, no outer office, no sign of a laboratory. Just a middle-aged man, conservative business suit, head fashionably shaved, sitting behind an uncluttered desk. He stood and offered his hand. "Mrs. Stevenson? I'm Dr. Damien."

She sat on the edge of the chair he offered.

"Our service is guaranteed," he said without preamble, "but it is neither inexpensive nor permanent."

"You wouldn't want it to be permanent," she said.

"No." He smiled. "Life would be pleasant, but neither of you would accomplish much." He reached into a drawer and pulled out a single sheet of paper and a pen. "Nevertheless, I must ask you to sign this waiver, which relieves our corporation of responsibility for anything you or he may do or say for the duration of the effect."

She picked up the waiver and scanned it. "When we talked on the phone, you said that there would be no physical danger and no lasting physical effect."

"That's part of the guarantee."

She put the paper down and picked up the pen, but hesitated. "How, exactly, does it work?"

He leaned back, lacing his fingers together over his abdomen, and looked directly at her. After a moment, he said, "The varieties of love are nearly infinite. Every person alive is theoretically able to love every other person alive, and in a variety of ways."

"Theoretically," she said.

"In our culture, love between a man and a woman normally goes through three stages: sexual attraction, romantic fascination, and then long-term bonding. Each of them is mediated by a distinct condition of brain chemistry.

"A person may have all three at once, with only one being dominant at any given time. Thus a man might be in love with his wife, and at the same time be infatuated with his mistress, and yet be instantly attracted to any stranger with appropriate physical characteristics."

"That's exactly—"

He held up a hand. "I don't need to know any more than you've told me. You've been married twenty-five years, you have an anniversary coming up . . . and you want it to be romantic."

"Yes." She didn't smile. "I know he's capable of romance."

"As are we all." He leaned forward and took two vials from the drawer, a blue one and a pink one. He looked at the blue one. "This is Formula One. It induces the first condition, sort of a Viagra for the mind."

She closed her eyes and shook her head, almost a shudder. "No. I want the second one."

"Formula Two." He slid the pink vial toward her. "You each take approximately half of this, while in each other's company, and for several days you will be in a state of mutual infatuation. You'll be like kids again."

She did smile at that. "Whether he knows he's taken it or not?"

"That's right. No placebo effect."

"And there is no Formula Three?"

"No. That takes time, and understanding, and a measure of luck." He shook his head ruefully and put the blue vial away. "But I think you have that already."

"We do. The old-married-couple kind."

"Now, the most effective way of administering the drug is through food or drink. You can put it in a favorite dish, one you're sure he'll finish, but only after it's been cooked. Above a hundred degrees Centigrade, the compound will decompose."

"I don't often cook. Could it be a bottle of wine?"

"If you each drink half, yes."

"I can force myself." She took up the pen and signed the waiver, then opened her clutch purse and counted out ten hundred-pound notes. "Half now, you said, and half upon satisfaction?"

"That's correct." He stood and offered his hand again. "Good luck, Mrs. Stevenson."

———

The reader may now imagine any one of nine permutations for this story's end. In the one the author prefers, they go to a romantic French restaurant, the lights low, the food wonderful, a bottle of good Bordeaux between them.

She excuses herself to go to the ladies' loo, the vial palmed, and drops her purse. When he leans over to pick it up, she empties the vial into the bottle of wine.

When she returns, she is careful to consume half of the remaining wine, which is not difficult. They are both in an expansive, loving mood, comrades these twenty-five years.

As they finish the bottle, she feels the emotion building in her, doubling and redoubling. She can see the effect on him, as well: his eyes wide and dilated, his face flushed. He loosens his tie as she pats perspiration from her forehead.

It's all but unbearable! She has to confess, so that he will know there's nothing physically wrong with him. She takes the empty pink vial from her purse and opens her mouth to explain—

He opens his hand and the empty blue vial drops to the table. He grabs the tablecloth . . .

———

They are released on their own recognizance once the magistrate understands the situation.

But they'll never be served in that restaurant again.

(2005)

Brochure

Who among us is not enriched by a return to our roots? Billions of people and others have gone to great expense and trouble to find their way back—not just to the place where they were born, but to the various worlds to which they can trace their distant ancestors and affines and primary clones.

But not one in a million has gone *all* the way back.

For many centuries since Old Earth was condemned as officially uninhabitable, it has been sitting unused, a reliquary for archaeologists and historians, and a "worst-case" scenario for terraformers—notoriously, the most unmarketable piece of real estate in Sirius Sector. Now, at the dawn of the 125th century, the Disney-Bertelsmann Consortium is proud to announce that Terra is returning to usefulness, ready to take a new and important place in the human and humanized universe.

(A "century" was once a significant fraction of the human life span, and for the first thirty or so twyops after the discovery of consciousness, centuries were used as a primary chronological unit.)

Beginning at midnight, 1021.9445 Two-Pop, with allowances for relativistic contraction (31 December 12400 Old Style), DBC will be offering monthlong Catastrophe Tours of Old Earth. A multigigacredit undertaking, Catastrophe Tours will thrill humans and others by re-creating the unique sequence of disasters that finally resulted in the Diaspora and Rebirth.

FEEL THE HORROR as trillions of anaerobic microorganisms strangle in an atmosphere that slowly poisons itself with oxygen! DBC's unique "Time Out" (∞) field compresses centuries into seconds, so that with your own eyes, or similar organs, you can watch the evolution of the tiny creatures who would become the rulers of a transformed planet.

SEE THE TERROR as a mighty asteroid crashes into the Yucatán Peninsula! With DBC's "Time Out" (∞) field, follow the shock wave in excruciating slow motion, as it circles the planet, destroying thousands of species and paving the way for the temporary primacy of mammals on Earth.

(DBC offers to sufficiently armored species the special option of "surfing" the shock wave; watching in real time as it pulverizes everything in its path. Individuals must be able to withstand impulses greater than one thousand gees and temperatures greater than molten iron.)

For a cooler time, FREEZE YOUR WHATEVER OFF as ice fields expand from the poles nearly to the equator! Again, DBC's "Time Out" (∞) field speeds up the process so that what was once an excruciating strangulation becomes a breathtaking crystalline transformation.

An optional winter sports package is available for suitably hardy species, although DBC takes no responsibility for your safety. Some of the animals are big, and all of them are hungry.

THRILL TO THE FOUR HORSEMEN Mortality Play as the "human" race, in its primal incarnation, is decimated time and again by war, pestilence, famine, and plague. They aren't real, of course, by modern standards, but their suffering is real enough!

LAUGH AT THE "FINAL TRUMP"—whose humorous double meaning will be explained—when a combination of ultimate weapons with greed finally ends war and suffering by eliminating nearly all potential victims! Customers with sufficiently developed appreciation of irony, and lovers of symmetry, will be amused by the rightness of the ultimate disappearance of oxygen, and the return of the planet to its original anaerobic owners.

Disclaimer: No advanced life-forms are harmed by this entertainment. The only creatures that still survive on Earth are a few hardy, rapidly mutating species, who thrive on disaster.

(2000)

Out of Phase

Trapped. From the waterfront bar to a crap game to a simpleminded ambush in a dead-end alley.

He didn't blame them for being angry. His pockets were stuffed with their money, greasy crumpled fives and tens. Two thousand and twenty of their hard-earned dollars, if his memory served him right. And of course it did.

They had supplied three sets of dice—two loaded, one shaved. All three were childishly easy to manipulate. He let them win each throw at first, and then less and less often. Finally, he tested their credulity and emptied their pockets, with ten sevens in a row.

That much had been easy. But now he was in a difficult position. Under the transparent pretext of finding a bigger game, the leader of the gang had steered him into this blind alley, where five others were hiding in ambush.

And now the six were joined in a line, advancing on him, pushing him toward the tall Hurricane fence that blocked the end of the alley.

Jeff started pacing them, walking backwards. Thirty seconds, give or take a little, before he would back into the fence and be caught. Thirty seconds objective . . .

Jeff froze and did a little trick with his brain. All the energy his strange body produced, except for that fraction needed to maintain human form, was channeled into heightening his sensory perceptions, accelerating his mental processes. He had to find a way out of this dilemma, without exposing his true nature.

The murderous sextet slowed down in Jeff's frozen eyes as the ratio of subjective to objective time flux increased arithmetically, geometrically, exponentially.

A drop of sweat rolled from the leader's brow, fell two feet in a fraction of a second, a foot in the next second, an inch in the next, a millimeter, a micron . . .

Now.

———

A pity he couldn't just kill them all, slowly, painfully. Terrible to have artistic responsibility stifled by practical obligations. Such a beautiful composition.

They were frozen in attitudes ranging from the leader's leering, sadistic anticipation of pleasure (dilettante!), to the little one's ill-concealed fear of pain, of inflicting pain, to Jimmy's unthinking, color-blinded compulsion to take apart, destroy . . . ah, Jimmy, slave of entropy, servant of disorder and chaos, I will make of you an epic, a saga.

I *would*, that is. I *could*.

But Llarvl said . . .

That snail. Insensitive brute.

Next time out I'll get a supervisor who can *understand*.

But next time out, I'll be too old.

Even now I can feel it.

Damn that snail!

———
• • •
———

The ship hovered above a South American plantation. People looked at it and saw only the sky beyond. Radar would never detect it. Only a voodoo priest, in a mushroom trance, felt its presence. He tried to verbalize and died of a cerebral occlusion.

Too quick. Artless.

Llarvl was talking to him "Bluntly, I wish we didn't have to use you, Braxn." His crude race communicated vocally, and the unmodulated, in-and-out-of-phase thought waves washed a gravelly ebb and flow of pain through Braxn's organ of communication. He stored the pain, low intensity that it was, for contemplation at a more satisfactory time.

He repeated: "If only we had brought someone else of your sort, besides your father, of course. Shape-changers are not such a rarity." He plucked out a cilium in frustration, but of course felt no pain. Braxn was too close; sucked it in.

"A G'drellian poet. A poet of pain. Of all the useless baggage to drag around on a survey expedition . . ." He sighed and ground his shell against the wall. "But we have no choice. Only two bipeds aboard the ship, and neither of them is even remotely mammalian. And the natives of this planet are acutely xenophobic. Hell, they're *omni*phobic. Even harder to take than you, worthy poet.

"But this is the biggest find of the whole trip! The crucial period of transition—they may be on the brink of civilization; still animals, but rapidly advancing. Think of it! In ten or twenty generations they'll be human, and seek us, as most do. We've met thousands of civilized races, more thousands of savage ones; but this is the first we've found in transition. Ethnology, alien psychology, everything"—he shuddered—"even your people's excuse for art, will benefit immeasurably."

Braxn made no comment. He hadn't bothered to form a speech organ for the interview. He knew Llarvl would do all the talking anyway.

But he had been studying, under stasis, for several hours. Knowing exactly what needed to be done, he let half his body disintegrate into its component parts and started to remold them.

First the skeleton, bone by thousandth bone; the internal organs, in logical order, glistening, throbbing, functioning; wet-red muscle, fat, connective tissue, derma, epidermis; smooth and olive, fingernails, hair, small mole on the left cheek.

Vocal cords, virgin, throb contralto: "Mammalian enough?"

"Speak Galactic!"

"I said, 'Mammalian enough?' I mean, would you like them bigger," she demonstrated, "or smaller?"

"How would I know?" snapped Llarvl, trying to hide his disgust. "Pick some sort of statistical mean."

Braxn picked a statistical mean between the October and the November Playmate of the Month.

With what he thought was detached objectivity, Llarvl said, "Ugly bunch of creatures, aren't they?" About one hundred million years ago, Llarvl's race had one natural enemy—a race of biped mammals.

With a silvery laugh, Braxn left to prepare for planetfall.

Braxn had studied the Earth and its people for some ten thousand hours, subjective time. She knew about clothes, she knew about sex, she knew about rape.

So she appeared on Earth, on a dirt road in South America, without a stitch. Without a blush. And her scholastic observations were confirmed, in the field, so to speak, in less than five minutes. She learned quite a bit the first time; less the second. The third time, well, she was merely bored.

She made him into a beautiful . . . poem?

She made him into a mouse-sized, shriveled brown husk, lying dead by the side of the road, his tiny features contorted with incredible agony.

She synthesized clothes, grey and dirty, and changed herself into an old, crippled hag. It was twenty minutes before she met another man, who . . .

Another dry husk.

Braxn was getting an interesting, if low, opinion of men, Bolivian farmers in particular; so she changed herself into one. The shoe on the other foot, she found, made things different, but not necessarily better. Well, she was gathering material. That's what Llarvl wanted.

She waited for a car to come by, reverted to the original voluptuous pattern, disposed of the driver when he stopped to investigate, took his form and his car, and started on her world tour.

Braxn tried to do everything and be everyone.

"He" was, in turn, doctor, lawyer, fencing coach, prostitute, auto racer, mountain climber, golf pro. He ran a pornography shop in Dallas, a hot dog stand at Coney Island, a death-sleep house in Peking, a Viennese coffeehouse, the museum at Dachau. He peddled Bibles and amulets, Fuller brushes and heroin. He was a society deb, a Bohemian poet, a member of Parliament, a *cul-de-jatte* in Monaco.

For operating expenses, when he needed small sums, he wove baskets, sold his body, dived for pennies, cast horoscopes.

Hustled pool.

The sweat drop had moved a hundredth of an inch. Must stop wasting time, but it's so hard to concentrate when it feels like you have all the time in the universe.

Braxn knew that he could remain in this state only a few more minutes (subjective) before he was stuck in it permanently. On the ship he could spend as much time as he wanted in mental acceleration, but here there was no apparatus to shock him out of it before trance set in. The trance would go on for more than a thousand years, such was his race's span of life. But to the six hoods he would age and die in a few seconds, reverting to his original form for an invisible nanosecond before dissolving into a small grey mound of dust.

He was seeing in the far infrared now, and definition was very poor. He switched to field recognition. The dull animals confronting him had dim red psionic envelopes, except for the one in agony, whose aura was bordered with coruscating violet flashes.

Electromagnetic. The ion fog around the leader's watch glowed pale blue. Leakage from the telephone and power lines made kaleidoscopic patterns in the sky. His back felt warm.

Warm?

He switched to visual again and searched the people's eyes for reflections. There—the little scared one—his eyes mirrored the fence, the Hurricane fence. Spaced with ceramic insulators . . .

He started to slow down his mind, speed up the world. The drop inched, fell to the ground with slow purpose; struck and flowered into tiny droplets.

Sound welled up around him.

"—eezuz Christ, he must be scared stiff!"

Braxn stumbled back toward the electrified fence, manufacturing adrenaline to substitute for his spent strength. His stomach knotted and flamed with impossible hunger. He received the pain and cherished it.

The leader advanced for the kill, bold and cocky, switchblade in his right hand, his left swinging a bicycle chain like a stubby lariat.

Braxn secreted a flesh-colored, rubbery coating over his body and, on top of that, a thin layer of saline mucus.

"Come, Retiarius!" he croaked.

"Huh?" The leader faltered in his advance, too late.

Braxn grabbed the bicycle chain and the fence simultaneously. There was a low, sixty-cycle hum, and the hood crumpled to the ground. He looped the chain around the scared one's neck and pulled him into the fence. Three to go.

The others had stopped, bewildered. Braxn, gaining strength at the expense of his temporary body, snatched the nearest one and hurled him into the fence. Another started to run, but Braxn used the chain as a bolo and brought him down. He dragged him screaming to the fence and shoved his face into it.

The only one left was Jimmy.

"Jimmy-baby!" The dim giant stood his ground, trying to understand what had happened, too sure of his own strength to be really afraid. He took a tentative step forward.

Now. The more fantastic, the better. He could do anything in front of this oaf.

Braxn kept the rubbery coating, but altered its reflective properties. Now it was flesh-colored to Jimmy. He kinked his hair, flattened his nose, broadened his lips, started to swell in height and breadth.

He was becoming a carbon copy of Jimmy—more true in the man's eyes than any photograph could be, for the specifications were coming from his own dim brain.

Thus the biceps were a bit larger, the face a little meaner, than a lying mirror would reflect. The teeth were square and white, and instead of the ugly mole on his cheek there was an incredibly virile scar that lanced down to his chin, catching the corner of his mouth in a perpetual arrogant sneer. He laughed, deep and hollow, mirthless.

"Whassa matter, you? Y'seen me before?"

Jimmy stood transfixed, a bewildered smile decorating his vacant face.

"Nuthin' faze you, Jim?" Braxn looked at the big Negro and cracked his knuckles. He let one finger fall off. It hit the ground, changed into a centipede, and scurried off. Jimmy followed its progress with awe. He looked up to his double again, smile gone, eyes narrowing.

Braxn dropped the patois. "Watch closely, Jimmy. You've got fear in you, like anybody else, and I think I know where to find it."

The strong, manly face blurred for an instant and came back into focus. The scar was a puffy infected seam that defiled a face no longer vigorous or handsome. It pulled down the lower lip to expose a yellow canine. The face was lined with a delicate tracery of worry and pain, the grooves growing deeper and more complex in front of Jimmy's horrified eyes.

The hair, sprinkled with grey, grew white and was gone except for a dirty stubble on the twisted, knobby chin. Face as body wasted away; wrinkled parchment stretched tight over a leering death mask.

Bloodshot eyes clot with rheum, cataracts cloud and blind them, the lids close and collapse inward and the body—real only in the minds of two disparate creatures—was mercifully dead.

The brown skin darkened further and released its life grip on the ancient body; the body puffed up again in macabre burlesque of its younger brawn. It lived again for a short time as maggots fed on its putrescence.

Then a dry, withered husk again, still standing upright; the last vestiges of skin and flesh sloughed off to reveal a brown-stained skeleton filled with nameless cobwebs. It collapsed with a splintering clatter.

On top of the pile of grey dust and bones, the yellow skull glared balefully at Jimmy for a long moment, and then, piece by piece, the whole grisly collection started to reassemble itself.

Before the clatter of Jimmy's footstep's had faded, his alter ego was whole and well again. The black-skin molecules had become charcoal-grey-Brooks-Brothers-suit molecules and Braxn, the very model of the young man on his way up.

Braxn scanned the still forms around him and found that they were all still unconscious. One, the little one, was dead. Probing further, Braxn dissolved a blood clot, patched an infarction, and shocked the still heart back into action. Pity to spoil good art—he liked the combination of cause and effect and dumb luck causing only the harmless one to die. Survival of the fittest, eugenics will out, and all that. With a mental shrug, Braxn walked off to find a cab.

* * *

"Oh, enter, by all means." Llarvl slipped into the Survey Chief's cabin with trepidation. He was in for a bad time.

The chief, who looked like a cross between a carrot and a praying mantis, got right to the point. "Llarvl, your reports stopped coming in several cycles ago. From this I infer that either a.) your scout is dead, not likely; b.) he got disgusted with your asinine questions, rather more likely; or c.) he went on one of his blasted binges and is busily turning the autochthones into quatrains and limericks. I find this last alternative the most probable, if the least palatable. He *is* a G'drellian, an adolescent at that. Do you know what that means?"

"Yes, sir, it means that he's in the aesthetic stage of . . ."

"It *means* he should have been locked up before we got within a parsec of this primitive world."

"But, sir, after his initial experiments he stopped killing them. Why, I *made* him stop. He might have drawn attention to himself."

"Your devotion to objectivity is most commendable."

"Thank you, sir."

"It shows that you know and appreciate the first rule of contact." He pressed a stud, and one wall became transparent. He gestured at the busy scene beneath them. "Are they aware of our presence?"

"Of course not, sir. That *is* the first law."

"Tell me, Llarvl. What sort of radiation would you suppose their eyes are sensitive to?"

The captain's addiction to obliqueness was most exasperating. "Well, sir, since their planet goes around a yellow star, their organs of vision are sensitive to a narrow band of radiation centered around the 'yellow' wavelengths."

The captain scraped his thorax with a claw. Llarvl interpreted this as applause. His race had forgotten sarcasm eons before the captain's had invented fire.

"You are a good study, Llarvl."

"Thank you, sir."

"So we make our ship transparent in these wavelengths, at great expenditure of power."

"Yes, sir. So the natives' development won't be influenced by premature knowledge of . . ."

". . . and with similar expenditure of power, we extend this transparency down into the longer wavelengths. Why do we do this, Llarvl?"

The little ethnologist was perplexed. Even the lowliest cabin boy could answer these questions.

"Why, of course, sir, it's to make the ship invisible to radar detection. Only it's not really invisible, it's just that the local implicit coefficient of absorption becomes asymptotic with . . ."

"Llarvl"—the captain sighed—"I learned one of those creatures' words the other day; and I suppose you've run into it now and then: catechism.

"Yes, sir." Llarvl squirmed.

"Now as far as I can tell, though I'm not a man of learning myself, this is a form of stylized debate; wherein one person asks a series of questions, whose answers are so simple that they brook no disagreement or misinterpretation. These answers, forced, as it were, upon the hapless interrogatee, lead to an inevitable conclusion, which gains a spurious validity through sheer tautological mass. Is that fairly accurate?"

Llarvl paused a second to retrieve the sentence's verbs, as the captain had mischievously, if appropriately, switched from English to Middle High German.

"Yes, sir, very accurate."

"Well, then"—the captain gave a gleaming metallic smile—"to borrow another of their delightfully savage concepts, the *coup de grâce*: How did we know that they had radar, long before we came into its range?"

"Radio broadcasts, sir, and television."

"Which means?"

"Mass communications, sir."

"Which means?"

"Sir, I'm aware of . . ."

"You're aware of the fact that our arty friend could gain control of this planetwide network, and, in a matter of seconds, destroy almost every intelligent being on the planet. Or worse, reduce them to gibbering animals. Or perhaps worse still, increase their understanding of themselves beyond the threshold . . ."

"Yes, sir." Llarvl could fill in the blanks.

"Then get out of here and let more capable minds deal with the situation."

"Yes, sir." The ethnologist started to scuttle toward the door.

"And Llarvl . . . remember that your captain, like most of the members of this expedition, normally communicates mind to mind, and can read your surface thoughts even when they are not verbalized."

"Yes, sir," he said meekly.

"Your captain may be a 'pompous martinet,' yes, but really, Llarvl: a 'vegetable that walks like a man'? Racism is, I think, singularly inappropriate in an ethnologist. Make an appointment with the psychiatric staff."

"Yes, sir."

"And on your way down, check at the galley and see if Troxl has a couple of years' work for you to do."

The captain watched the disconsolate creature scurry out, and settled down at his desk. He passed a claw over a photosensitive plate.

"Computer," he thought.

"Here, Captain."

"Where the hell is that G'drellian poet?"

The machine thought a low hum. "I can't find him. He must be generating a strong block. You know a G'drellian can synthesize 'dummy' thought waves exactly out of phase with his natural pattern, and by combining the two patterns . . ."

"How do you know he isn't just on the other side of the planet?" A computer will talk on one subject forever, if you let it.

"Using the planet's satellites as passive reflectors, I can cover 80 percent or more of the planet's surface, and by integrating the fringe effects from . . ."

"I believe you. Then tell me; where is his old goat of a father?"

"Meditating in the meat locker, in the form of a large stalagtite, as he has been, I might add, ever since you . . ."

"All right! Have Stores send me up a winter outfit. I'll have to go and try to blackmail him into telling me where his blasted progeny is."

Give me a thousand humorless ethnologists, thought the captain to himself; give me a thousand garrulous computers, but spare me the company of G'drellians. Even on G'drell, they confine the adolescents to one island, to work out their poetry on worms and insects and each other.

A survey expedition needs a G'drellian, of course; a mature one to solve problems beyond the scope of the computer, but —

Damn that Brohass! He must have known he was gravid when he volunteered for the trip. How do you deal with these creatures, who seem to live only to torment other people with their weird, inscrutable sense of humor? Brohass knew he would undergo fission, knew his offspring would reach adolescence in midvoyage, and probably contrived to send the ship to a planet where . . .

The captain's reverie was broken by the robot from Stores. "The clothing you requested, sir."

"Put it on the hook there." The robot did so and glided out of the room.

I should have had it delivered to the locker, thought the captain; clothing was tantamount to obscenity to many of the crew members, and one must maintain dignity . . .

"Yes, one must, mustn't one," thought the computer.

"Will you go do something useful?" The captain threw up a block in time to miss the reply. He jerked the clothes off the hook and strode out of his cabin, letting out occasional thoughts about the ancestry, mating habits, etc., of the machine that was the ship's true captain.

<hr/>

• • •

<hr/>

"Fasten your seat belts, please." The slender stewardess swayed down the aisle, past a young man with a handsome, placid face and a Brooks Brothers suit. "Landing at Kennedy International in three minutes."

Braxn did as told, shifting the heavy attaché case from his lap to the floor. Two hundred pounds of gold bullion would buy a great deal of prime time.

They landed uneventfully. Braxn took a helicopter to the Pan American Building, went down to the 131st floor, and into an office with gold leaf on the frosted-glass entrance, proclaiming Somebody, Somebody, and Somebody, Advertising Counselors.

He came out two hundred pounds lighter, having traded the gold for one minute of time, nine o'clock Saturday night (an hour away), on all of the major radio and television networks. A triumph of money over red tape, his commercial would be strictly live, with no chance of FCC interference. And his brand of soap would certainly make the world a cleaner place for a person to live in.

Alone.

• • •

The captain donned his thermal outerwear and entered the massive locker. Sure enough, there was a huge blue stalagtite suspended from the ceiling. He addressed it.

"Brohass," he thought obsequiously, "would you serve your captain?"

The huge icicle fell and splintered into several thousand pieces. They reassembled into a creature who looked rather like the captain.

"What would you do to me if I said 'no'?"

"That's ridiculous," said the captain, somewhat emboldened by facing a familiar shape. "No one can do anything to harm you."

"All right, that settled, will you please *go* and let me get back to my conversation."

Curious in spite of himself, the captain asked, "Who are you conversing with? You don't generally think with the other crew members."

"My father has found a particularly humorous ninth-order differential equation; he is explaining it to me, and I would like to devote all of my energy to understanding."

The captain shivered, not just from cold. Brohass's father had been dead for thirty years. But half of him would live as long as Brohass lived; a quarter would live as long as Braxn, and so on down the line. It was unsettling to more mortal beings that a G'drellian maintained an autonomous existence, within his descendants, for tens of thousands of years after physical death. Whether a G'drellian would ever die completely was problematical. None yet had.

"This won't take much of your time. I want you to locate Braxn and give him a message."

"Why can't you find him yourself?"

"It's a rather large planet, Brohass, and he's thrown up a strong communication block."

"We're on a planet? Which one?"

The captain thought a long string of figures. "They call it 'Earth.'"

"I'm afraid I'm unfamiliar with it. Please open your mind and let me extract the relevant details."

The captain did so, with chagrin. Brohass could easily have asked the computer, but his people were born voyeurs, and never would pass up a chance to probe another's mind.

"Interesting, savage—I can see why he was drawn to it. Incidentally, your treatment of Llarvl was shameful. In his place, *you* would have lost control of my son just as quickly.

"And your knowledge, captain, of the people on this planet, is encyclopedic, but imperfect. You misunderstand both catechism and tautology, you used the expression *coup de grâce* where *coup de théâtre* would have been more fitting, and your Middle German would send a Middle German into convulsions. Furthermore, you *are* an ambulatory vegetable.

"To your credit, however, you were correct in assessing my son's plans. He is now in possession of a minute of 'time,' as they say, on the planet's communications network.

"Funny idea, that; beings possessing time rather than the other way around . . ."

"Brohass!"

"Captain?"

"Aren't you going to do anything?"

"Interfere with my child's development?"

"He's going to *kill* several billion entities!"

"Yes . . . he probably is. Mammals, though. You have to admit they'd probably never make anything of themselves, anyhow."

"Brohass! You've got to stop him!"

"I'm pulling your spindly leg, captain. I'll talk to him. Just once, just once I would like to have a captain who could take a joke. You know, you vegetable people are unique in the civilized universe in your . . ."

"How much time do you have?"

"Oh, two thousand three hundred thirty-eight years, four days and . . ."

"No, no! How much time before Braxn gets on the air?"

"If Braxn got on the air, he would fall to the ground, even as you and I."

The captain made a strangling noise.

"Oh, don't bust a root. I have several seconds yet." Brohass reverted to his native formlessness and sent a piercing tendril of thought through his son's massive block.

"Braxn! This is your father. Will you slow down just a little bit?"

Braxn concentrated, and the bustling studio slowed down and froze into a tableau of suspended action. "Yes, Father. Is there something I can help you with?"

"Well, first, tell me what you're doing in a television studio."

"At the minute of maximum saturation, I'm going to broadcast the Vegan death-sign. That's all."

"That's all. You'll kill everybody."

"Well, not everybody. Just those who are watching television. Oh, yes, and I've worked out a phonetic equivalent for simultaneous radio transmission. Get a few more that way, if it works."

"Oh, I'm sure you can do it, son. But, Braxn, that's what I wanted to think to you about."

"You're going to try to think me out of it."

"Well, if you want to put it that way . . ."

"I bet that joke of a captain put you up to it."

"You know that that vegetable who walks like a man . . ."

"Hey; that's a good one, Father. When'd you—"

"—neither he nor anyone else on this tin can could make me do anything that I . . ." Brohass sighed. "Look, Braxn. You're poaching on a game preserve. Worse, shooting fish in a barrel. With a fission bomb, yet. How can you get any aesthetic satisfaction out of that?"

"Father, I know that quantity is no substitute for quality. But there are so *many* here!"

"—and you want to be poet laureate, right?" Brohass snorted mentally.

"There's something wrong in that? This will be the biggest epic since Jkdir exterminated the . . ."

"Braxn, Braxn; my son—you're temporizing. You know what's wrong, don't you? Surely you can feel it."

Braxn fell silent as he tried to think of a convincing counterargument. He knew what was coming.

"The fact is that you are maturing rapidly. It's time to put away your blocks—sure, you can go through with this trivial exercise. But you won't be poet laureate. You'll be dunce of the millennium, prize buffoon. You're too old for this nonsense anymore; I know it, you know it, and the whole race would know it eventually. You wouldn't be able to show your mind anywhere in the civilized universe."

He knew that his father was telling the truth. He had known for several days that he was ready for the next stage of development, but his judgment was blinded by the enormity of the canvas he had before him.

"Correct. The next stage awaits you, and I can assure you that it will be even more satisfying than the aesthetic. You have a nice planet here, and you might as well use it as the base of your operations. The captain is easily cowed—after I assure him that you no longer wish to, shall we say, immortalize these people in verse, he'll be only too glad to move on without you. We'll be back to pick you up in a century or so. Good-bye, son."

"Good-bye, Father."

The filament of the green light on the camera facing him was just starting to glow. He had something less than a hundredth of a second.

Extending his mental powers to the limit, he traced down every network and advertising executive who knew of the deal he had made. From the minds of hundreds of people he erased a million memories, substituting harmless ones. Two hundred pounds of gold disappeared back into thin air. Books were balanced.

Everyone in the studio had the same memory: Five minutes ago a police-escorted black limousine screeched to a halt out front, and this man, familiar face lined and pale with shock, stormed in with a covey of Secret Service men and commandeered the studio.

Braxn filled out his face and body with paunch. The man who owned this face died painlessly, as soon as Braxn had assimilated the contents of his brain. The body disappeared; his family and associates "remembered" that he was in New York for the week.

A finger of thought pushed into another man's heart and stopped it. Convincing—he was overworked and overweight, anyhow. But to be on the safe side, Braxn adjusted his catabolism to make it look as if he had died ten minutes earlier. He manufactured appropriate cover stories.

All this accomplished, Braxn let time resume its original rate of flow.

The light winked green. A voice offstage said, "Ladies and gentlemen"—what else could one say—"the, uh, vice president of the United States."

Braxn assumed a tragic and weary countenance. "It is my sad duty to inform the nation . . ."

Nine stages in the development of a G'drellian, from adolescence to voluntary termination.

The first stage is aesthetic, appreciation of an Art alien to any human, save a de Sade or a Hitler.

The second stage is power . . .

(1969)

Power Complex

The president of the United States was an alien.

Now it says right here in the Constitution—Article II, Section I, Paragraph 5—that "No person except a natural born citizen, or a citizen of the United States" can be president.

Ross Harriman was what they called him, and he let them call him that, as his own name had a decidedly foreign flavor to it.

They thought he had been born in Madison, Wisconsin, in 1945; and after a half century of reasonably honest living and politicking, had come to be vice president. On the death of President Ashby last week, Harriman became president.

In point of fact, Harriman, who called himself something that sounded like Braxn, was not born at all. He was budded about six months ago on an interstellar survey ship just out of the Vega system and eased into the first stage of maturity about a week before they got to Sol system and went in orbit around Earth.

The problem of Braxn's nationality would have interested quite a few people, as there was a pregnant woman on Tranquility Base, and there would no doubt soon be another on Tsiolkovski. The *jus sanguinis* argument was somewhat simplified in Braxn's case, as he had only one parent, his bud-father Brohass, who was a pure-"blooded" G'drellian. The *jus soli*, or place-of-birth, argument, however, was most complicated—Braxn was born somewhere on a non-Euclidian geodesic stretching from Vega to Earth through seventeen distinct (of course) dimensions.

Braxn could probably have made a point for claiming to be a citizen of either Vega system or Sol system. But the inhabitants of one were pre-literate gibbering savages, and the inhabitants of the other not much better, so he let the option go and remained a G'drellian.

Outside of legal fiction, of course, Braxn could only be a G'drellian, and would never wish to be anything else. The inhabitants of G'drell were about the most gifted creatures in the galaxy: the best shape-changers and quickest learners, very good philosophers and mathematicians, virtually (absolutely, they claimed) immortal, powerful telepaths, competent humorists, sometimes talented weather forecasters and inventors. A G'drellian invented the drive which all interstellar ships use—it has a moving part but doesn't wear out. Neither does it use anything so cumbersome as fuel. Every adult G'drellian understands the principle behind the drive. But they've never been able to explain it to anybody else, or so they claimed.

So at an age when a human child is barely able to focus his eyes and reach for a bottle, Braxn was teaching quantum mechanics to a class of Oxford upperclassmen. When that got dull, after one afternoon, he became a cutthroat bandit on the Trieste waterfront. That lasted almost a whole day. And so on.

In this first stage of his development, Braxn, like all G'drellian children, was after a variety of experiences. The one thing common to all of his little experiments in living was that he either inflicted or experienced pain or discomfort—from simple embarrassment to excruciating death. These sensations he arranged in a system of esthetics that was incomprehensible to mere humans.

To an adult G'drellian, however, they were on the order of finger paintings.

Throughout this childish stage the immature G'drellian is protected from real harm by a considerable ability to manipulate time and space, matter and energy, by purely mental effort. He could repair damaged tissues by transmutation of any available matter, or, if given warning, could simply teleport out of harm's way.

Learning about pain, Braxn destroyed several hundred sentient creatures. And in his lovable childlike way, he felt no more remorse for them than a zoologist feels for the specimens he dissects. Less.

There came a time when Braxn had reached a plateau of sophistication in dealing with the illusions (to him) of pain and death. At this point, he was ready to pass on to the next phase of his education—the manipulation of power.

At this particular moment of history (the last decade of the twentieth century), there were two laboratories of sufficient size and scope for Braxn to use as a base for his investigation of power. One was the fifty-two United (everybody keep a straight face) States of America and the other was what was loosely called "The Eastern Bloc": forty-nine or fifty (the number changed every now and then) countries and fractions of countries who at least paid lip service to the ideals of Marx and/or Mao and/or Lenin.

When Braxn had to make the decision, he was in New York, which is closer to Washington than Novymoscva. The effort required to teleport was more important to him than the miniscule difference he saw between communism and capitalism, between oriental inscrutability and occidental brashness. So he became president.

It took him less than a microsecond to elect himself.

First he killed the president by the simple expedient of wishing a heart attack on him. He disposed of the vice president after duplicating the latter's body and brain and was swished into office by the law of succession. The period of confusion after the president's death, Braxn reasoned, would cover any mistakes he might make out of inexperience. Besides, he had at his disposal all of the political acumen stored up in the former vice president's brain.

Unfortunately, as is often the case with vice presidents, this was not much. But the personal details were useful.

Braxn stumbled through the first hours of office, giving a convincing imitation of a bewildered Ross Harriman suddenly weighed down by grief and a crushing burden of responsibility. By 3:00 A.M., after numberless conferences, speeches, comfortings, and a few genuine surprises—China turned out not to have been behind the newest Pakistan conflict—the army of advisors, well-wishers, reporters, and opportunists let the new chief executive retire for the night.

———

Of course, being a G'drellian, Braxn needed sleep no more than he needed pollen or diesel fuel. But he was glad to get away from public scrutiny so he could relax in a more comfortable shape.

Once satisfied that his suite was free of bugs and that he was in no danger of sudden interruption, Braxn mentally reviewed the shapes available in his repertoire. He settled on being a Persian rug. He had been one before and enjoyed the musty taste and the soothing colors and the fuzzy feel of air washing over him. He set his mind in the Persian rug pattern and *pushed*.

Nothing happened.

He *pushed* in the old familiar way, but instead of rolling out on the floor in a riot of rich colors, he stayed the same shape and the air in front of him shimmered and solidified into an image of Brohass, his father. He held up a tentacle.

"Don't try to say anything, Braxn old bud, because the following is a recorded announcement, which you triggered by trying to change shape.

"I don't know how long you stayed in that dumpy Harriman body before you decided to slip into something more comfortable. Doesn't really make any difference. You're stuck with Harriman for a while, with one important exception.

"While you were an infant, in the aesthetic stage of your development, you did quite a bit of violence to your environment. This was necessary, for reasons that will one day be quite clear. While you were on your rampage, you had to be protected from the possible consequences of your violence—thus you were given certain of the powers of an adult G'drellian. These included, but were not limited to, transmutation, teleportation, telekinesis, and the ability to read and manipulate the minds of others. These powers are ebbing in you, and in a short while you will find you have none of them. With, as I said, one important exception."

"Dad—"

"There is, of course, a good reason for this. The present stage of your development involves the manipulation and appreciation of power, both in the abstract and the concrete, personal sense.

"Being virtually omnipotent, at least by the standards of this planet's aborigines, you could no more learn about power than one could learn to be a gourmet, continually gorged with food. Thus, for your own good, these powers have gone into a dormant cycle—they are there, but you can't use them.

"You will *never* get them back unless you successfully complete this phase of your growth. Don't—"

"The . . ."

"—interrupt. The exception. Most organisms who are relatively powerful, in relation to the challenges of their environment, are shielded from an appreciation of their power by an inability to directly feel the effects of wielding that power. You, son, won't be limited in this wise.

"The exact mechanism I am using to implement this, I will leave for you to discover. Just one word of warning.

"You can die here." The word "die" laid an icicle next to Braxn's spine. He had seen things die, hundreds of them, but it never occured to him that— "Yes, you can die. G'drellians *are* immortal, but only after the fourth phase. You may die, and to be perfectly frank, it would upset me no more than if you had aborted as a bud. You are still an imperfect, unformed organism.

"But you show promise, son. I'm looking forward to seeing your progress, some months or years from now, when the ship returns. Until then, learn and grow."

The image of the octopoid figure faded out, and the phone chimed. Braxn glared at it and savagely punched the FULL VIEW button.

"Mr. Harriman, sir, Senator Tweed, uh, he says he has to see you immediately."

"Damn it, Fred," Braxn exploded in a way that was calculated to show it was calculated, "tell Tweed he can see me in the morning. It's been too damn rough a day to sit up here and choke on that infernal cigar smoke!"

"Well, sir, not meaning to, appear to, uh—"

"*God* damn it, Fred, you never minced words with the Old Man. Show me the same consideration. Spit it out."

"Sir, Senator Tweed *is* the majority leader—"

"And I'm the minority president."

"Yes sir, and he's very conscious of protocol, or at least outward forms—you *must* see him before any other member of Congress—"

"Jesus Christ," Braxn slid the old-fashioned horn-rims off his face and knuckled an eye in a well-known gesture. "Mana."

"Sir?"

"I've got mana. Anthropologist's word." Fred looked at Braxn in a subtly different way. *You ignored old Harriman while you were Ashby's right hand; surprised to find out that he might be more than just a harmless puppet?* "He wants to be first in line while the magic's still fresh . . . or—something, I read about it somewhere." He looked thoughtfully at Fred's image. *He knows I'm backing off. Does he know I know he knows—* "Hell, send him in. Call the plant and have 'em turn the airco all the way up. Make it as noisy as possible." He grinned sweetly at the screen. "Maybe the old bastard forgot his hearing aid!"

A Secret Service man conspicuously armed with a high-energy laser tube opened the old thick oak door and ushered in Arthur Tweed. He was an old man who in the right light could have looked like an old woman, shoulder-length stringy silver hair against wrinkled, craggy features. But he never stood in the light that way, not in public, any more than he would allow his shoulders to slump or his gait to falter.

He strode through the door not at all like an octogenarian kept up six hours past his bedtime. He crinkled a smile at Braxn that lasted until the door whispered shut. Then eighty-three years dropped like a mantle on his frail body, and the grin became a winsome spinster's smile. Braxn ignored this as he had ignored the college-boy routine. Just another part of the act; the old man knew that not even politicians were immune to pity.

"Good of you to see me at this hour, Ross."

Braxn raised an eyebrow. Tweed had known Harriman for eighteen years, and had never used his first name before. He waited just a fraction of a second longer than was polite, before replying, "My pleasure . . . Senator. Please pull up a chair." Purely rhetorical; the man looked as if he couldn't pull up a weed without keeling over. He perched himself on the edge of an overstuffed chair to Braxn's right.

"I've already offered you my official condolences, but please let me . . ." Braxn cut him short with a wave of the hand.

"Skip it. You didn't like the old bastard any more than I did."

"Uh . . . huh!" The senator slid back in the chair. "Huh! Huh!" It took Braxn a second to realize he was laughing. "That's what I like— huh! huh!—a man who speaks his mind—huh!"

Just what you don't like, you old trickster. Tweed reached into his vest pocket and extracted a short black Toscani cigar. The sulphurous vapor from the wooden match was balm to the nose, compared to what followed. Providentially, the airco cut in at just the right moment, loudly. Tweed looked at him through narrowed eyes.

"Can't be feeling the heat, Ross?"

"No." He pushed an immaculate silver ashtray across the desk to Tweed. "Just a social visit, or . . ."

"Mnh. Well. No. That is. A bill, the Selective Service renewal, Ashby was going to sign it tomorrow . . ."

"Really?" Braxn smiled.

"*Yes*, damn it!" He shot forward and leaned back again. "He . . . we talked him into it."

"*Tripling* the draft call?"

"Of course. If we don't, West Pakistan's bound to go under."

"Bullshit." Braxn took a cigarette out of the ornate case on the desk and waved it alight. "Ashby never believed that. If you believe it, you've been listening to your own speeches too uncritically."

"Huh! Nevertheless. I think you may want to reevaluate your own position, Ross."

"Cut-and-dried, Arthur. It's another Vietnam. We're pulling out as soon as—"

"Ross, you were a military man, weren't you?"

"You know damn well I was. West Point."

"Oh yes. Purple Heart. Silver Star. For bravery. *In* Vietnam."

"That's right."

"You were a real crackerjack combat officer."

"Get to the point."

"Yes." He blew a leisurely ring that floated a foot and broke up in the air currents. "A man has to have military service before he can even think of running for office. It's the American way. Combat, preferably. I was in Korea, of course."

"Of course."

"Yes. A, uh, man came to my office tonight. With a series of photographs."

"How intriguing."

"The man was your copilot, Ross. On the mission when your helicopter went down and you won the Silver Star, defending it."

"And?"

"The photographs indicate that you were not shot down, but were grounded by mechanical failure. And that your wound was self-inflicted."

"Get out."

"Now just a minute, Ross . . . I don't for a second believe . . ."

"Out."

"I was just . . ."

"Listen, Tweed. Any military doctor can look at that wound, even after thirty years, and tell you that it came from a .50-caliber machine-gun bullet. A man can no more 'self-inflict' a .50-caliber wound than he can shoot himself with a howitzer."

"Ross, Ross, I *know* that. I told you, I don't for a moment believe him. But you know as well as I that once the accusation is made, any—"

"What do you, does he, want?"

"He's a fanatic militarist, Ross. He wants you to sign the draft bill."

Braxn laughed, one short bark. "I'll think about it. Tell him I'll think about it." He rose and glowered down at the little old man. "It was a pleasure speaking to you, Senator."

Tweed levered himself out of the chair and laid the smoldering cigar in the little silver bowl. "I hope you'll . . . be in touch with me."

"Good-bye, Senator." When the man had disappeared behind the mass of oak, Braxn punched the phone. "What do we have on the old Tweed?"

"Almost nothing, sir. He has a mistress, but he's had her for thirty years. She's ugly as sin."

"That'd gain him more votes than it'd cost him. Put some of the staff to work on him. Then you get some sleep. I'm going to do the same."

Braxn left his office and, accompanied by the ubiquitous Secret Service guard (not even the White House was considered safe, after the audacious Agnew assassination attempt), retired to his personal quarters. At least the guard stayed outside the door.

"Thanks, Roger." He closed the door gently so as not to awaken Harriman's wife, presumably asleep in the master bedroom. They wouldn't be moving upstairs to the executive apartments, of course, until Elizabeth Ashby had moved out.

He went into the study and sat at the huge desk. The antique overstuffed swivel chair groaned and squeaked a pleasant fugue of old bearings and new leather. He started at the top of the big stack of papers in the IN box.

"Ross?" Standing in the door, in the half-light from the desk lamp, Linda Harriman looked almost pretty. She stepped closer, and the illusion vanished.

"Morning, darling." Braxn watched her approach, putting on Harriman's smile of genuine affection. Thirty years before, people had whispered "political suicide" when Ross went out and married the homeliest girl in Madison society. But the years that had blunted the fragile beauty of her contemporaries had been kind to her, softening planes and juts into gentle curves.

"You shouldn't be up." She took the cigarette from his mouth and laid it in the ashtray. "It's going to be a hard day tomor—today."

"I got a nap earlier." He half turned back to the desk.

She tugged a curl of his hair. "Liar." She smiled. "Try to get some sleep before you jump into the fray again."

"Okay." He chuckled and squeezed her hand good-bye.

When she was gone, Braxn started to riffle through the hundred pages of synopses Ashby's staff had prepared: summations of bills, personal requests, appointments, all needing action in the next week or ten days. Luckily, Harriman had a reputation for being a fast reader (with regrettably shallow comprehension).

In a half hour he had memorized the synopses and decided on tentative courses of action. He reached for the phone and tapped out Fred's combination.

An unfamiliar face peered out at him and seemed about to phrase a nasty comment, then saw who he was. "Oh! Mr. President—Let me get Mr. Aller."

"Don't wake him up on my account. Just checking on something."

"He's awake, sir, I'll get him." After a minute, Fred Aller filled the screen with his unkempt sparse white hair, salt-and-pepper stubble, and piercing grey eyes.

"Damn it, Fred, I told you to get some—"

"I know, sir. Something big came up."

"About what?"

"Might be something we can use on Tweed."

"And I wasn't called?" Braxn growled.

"Mr. President, I thought you were asleep, too; you need it as much as I do." His eyes clicked that quarter of an inch out of line that showed he was staring at the screen. "Maybe you didn't need it as much. Still have TV makeup on?"

"No, hell no. Got some uppers from the doc. What's the scoop on Tweed?"

"Same thing he wants to pull on you. Of course we have spies—"

"What!"

"—not in your office, sir, in his. Holographic infrared laser bug, with its optical locus in the glass over an eighteenth-century painting that he thinks has been hanging in front of his desk since the Roosevelt administration. The first, Teddy."

"Same thing . . . his war record?"

"That's right, sir, but in his case it's more or less true. He was commanding a frontline infantry platoon in Korea, and got fragged, hit by a—"

"—grenade, yeah, I know what 'fragged' means."

"Rifle grenade. Anyhow, he was evacuated to the rear for treatment, where they taped him up and *then* sent him to a hospital in Japan, diagnosing neuresthenia."

"Shell shock?"

"Right. That could cost him a few vet votes right there. Lots of people think that shell shock is just a nice word for cowardice. This isn't on his medical record, by the way: he covered his tracks pretty well.

"But that's not half of it. He lounged around Japan for a month—whoring it up—and then got transferred back Stateside, where he got a Pentagon job, reporting to Walter Reed once a month for examination."

"I don't know," Braxn said, "it's good stuff, but it's too diffuse. An awful lot of people wouldn't see anything particularly reprehensible about any of that."

"Ah, sir, but the clincher . . . the way he got out of Japan. The second-in-command in that hospital was his *uncle*—whom he later got appointed to a high place in the Public Health Service . . . a post he held for only three months before being discharged for gross incompetence and dishonesty."

"Hah!" Braxn slapped a palm on the desk. "That might do it. Can you get me a package of evidence? Xeroxes and such, before noon?"

"Already made up, sir."

"Wonderful. Call the old bastard's secretary and tell him . . . the president desires the senator's company for lunch tomorrow."

———————

The White House chef had prepared a mild Chicken Kiev, in deference to Tweed's aging entrails, which the two men washed down with a white Bordeaux, 1983; a good year, but not quite as good as the most junior senator would have gotten, had he belonged to the president's party.

Both men were in formal black, as, soon after lunch, they would have to get into their respective black limousines and join the cortege bearing Ashby's remains down Pennsylvania Avenue Mall (cleared of pedestrian traffic for the occasion), twisting around to the Lincoln Memorial, and across the bridge to Arlington Cemetery. Braxn reflected that Tweed wouldn't have any trouble looking appropriately sad, once he saw the contents of the manila folder sitting in the backseat of his waiting limousine.

After lunch Braxn escorted Tweed to the secluded atrium that Ashby had had built, just after his inauguration. It was a pleasant green place to go to relax and was incidentally filled with disruptors and noise generators in every frequency, making it theoretically impossible to bug. The slight hiss and hum where the little watchdogs spilled over into audible frequencies was nicely masked by a soothing miniature waterfall.

Braxn produced brandy and offered the old man a Havana.

"No thanks, Ross. I used to smoke 'em—before you were getting started in politics . . . but Castro. Had to lose my taste for them." He accepted the brandy, though. Braxn lit up a Havana and Tweed ignited a black-rope Toscani.

"A pity to rush a good cigar," Braxn said, taking a deep puff and letting the smoke trickle out of one corner of his mouth. "But I suppose we have some business."

"Business, yes. Yes."

"Your, uh, your photographer friend . . ."

"Yes, hum, he says he's having bids submitted by TIME/LIFE and—"

"Damn!" Braxn jumped out of his chair.

"Calm down, calm down, Ross. You aren't implicated yet. All they know is that it's a scandal involving a 'high government official.' They'll be bidding against the *Times*, WPI, and Scanlan Syndicate."

"And if I comply with your—*his* demand, what does he tell the firm that wins the bid?"

Tweed chuckled, a sound somewhere between a death rattle and a pant. "Don't worry, Ross. We have an alternate—"

"To throw to the wolves. So another Liberal Democrat, instead of me, gets the gaff. An unattractive dilemma, Senator."

"No, no, no . . . *not* a Lib, Ross. One of my own."

"Not *Sam*!"

Tweed answered with a death's-head grin wreathed in grey smoke.

"God! You are—you're the most . . ." Braxn sat down and puffed his cigar back to life. He spun around to stare at the manicured lawn and smile.

He came back around, puffing away, staring at Tweed through a blue fragrant nimbus . . . then he jerked the cigar out of his mouth and laughed, one explosive cough. Tweed jumped.

"Tweed. Oh, Tweed . . . I don't know how many really big mistakes you've made in your career, but this one has got to take the prize. You don't lean on a *president*, not this way."

"On the contrary," he said quietly, "I've made a career of it."

"There's a manila folder on the seat of your limousine. You go down and read it, and then decide whether you—"

Tweed smiled. "Bribery?"

"What a coarse word. No, no money involved, just a trade. Something similar to the commodity you hold."

"Impossible, Ross. There's no way for you to trade your political future for mine. I won't be running next—"

"Bullshit. You've been threatening to retire for twenty years. You could no more stop running than an animal caught in a forest fire."

Tweed finished off his brandy in one gulp and stood up. "You young . . . look, Ross, you're out of your *league*. Why don't you just—"

"Why don't *you* just read the damn thing, and we'll talk tomorrow."

"Maybe. I may have an appointment with the ladies and gentlemen of the press." Tweed turned on his heel and stalked out.

Braxn felt a coldness in the pit of his stomach and was startled to realize that it was fear. He'd never been afraid before, and now he was afraid of this decrepit old man. He swallowed some brandy, and the fire fed the coldness.

"Mr. President?"

"Ah, come in, Fred. Have a drink: it's going to be a long ride."

"Thank you, sir." He poured a couple of fingers and sat in the chair Tweed had just vacated. "I've made up a list, here, you'll want to check." He handed Braxn a sheet of paper. "No banquet, of course, after the state funeral. These are just the people we're inviting to dinner."

Braxn tried to study the list, the representatives of some twenty countries. But he couldn't seem to focus his mind on it. Suddenly the world *split*, and he knew what his father had been talking about. It was as if only the left side of his body was here in the atrium, talking to Fred—and the right side was walking down the steps in front of the White House, inhabiting an old body full of aches and twinges, looking at the cherry blossoms with a rheumy, jaundiced eye, nose and mouth full of bitter Toscani cigar smoke.

That young upstart that pup Harriman he thinks he can scare me, ME for shit's sake I ought to—

Chauffeur opening rear door, touching his cap. "Thank you, Harry."

"God knows I'd like to invite Ramos," Fred was saying. "But if Cuba comes, then what are we going to do with Germany? And if Germany and Cuba get together—"

Tweed took a deep sniff of the musty felt smell and was grateful for the thousandth time that he had had that nasty fake leather upholstery taken out. The crisp yellow envelope violated the grey fuzzy calm of the interior. *I'm not going to look at it. I'm not. We'll just go ahead the way we planned and the devil take . . .*

"I don't see why we can't have two dinners," Braxn said, "or a tea and a dinner. They're all political realists, they can appreciate the situation we're in—look, we can have a tea right after the funeral, with Cuba, Britain, Canada—here, the ones I put an X by, the ones who are unequivocally—"

Tweed picked up the envelope and broke the plain
seal on it. The engine started. *Hell, might as well see—*

> "—and then the dinner would be a formal proto-
> col affair; the unaligned, the sceptical, the ones who
> are outright enemies—"

> "You know, sir, it's unconventional, but it might
> just—"

*—my uncle Jesus Christ I didn't know he was my
wife's uncle until after I got out and he came and told
me he'd blow it all up if I didn't give him—*

> "I know it'd work, God damn it . . . sorry, Fred,
> I've been under a terrific—"

*—and he fucked up and I had to get rid of, quick
court-martial, insane asylum, covered my tracks so
well hadn't even thought GOD MY ARM—*"Harry!—
Stop—my—arm—"

> "What's wrong, sir, what—"
> "Nothing, Fred, a, a . . . spasm, in my arm,
> fatigue—"

Paralyzing pain creeping past the shoulder, crawling *Oh Jesus Jesus God another heart attack stop
smoking fuck drinking Jesus fuck* "God—Harry—"

> "Sir, you better let me get the doctor, you look
> positively—"
> "No sweat, Fred, I, it's happened a dozen times . . .
> before. Doctor said, he said—" *Cold fist—*

Cold fist in the middle of his chest, icicle spike nail-
ing him to the seat *When did I lie down?* Fuzzy grey

felt ceiling looks on fire, sky-rockets, stars exploding
there, door slams, door opens, Harry unclips tie and
opens front of shirt.

"What is it, sir, another attack?"

> "Maybe I'd better lay, lie down for just a
> minute . . . Harry, uh, Fred, would you come, go
> please and get me a glass of water—"

*Oh God sweet Jesus God the pain fuck pain
Mother* "Mother."

The left-hand side of the universe welled up crimson and faded out
and Braxn sat up, rubbing his arm, then kneading his chest. Fred came
tearing in with a glass.

"It's all right, Fred." Braxn held up a hand, waving, refusing the water. "As I say, it's happened—"

Fred's sleeve buzzed. He set the water down and talked to his
bracelet. "I'm busy, damn it. What? What!"

"Tweed's had a heart attack. Right in front here."

Braxn didn't move a muscle. "Get that dossier."

"God, that's right, that's what—" He spoke to the bracelet. "Manila
folder on the seat of Tweed's car. Get it if you have to steal the *car*."

"Guess I'd better go down. Make sure the area's cordoned off. And
have somebody grind out a short speech for me to give to the reporters."

"Guess Tweed's too old for another transplant, or an implant."

"Probably."

"Hopefully," Braxn whispered. The two of them went off to the elevator.

Other members of the cortege were standing around, buzzing in a
low murmur, mostly French and English. It looked like a theatre-of-the-
absurd funeral, as if a state figure had died on cue, rows of black limousines and platoons of mourning dignitaries already arranged for; or as if
the body had been on the way to its hearse and had been carelessly
dropped on the sidewalk.

The only man not dressed in black was the White House physician,
wearing a conservative twill one-piece.

"Any chance?"

"No, Mr. President. He's been on borrowed time and tissue for fifteen years. At his age, with his habits, it should have worn out long ago."

Braxn looked at the old man he had just fought with and killed. Greyish skin, blue lips pulled over a wide, surprised yawn, eyes red slits where somebody had closed them, hands dead white claws on scrawny exposed chest. Smell of cheap cigar smoke competing with embarrassing evidence of final peristaltic surge.

A ground-car ambulance pulled up over the front lawn and, after they had taken the body away, Braxn got into the limousine directly behind the hearse and led the cortege off across the river.

––––––

Not too surprisingly, even after a lifetime of scrupulous churchgoing, Tweed admitted in his will to having always been an atheist and wanting no part of the barbaric practice of having his bones planted in magic ground. Instead he preferred antiseptic cremation, his ashes to be scattered in the Potomac by his lifelong companion, chauffeur, manservant, Harry Doyle.

Unfortunately, the Environmental Services Commission pointed out, that was against the law. Gently but firmly they reminded Tweed's estate that the Potomac is not the Ganges. At least not in Washington.

Of course, the Potomac also runs through Maryland on its course to the Chesapeake Bay. So Harry was dispatched with the urn to nearby Charles County, to go to Indian Rock and scatter Tweed's ashes not so very far downstream from his beloved Capitol.

(Harry, who had always hated the old man's guts, got as far as Waldorf, where he flushed the ashes down a toilet in the men's room of a Gulf station. Then he drove on to Indian Rock and drank a six-pack while watching the Potomac flow sluggishly by.)

––––––

After the funeral, the tea went quite well, and even the dinner afterwards, with all the enemies and switch-hitters and unaligned, was only occasionally marred by dignified argument, strained through the teeth.

During the tea, the West Pakistani ambassador implored Harriman to sign the draft bill. Braxn told him bluntly that the bill in its present form, tripling the draft call, would just put too severe a strain on American manpower. Besides, it would be political suicide—a Gallup taken the week before showed that 49 percent of Americans wanted us to withdraw the seventy-five thousand advisors already there . . . and 11 percent wanted us to throw our support over to East Pakistan and Tibet!

Accordingly, the next day Braxn vetoed the bill, as almost everybody but Tweed had expected. The veto was quietly but with lightning speed approved by the House.

A compromise bill, doubling the draft quotas, had been introduced earlier. It fizzled out by negative vote on engrossment and third reading.

The third and final draft bill was a complicated mess of new apportionment criteria, full of obfuscatory rhetoric and pages of figures. But if you sat down with a blue pencil and an adding machine, you'd find it boiled down to another compromise: essentially providing for a 1997 draft call of eighty thousand rather than sixty thousand.

"This bill here," Braxn said, tapping the folder with a pencil, "is about the best you're going to get out of this Congress. I'm not sure that you'll get even this, though. I, for one, need more justification than Pakistan."

"You've *got* it, sir!" The man who said it was a burly, bullet-headed, handsome soldier with so many stars on his shoulders that he only had to call one man "sir."

"The general's right, Mr. President." The secretary of defense was a slim, bland-looking man who looked as if he might be an insurance executive or the dean of a small law school. In fact, he had been both. He had never been a soldier. "We realize you probably haven't had time to read the entire report—"

"I've read it. I'm still not convinced."

"Well, it convinced *me*," the secretary said. "We've got to think of the future—"

"—in the light of the 1995 Geneva Accords, especially," the general interrupted. "We're going to be headed for bad trouble if—"

"Wait, wait." Braxn waved a hand at both of them. "I understand the argument. You assume there will never be another Two Chinas War; that the Geneva Accords forbidding the use of . . . certain weapons in international conflict, make our technologically oriented weaponry obsolete. That we ought to retool downwards, train fewer troops—*no* troops, eventually—in the use of sophisticated weapons . . . in effect, 'detoxify' our military back to, hell, all the way back to World War II—"

"Sir, that's not it at all. Begging your pardon, sir . . . we plan to keep the modern weaponry in the event that the Accords break down. But more and more men have to be allotted to Infantry and regular Artillery if we're going to be able to cope with these brushfire wars with backw— with small countries."

"And to be baldly frank about it," the secretary said, "we need Pakistan, we need to not only stay there but increase our involvement, up to fourfold—otherwise, we aren't going to have the nucleus of experienced noncoms and officers we'll need if a *real* war comes up."

"I think you're both unduly alarmed. General, approximately what percentage of our forces are combat veterans?"

"Well . . . sir, damn it, nearly sixty percent. But that doesn't mean anything! Most of those men got their combat experience in the Two Chinas War . . . and you can't blame them for thinking in terms of nukes and lasers and disruptors—not bullets and C-6 and lousy five-hundred-pound bombs! They're just plain ill equipped—"

"Then haul 'em back and teach 'em, General! Oh hell"—he tossed the pencil down on the bill—"I assume you both know that this bill is going to pass, whether I veto it or not. By the narrowest of margins, of course; the Senate wants a stronger military, but it doesn't want to seem hawkish to the folks at home. To the people who are going to *be* drafted.

"I'll think about it. I'll *keep* thinking about it. Gentlemen, I hate to seem abrupt, but we just aren't getting anywhere. Besides, I have some very important handshaking to do . . ."

Both men rose. "Well, thank you for taking time out to listen to us, sir," the general said. "Again, I urge you to—"

Braxn cut him short with a wave and a smile. "I may. Good-bye."

As soon as the men disappeared, Braxn took out his pen and looked at the document, without seeing it. *I wonder if either of them understands,* he thought, *that it's not really a military question at all.* It had to do with his relations with Congress. Since he had gotten to the presidency essentially through a governorship, he didn't have many real friends in the legislature.

There would be a lot of noise when the public deciphered it and found out that it meant larger draft calls all around. He could make them pass it over his veto, and come out lily white. Or he could sign the damn thing and take some of the heat off Congress.

The old-fashioned flat-nib fountain pen scratched loudly on the parchment. *Anachronisms*, Braxn thought, and he punched his secretary's desk.

"Send in the Scouts and feed me the speech." He turned up the gain slightly on the receiver built into his eyeglass frame. This was the last formal appointment of the day.

It took about ten minutes, parroting the words and actions that his secretary fed to him. Twelve Eagle Scouts in full regalia, their scoutmaster in mufti. Braxn amused himself by imagining what the spindly little man would look like in the traditional shorts and Teddy Roosevelt hat. From Harriman's memory he dragged up a half-century-old image of Wally Cox playing *Mr. Peepers.*

After they had gone, he punched Fred's combination.

"Oh, hello, sir."

Without preamble: "I signed the goddamn thing."

Fred nodded soberly. "No choice, really. Let's hope Congress handles it right."

"Well, I'm knocking off for the night." Braxn reached for the switch.

"Oh wait, sir, just a second . . . one thing, uh, might not be too . . . uh."

"Well?"

"Well, one of my men got the dossier on Tweed, slipped it off the backseat while everybody was watching the old man die. I checked it over, though, and the last page is missing. A Xerox of an old photostat of his Army psychiatric profile."

"You rechecked the car?"

"We took the damn thing apart, couple of hours ago. No sign."

"I guess we just sit tight. What about the helicopter pilot?"

"No sweat . . . we found him this morning, holed up in a fleabag hotel in Philadelphia. He was scared, sir, really almost out of his mind. He was sure we'd killed Tweed and were after him. We persuaded him otherwise."

"Not too convincingly, I hope."

"Naturally not. We also purchased the article from him, just as a safeguard. Ten thousand bucks—about a tenth what he was going to get.

Took the money out of the party's campaign fund, chalked it up to 'ghost writing.' "

"All this and a lousy sense of humor, too?"

"Yes, sir," Fred said with a little smile.

After they punched off, Braxn returned the draft bill to its black leather case and gave it to his secretary on the way out, instructing that a courier run it over to the Speaker's office. He knew the old geezer wouldn't be there this late, though: probably over at II Caesars', soaking his brain.

His wife met him at the door, trading him a glass of chilled Tavel '88 for his coat. They were still in the downstairs apartments; Braxn knew that Harriman would have wanted to stay there as long as possible.

"Hard day today, dear?"

"Hmmph." He sat down in an overstuffed recliner. "Conferences. Audiences. Two secretaries, four congressmen, a general, two ambassadors, and twelve Macedonians in full battle array. Actually, I think they were Boy Scouts."

"Sounds exciting."

"It was, I must have woken up twice. What's for dinner?"

"Oh, Rosa's fixed something special." She spoke into her watch. "Rosa? When may dinner be served?"

She put the watch up to her ear for a second. "Whenever you're ready."

He had just picked up a copy of the *Star* nitefax. He refolded it along the original crease and tossed it down. "Let's go. I could eat a can of dog food."

"That won't be necessary for a while, I hope."

While they were walking to the dining room, the world shimmered and split again.

It was dawn in Barisal, the least likely time for an ambush; besides, most of the fighting had been confined to the city proper, so the Americans *we'd been so glad to get out of those damn streets let the gooks fight for their own city said this goddamn jungle patrol was gonna be a picnic fuck you colonel wish you were here with*

"Is something wrong, dear?"

"No, I—I just stood up too fast. Drinking too much coffee, not enough sleep, I guess."

Jesus Christ did we ever walk into it a classic box from three sides heavy .65-calibers sprayed tiny anvils, making a ceiling of lead never more than three feet off the ground. Men were screaming in pain to the left and right, and just ahead Lieutenant Hernadez was thrashing around in the elephant grass with a sucking chest wound.

"Excellent," Braxn said, chewing mechanically. "Tell Rosa I wouldn't trade her for a Lib majority in Congress."

"Take it easy, Lieutenant—I SAID TAKE IT EASY— there." He got the man to stop squirming long enough to stop the sucking with the plastic from the bandage wrapper *Okay, now the bastard's chest might fill up with blood, but at least I won't have to listen to that horrible shhik-shhik*

"Well, if any Dixiecrats come by, we'll tell 'em it's *Taiwan* duck . . ."

Now the bandage over the plastic and run the strings behind the lieutenant's back *God they could have made these strings a little longer where the fuck is a medic* "Ten-six! Ten-six, God damn it!" Down flat, burst of fire seeking out his voice . . .

"You really *do* seem distracted, dear."
Braxn took off his glasses and polished them with his napkin.
"Really nothing, Linda . . . but I wonder if you could get me an aspirin?"

Captain Brown crawled up through the fog and smoke, moving on his back like a swimmer trying to do a backstroke with his shoulders. "Fall back and get me a medic." His left hand cradled his right, blood gushing from the stump of a thumb. "Hernandez KIA?"

Jesus Christ by the book all the way "Not yet, sir. Just about."

"No wonder we haven't got any fuckin' support, get me his maps, they're in the right leg pocket. Then GET THAT—"

> Braxn stared at a forkful of rice, then levered it into his mouth. "Oh, thank you, dear." He washed the tablets down with ice water.

The medic was in a shallow depression behind a stand of saplings, bandaging a tall Negro flanker whose lower jaw was shot off, thick blood drooling around the pressure bandages.

"Where you hit?"

"Not me, Doc—the captain's bleeding pretty bad from a hand wound and Lieutenant Hernandez got shot in the chest—"

"Motherfucker musta stood up."

A burst of machine-gun fire rattled through the saplings. The medic cringed down, but the big Negro just lay there, eyes filming.

"Fuck 'em both." Doc pushed a morph-plex syrrette through the dying man's sleeve, blood-slick and shiny. "Let's go."

> "—just a combination of a headache and a stomach ache."
>
> "Maybe you shouldn't be taking aspirin, then."

An artillery spotting round popped maybe two hundred meters away. The captain was lying beside a dead radioman, talking on the horn while he looked at the map. "Drop one-zero-zero and fire for effect, one-two over and out." He hung up. "You fellas better dig a deep hole. That's comin' in right on top—"

> "Oh, *now* look! You've got that orange sauce on your sleeve. Let me take some cold water to it before it sets."
> She patted at the stain. "Are you *sure* you're feeling all right?" she asked nonsensically.

O God Jesus Christ make it stop the ground fell away and slapped back, twice, four times *so loud* so loud you didn't hear it with your ears but with your lungs and guts and bones and balls—

> Braxn rose from the table and supported himself with a hand on the chair back. "I'm going to lie down for a while."
> "Let me rub your back."
> "No!—no, finish supper; I'll just lie on the couch for a—"

"TEN-SIX—DOC! Ten-six?" *Look at Doc over there without a head he was always a lazy fucker wonder why it doesn't hurt I always thought it'd hurt so much but you can't put 'em back in they keep slipping around and between your fingers almost no blood . . .*

> "I better call Dr. Dean . . ." "No, no, it'll . . . pass." "I'll call him."

so weak Holy Mother Mary of NO I'm not gonna I don't wanna God God it hurts now maybe if I put some dirt on my hands they'll "TEN-SIX" *they won't slide out so easy and I can stuff Holy Mary God of shit fuck it hurts, what's the use*

Not as easy as it used to be but the involuntary
telepathic link helps—push . . .

Braxn was lying in a stand of elephant grass, grey-white smoke clinging to the ground around him, the soft yammer of battle sounds whispering in his ears. Bluish bloody intestines spilled out of a foot-wide wound
in his abdomen.

He willed his hands sterile and carefully rolled the guts back into the
abdominal cavity. With his fingers and his mind he debrided the wound
and held the bloody lips of it together for a few seconds until it healed.
He cleansed himself internally against peritonitis, then fixed the broken
eardrums.

Now for the larger problem. Could he still affect the rate of subjective time flow? He concentrated on slowing down this little corner of the
universe. Make it lazy. Come on, Reality, isn't it hard to support a war? So
much noise and confusion. Easier just to let it all . . . run . . . down . . .

A machine gun about ten meters in front of him was firing at a hysterical cyclic rate—*dubdubdubdub*—belt-fed, rattling off a thousand
rounds per minute. After about a hundred rounds it started to signal the
results of Braxn's efforts.

Dubdubdub-dub-dub—dub—dub, doob, doob . . . doomb. Thud.

Braxn stood up and walked through the grass to the machine gun. He
was halfway there when a bullet crawled through the air toward him,
moving with the speed of an overfed bumblebee. He caught it between
two fingers and lifted it—it was heavy with fossilized kinetic energy—and
released it above his head. It glided on.

Another bullet was just coming out of the muzzle when he reached the
gun. He swatted the slug into the ground. No wonder the gunner had been
firing hysterically—a piece of shrapnel had hit him in the face and spirited
away his nose and half a cheek. He was in profound shock and dying.

Braxn took the necessary elements from nearby plants and insects
and a pinch of dirt and fashioned the man a new nose and cheek. Of
course, it wouldn't look exactly like his old one, but at least it was consistent with Pakistani somatypes.

The gunner's loader, the man who keeps the belt of ammunition feeding into the gun, was splayed out behind the gun with an ugly wound in
his throat. Braxn healed the hole in the trachea, closed the wound in the

neck and teleported the inspirated blood out of the man's lungs. Then he visualized the bolt of the machine gun and made the firing pin disappear. He started to wander through the battle area.

A hand grenade hung suspended in midair, imperceptibly rotating and falling. Braxn plucked it out of the air and unscrewed the top assembly. He snapped off the blasting cap inside, then screwed the thing back together, its firing mechanism useless, and let it continue on its way.

In all, Braxn deactivated sixty-three rifles and pistols and four machine guns, eighty-one hand grenades and two grenade launchers. He revived seven dead men and healed the wounds of fourteen others. One person, who had evidently sustained a direct hit from an artillery shell, he had to leave the way he found him—there were no pieces larger than a section of liver to work with. The all-important brain cells were disorganized and scattered over an eight-meter radius.

Braxn returned the soldier's body to the stand of elephant grass. As a final touch he cleaned all of the blood and smoke from the battleground. He lay down and pushed his persona back into Harriman's body.

> *Ugh, what's that? Of course, of course, this body's dead—or at least not alive. It wasn't alive when I took it over. What a bother ... have to reprogram the brain—*

So quiet all of a sudden ... wait! I was hurt, I was dying but O God, sweet Jesus ...

> *... must be careful in the future—if I leave this body again—not to leave it too long. It'll start to smell ...*

"I know, goddamn it. I can't get my fifty to work either—stop those bastards—"

Braxn stood up Harriman's body and experimentally wiggled it around and stretched. Everything seemed to be in order, but numb and aching. He shuffled back into the living room. Linda was sitting on the couch, not-reading a magazine.

"Oh, Ross. You look just awful—come and put your head in my lap."

Braxn did so to humor her, found it felt good. "I checked on you while you were sleeping. You looked so—well, so *bad* that I called Dr. Dean."

"Ah. Well. It's not that serious. But—" Braxn closed his eyes and shook his head. "The bill."

"What was that, dear?" Linda was stroking his forehead with a cold wet napkin.

"The draft bill. I shouldn't have let it through."

"Didn't you veto it day before yesterday?"

"No. That was a different one, not as sneaky. This one just reapportions various Selective Service districts."

"But it still increases the draft?"

"Overall, yes. Lowers it in some noisy districts."

Linda dipped the cloth in water again. "Well, I agree. You should've vetoed it—those poor boys. Don't you remember how you felt after . . ."

"Yes. Yes, I remember." He squeezed a hand over his eyes. "Maybe that's what's bothering me—

"But it's more complicated than that. God, if I vetoed that bill, I'd get nothing, absolutely nothing out of this Congress, for the rest of my term."

"Still—"

"Oh, still, *still*! You know a president can't do everything the way he wants, the way he knows is right, thinks is right . . ."

Dr. Dean came in, followed by a worried-looking Rosa.

"Good evening, Linda, Rosa." He moved a fake Italian Provincial chair over beside the couch and sat down. "What seems to be the trouble?"

"It's nothing, Joe. Really noth—"

"He almost fainted at the dinner table, Doctor."

"Linda . . . just a combination of not enough sleep and too much coffee."

"Well, roll up a sleeve and I'll check the hydraulic pressure."

He wrapped a slender tape around Braxn's arm and checked the numbers on a digital readout in his bag. "Normal . . . pulse a little low, but nothing to worry about. Here." He peered at Braxn's retina with an ophthalmoscope. "Yes, it definitely is an eye." He checked knee-jerk reflexes and took a blood sample.

"I'll put this juice in the Mixmaster upstairs. Don't expect to find anything, though—I think your diagnosis was correct, Dr. Harriman. Fatigue, possible overdose of caffeine and nicotine. Taking any other drugs?"

"Not since those uppers you gave me last week."

"Last ones you'll get, too. Take my advice, Ross, and try to cool it a little bit. These eighteen-hour days are driving your staff crazy.

"Besides, you're stuck with this job for three more years, maybe even seven. You won't even make it to election year unless you slow down."

"Hogwash. I've never felt better in my life."

"I wish you knew how many people have said that to doctors and keeled over dead the next day. Your *mind* thrives on work, Ross, but your carcass is just the same old kind of inefficient machine everybody trundles around in."

"All right, Joe, I'll think about it. I promise to sleep until six at least one day a week."

"Well, that's something. Linda, make him stick to it."

———

The next morning Braxn found a note on his desk. "Urgent you get in touch soonest—Fred." He punched him up.

"What's happening, Fred?"

"God, sir, too much. You know that missing page from the dossier on Tweed?"

"You found it?"

"It found us. In the person of Harry Doyle, Tweed's old chauffeur."

"Surely he can't—"

"Reconstruct what happened? I'm afraid he did—he knew that Tweed was reading something that we gave him when he keeled over. Afterwards, he tried to find it, and only came up with the one page. It'd slipped down behind the seat."

"Did he say what he's going to do with it?"

"That's the scary part. He said he's 'not decided,' but he didn't even hint about taking a bribe. He's a nut, sir, and he hates politicians—when he came to Washington twenty-five years ago, he had political ambitions, took a job driving for Tweed just to tide himself over. Never got any further."

"What a mess." Braxn stared into space for a second, then lit a cigarette. "Any ideas?"

"Yes, sir . . . we could pull Tweed's trick on him."

"Have him committed? Fred, this isn't 1958. Where would you find an old-fashioned insane asylum?"

"Switzerland. Bern. *Institut fur die Sinngesundheit*—it's a fairly new spa, but it has old-fashioned ideas, like total isolation of the patient until he gets well."

"And in Doyle's case . . ."

"Poor fellow. Really a deep-rooted psychosis."

"I don't really like it, Fred. It sounds awful Big Brotherish."

"I don't care for it either. But the alternative, the scandal, would be worse. For you *and* the country."

"We can't just make a person drop out of sight like that."

"Ah, but we can, we can—all above-board and legal. His mother—she's sixty-eight, lives in Sioux Falls and is also a nut—would be glad to sign the papers. She tried to get him committed eight years ago."

"You're thorough, Fred."

"Yes. We have a man in Sioux Falls with a Swiss passport and a German accent. He has contracts that give very attractive terms, and will meet Mrs. Doyle at a Woman's Club meeting tomorrow.

"We also took the liberty of putting a little something in Doyle's dinner last night. He'll be heavily sedated for twelve hours yet."

"And if I give the word, he wakes up in Switzerland."

"That's correct."

"What about the rest of his family?"

"Never married, father dead. No friends to speak of."

"Okay, go ahead. But I have a feeling it's going to backfire."

Fred shrugged. "It seems tight enough. And it's reasonably humane. In the Eastern Bloc they'd just haul him in and shoot him."

"Well, in China maybe." Braxn took off his glasses and rubbed his eyes. "In Russia, they'd bundle him up and send him off to an asylum in Siberia. Or maybe Switzerland."

———

For the next week, Braxn went through the "double living" phenomenon daily.

As the result of a bill approving the (further) devaluation of American currency, he lived with a Mexican peasant who had been making a marginal income by working in the United States, in Laredo, and crossing the border back home each night. When the value of the dollar went down, he found that his paycheck was no longer a marginal living for his family, even before his pay was cut to preserve his employer's profits.

To cut down on federal welfare expenses, he made it impossible for a family to get food stamps if the total family income was over $3,000 per adult member, $1,000 per child, per year. For a conventional family of two adults and two children, this was quite equitable, the average U.S. family income being $14,000 per year. But Braxn had to live through the situation as it presented itself to a forty-eight-year old ex-prostitute trying to support four children, working as a custodian for a mere $7,500 per year. She solved her problem by teaching her twelve-year-old daughter the trade, and finding old gentlemen who were willing to pay a premium for her services.

A bill terminating funds for a space research project made him share the body of a chemist, who couldn't tell his wife he'd been fired and instead filled a five-hundred-milliliter flask with sulphuric acid and managed to get most of it down before he died.

A presidential directive ordering energy workers in New York City back to work resulted in a brief but bloody shoot-out between the "loaf-ins" and the National Guard. Braxn got to "be" a teenage Guardsman who didn't want to live through an emasculating pistol wound in the groin, but did.

"All right, Secretary, you have about ten minutes. Start talking."

The secretary of defense lowered himself into a chair, gently. Probably has hemorrhoids, Braxn reflected. "Mr. President, my staff informed me this morning of a very disturbing rumor—"

"It's true."

"Uh. Ha-ha. No, this . . . can't be true, sir. The rumor concerns a pullout of—"

"Yes." Braxn slid a five-page report across his large desk. "When I heard you were coming, I had a copy of this made up, for your enlightenment."

The secretary picked it up and glanced at it. "We—we're ending our involvement in Pakistan?

"Correct."

"But only—only a couple of weeks ago you—"

"I reluctantly signed a bill raising the draft call by a third . . . but not for the defense of a corrupt Asian regime, and *not* so your brass hats could get experience, playing soldier with the lives of American boys. It was to enhance our *overall* defense posture. Emphasis on *defense*. Of America, not Zambia or Paraguay or West Pakistan.

The Secretary shook his head slowly from side to side. "This is a . . . a horrible mistake."

"No, this is the avoidance of a mistake. Almost every other country learned its lesson from the Two Chinas War. Time we figured it out, too."

Shimmer and split.

"Is it all right if I have another drink?"

"All right, Doyle, but I wish you'd try to get some sleep after we change at Kennedy."

"You know better than that, Mr. Secretary. China will be anything but happy—they don't . . .

"I'm sorry, sir, but we'll be in our landing pattern in a couple of minutes."

"That's all right, thank you anyhow, miss." *Got to make my plane at Kennedy. I'll never get another chance at that bastard Harriman . . .*

"What are you going to do with all that Army back in the States?" The secretary was up and pacing around. "Mark my words, without an actual war—"

He can't clap me away in some loony bin fulla Krauts
"Smooth landing."
"*Ja.*"

"There's no need discussing it. It's an executive order, and you may either comply or submit your resignation.

Short one that time, Braxn thought.

"I'm not resigning. Not yet. I wouldn't give you the satisfaction."

"Don't misunderstand me, Mr. Secretary," Braxn said smoothly. "I want you to stay on; I need men of experience, discernment. But I'm not

Ashby, I have different ideas, some of which fall into your sphere." Braxn stood. "I'm only telling you that you can learn to work with me if you wish. Otherwise . . . the sooner you leave, the less prejudicial it will be to your political future."

"Hmn. You'll be hearing from me, Mr. Harriman."

"I expect to," Braxn said to the man's back.

As soon as he'd left, Braxn stabbed a finger at the phone.

"Good afternoon, sir. What can I do for you?"

"Got to speak to Mr. Allen. Very urgent."

"Mr. Allen's in Chicago. I'll see if I can patch through, and punch you back. All right, sir?"

"That's fine." *Got to find out what's with Doyle,* Braxn thought. *How'd he get out, what's he doing in an airplane with a German—*

Fred's image on the screen was poor quality and rolling. "Yes, sir. What can I do for you?"

"Are you alone?"

"No, sir, I'm in the mayor's limousine, with the mayor. Would you like to say hello to him?"

"Certainly." *Hell no.* "Hi, Phil, how're things going?"

"Well, Mr. President"—a flaccid fat face came on the screen—"not too well, actually. The labor situation . . ."

"Ah, yes, I know—that's why I sent you Fred: he's my right arm and half my brain . . . in fact, I can't get along without him. Can you spare him for about an hour?"

"Sure thing, sir. Fred, we're pretty near your hotel—just take you there?"

"Fine," Fred said off camera.

"While I've got your ear, Mr. President . . ." Braxn half listened to the old criminal for a couple of minutes. Then he said good-bye, and seconds later Fred punched him from the scrambled phone in his hotel room.

"What's up, sir? World War III?"

"Not till next week. Fred . . . do you believe in intuition?"

"Hmm . . . neutral. What, get a flash about something?"

"Something like that. Maybe I'm all wet: if so, I apologize for tearing you away from your pleasant companions—"

"*Quite* all right, sir. I was getting cancer of the eardrum."

"Anyhow, it's about Doyle."

"Doyle?"

"Tweed's man—when did you last get a report on him?"

"Oh, that, that—haven't heard anything since they told me he was definitely safe behind bars. Sir, you shouldn't worry. He's lost to the world until—"

"Still, I *am* worried. Take long to check?"

"Well, we shouldn't, we ought not to call the hospital directly. I'll have my German call his mother first."

"Do what you think best, Fred. But do it *quick*. I can't explain, I have this feeling . . ."

"Of course, sir." The tone of his voice might have said *been waiting for the old man to crack, knew he couldn't keep it up*. "We'll get right on it and punch you back."

"Fine. I'll be here in my office."

After a few minutes, Fred came back on the screen, worried and perplexed. "Sir, it's . . . it's *weird*. We tried to get his mother and patched into a funeral home. She died yesterday. My man's calling—wait—"

Fred looked to his left, evidently at another screen. "God. But they had orders . . ."

"Has it left . . . *arrived*! Check the roster for the connecting flight—right."

He produced a handkerchief and passed it over his face. "Sir, if you ever get another flash . . . *listen* to it!

"His mother died and the *Institut* decided that he was stable enough to attend the funeral, take care of the arrangements. They sent him to the U.S., accompanied by an aide.

"The plane—God!—the plane landed twenty minutes ago, in New York . . . my man's checking their connecting flight; it's pretty close—"

He looked away again. "Shit!" Braxn was amused in spite of himself. Fred was always so cool. "The flight to Sioux City has loaded. They aren't aboard. I'll keep checking."

"Okay. I'll keep worrying. Punch me as soon as anything happens."

Split again:

Sorry to have to do that, he never hurt me he was always very nice. The jet noise tripled and he tilted back, airborne.

*No need to worry. He's just one man. I have a
whole army—*

*Always wanted a Weatherby, buy me a Weatherby
and a twenty-power Bushnell get Harriman, haven't
killed a man since all those gooks always wanted to kill
a man on my own . . .*

"Fred! What is it?" He looked pale. "Haven't found Doyle . . . but
the police found his aide, Herr Kramer, his . . . his throat cut with a razor
blade, in a stall in the—"

*Except for Kramer, sorry about him, he was al-
ways very nice.* "Gin and tonic, please." *Weird machine, cheaper than girls, cheap bastard airline.*

"—get hold of yourself! Get somebody to make an
anonymous punch to the police, say he saw a man with
blood—"

*They'll never catch me, have it all figured out good
thing the old bitch died yeah they'll catch me after I do
it I'll be famous they'll hang me but . . .*

"—and check the shuttle, the Washington shuttle,
he wouldn't stay around the airport very long after—"

*bigger than Khan bigger than Oswald, bigger than
Booth! That damn plastic won't do any good against a
.658 Magnum shatter it get Harriman's ass . . .*

"Sir, the shuttles out of Kennedy are fully automated, have been for
two months. Not even a stewardess, just an automated drink tray. All we
can do is watch at Dulles."

"Okay, set it up. Better watch Friendship, too."

"Right." Fred punched off, and Braxn tried to concentrate on the thick
report in front of him. *Just let them take care of it, what can one man do . . .*

. . . to optimize all the ecological parameters, this committee decided to situate the experimental station first in a northern temperate rural region, then in a northern temperate urban region, then in . . .

"Mr. President?"

Braxn opened the line to his secretary. "Yes?"

"Your appointment with the secretary of the interior is in ten minutes. Do you want—"

"No, God, I haven't even finished reading the report. Look, Joyce, something has come up in Chicago, something important. I'm staying in touch with Mr. Aller, trying to keep on top of it. Cancel all of today's appointments, tell 'em I'm not in." He stood up. "In fact, I won't *be* in. I'll be in my office downstairs."

"All right, sir."

Linda wasn't home; she was spending a few days in Wisconsin, visiting grandchildren. That simplified matters. Braxn told the guard at the door that he wasn't in, to anybody.

He poured a glass of wine and sat down at his desk, with the thick report unopened in front of him. He stared at the phone for a few seconds, then punched Fred.

"No word yet, sir."

"Nothing?"

"No, sir . . . The New York State Police are doing a dragnet through Kennedy; all the airlines have his description. If he hasn't left Kennedy, we'll find him soon."

"We? Or the police?"

"Sir?"

"If *they* catch him, they'll hold him for homicide. He's sure to shoot off his mouth. Headlines for a week."

"God." Fred slapped himself twice. "I'm not *thinking*."

"That's all right, Fred. It was my idea to feed his description to them—what do you think the chances are, that he's still there?"

"Well, it gets more likely with every shuttle that lands without him. Another hour at the most, and we'll be able to say he definitely didn't—"

"Didn't take the shuttle to Washington or Baltimore. Could he have slipped on another automated flight, before his description went out?"

"Oh . . . it's possible, sure. The other shuttles are, let's see, Newark,

Boston, Hartford, Philadelphia . . . might be one to Richmond, but I doubt—"

"Any way to check them?"

"Newark and Boston, at least, probably have a camera like the one at Kennedy, takes pictures of all the people debarking from the shuttle, because of smuggling. I'll check all of them."

"Well, that's a start. Go ahead."

Harry Doyle got off the shuttle in Boston and took a limousine to Cambridge. Knowing he couldn't buy a gun with Kramer's identification, he waited in a bar until he saw a man about his own age, height, and build. He followed the man home to his apartment, rang the bell and when the man came to the door he slashed out with the razor blade—a technique he had practiced mentally a thousand times in Switzerland—pushed the silently dying man inside, was grateful that he was alone, took the man's wallet and memorized his new date of birth and social security number, locked the door behind him, and went on down the street.

He called five sporting goods stores before he found one that had the Weatherby .658 Magnum, an elephant gun that was really overkill, even for elephants. He said he would be there in half an hour, and he was.

It took over half of Kramer's American money to buy the Weatherby and the scope and a box of shells, and shooter's mitts and a case. When it was all wrapped in brown paper and tied up in a bundle, it didn't look like a gun at all. He left it in a locker in the bus station and went to the public library and looked in Section B of the Sunday *Washington Post* and found the president's itinerary for the week. He would be present at the dedication of the new Peace Corps school in Columbia, just outside of Washington. So would Harry.

————

. . . our conclusions were that this type of EE station has an optimum balancing effect in areas on the periphery of an urban heat sink, but closer to the urban mass or more . . .

The phone chimed, and Braxn punched up visual.

"Well, sir, we got results from Newark and Hartford. The camera at Boston had been taken down for repairs. Nobody who looks like Doyle—"

"Is there any way to check Boston?"

"Ah . . . not after four hours, sir. Big town with efficient rapid transit in and out. If he slipped through the Boston shuttle while the camera was down—it's fixed now—then he could be anywhere on the East Coast."

"That might make it easier . . . in a way, not to find him, but . . . I guess we can assume he's 'crossed state lines pursuant to the commission of a—'"

"The CBI?"

"Yes. Might as well, we have more control over them than the—contact the CBI, tell them all you have that's, uh, safe . . . tell them that he's a murderer and is suspected of high treason, is armed and dangerous."

"And to not risk trying to take him alive."

Braxn chewed a nail, thoughtfully. "I think that would be best. Tell the director he can call me for verification. Patch him through your scrambler, though."

"Sir, um, maybe you ought not to make any public appearances until we nail him. He is desperate and—"

"Yes, I had planned to curtail my . . . peregrinations—I'll keep the appointments, I think, that are in the Washington area . . . trust the Secret Service and the CBI. I've got two speeches in town this week, and that one out in Columbia. The rest I'll postpone or arrange for a substitute. (To look more like a traveler, Harry bought an old suitcase in a pawnshop and filled it with newspapers and a supply of sandwich material. Then he went to a trucking firm and traded a twenty-dollar bill for a lift to Baltimore on a big ground effect rig.)

"Joyce, who wrote this Peace Corps speech?"

Her image went off the screen for a second. "Philip O'Hara, that new boy from Yale."

"Tell him I need a rewrite—the language is fine, continue in that vein, but I want more about 'the administration's changing priorities'—and I want it worded so that young people will think the Peace Corps will be an alternative to the draft, but older people will see it as just a two-year deferment."

"Uh, sir—do you know which it'll be?"

"Probably something in between. Certainly, someone who takes two consecutive tours will be too old for the draft when he gets out."

"But you don't want that said explicitly."

"God, no!" A chime rang. "Have to punch off, Joyce." Braxn turned to the other phone. "What is it, Fred?"

"Just a progress report. Little enough progress—but we do have the CBI'S full cooperation: the director assigned a force of 122 men to the job."

"Good." Harriman had always been leery of the amount of power the CBI had accumulated—it had too much in the beginning, when they'd merged the old CIA and FBI—but now Braxn was glad to have it on his side. Most C-men came close to the public image of the remorseless, thorough, incorruptible automaton. There wasn't a man on earth who could elude 122 of them for any length of time.

(Harry got off at a trucker's stop just north of the outer Beltway, and hitched a ride to Towson. Five minutes after he left, two expressionless men in charcoal coveralls came into the truck stop with a description of him. Luckily, the waitress on duty didn't like cops.)

The week before, Braxn had approved a measure closing some loopholes in the Capital Gains Law. This week, he lived through a businessman fidgeting, worrying, waiting for his secretary to go to lunch, whereupon he opened a window, stepped out and jumped 1,236 feet into a busy Dallas intersection. An experienced skydiver, he aimed for a red convertible, and just missed.

(Harry rented a car in Towson and drove out in the country. At an old stone quarry, he paced off a hundred meters and fired twelve rounds, getting the scope zeroed in. The gun was awesomely loud. He was gone fifteen minutes before the Towson police came to investigate. They figured it was just some kids raising hell.)

"It was just an unfortunate coincidence," Fred was saying. "The man was a dead ringer for Harry Doyle, and when the agent stopped him and identified himself, the fool tried to run."

"And he burned him down on a busy corner in Philadelphia," Braxn said.

"That's right, sir. We're lucky he was a good shot. An amateur with one of those pocket lasers would have killed a dozen innocent bystanders."

"Instead of just one."

(Harry drove to Columbia and located the new Peace Corps school. He noted the position of the bleachers and drove on by without stopping.

Tommy Tommy Tommy Tommy you wasn't doin' nothin' just walkin' down the street an' they shot you for doin' nothin'

God damn you Tommy, woman. I Harry Doyle why can't I control this damn thing

"He look just like he sleepin'."

———

(He parked the car in the lot behind an all-night drugstore and waited in the car until it got dark. Then he stepped inside briefly to puchase a small flashlight and a bottle of fingernail enamel. Outside, he painted the button lens of the flashlight with enamel, so it gave off a very faint red glow.

(Harry sneaked across a golf course to a water tower: naturally, the highest point around. He found a breach in the chain-link fence and wiggled through with rifle and lunch bag.

(Using his light sparingly, Harry found the steps that spiraled up the side of the tower and tiptoed up. At the top, there was a catwalk that went all the way around the tank. From one point, he could look down and see the pattern of light and shadow that was the new school and bleachers, not half a mile away.

(On the far side of the catwalk there was a small toolshed, unlocked. Harry went in, closed the door behind him, and lay down. So he'd carried the hacksaw blade all the way up there for nothing. Who would've guessed he could be so lucky?)

"I don't believe in luck, Fred. There's incompetence somewhere along the line."

"They're doing all they can, sir. The director assigned another team of a hundred men to the hunt."

"Maybe he's lying low for a while, on the West Coast or in Canada—"

"We have men there, and there. And in Mexico and Cuba."

(When Harry woke up there was a bright line of sunlight shining under the door. He ate a stale sandwich and sipped water from his canteen.)

"Almost time to go, sir."

"Thank you, Joyce. You watch on the video and feed me the speech after I finish my opening remarks." Braxn heard the helicopters' engines starting, up on the roof.

(He heard the footsteps long before the man got to the shed. When the door opened, Harry was standing to one side, rifle held horizontal, butt first, at eye level. The Secret Service man stepped in, laser in one hand and flashlight in the other, and probably never felt the twenty-pound club strike his temple.

(Harry considered taking the laser, but decided it wasn't accurate enough at eight hundred meters. He heard the flutter of helicopters and crawled over the agent's body and started around the catwalk.)

Braxn looked out the window and saw the green field, the school, the bleachers slowly rising up to meet him. He mentally reviewed his opening comments, going over the ways they would have to be modified, according to who had or had not shown up.

(He crawled to his firing position just about the same time as the helicopters touched down. He put a handful of ammunition in front of him—the rifle worked like a double-barreled shotgun; had to be reloaded after every second shot—and focused the scope on the door of the white helicopter.)

Braxn let two of the Secret Service men precede him then he stepped out onto the grass, Fred following, and then:

There's the bastard! Breathe and hold. now ...
Crosshairs swing over and settle on Harriman's chest—

Braxn jumped to the right. *No place to hide ...*
swing to the left

Aim for the top of his head not sure how far it'll drop but only has to hit his big toe and he's dead—

"You can die here," Father said. Jump left—

Swing right—

Fred caught Braxn's arm in a tight grip. "Sir! What's—"

now

Let go! "Let go!"

The force of the bullet jerked Braxn from Fred's grip and his right shoulder erupted in a spray of blood and muscle and bone splinters. His body turned a half somersault in the air and he landed heavily just as the sound of the shot, rolling thunder, reached him, and then the second bullet dug a furrow inches from his head.

Lasers crackled and filled the air with ozone while the doctor did something to stop the cephalic and brachial veins and the brachial artery from oozing and spurting blood. He gave a quick injection for shock just as the third bullet whirred by his ear. The fourth hit a Secret Service man in the abdomen, killing him.

Harry chambered two more shells and smiled. They might get him sooner or later but, as he had figured, those lasers just wouldn't reach. He put his eye to the scope and looked for a good target.

He didn't see the Secret Service agent who had jumped back in the helicopter, as he poked the snout of a 30/06 Mannlicher target rifle out the door. Harry was just starting to squeeze the trigger as the relatively small bullet from the agent's gun fortuitously struck the end of his telescopic sight. The metal eyepiece slammed back, putting out Harry's eye very painfully.

He stood up raging, blood streaming from his eye, and fired two wild unaimed shots before the second small bullet opened a bloody rose in the center of his chest. The bullet passed on through and penetrated the metal skin of the water tank and a jet of water pushed Harry off the catwalk.

———

"Son! Wake up! This body is dying." The illusion of a friendly octopoid figure floated in front of Braxn's eyes, not quite as real as the bright light and anxious masked people hovering over him; green tunics smeared with blood.

"It hurts, Father."

The surgeon didn't look up, but one of his assistants turned bright eyes to the president's face.

"I know you are probably in pain," the prerecorded, hypnotically implanted image said. "Remember your learnings and ignore the pain. You may be able to escape.

"If you have learned enough about power, if you've learned enough from *both* sides, you have no further use for this body. Try to reach out and find another. *Try!*"

Braxn tried, but the pain was too much of a presence, a crushing weight.

"This pain is not mine," he said aloud. "This pain belongs to this body." He took that thought and pulled it, stretched it until it lay over the dying organism like a shroud. The pain didn't fade, but it slowly became less important. He reached out and *pushed*.

The surgical mask was rather tight and tasted slightly of lipstick. Scrubbed down in too much of a hurry. Good to be in a young woman's body, after that—

"Scalpel!" the surgeon said. "God . . ." With hands that were his and not-his, Braxn slapped a scalpel into the doctor's waiting palm.

"No heartbeat." He made an incision, deep, in Harriman's chest, held it open and plunged his gloved hand in to try to massage the heart back into action. Braxn knew it was useless; Harriman had died of spiritual abdication.

Eventually he stopped trying. He stripped the gloves from his hands and pulled down his mask. With an opportunity to say something that would ring down through the ages, the doctor just shook his head, whispered an earthy syllable, and stalked out.

Afterwards, washing up, Braxn was still enough of a politician to wonder whether that doddering old fool of a Speaker would have the grace to step out of the line of succession.

(1970)

Fantasy for Six Electrodes
and One Adrenaline Drip

(A Play in the Form of a Feelie Script)

ESTABLISHING SHOT I: Slow DOLLY down buffet table loaded with rare and expensive foods. Linger on certain items: purple Denebian caviar in crushed ice with pattern of thin lemon circles; a whole grouper jellied in crystal aspic; pepper-roasted bison haunch, partially sliced, pink and steaming; platoons of wine bottles ranked at end of table, some on ice (use stock SMELL for simulated items, linen tablecloth FEEL down to wine bottles; switch to cool smooth moist glass FEEL at end).

NARRATOR

SEXY CULTURED VOICE

> There are almost ten million people on Earth with personal worth over ten million credits. Nine million, Nine hundred and ninety-nine thousand of them are just too poor to be invited to this party.

PAUSE AT BISON HAUNCH

> Of the remaining thousand, say, roughly half are too new to the game of superrich to be considered.

SUBLIMINALS: Feel and smell of money.

> Half of the eligible five hundred either have unfortu-
> nate politics or are simply disliked by the host.

SOUND UNDER NARRATOR: polite early cocktail party chatter.

> The rest were all invited. Many were off-planet,
> some did not care for the host, some had pressing
> business elsewhere. Eighty-three of them have never
> appeared in public, and this party seemed too
> public.
> Ninety-four came, some with wives or husbands or
> concubines or friends; a total of one hundred and
> fifty-one fortunate people. We are interested in only
> a few of them.

CUT from wine bottles to HAZLIK. HOLD glass FEEL in right hand.
SOUND UP. FEEL expensive clothing on SOMATIC: Healthy though no
longer young male body. TASTE of fine wine and SMELL of good dope.
ADD SOMATIC: Dope 0.20.

TIGHT on HAZLIK, who is talking animatedly, but his voice is lost in
SOUND.

NARRATOR

> You have never heard of Theophilus Hazlik. His
> anonymity costs him over ten million credits per
> year. He owns an interstellar shipping agency, seven
> industrial combines, and two countries on two plan-
> ets. One of them is on Earth.
> He is the host.

CUT TO: MEDIUM TWO SHOT of HAZLIK and CELIA OBRAVILLA.
FEEL dopestick in CELIA'S left hand, HOLD glass FEEL in right. FEEL
cool airco breeze on exposed breasts, silk cape over shoulders, silk
trousers, and no underclothing. Mix TASTE good dope and wine. SO-
MATIC: Dope 0.30, female sexual tension 0.10. (CELIA is about forty

but looks half that. See if Special Effects can get across a somatic sublim-inal of cosmetic surgery; face and body).

NARRATOR

Celia Obravilla. Born into big money, married big-ger. Husband died and she invested wisely. She would be the most sought-after woman at the party . . . except there were certain questions about her husband's death . . . of course, it would be gauche to suggest . . . and dangerous . . .

SOUND UNDER and TIGHT ON CELIA.

CELIA

GESTURING WITH DOPESTICK

. . . tiresome, tiresome. I told him, Professor, if *I* can't buy it, nobody can; and if it can't be bought, I don't want it.

SOUND UP and CUT to SAUL MORENO. He is a small dark man, sit-ting alone in a corner. FEEL tight formal clothes that don't quite fit, heat from coffee mug in right hand. TASTE aftertaste of bitter coffee. SO-MATIC NULL.

TIGHT ON MORENO.

NARRATOR

You might have heard of this man, if your profession involves prostitution or wholesale distribution of smuggled interstellar goods. He is Saul Moreno . . .

MORENO sips coffee. TASTE real coffee flavored with honey and car-damom.

NARRATOR

. . . and he is not the only criminal here. For instance—

CUT to FREDRIKA OBLIMOV, talking seriously to someone off-camera. She is very old, but beautiful in a cool, elegant way. SOMATIC: generalized aches and twinges of old age. Strong TASTE of gin, though she isn't holding a glass. SUBLIMINALS: feel of spiderwebs and smell of mildew.

NARRATOR

> This is Fredrika Oblimov, who is the oldest person at the party and probably the most dangerous. She owns an army, but it is not a conventional one. She has made a moderately large fortune by arranging to have very important people murdered. These by verbal contracts, paid in advance, books juggled in advance to hide her fee, hypnotic wipe of memory of agreement. No money-back guarantee, but she claims never to have failed. She has a contract on one of the people at this party.
> Watch now: she is telling a joke.

SOUND OUT and explosive laughter. CAMERA CUTS from person to person, six people standing around FREDRIKA, all laughing desperately. FEEL, SMELL, TASTE, SOMATIC: NULL. HOLD SUBLIMINALS and ADD ADRENALINE: 0.10.

CAMERA HOLDS on seventh man, who is not laughing, but has a small innocent smile.

NARRATOR

> Do you see this man?

HOLD NULL and SUBLIMINAL DISSOLVE to SUBLIMINAL: Feel of cold marble and ADD ADRENALINE: 0.12. DOLLY to BIG CLOSE-UP on face: no movement whatsoever except eyes, slowly scanning from left to right.

NARRATOR

> He works for Fredrika. Or, if you prefer, he is her husband. This week.

CAMERA PANS down arm to left hand. BIG CLOSE-UP on hand, thumb rubbing across fingertips.

NARRATOR

This is not a hand. It's a prosthetic device: the finger-nails are harder than steel and keener than razors. Underneath the fingernails, a fast-acting nerve poison.

ADD ADRENALINE: 0.15 and ADD somatic SUBLIMINAL: Nausea. SOUND UP as laughing dies.

NARRATOR

He is careful whom he touches.

CUT TO: MEDIUM SHOT of FREDRIKA and the people surrounding her.

FREDRIKA

You are all so kind.

CUT TO: MEDIUM SHOT of HAZLIK. FEEL, TASTE as before, ADRENALINE and SUBLIMINALS OUT.

HAZLIK

LOUDLY, WELL OVER SOUND

All right, everybody. Let the feast begin!

FADE TO COMMERCIAL.

COMMERCIAL. (One minute Stiffener © spot)

FADE IN ESTABLISHING SHOT II: Same scene as first establishing shot, but buffet table is now a confusion of empty serving dishes, picked bones, empty bottles, etc. SMELL and TASTE: Good food and drink, tang of dope and tobacco smoke. SOMATIC: Pleasantly full, satisfied feeling. SOUND of slightly more animated conversation over subdued clatter of dishes and servants clean off table.

CUT TO: MEDIUM SHOT of HAZLIK standing, talking to an attractive woman seated on a cushion. FREDRIKA and her companion approach.

FREDRIKA

Pardon me, Theo . . .

CUT TO: MEDIUM CLOSE-UP of HAZLIK as he turns, carefully does not react, smiles warmly. SOMATIC: Small shiver and ADRENALINE: 0.05.

HAZLIK

Ah, Fredrika.

CUT TO: MEDIUM GROUP SHOT of HAZLIK, FREDRIKA, and COMPANION.

FREDRIKA

Theo, I don't think you've met my husband, George.

HAZLIK knows exactly what GEORGE is. As they shake hands: ADRENALINE: 0.10, SUBLIMINAL: Feel and smell of clotted blood. FEEL of rough skin against rough skin.

HAZLIK

URBANE: HONEST OPEN SMILE, CRINKLED EYES.

My pleasure.

GEORGE

COLD SMILE

Yes.

MEDIUM TWO SHOT from George's point of view: HAZLIK and FREDRIKA silently regard each other just a moment longer than politeness would allow. ADRENALINE, SUBLIMINAL OUT. SOMATIC: Nerve in neck begins throbbing.

HAZLIK

QUESTIONING

Business has been good.

FREDRIKA

No worse than usual.

PAUSE AND IRONIC SMILE

Men still pay for my services. Fatal attraction.

HAZLIK does not smile. ADRENALINE: 0.12, SOMATIC: Nausea of fear. HAZLIK drinks large gulp, TASTE and SMELL of warm brandy going down. NAUSEA UP and ADD SOMATIC: gagging reflex.

HAZLIK

COUGHS

Pardon me. (COUGHS AGAIN) Have to cut down on my dope.

FREDRIKA

I can recommend a good hypnotist.

HAZLIK

CATCHING REFERENCE TO F'S BUSINESS METHODS

I've tried that. Several times, I think.

FREDRIKA

MERRILY, GLIDING AWAY

You're right, you're right.

SUBLIMINAL: Feel of cobwebs and sound of batwings.

HAZLIK turns back to young lady. ADRENALINE HOLD and SUBLIMINAL OUT. SOMATIC: Male sexual tension 0.10.

INTERCUT CLOSE-UPS, HAZLIK and GIRL.

HAZLIK

You were saying?

Girl is wearing gossamer chemise. FEEL of silk against nipples and thighs. SOMATIC: Female sexual tension 0.20. SMELL of vaginal musk and perfume. GIRL runs tongue between lips rapidly. TASTE and FEEL of warm flesh.

GIRL

Not what I was saying. What I was thinking . . .

HAZLIK

BACK IN CONTROL

Do you think often?

GIRL

IGNORES JIBE

I was wondering what it would be like to make love to a billionaire.

HAZLIK

SOMATIC: Male sexual tension 0.30.

Seven times over.

GIRL

CONFUSED

Seven *times*?

HAZLIK

CHUCKLES. SOMATIC: Male sexual tension 0.40.

No, no—seven billion.

GIRL

GIGGLES

I thought . . .

HAZLIK

SOMATIC: Male sexual tension 0.50, SMELL: Male musk, FEEL: erection fighting clothes.

LAUGHS

Anything's possible.

LAP DISSOLVE to HAZLIK and girl making love on lawn.

(Avoid stock intercourse stimulus/response package. The important thing to get across is the idea that Hazlik is sexually potent yet emotionally empty.)

(Consider the following sequence merely as a guide to the director. Much, of course, depends on the individual actors' feeling for one another—Stiffener © or no!)

STROBE ALTERNATION

GIRL: FEEL: soles of feet, buttocks, shoulder blades, back of head all on grass—going back and forth a couple of centimeters with each thrust; HAZLIK'S chest hair rubbing against breasts, hairy legs gently abrading inside thighs; slightly painful bumping contact between pubic bones, faces not in contact, his hands pressed against small of back. SMELL: Male musk under dope and wine. SOMATIC: Penis rigid inside vagina, active but controlled, very long thrusts alternating with short quick ones; her sexual response during minute of ALTERNATION before orgasm equals $0.50 + .006667t(\sin\{t/7.78\})$, t in seconds. Then four orgasms, decreasing in intensity as they increase in painfulness, separated by 8, 6, and 4 seconds . . . then SMELL: Female musk UP and add perspiration. FEEL: Pain from pubic bone contact UP on last two orgasms. SUBLIMINAL: Taste of blood HAZLIK: FEEL: Elbows to forearms on grass, sharing weight with knees. Fingertips move from buttock cleavage to lumbar dimples. Vagina is almost excessively moist; penis slipping forward and back with almost no resistance. Breasts moving regularly, deforming under his chest. Toenails digging into dirt. SMELL: Vaginal musk and perspiration, grass. TASTE: Aftertaste of good dope and brandy. SOMATIC: Constant male sexual tension 0.75 throughout preorgasm minute (distracted, enjoying stiffness of penis more than he is the loving). Slightly painful rhythmic contact between testicles and GIRL'S buttocks. Simultaneously with GIRL'S last orgasm, HAZLIK ejaculates without joy. SUBLIMINAL: Carrying heavy weight. *BOTH*: Stock SOUND of intercourse.

HAZLIK and GIRL remain joined for about thirty seconds, panting wordlessly after last orgasm. FADE OUT HAZLIK: FEEL, SMELL, SOMATIC. GIRL: FEEL: HAZLIK slipping out of her, she clasps legs over his body.

                              GIRL

        You were very good.

                             HAZLIK

PATS SHOULDER AWKWARDLY AND SLIPS OUT OF HER

        So were you, child.

                              GIRL

LITTLE VOICE

        Don't you want to talk? Sit here a minute and . . .
        maybe . . .

                             HAZLIK

DRESSING, CHUCKLES

        Not right now, no . . . I'm host of this thing, remember? Have to get back and mix.

GIRL stretches out on her side, watching HAZLIK dress. FEEL: Grass prickling arm, head on arm, puddle of sweat trickles out of navel, stock postcoital stickiness and languor but SOMATIC: Female sexual tension 0.20 (vaguely unsatisfied). SUBLIMINAL: Female orgasm 0.05, feel of feathers stroking places that can't be reached.

                              GIRL

        I . . . of course.

LONG TWO SHOT as HAZLIK stretches and yawns hugely, smiles at GIRL and says good-bye with casual wave. CAMERA FOLLOWS as he returns to party. He passes several other couples making love, but of course pays no attention, except to exchange spoken greeting with one man.

CUT TO: LONG SHOT, party interior. SMELL: Dope and tobacco smoke, incense, crowd odor very slight, alcohol and coffee. There are about sixty people standing and sitting around in small groups. HAZLIK enters through inconspicuous automatic door, walks toward bar. SOMATIC: Thirst, nervous energy. SUBLIMINAL: Male sexual tension 0.05.

HAZLIK

TO BARTENDER

> Double wine punch, ice.

MEDIUM TWO SHOT as CELIA approaches HAZLIK'S back. ADRENALINE: 0.10, SUBLIMINAL: Feel of hands squeezing HAZLIK'S throat.

CELIA

> Having a good time, Darling?

HAZLIK

TURNS

> Ah, Celia. Darling. Yes, a wonderful time.

CELIA

TO BARTENDER (OFF)

> Cold bhang, please . . . Thank you.

CELIA moves in very close to HAZLIK, smiles.

CELIA

OVER GLASS, VENOMOUS WHISPER

> You old goat . . . that . . . *child*!

                                    HAZLIK

ARTIFICIAL SMILE. SUBLIMINAL: Buggery, violent rape.

>   I didn't know you'd had experience with goats, too,
>   darling.

                                    CELIA

>   Only you, my dear.

Tense silence for several seconds. TASTE: Cold bhang, spiced wine. SO-
MATIC: Dope 0.05. ADRENALINE down and OUT.

                                    HAZLIK

SOFTENING SLIGHTLY

>   She was something special to you?

CELIA gulps half of her drink and looks away from HAZLIK, ab-
stracted. SOMATIC: Dope 0.10.

                                    CELIA

>   Once.

SUBLIMINAL: Fear spectrum slowly UP to SOMATIC: Stomach tight-
ens, ADRENALINE: 0.20 as HAZLIK remembers CELIA'S reputation.

                                    HAZLIK

SLOWLY

>   I'm sorry. I really am . . . there was no way I could
>   have known.

                                    CELIA

LOOKING AT HIM STRANGELY.

>   No.

CELIA walks away as HAZLIK studies his drink. SOMATIC: Fear spectrum fade DOWN and slowly OUT. HAZLIK walks off in other direction. CAMERA FOLLOWS for a short distance. HAZLIK idly stops to

watch a dice game in progress on a table which is a large block of natural crystal. The three dice clatter down and come to a rest: fifteen. Mixed murmurs of approval and unhappiness. Money changes hands. SUBLIMINAL: Feel, smell of money. SOUND of money crinkling.

PLAYER

High up *sans* thirteen.

OTHER PLAYERS

Cover high.
Low middle.
High middle.
Low field.

PLAYER

Thirteen, somebody.

HAZLIK

How much?

PLAYER

One thou . . . oh, Hazlik. Good party. Why don't you wait for a field?

HAZLIK

Ah . . . luck is luck.

While HAZLIK takes wallet from cape pocket, MORENO approaches, comes up very close.

TIGHT TWO SHOT as MORENO speaks softly to HAZLIK. SMELL: Strong coffee on breath.

MORENO

WHISPERS

Hazlik. I have to talk to you.

HAZLIK hands single bill to PLAYER, turns back to MORENO.

                          HAZLIK

A LITTLE ANNOYED

         Can't it wait?

                          MORENO

         No. Not at all.

HAZLIK turns back on game as dice clatter. CAMERA FOLLOWS as he
walks off with MORENO.

                        PLAYER (OFF)

         Fifteen *again*!

                          HAZLIK

AS THEY WALK

         Well?

                          MORENO

LOOKING AROUND

         One of your guests, um . . . (WHISPERS) have you
         met Fredrika's escort?

                          HAZLIK

EXPRESSIONLESS

         Yes. Pleasant fellow.

                          MORENO

         Can we go somewhere in private?

                          HAZLIK

SHRUGS

         The outside balcony. Here.

They both step into a lift zone and float to the second floor.

SOMATIC: Stomach dropping reinforced by ADRENALINE: 0.10. HAZLIK opens manual door and steps outside. MORENO follows.

LONG SHOT past HAZLIK as he goes to edge of balcony and looks out over grounds. The full moon is up; acres of neat grass, landscaping, formal gardens. SMELL: Flowers, grass. SOUND: Crickets, far-off jungle noises, MORENO'S footsteps as he comes to join HAZLIK.

TIGHT TWO SHOT on MORENO and HAZLIK.

> MORENO

You keep the jungle away quite well.

> HAZLIK

Yes. I wish I could pattern my life so. (SMILES) Fredrika?

INTERCUT CLOSE-UPS MORENO and HAZLIK.

> MORENO

Her "George." He worked for me once. I had to discharge him.

> HAZLIK

STILL GAZING OVER GROUNDS

For good reason, I'm sure.

> MORENO

He killed a man.

HAZLIK laughs, a short bark, and looks at MORENO, wryly.

> HAZLIK

You've never killed a man.

MORENO snorts and walks a short distance away. He talks into the night.

MORENO

I'm not talking about business. He killed this man for pleasure . . .

PAUSE. SUBLIMINAL: Spiders crawling through filth.

after making love to him. I later found . . . (PAUSE) that he had done it before. Also to women.

HAZLIK

LIGHTLY

He seems a man well suited to his profession.

HAZLIK turns his back to the railing and studies the party below, through the glass doors. SOUND: Faint party noises.

HAZLIK

What has this to do with me?

MORENO

Everything and nothing. (TURNS) There *will* be murder here tonight. She wouldn't have brought . . . him . . . as a social ornament.

HAZLIK takes out a dopestick and has trouble waving it alight. TIGHT on HAZLIK as he blows the tip into flame and sucks. SOMATIC: Dope 0.40 then UNDER to 0.10.

HAZLIK

This is the most private of private property, on Earth. She will play her games and there will be no trouble, unless somebody wants to make trouble. With her, not many would.

MORENO

Don't you care who is going to die in your own house?

HAZLIK

I don't care to *know*. Not ahead of time.

MORENO

Not even if it's a friend, or someone you love? Not even if it is yourself?

HAZLIK turns around again, slowly, and throws dopestick over balcony edge. He watches the spark fall and die.

HAZLIK

Fredrika is bold. But she is not stupid. (PAUSES) Besides, how could *you* know who her . . . intended is?

MORENO

SHRUGS

I don't. But I have men here, too.

HAZLIK

COLDLY

Were they invited?

MORENO

Yes. You said to bring a friend. I brought a very good friend. So did Porfiry Esterbrook, and so did . . .

HAZLIK

I see. How many?

MORENO

Enough to isolate . . . "George" . . . and ask him some questions.

HAZLIK

TO HIMSELF

You aren't doing this for my sake. (ADDRESSES
MORENO DIRECTLY, SHADE OF MENACE) Exactly what is going on?

MORENO

That also may be one of those things that you don't
wish to know.

MORENO sees HAZLIK'S face and realizes he's gone a little too far. SO-
MATIC: Stomach tightening and ADRENALINE: 0.20.

MORENO

LONG PAUSE, SWALLOWS

All right. A . . . a power struggle, so to speak. No—
an extermination! (SPEAKING WITH PASSION
FOR THE FIRST TIME) The old bitch has got to
go! Our lives are . . . too complicated, too uncertain. Get rid of her, and—

HAZLIK

I believe she has been useful to me in the past.
You've probably used her services, too. One never
remembers, of course.

MORENO

ANGRY

No. Never.

HAZLIK

It certainly was convenient to your industry when
Mlle. Legrange passed on.

MORENO

Yes. But I never would have hired that old hag to do
it. It was a fortunate accident.

HAZLIK

LIGHT LAUGH, SOMEHOW EVIL

> Our little world is full of accidents that turn out to favor one or the other of us. Fredrika is behind most of them.

MORENO

FACE SET

> But not Mlle. Legrange.

HAZLIK

> As you wish.

The two men stand in silence for twenty seconds. HAZLIK takes out a dopestick and then returns it to the pack.

HAZLIK

> At any rate . . . you wish to enlist my aid, against Fredrika?

MORENO

> Not directly. I'd like some guarantee that you won't interfere, though.

HAZLIK Silent.

> Do you still have those, uh, small rooms . . . underneath the place?

HAZLIK

> The soundproofed conference rooms? Of course. Would you like one?

MORENO

> Yes! If we could get him . . .

HAZLIK

I don't want to hear about it. Not until afterwards.
And never, unless it directly concerns me.

MORENO

Excellent. I'll tell—

HAZLIK

Wait. I go first.

HAZLIK leaves. CUT TO: BIG CLOSE-UP of MORENO, smiling now.

FADE OUT to COMMERCIAL.

COMMERICAL: One-minute Stiffener © spot.

FADE IN: ESTABLISHING SHOT III: MEDIUM, GROUP SHOT of
FREDRIKA and GEORGE with several other people, talking. A white-
coated servant glides up to FREDRIKA and whispers something to her.
She goes away with him. GEORGE begins to follow, but THREE MEN
pass between them.

BIG CLOSE-UP on right hand of FIRST MAN, who is holding a small
ampoule.

TIGHT TWO SHOT of FIRST MAN and GEORGE as FIRST MAN
squeezes ampoule and a jet of colorless fluid sprays into GEORGE'S face.
It is "come-along" gas. SMELL: Ammonia; FEEL: Icy splash on face.

GEORGE reaches out with left "hand" but barely brushes man's arm.
GEORGE gets a funny passive look, his hand drops back, and he stands
still.

FIRST MAN

WHISPERING

Now, George, just follow us.

TIGHT GROUP SHOT of the THREE MEN herding GEORGE away.
CAMERA FOLLOWS for a short distance.

CUT TO: MEDIUM TWO SHOT of FREDRIKA and SERVANT. She is arguing with him and doesn't notice GEORGE is headed the other way.

CUT TO: LONG SHOT of downstairs room as THREE MEN and GEORGE enter. The walls and ceiling are covered with a mossy substance; the soundproofing. There is a conference table in the center of the room. The chair at the end of the table has manacles attached to the arms. SMELL: Dry "chemical" odor of soundproofing. SUBLIMINAL: Feel scratchy dry moss, smell brimstone and rotting flesh. ADRENALINE: 0.10 and OUT.

CAMERA FOLLOWS FIRST MAN and GEORGE to the end of the table.

FIRST MAN

You sit here.

TIGHT ON FIRST MAN as he grips edge of table, wobbles. SOMATIC: Extreme nausea, fire in right arm.

SECOND MAN (OFF)

What's wrong?

FIRST MAN

I   don't . . . know . . . he   must   have . . . gotten (CHOKING SOUND)

MEDIUM GROUP SHOT as FIRST MAN falls to floor, begins jerking around. SECOND MAN moves to help him, stops. Looks up at GEORGE, who is watching the whole thing with quiet interest.

SECOND MAN (TO GEORGE)

Did you do that?

GEORGE

INNOCENT SMILE

Yes. Nerve poison.

TIGHT ON FIRST MAN as he expires noisily, messily on floor. SMELL:
Vomit; SUBLIMINAL: Taste of vomit, extreme nausea, SOMATIC:
White-out.

THIRD MAN

God.

SECOND MAN

SWALLOWS, TRYING TO STAY CALM

How did you do it?

GEORGE

I told you. Nerve poison.

THIRD MAN

Let's fasten him down and loosen him up.

SECOND MAN

So do it. The manacles.

THIRD MAN gives SECOND MAN a hard glance, goes cautiously to
GEORGE. He stands just out of arm reach.

THIRD MAN

Put your arms up on the arms of the chair.

GEORGE obeys without hesitation, but moving slowly. ADRENALINE:
0.15.

THIRD MAN

All right. Stay that way.

ADRENALINE: 0.25. GEORGE'S hands are lying palm up on the chair
arms. BIG CLOSE-UP as THIRD MAN turns right hand over and latches
manacle (SOUND: Loud click and SUBLIMINAL: Metal tightness
around wrist) over wrist. He reaches for left hand and GEORGE closes
hand over his. MICRO CLOSE-UP shows fingernail slitting flesh.

TIGHT TWO SHOT of GEORGE and THIRD MAN as THIRD MAN jerks his hand away.

THIRD MAN

Ouch! (TOUCHES CUT TO MOUTH) Some fingernails this guy ... (SHARP INTAKE OF BREATH) He ...

BIG CLOSE-UP on THIRD MAN'S face. ADRENALINE: 0.35.

SECOND MAN (OFF)

Sit down. Don't move—I'll get some atropine.

LONG GROUP SHOT: GEORGE watches passively as SECOND MAN runs from room. THIRD MAN sits down cautiously. ADRENALINE: 0.40.

THIRD MAN

Will atropine work?

GEORGE

If he gets back in time.

ADRENALINE: 0.50 and OUT.

CUT TO: TIGHT GROUP SHOT of MORENO, HAZLIK, and others sitting at crystal table playing dice. SECOND MAN hurries up to MORENO, whispers.

MORENO

TO HAZLIK, ACROSS

Do you have any atropine in the place?

INTERCUT CLOSE-UPS, HAZLIK and MORENO.

HAZLIK (COUNTING MONEY)

ANNOYED

What?

MORENO

Atropine! Uh . . . a drug overdose.

HAZLIK (TO SECOND MAN)

There might be some. Ask the butler.

HAZLIK (TO MORENO)

One of your men popping on duty?

MORENO

Not really . . . it's more, uh, concerned with what we discussed earlier.

HAZLIK

The woman?

MORENO

Her man, actually.

HAZLIK

STANDS CASUALLY

Let's go take a look.

CUT TO: LONG SHOT past MORENO and HAZLIK standing in door of conference room. THIRD MAN is sitting with his arms wrapped around himself, deathly pale. GEORGE is exactly as we left him: one wrist manacled, monumentally unconcerned with everything. Corpse of FIRST MAN has skin like marble, has gone into *rigor mortis*. (Note: ask State Correction Board whether we can get two young Terminals to play the parts of FIRST and THIRD MEN.)

ADRENALINE: 0.50, somatic SUBLIMINAL: Nausea and angina. SMELL: Vomit and feces.

THIRD MAN

Atr— . . . atropine?

HAZLIK

BRUSQUE

> Maybe. Coming.

MORENO

> What did he do? Protter said something about his hand.

THIRD MAN

> I don't think it's a hand. It's a p-pross. Nerve, ah, nerve p-poison under the finger . . . nails . . . sharp . . . oh God—

THIRD MAN flops down on floor, rigid, and begins beating arm on floor. He jerks several times, vomits explosively, and dies. SMELL: As before, UP and DOWN. Stinger of ADRENALINE: 0.80 and OUT. SUBLIMI-NAL: Drowning in filth.

MEDIUM TWO SHOT of HAZLIK and MORENO standing in door, staring. PROTTER (SECOND MAN) runs up to them from behind.

PROTTER

OUT OF BREATH

> I've got the . . . oh.

SMELL: Down to strong SUBLIMINAL.

HAZLIK

> Let me have that. (SPEAKS INTO BRACELET) San-dler. This is the boss. Got some garbage to be taken out, in Conference A. (LISTENS) That's right. (TURNS A MICRODIAL on the bracelet) Johns, this is the boss. Get an interrogation team down to Conference A, sooner. (LISTENS) Doesn't make too much difference. Right.

TO NOBODY IN PARTICULAR

It had to come to this, sooner or later.

HAZLIK (TO MORENO)

You were right. We've allowed Fredrika too much.

MORENO

Yes. (TO PROTTER) You can go.

PROTTER shuffles, lost, down the hall and HAZLIK and MORENO stand outside door and smoke. SOMATIC: Dope 0.25, SUBLIMINAL FADE to OUT.

Four men hustle up, with stretchers and a sanitizer. They go straight through the door without saying a word to either man. High-pitched humming, sanitizer SOUND. HAZLIK shouts over:

HAZLIK

Stay away from the man in the chair.

CLOSES DOOR SOUND OUT abruptly.

HAZLIK sits down on floor; then MORENO does also. Soon the four men come back out, bearing the stretchers. Again, they show no sign of seeing the two.

HAZLIK

Just when everything was going so well. (PAUSE)

UNSENTIMENTALLY

Moreno, do you consider yourself a happy man?

MORENO

UNCOMFORTABLE

Well . . . I suppose so. I have all that I need . . . and I keep busy.

HAZLIK

LOOKING AT ATROPINE SYRETTE, FIDDLING WITH IT

Until a few weeks ago, I would never have called myself . . . happy . . . there was a strange—

WITH SUDDEN VEHEMENCE (ADRENALINE: 0.25)

—a *weight* on my soul, Moreno! An actual weight of, I don't know; sorrow, guilt . . . questioning whether I might not have been . . . different. (PAUSE) But one day; three weeks, a month ago, I woke up one morning and it was all gone, I was free. That's when I decided to throw a party. (PAUSE) But now I feel it coming back.

SOUND of footsteps approaching; HAZLIK looks up.

                    HAZLIK

GETTING UP

Ah, Johns. We have a little problem.

MEDIUM GROUP SHOT past HAZLIK and MORENO to the interrogation team: JOHNS and his two assistants, FRIEDMAN (male) and O'HARA (female).

                    JOHNS

We'll do what we can, sir. Have you met O'Hara and Friedman?

                    HAZLIK

No, I haven't.

                    JOHNS

They're very good.

                    HAZLIK

WITH A WAVE OF HIS HAND

I trust your judgment in these things. Follow me.

All five enter the "conference" room. HAZLIK walks over to stand (not too near) by GEORGE.

HAZLIK

This man works for Fredrika Oblimov . . . George.

GEORGE

Yes?

HAZLIK

What sort of work do you do for Fredrika?

GEORGE

SMALL SMILE

I am her husband.

HAZLIK (TO MORENO)

What did they drug him with?

MORENO

If they followed my instructions, it was come-along gas.

HAZLIK

Makes sense. He doesn't really have to tell the truth, then. Not even to a direct order.

JOHNS

We can fix that, sir.

HAZLIK

IMPATIENTLY

Of course you can. But nothing so crude as dissolvers or triple-scop. I want to be able to return him to Fredrika no worse for wear, except for a lack of memory . . . of these proceedings. Can you do that?

JOHNS

DOUBTFUL

How soon would he have to be returned?

HAZLIK

No more than an hour.

JOHNS

I don't know . . . that lets out most of our drugs. We can keep him on come-along, of course, and he won't remember . . . but it won't make him talk.

O'HARA

Let me work on him.

JOHNS

All right.

O'HARA approaches GEORGE without caution.

HAZLIK

Watch out! His left hand's a pross. Nerve poison under the fingernails.

O'HARA (TO GEORGE)

SULTRY

Now, George. Is that right?

GEORGE

LITTLE-BOY SMILE

Uh-huh.

O'HARA

Now, George, turn your hand over, palm down, and don't touch me while I fasten your arm to the chair.

GEORGE

All right.

O'HARA binds him without any trouble.

O'HARA (TO HAZLIK)

Exactly what do you want to know?

HAZLIK

He's here to kill somebody. You know about Fredrika's contracts? (SHE NODS) I want to find out who the victim is supposed to be—and who contracted for it, if *he* knows.

O'HARA

SOFTLY

George, who did you come here to kill?

GEORGE

SINGSONG

I'm not . . . sup-posed . . . to tell.

O'HARA

You can tell *me*, George. I'll keep it a secret.

GEORGE

PETULANT

Huh-uh!

O'HARA

LOOKS UP

Friedman. Bring the kit over.

HAZLIK

No marks!

JOHNS

Don't worry, sir. They're too good for that.

FRIEDMAN

CROSSING OVER

That's right, sir. Direct stimulation of the pain centers in the brain, the newest thing. Doesn't leave a
sign.

O'HARA

Now this man is going to hurt you, George. I can't
stop him from hurting you unless you tell me whom
you came here to kill, and why.

GEORGE

GIGGLES

He can't hurt me. Fredrika told me, nobody can hurt
me if I don't want.

FRIEDMAN

Probably a simple hypnotic injunction.

SQUEEZES GEORGE'S EARLOBE BETWEEN FINGER AND
THUMBNAIL

No reaction. Well . . .

FRIEDMAN opens up black case, brings out a small limp net of wire
mesh. He shakes it out.

I think this will bypass it.

FRIENDMAN lays net over GEORGE'S head and secures it with a chin
strap. He takes out a little box with a dial on it.

FRIEDMAN (TO O'HARA)

Ready?

O'HARA

LICKS LIPS, STARING AT GEORGE INTENTLY

Yes . . .

BIG CLOSE-UP of little box. FRIEDMAN turns dial to first setting. BIG CLOSE-UP on GEORGE'S face. Beads of sweat break out on his forehead. SOMATIC SUBLIMINAL: Steel band tightening around chest.

DOLLY BACK to TIGHT TWO SHOT, faces of GEORGE and O'HARA. SOMATIC: Female sexual tension 0.20.

O'HARA

It hurts, doesn't it, George.

GEORGE

SMALL VOICE

Yes, it hurts.

O'HARA

Whom are you going to kill?

GEORGE

CHILDISH DEFIANCE

That's for me to know and you to find out.

O'HARA glances at FRIEDMAN, and he adjusts dial upward with audible click. HOLD SUBLIMINAL and ADD SUBLIMINAL: Little finger being pushed back to breaking point.

BIG CLOSE-UP on O'HARA'S face, smiling. Sharp intake of breath from GEORGE (OFF).

O'HARA

Whom are you going to kill?

GEORGE

Stop it. Make him stop it.

O'HARA

Whom are you going to kill?

GEORGE

Make him stop.

O'HARA

MOVING EVEN CLOSER TO GEORGE, SMILING

More.

HOLD SUBLIMINAL and ADD SUBLIMINAL: Knitting needle being pushed through thigh. GEORGE moans. SOMATIC: Female sexual tension 0.40. BIG CLOSE-UP on O'HARA, panting through her nose, teeth clenched.

O'HARA

Whom are you going to kill?

GEORGE

I . . . can't . . . say.

O'HARA

More . . .

Click and HOLD SUBLIMINAL and ADD SUBLIMINAL: Extreme pressure on testicles. SOMATIC: Female sexual tension 0.75.

MEDIUM TWO SHOT of GEORGE and O'HARA. GEORGE has head thrown back, features contorted, screaming; O'HARA leaning over him, hands on his forearms, shouting into his face:

O'HARA

AT THE TOP OF HER LUNGS

Whom are you going to kill whom are you going to
kill whom are you going to kill?

HAZLIK (OFF)

WHISPERS

> God.

FRIEDMAN

CALMLY, ACADEMICALLY

> This level of pain is greater than that experienced by
> one who burns to death.

JOHNS

SLIGHTLY BOTHERED

> You might as well try something else. This isn't go-
> ing to work.

FRIEDMAN

> You're probably right.

GEORGE'S screams stop abruptly. SUBLIMINALS OUT.

O'HARA

> Whom are you going to kill whom are you going to
> kill whom are you?

O'HARA slips lithely off him and holds hand out to FRIEDMAN.

O'HARA

> Quickly.

FRIEDMAN HANDS her a small ampoule. She grabs GEORGE by the
hair—his head is lolling and he's whimpering like a child—and holds his
head up while she crushes ampoule under his nose. Immediate SO-
MATIC: Male sexual tension 0.70, SMELL: Full-strength Stiffner ©.

O'HARA

TEASING GROTESQUELY

> I've got something you wa-ant.

GEORGE looks at her sickly and takes in ragged breath. SOMATIC: Male sexual tension 0.75.

GEORGE

HOARSELY

Come here.

O'HARA

Not until you tell me. Whom did Fredrika order you to kill?

FULL-BODY SHOT of O'HARA past GEORGE. O'HARA pulls shift over her head and, underneath, is wearing only a little wisp of bright material which clings wetly to her. She has a ripe young figure, shiny with perspiration. SOMATIC: Male sexual tension 0.85, painful erection.

O'HARA

Who-o-o?

GEORGE shakes his head violently, incapable of speech or not trusting himself. A little salvia has trickled out of the corner of his mouth. O'HARA approaches him and kneels, begins caressing the back of his hand with her breast. FEEL: Featherlight touch of breast on back of hand which is struggling to clutch but unable to turn over. SOMATIC: Male sexual tension 0.93. SMELL: Female, male musk.

O'HARA

Just one little name, and I'll take care of you.

O'HARA stands and turns her back to GEORGE; slowly slides final garment down. SOMATIC: Male sexual tension 0.95.

O'HARA (FACING AWAY)

Just tell me, George.

GEORGE groans something intelligible. O'HARA turns and, in a quick smooth motion, mounts his hand and begins rubbing back and forth. FEEL: Slippery labia, unnaturally hot and wet. SMELL: Female musk UP.

SOMATIC: Male sexual tension 0.99; unbearable, gut-wrenching frustration.

                              O'HARA

HUSKILY

> If you want . . .

                              GEORGE

SCREAMS

> Haz-lik! *Hazlik!*

FEEL, SMELL, SOMATIC all OUT. O'HARA slides off GEORGE and slips back into clothes. FEEL: Wetness on back of hand turning cold and sticky as HAZLIK crosses in blind fury. ADRENALINE: 0.75.

                              HAZLIK

BARELY CONTROLLED

> You are going to die . . .

TIGHT TWO SHOT: HAZLIK and GEORGE. HAZLIK has produced a shooter and is holding it at GEORGE'S head. He lowers aim, pointing it at his groin.

> . . . and it's up to you whether you die quickly or in
> great agony.

                              GEORGE

Don't . . . don't kill . . .

                              HAZLIK

Who ordered the contract? Who wants me dead?

                              GEORGE

I don't know, she never tells me, please, *please* don't
kill . . .

MORENO (OFF)

He's probably telling the truth, Hazlik.

HAZLIK thumbs safety on shooter; it begins to hum. ADRENALINE:
Down to 0.50.

HAZLIK

You're right.

HAZLIK turns to face MORENO and drops shooter in tunic pocket.
ADRENALINE: 0.35.

HAZLIK

Let's go talk to Fredrika.

JOHNS

Shall we kill him?

HAZLIK

Eventually.

TO O'HARA, LEERING

You may practice on him first. Don't worry about
marks.

CUT TO: Main room again. Party going full swing, people laughing and
chattering. FREDRIKA is seated near the bar, looking deadly. DOLLY in
for TIGHT GROUP SHOT as HAZLIK and MORENO approach.

SOUND UNDER and HOLD ADRENALINE.

FREDRIKA

COLDLY, TO HAZLIK

Where is my husband?

HAZLIK

He's enjoying his own private party right now.

MORENO

And being positively garrulous.

FREDRIKA

Oh? I'm glad to hear that. I was afraid he wasn't having a very good time.

MORENO

HISSES

He still—

HAZLIK

INTERRUPTING

He talked, Fredrika. I know he came here to kill me. *You* came here to kill me.

FREDRIKA

WHISPERS

You fool. Both of you, fools.

MORENO

No, dear, for a change you play the fool. This time you went too far.

FREDRIKA

VENOMOUS

If you kill me, an army will be at your door by dawn.

HAZLIK

By dawn, I will have an army here to meet them.

MORENO

Two armies.

HAZLIK

Perhaps, though, if you will tell me who contracted
for my death . . .

FREDRIKA

You know I can't do that.

HAZLIK

This one time; this last time, you had better.

FREDRIKA

LOOKING AT MORENO

Alone.

HAZLIK

All right. (TO MORENO) You will excuse us?

MORENO makes exaggerated bow. FREDRIKA and HAZLIK leave wordlessly. MORENO watches them go and speaks softly into his bracelet.

CUT TO: TIGHT TWO SHOT of FREDRIKA and HAZLIK alone in a
corridor. HAZLIK opens an ornate, old-fashioned manual door.

HAZLIK

WRYLY

My chambers.

LONG SHOT past HAZLIK and FREDRIKA to opulent bedroom; a
fantasy of glass and velvet and silk. SUBLIMINAL: Feel of velvet and
silk, sound of fine glass tinkling. Slight SMELL: Dope. SOMATIC: Dope
0.08. A tall, beautiful girl sits naked on the couch by the bed, smoking
dope and reading. Unruffled, she puts down the viewer and slips a house-
coat over her shoulders; crosses to exit between HAZLIK and
FREDRIKA.

HAZLIK

I'll call for you later. (MOTIONS TO FREDRIKA)
Have a seat, dear.

HAZLIK crosses to a large bar and selects a fine decanter.

HAZLIK

Brandy?

FREDRIKA

Just a taste.

HAZLIK pours two small glasses of brandy, his back to FREDRIKA, watching her in a mirror. She doesn't move. He reaches in tunic pocket and takes out his shooter. SOUND: Soft hum; still activated. He crosses to FREDRIKA with shooter in right hand and drink in left.

HAZLIK

Distilled from the finest Antarean vintage.

FREDRIKA accepts, not looking at shooter, and takes a small sip.

FREDRIKA

It travels well.

HAZLIK returns to the bar and gets his glass, then sits on bed about two meters from FREDRIKA. He empties the glass in one swallow. TASTE and SMELL: Fine brandy; SOMATIC: Liquor burning on its way down.

HAZLIK

Well?

FREDRIKA

The man who contracted for your death is one of
my oldest and most valued customers.

HAZLIK

Was. As our friend pointed out, you are no longer in the business. (PAUSES) You may yet live, though.

FREDRIKA

LAUGHS SOFTLY

You can't allow me to live.

TAKES LONG SLOW SIP OF BRANDY

Neither can Moreno.

FREDRIKA reaches up and takes a long pin out of her hair. The hair falls in a soft white cascade around her shoulders. She was very beautiful once.

HAZLIK

RAISING SHOOTER

That pin is a weapon.

FREDRIKA

With proper knowledge, anything is a weapon. (PAUSES) Don't worry. I won't throw it at you.

HAZLIK

More of your nerve poison?

FREDRIKA

Oh, you found out George's little secret? How many men did it take?

HAZLIK

Two. We have atropine now, though. (TAKES AM-POULE OUT OF HIS POCKET AND SHOWS IT TO HER) You might as well tell me who your customer was. If nothing else, I can promise you a pleasant death.

FREDRIKA

Having made a lifelong study of the subject, I can
assure you that there is no such thing as a pleasant
death. Not even painless death is pleasant, not even
for an eighty-year-old woman.

FREDRIKA stands and begins walking. For once, she looks as old as she
is. CAMERA FOLLOWS as she talks, fiddling with the pin.

FREDRIKA

You don't recall the last time you contracted for my
services.

HAZLIK (OFF)

Of course not.

FREDRIKA

It was a most unusual request. Also very difficult.
But I accepted the challenge.

HAZLIK (OFF)

So? You were paid well, no—

FREDRIKA

I wouldn't have risked it if it hadn't meant so much
to you. I've always respected you, Theo; loved you
in my own way.

ADRENALINE: 0.20. SUBLIMINAL: Rattlesnake coiling.

FREDRIKA

You were very disturbed, agitated. You had tried a
multitude of other possible solutions before coming
to me. None of them was satisfactory.

ADRENALINE: 0.40. SUBLIMINAL: Guillotine rising, rusty squeak.

HAZLIK (OFF)

What has this to do—

FREDRIKA

Patience. Old people do rattle on.

FREDRIKA stops walking a little more than an arm's length from HAZLIK. ADRENALINE: 0.50, SUBLIMINAL: Losing balance on edge of cliff.

FREDRIKA

You were afraid that your empire was going to crumble because of the weakness of one man.

FREDRIKA points pin at HAZLIK, as if for emphasis. ADRENALINE: 0.60. SUBLIMINAL: Tied to stake and flames licking at feet.

FREDRIKA

You arranged for that man to be killed. One month ago this night, you arranged it. Because he had just turned fifty and was sad and afraid and knew that his empire soon would be down around his ears, and was not strong enough to commit suicide, he— you, Theo—*you* hired me to be your instrument of suicide.

FREDRIKA rests point of pin lightly on HAZLIK'S chest. ADRENA-LINE: 0.70, SUBLIMINAL: Falling in darkness.

HAZLIK

You're insane.

FREDRIKA

No, Theo. Your subconscious knows. Put down the shooter.

HAZLIK puts muzzle of shooter against FREDRIKA'S abdomen. ADRENALINE: 0.85, HOLD SUBLIMINAL.

FREDRIKA

No difference.

FREDRIKA leans on the needle and, at the same instant, HAZLIK fires. FREDRIKA explodes, cut in two.

TOTAL SENSORY NULL as HAZLIK stares at pin, a couple of centimeters sticking into his chest. He drops the shooter into the confusion of gore all over the rug and takes the atropine ampoule out of his pocket.

Then HAZLIK throws the ampoule away and shoves the pin the rest of the way into his chest.

ADRENALINE: 1.0.

SOMATIC: Male orgasm 1.0.

SMELL, TASTE, FEEL, HEAR, SIGHT all UP with white noise TO: FULL SENSORY OVERLOAD.

FADE TO BLACK.

CREDITS.

COMMERICAL.

(1972)

Notes on the Stories

The title story of this collection ran a winding path from conception to delivery. Like one of the others here, it started with a letter from my old friend Robert Silverberg, inviting me to write a story for an anthology. This was *Far Horizons*, with the daunting subtitle "All New Tales from the Greatest Worlds of Science Fiction." He was asking writers who had created classics in the genre to revisit their worlds and write novellas set in them.

In my case it was *The Forever War*, and it was a wonderful opportunity. Editors and others had been after me for twenty years to write a sequel to the novel, and my response had always been no, the novel's complete as it stands. But I always wanted to write a novella about what happens after the novel ends, and here was Silverberg offering me the chance, and for more money than the novel's original advance.

I got twenty or thirty pages into it, though, a novella I was calling "Forever Free," when I realized that it begged to be expanded into a novel, an actual sequel. I wrote Silverberg and asked how soon the material could be reused, and he said three years. That was too long; it was time for me to send out the next book proposal.

So I turned "Forever Free" into the book proposal, same title, and looked for another angle on the novella. It was immediately apparent. In the last part of the book, the main characters Marygay and William are separated, and we follow William's story. What happened to Marygay?

It was fun to write her story, both as a bridge to the sequel and as an oblique commentary on *The Forever War*, twenty years later.

———

I don't often write fantasy (except insofar as science fiction is a subset of fantasy), but every now and then a fantasy idea tickles my fancy. I got a request from Jean Rabe to write a story for *Renaissance Faire*, a book of stories set in those odd modern worlds of make-believe.

I'm not a big fan of the anachronistic gatherings, but my wife loves them, and I let her drag me along, and do enjoy myself once I get there, the mead and junk food and interesting costumes and old music. The music gave me an entrée into a story.

For years I've had in my "crazy ideas" file a clipping from *Acoustic Guitar* magazine, about the lives and times of those odd performers who hire out as "sidemen"—mostly unsung heroes of live music and records, who sit in to fill lacunae in visiting bands or to beef up the background for a recording session. It's a precarious life, but full of variety, and as a freelance writer, I feel a kind of bond with people who wind up there.

I've also been an amateur musician since grade school, and in a couple of insane periods in my youth considered doing it for a living. Fortunately, no amount of yearning can make up for a lack of talent, so I was never given an opportunity to ruin my life in that particular way. One of the pleasures of writing stories, though, is the license to put on a manic disposition and imagine who you might have become if things had worked out differently. "Diminished Chord" let me venture out into that territory.

———

"Giza" is one of two stories that appear here courtesy of my classes at MIT. I start out the semester with an assignment that seems arbitrary, even cruel: I give each student a theme chosen at random from the table of contents of Peter Nichols's excellent *The Science in Science Fiction*, and make them write the opening couple of pages of a story based on that. If you don't know anything about antimatter or generation ships or werewolves, hey, look it up. You didn't get to MIT from a coupon on a cereal box.

As partial compensation, during the break in the middle of the three-hour meeting, I have them get together and agree on whatever topic seems to be the worst, and give it to me to write. This particular year, the students were especially cruel, and made one up: asteroid psychology. I said sure, and then wandered off to wonder what I had gotten into. The psychology of a rock?

The book *Writing the Natural Way*, by Gabriele Rico, has some interesting tips, and one I pass on to my students is the idea of trying to visualize a story by making a graphic map of its characters, ideas, settings, whatever—a way to get your brain out of thinking of a story as a sentence-by-sentence structure, and seeing it as a broader gestalt. I did that, writing ASTEROID inside a circle on the left and PSYCHOLOGY inside a circle on the right, and then free-associated on the two words, trying to find a commonality.

I doubt that I spent fifteen minutes on it before the idea for the story crystallized, almost entire: an asteroid can't have a psychology, but the people trapped inside one could, and it would be toxic.

The time of writing is relevant. It was the week after 11 September 2001.

———————

"Foreclosure" was another story from the random-topic assignment, but this past year the students were more kind and merely gave me a topic that was so overworked it seemed impossible to come up with anything new: terraforming, changing inhospitable planets into Earth-like ones.

———————

Sometimes this writer/teacher's life isn't too rough. The day after that class, my wife and I got on a plane to Barcelona, where I was to give a speech and then take it easy for a while. Two old friends, Joan Manel and Mercé, had traded their flat in the city for a beach house in Cubelles, the resort town to the north, and they invited us to kick back and relax for a week.

So there I was, sitting on a blanket on this gorgeous topless beach, not a cloud in the sky or a care in the world, and of course my thoughts turned to terraforming, because deep inside this jet-setting sybarite is an American Puritan workaholic. I took out my Moleskine notebook—that I should even have it on the beach condemns me as hopeless—and decided to make a list of every terraforming theme I could remember, and see whether that would generate an idea for a new one. It worked. The list, which didn't take a half an hour of Spanish sun, is kind of interesting:

Playing God
The ultimate in pollution
Unwitting horror
Greed
Insane colonialism
Need to abandon Earth
Geometric increase (von Neumann machines)
Earth as a result of terraforming
Accidental terraforming (garbage taking over)
Terraforming as trivial hobby

Aliens xenoforming Earth
Doing Mars, Venus, Luna for mining, etc.
Moon partially terraformed
Earth retroterraformed after disaster
Very slow terraforming

—which led to the story. I wrote down "Maybe nobody has done this one—terraforming on such a slow scale that it looks like planetary evolution. The aliens come back to claim Earth, now that it's "done," and their claim is legal; humans are an accidental by-product and are screwing up the process. They have to be educated so they know why they're being destroyed. "Foreclosure"—people have a thousand years to leave the Earth.

I chose as a viewpoint character my late mother-in-law, a wonderful woman who left a bad marriage and reinvented herself as a hotshot real estate agent.

———

"Four Short Novels" was another story generated by a Robert Silverberg request. The French publisher Flammarion wanted an anthology of stories that take place a thousand years from 2001, called *Destination 3001*. Unspecific enough that I could say yes and table it until an idea occurred to me.

This is unusual: I don't have the faintest idea where the story came from, but I know the exact instant when it occurred to me.

I'm a fairly serious bicyclist, and one chore bicyclists do is "interval training," which is a fancy way of saying "go up hills." I was laboring up one beautiful hill here in Gainesville, Florida, trying to keep my cadence up without descending into granny gears, when the structure of the whole story came to me in a hyperoxygenated flash. By the time I finished with the hills, I knew what the first and last sections of it would be, and wrote a paragraph describing them as soon as I got home.

I wasn't able to write it right away, though, because I was racing a deadline on the novel *The Coming*. I got that put away and we hopped on a plane to Australia, for the World Science Fiction Convention in Melbourne. After that convention, we were invited up to Airley Beach, a lovely resort town just off the Great Barrier Reef, which we'd visited back in the eighties with Australian fan and critic Eric Lindsay. Eric had had the good sense to move there, and he invited a small mob of us up to continue the party that had started in Melbourne a week before.

I suppose the old Puritan gland, again awakened by cloudless skies and topless women, drove me once more to my notebook, and I wrote the story in three or four easy mornings. Perhaps I ought to move to a topless beach and start making a living as a short-story writer.

"For White Hill" is probably the most complex story in this book, and is my personal favorite, for various reasons. Greg Benford wrote to five "hard" science-fiction writers—as a short definition, you can say that hard SF uses real science—and asked us to write novellas for an anthology called *Far Futures*, stories set at least a thousand years from now.

Looking back at the notes for this story, I see that initially I had suggested a much different one, concerning time travel. Here's a letter to Greg, who is a professional physicist:

Many thanks for yours of 12 July re Lyapunov exponents. etc. I'm late answering because it arrived just after we left for Europe. Sweden and Denmark, loverly.

It's an interesting constraint. Tell me whether I might get around it in this wise:

Chaos noodges the planets around so that their position is basically unknowable beyond a few million years of launch time. This does play hob with my wanting to have each jump orders of magnitude longer than the previous one. Or does it? After the first couple of jumps—a mere few thousand years into the future—it would be duck soup for them to enclose a snazzy space ship inside the time machine's radius of influence. Here you go, right off the rack. Our hero takes care of chaos etc. by zooming up orthogonal to the plane of the ecliptic and doing his time travelling way up there, deliberately missing the Earth by tens of A.U.'s. Then he finds Earth and goes back down and lands, to see what the Morlocks are up to.

Furthermore, the protagonist has planned for this ahead of time. He knews he's on a one-way leap into the unknown, and he's gambling that technology will save him before chaos destroys him. What a guy!

Possible?

Let's have a glass of good wine in San Francisco and mumble over these and other things. You have a deadline yet?

That turned out to be the novel I'm writing now, twelve years later: *The Accidental Time Machine*. I'd forgotten that Greg was in on its inception.

I drifted over into another direction, though. I'd been thinking about writing a novella about the future of art, anyhow, so why not do it for Greg? The structure of it, I stole from the best of sources.

When I was in the middle of the book *Forever Peace*, I was slowly reading *The Art of Shakespeare's Sonnets*, by Helen Vendler. I had real issues, as they say, with her approach to the text, but it was a good read and a good way to start writing in the morning: I would copy out a sonnet by hand, and then read her analysis while the tea was brewing, and then turn to my own book with the same pen. (Some of us hard-science guys slightly believe in magic.)

In the course of that exercise, I noticed that some of the sonnets had a compelling narrative thrust; in particular Number 18, possibly the best-known poem in the language: "Shall I compare thee to a summer's day?" I decided I would write a novella in fourteen sections, each one based on a line of that poem.

I wanted to make it just possible for a careful reader to figure out the source. Numbering the sections 1 through 14 would make it too easy, so I invented a base-14 number system to be decoded. The title "For White Hill" is another clue; Shakespeare dedicated the 1609 printing of the sonnets to W.H., their "onlie begetter." Finally, the short last section is a pretty direction evocation of the final line—"So long lives this, and this gives life to thee."

(There's also a writing pun in the names of the main characters—Waterman and Montblanc [roughly "white hill"] were the brands of fountain pens used to write the story. I know, that's beyond the pale.)

For anybody with a morbid interest in the calculations and logic that go into a story like this, I put eight pages of notes at http:home.earthlink.net/~haldeman/forwhitehillnotes.htm. I trust the story can be enjoyed without all that stuff, though.

————

The plot for "Finding My Shadow" also came from verse, but this time a popular song. Along with a number of other science-fiction writers, I met singer/songwriter Janis Ian at a World Science Fiction Convention in Montreal—she had been in correspondence with Mike Resnick over one of his stories, and he talked her into coming.

We were all kind of fascinated by her bubbly enthusiasm—I mean, half the people I know are science-fiction writers, so they're no big deal—and delighted when she subsequently sent a bunch of us a stack of her CDs, with the suggestion (Mike Resnick's idea) that we write stories based on the lyrics, for a book eventually called *Stars*. Her "Here in the City" suggested to me a dark vision of urban apocalypse, which I placed below and within my beloved second home, Boston.

————

"Civil Disobedience" is another urban apocalypse, this time set in the Washington area, where I lived from grade school through high-school graduation, and later for five years of college. Ernest Lilley was putting together an anthology of future Washington stories and, knowing I'd grown up there, asked me for one. I said sure, and more or less forgot about it. The deadline just came due as I was starting to write these story notes, so I tabled them and wrote it.

I'm not alone in being angry at and scandalized by the current administration, so a story set in Washington had to be political. The immediate impetus of it was the establishment's blithe dismissal of warnings from mainstream British scientists that catastrophic flooding from global warming could be only a few years away. I suppose they think they will be saved by the Rapture, or their fortunes.

———————

Now we come to two stories that were written to "illustrate" paintings. I was waxing nostalgic for the days when a science-fiction magazine editor would send you a photocopy of a painting that would be on the cover someday, and have you write a story around it. I once won a Hugo for one of those, "Tricentennial," in the July '76 *Analog*. Gordon Van Gelder, editor of *The Magazine of Fantasy and Science Fiction*, heard my plea, bought a painting he liked, and sent a copy to me. The artist Max Bertolini gave me permission to publish a link to a copy of it: http://home.earthlink.net/~haldeman/FSF_art.jpeg.

It's a good painting, and suggests any number of stories. Two scientific problems presented themselves immediately: the air has a green cast, and the shadows indicate that there are two suns. So only a certain set of orbits would work, and I had to postulate some aliens who could breathe chlorine, or at least tolerate it in a concentration where it was visible. (A human can't, nor can any living organism I know of; it was an effective weapon in World War I because it would sink down into trenches and bunkers and poison people in fairly low concentrations.)

So I juryrigged a planet and some aliens who could live there, and who might construct the huge stone artifacts in the cover illustration—for those of you who don't have a computer at your elbow, it's two space-suited people looking up at three identical large alien faces carved out of rock, with a tanklike vehicle behind them.

"Memento Mori" was an interesting challenge from Dave Gross, who had just taken over the editorship of the venerable *Amazing* magazine. Among the new things he wanted to do was a feature called "A Thousand Words," where an author would be given a picture and asked to write a thousand-word story—not 999 words or 1001, but exactly a thousand. It seemed difficult but not impossible. I do a lot of formal poetry with more or less arbitrary restrictions, and in fact I'd done exactly-100-word stories (called drabbles) twice for a British charity.

Dave sent me four paintings, and I chose the one by David Rankin, who kindly allowed me to post a scanning of it at http://home.earthlink.net/~haldeman/Mmori.jpeg.

"Brochure" and "Heartwired" were both written as short diversions for a series in the science journal *Nature*. All the editor required was that they be amusing, short, and contain some actual science. The first, "Brochure," was part of a millennium project. The series was well enough received that they did a repeat.

It's kind of humbling to have a story in a magazine most of whose contents you have no chance of understanding.

"Out of Phase" is the first science-fiction story I sold, back in 1969, and "Power Complex" was its 1970 sequel. They didn't appear in earlier collections of my short stories because I intended for them to be the first two chapters of a novel.

I kept them in the back of my mind for a while, but after thirty-some years the back of my mind got pretty far back. I looked at them while putting together the stories for this volume and realized with a shock that I can't use them for that novel anymore, because their main character is too similar to the Changeling in my 2004 novel *Camouflage*. I had unconsciously plagiarized myself!

There's a lesson for beginning writers in the history of "Out of Phase." It's the first story I wrote in a fiction-writing course I took, my last semester in college. (I got an A. The other SF story I wrote for the class became an episode in the *Twilight Zone* series.)

Right after that semester I graduated and was drafted and sent to Vietnam. Like most other draftees who went there, I spent one year in combat and then came back to a month's leave—so-called "compassionate" leave, which I think means that your family, rather than the army, gets to deal with your problems.

One thing I did that month was type up those two stories and send them out to the science-fiction magazines. I was rejected by both *Analog* and *The Magazine of Fantasy and Science Fiction*, but when Frederik Pohl at *Galaxy* saw "Out of Phase," he sent me a little note saying that if I could boil the first four pages down to one, he'd look at it again.

In fact, I boiled those pages down to the one word, "Trapped." I sent it back, and knew from magazines about writing that I should include a cover letter with a bare minimum of information. It went like this: "Dear Mr. Pohl: Here is the story with the changes you requested."

It turned out, though, that Mr. Pohl had quit as editor of *Galaxy*, and his last-minute replacement was a man who hadn't seen a science-fiction magazine in twenty years. He didn't know Haldeman from Heinlein, so when my story came in with that cover letter, he probably bought it without even reading it.

The lesson to the beginning writer is clear. Just keep track of magazines' hiring and firing in journals like *Locus* and *Publishers Weekly*. When somebody leaves a magazine, shoot his or her successor a story with a cover letter addressed to the recently departed. "Here is the story with the changes you requested" could start you on a career that could result, thirty-five years later, in a confession like this.

———

I started writing just a little too late to get into Harlan Ellison's groundbreaking anthologies *Dangerous Visions* and *Again, Dangerous Visions*. "Fantasy for Six Electrodes and One Adrenaline Drip," written in 1972, was going to be in *The Last Dangerous Visions*, and make my name a household word. I could have been the Father of Cyberpunk, seven years before William Gibson's "Johnny Mnemonic." Or maybe not.

At any rate, the last of the dangerous anthologies never saw print. I lost this story for ages, since it was written before computers made it easy to keep track of things. Then the University of South Florida offered to collect my papers, which sent me rummaging through dusty old boxes.

In one of the boxes I found a carbon—that's what we used when "Xerox" was the name of a villain in Buck Rogers—of the story, and I still like it, though perhaps it's more quaint now than dangerous.

Joe Haldeman
Gainesville, Florida, 2005